RENEGADE IMPERIUM: BOOK 2

CARNAGE AND COURAGE

JON FRATER & A.K. DUBOFF

Published by Epic Realms Press
Cover Copyright © 2024 Vivid Covers

ISBN-10: 196561406X
ISBN-13: 978-1965614068

0 9 8 7 6 5 4 3 2 1

Produced in the United States of America

TABLE OF CONTENTS

PART 1

STRICTLY BUSINESS

1

EVERYTHING IS A CONTEST

CAPTAIN AURA STOOD at the opening of the Sa-Zen ashram on Valdos III. The stone building was part of an ancient monastery, one of many located in the largest of the planet's deserts. Over the past two months—since the violent confrontation with her past as a TSS Agent—she'd come to think of the place as a retreat from the galaxy and from her alter ego, space pirate and interstellar thief Mother Carnage.

The truth was that Valdos III agreed with her. The people weren't especially friendly, but they were brazenly social and unceasingly polite. Besides, she had grown to love the stonework and architectural designs that permeated the cities here. She only wished the landscape and people weren't so *drab*.

"Sand-colored clothing. Sand-colored food. Sand-colored sand." Aura sighed as she pulled her Valdan spirit robe close around herself.

Hammurabi pulled up the hood of his robe. "Don't you

mean *Thand*-colored?"

On the other hand, she preferred drab to idiocy. "Ham, you're a twit."

"Aura, you're a bore. Sand is sand, just deal with it. Besides, you needed this vacation."

"My ship and crew needed the vacation. The *Emerald Queen* needed upgrades and repairs, and new crew vetted and approved. We've spent two months doing that. I need to get back to work."

"You need to make sure your new security contingent is settled in first."

Ham's personal soldiers, the Scorpions, were in the process of doing that already. Quartermaster Tabor Laski and First Officer Lom Mench had arranged it. A dozen of the telekinetic adepts were already on board the *Emerald Queen*; they had been assigned quarters and were being worked into the crew's daily routine.

"It's being seen to," she said.

"You also needed to sit down with a Gifted monk and get your brain back into fighting trim," Ham insisted. "You got your ass handed to you. Not a great look."

And there her mood went, out into the sand dunes. "I know, I know. I spent too long out of practice. It won't happen again."

"I hope not," a new voice said from behind them. Sargon pulled his own robe around his tall, thin body more tightly. The rising wind whipped bursts of sand across the ashram which itself was the color of… sand. "You know, Aura, Gilgamesh brought you into New Akkadia because he believed that you could be a major part of its promise. He convinced us of it. It'd be a shame if you fell short of that goal."

Aura smiled brightly at him. He was smart and inventive,

but he had few social skills, despite his tall stature. She struggled to take him seriously when he spoke like this to her. But he was Gil's friend, and she had to remain civil. For now. "Really? I thought it was because you needed a commander you could trust," she snarked.

"That, too."

Ashurbanipal joined them; his hood was down, his robe was open, and the wind played havoc with his clothing and wavy brown hair. Ash seemed to relish the drubbing from the environment. "You know, sand is a big deal to the Valdans," he said. "There are something like two thousand different kinds of sand on this planet. It's essential to the local economy. Some types are extremely useful in industry, some are prized ornaments, some are used in local trade. The TalEx corporation has a mining site in the deep desert that pulls the grit out of the air and compresses it into stone. Very highly prized as a building material."

"Stop it, Ash," Ham said. "I think I like you better when you talk through an AI avatar on the Dark Net."

"And rob you of my sparkling personality? Never!"

"Have you even stepped one foot into a meditation salt room since you arrived?" Ham asked.

"I spend my time in the gold vault."

"Typical. You're as spiritual as a leeca," Sargon sneered.

"But I'm rich. We'll all be far richer if New Akkadia falls into place like we planned," Ash insisted.

Aura stepped closer to Sargon. "You should remember that New Akkadia can only succeed as long as the TSS stays far away from you. The *Emerald Queen* can help maintain the illusion of control you want to project to local Enforcers and functionaries. But if a proper battleship shows up, it'll all fall apart."

Sar turned his head, his expression one of boredom. "And?"

"And I wonder sometimes if you've thought all this through as well as you think you have."

Sargon patted her hand. "Don't worry, Aura. It's taken care of. We'll pick more targets, you'll take what we need and threaten a few troublemakers. It'll be fine. Just be sure to meet us at Boragin on schedule. Ham and I have a meeting with their prime minister that can't be delayed."

Aura remembered they'd passed by Boragin on the way to Diphous. "Boragin is a Makaris Dynasty planet, isn't it? Agricultural?"

"Very much so. Some of the most advanced growing techniques in this part of the galaxy are used there."

"What can they possibly offer us?"

"Food, obviously," Sar said. "We paid for delivery, and they stiffed us. Then to add insult to injury they convinced their neighbors to refuse our buy offers on the open market. Ham and I are going to hand them a carrot, but if they don't see the error of their ways, you'll be on hand with a very big stick."

Now we're attacking farmers. Wonderful. "Sounds delightful."

"A good meal is better than the finest coat," Ham said sagely.

"In the meantime, you have studies to attend to," Ham said.

Aura bobbed her head. Ham was right about that. "Let me see you boys off. Gil speaks highly of your ship, Sargon."

"As he should. *Nineveh* is a work of art," Sar admitted.

"My *Tiamat* is nicer," Ham insisted. "More efficient design and a better-looking AI."

"Only you like that kind of thing," Sar said. "No one buys

a yacht because it's *efficient*."

"Very much so," Aura quipped. "Look at Ash's ship. Any less efficient and it wouldn't fly."

"Finally, Aura, you and I agree on something. Ash's *Ishtar* looks like a spinning top. I have no idea why you went with that design," Sar said.

Ash looked hurt. "It's supposed to look like an ancient temple," he said.

"Bah! A yacht should be sleek and luxurious."

"With a beautiful AI in attendance," Ham agreed.

Sargon began expounding on all the benefits of travelling in style. All Aura knew was the same Lynaedan shipyard had crafted yachts for all four of the Mesopotamians, complete with their own over-endowed female AI servants. Typical.

She walked the men to the edge of the landing field outside the monastery and watched as they faded from view, swallowed by the environment. The only way she knew they'd made it to their respective playthings was when their yachts lifted off and took flight. Good riddance.

Back inside the monastery she shed her outer robe and returned to the chamber where she'd left Gilgamesh. She found him exactly where she'd last seen him, in a lotus position in a heated room surrounded by salt walls. She could sense his breathing and heartbeat; when his pulse rose a bit, she knew he'd noticed her. She concentrated on using her telekinesis to scoop up the loose dust and sand on the floor, then formed it into a ball and dropped it on his head.

To his credit, he reacted quickly—forming a telekinetic shield and flinging the cloud back into the air. "Most people just say hello when they enter a room," he said.

"Hello, then," she whispered and settled against him. She had to admit that spending time with Gil had been something she'd needed. "Your partners have gone on to Boragin. I'm to meet them there in the *Queen*."

"Good. Thank you for dealing with them."

"I didn't *deal* with them. I just made some small talk, stroked their egos a bit, and watched them leave. I'll need to be on my way soon, too."

"Same difference. I needed the space," Gil sighed.

Aura put her hand on his thigh. "This business with Boragin worries me. We've stolen plenty of valuables from the Talsari Dynasty already, but this time we're going after a planetary government. New Akkadia is becoming known to the Empire at large, and they're going to think we're dangerous."

"I wonder about that, too. Those three do seem to be looking for trouble now, don't they?"

"Yet, you still want to be part of their group."

Gil shook off the last of the sand and opened his eyes. He'd gotten back into his own training among the Valdans. He'd never be anything more than a mid-level Trion as far as his rating went, but he wasn't defenseless. "It's a big group now. We have controlling interests in commerce, government, and industry on nine worlds. Now, Sargon is putting together a meeting with a major financier to create a sector-wide investment company. There's a ton of money to be made there. Wealth like that will take us to the next level. It could help us grab another five or six worlds."

She loved the excitement that talk of New Akkadia brought to his face. However, she was starting to loathe how the project was eroding his soul. "Gil… we made a ton of money already. We're both set for life. Is there anything you want to do *besides* fill a warehouse with credit chips?"

"Yes. Everything! If you have enough money, you can do

absolutely anything you want."

Anything except bring her dead crewmates back to life. She'd gone along with the dream of New Akkadia as a tribute to those who hadn't survived *Triumph*'s collision with Gil's starship. How was her making multiple fortunes an honor to their memory? "I think I've had enough of the rat race," she admitted. "I've thought about cashing in my chips and retiring somewhere."

"What are you going to do then, Aura? Write your memoirs? The Life and Times of Mother Carnage? You're a wanted criminal."

Aura lay on the warm stone and stared at the ceiling. She hadn't noticed the fine tiling before. Its pattern became immediately apparent: the open flame of the Scorpions. "Bomaxed right. I'm a woman with a past. Even more reason to think I've earned a rest."

"You'd be bored out of your mind in a year." He scoffed, lying down next to her.

She turned onto her side and kissed him. "Maybe a year with nothing to do would be nice. I think we both deserve some time off. Sargon and the others can get along without us."

"I'm not abandoning the dream, Aura. I'm in it. I have to see it through."

"Which dream? Ours or Sargon's?"

"There's only one dream: New Akkadia."

She felt the air go out of her lungs and pull part of her optimism about the future with it. The man she'd learned to trust and follow across the galaxy was gone. She didn't know this guy and wasn't sure she wanted to. "Trouble is, no matter how much money and power you amass there's always someone out there with more of it. The contest never ends."

"Aura, it's about the right of self-determination. Not a contest."

"Gil, to men like Sargon, Ham, and Ash, *everything* is a contest."

—   —   —

Agent Lee Tuyin stood before Lead Agent Saera Alexri with the same unpleasant sense of failure he'd experienced at their last meeting in her office.

"I am not thrilled with what I'm seeing in this latest report, Lee," she said.

"We *are* making progress," he assured her. "Officer Godri and I surmised that since Hammurabi—"

"That would be Kaja Akanis," she noted wryly.

"Yes, ma'am. Since he had a relationship with the Scorpions which is a group of assassins from Valdos III, it made logical sense that they would have returned to that planet to go to ground while recovering from the damage my team did to the *Emerald Queen* and Agent Aura Thand."

"*Former* Agent."

"Yes, ma'am."

"I agree, it tracks. What did you find?"

"In fairness, we're bumping up against numerous obstacles," Lee admitted. "The Valdan government has been less than cooperative in supporting our investigation. Every time we think we have a lead on a Valdan institution that's offering the Scorpions support, the planetary government claims either the institution is irrelevant or doesn't exist. They've even claimed the Scorpions themselves don't exist or if they do—they are no threat. Frankly, ma'am, it's infuriating."

"I think I finally understand your problem," the Lead Agent said. "The group you identified as the Scorpions is part of a much larger anti-Talsari group that has issues with TalEx's activities in the Valdan great desert. Lots of mining opportunities present themselves, and the Valdan government wants the development money that comes with them. But they don't want the problems with local inhabitants who couldn't care less about TalEx but take up arms against the corporation. It's a mess. It's not going away."

Lee sighed. "I'm not sure how to move forward under these conditions, ma'am."

"Nor am I. But I can at least take a somewhat more active role in this. I can do what I can to manage the politics of the situation on Valdos. But in return I need you to get something substantial regarding Aura Thand. She's had some success, and she's getting bolder. This setback you inflicted on her two months ago isn't going to last. I think you've figured that out already."

"I have, ma'am."

"Good. How is Officer Sley handling all this?" she asked.

"She went back to Greengard after the *Emerald Queen* jumped away. We're in contact with her, but until we've secured a solid lead that might require her insight, she seems content to stay on Greengard with her family."

"You'll forgive me for feeling a bit of relief at that news. She can stay on Greengard as long as she likes."

"Yes, ma'am."

CREATIVE ACCOUNTING

COLIN COVRANI'S CHEST constricted when his handheld beeped with an incoming call from the bank. He took a deep breath of fresh air and looked out at the city below his balcony. "Hello?"

"Colin! Good morning. My name is Emily Govrin. I'm your new account manager."

Passing me off to someone new again? Everyone seemed to view him as a problem, and the fact that she was trying to cover for it with a chirpy voice soured his mood. There was nothing happy about his family thinking that he needed protection from himself. *Fine, she's being paid to manage me, so let her earn her salary.* "It's a pleasure to meet my new nanny," he said.

"Oh, please. Your previous account manager, *she* was a nanny. I'm just here to remind you of your responsibilities and obligations."

"Like not spending the family fortune all over the galaxy."

"Exactly!" she squealed. "I see we're on the same page.

That's a great start!"

Colin wondered what Emily looked like. She sounded like she was fifteen years old, probably a blonde. But she had a sarcastic edge to her... maybe a redhead. "How can I help you today, Miss Govrin?"

"I'll tell you. In going through your file, I found a number of purchases that raised questions. You already mentioned your debt to the bank—which you covered with your savings account. But there was one outstanding debt. Who exactly is *Decius*?"

"He's a J-10 small package trader. I bought him last year." *My special project. Decius* wasn't a great starship. There were roomier, more expensive models out there, but *Decius* was *his*.

Emily didn't hesitate. She probably had no idea that a 'small package trader' was a euphemism for 'smuggler's ride'. "I see... Yes, here's the purchase note. A quarter-million credits is still owed. You're paying him off in installments?"

"Yeah. Twenty thousand comes out of my account every month to cover the payment. I figure he'll be all paid off in a little more than a year."

"Love it. And that money comes from...?"

"I receive a stipend from the family account."

"Excellent, I'll make a note of that." She paused for a moment. " All right, I think we're all set for now. Let's stay in touch."

"Sure."

"Thank you for your time, Colin. I'll have my assistant give you a ring in the future to set up a proper appointment. Have a great day!"

—

The good mood Colin had awoken to was ruined. Fortunately, a hearty meal usually helped his spirits.

As he made his way to breakfast, his mother, Yelena, intercepted him in the hallway. "Colin, come inside for a moment, will you?"

"To your office?"

"Of course, why not?"

"Well, when I was ten I tried to hand you a cup of juice in here, then I accidentally spilled it on your desk. You told me to stay out from then on. I stayed out."

She snorted. "I don't remember *any* of that. Come on. You don't have any juice now."

Well, I *remember it like it was yesterday.*

He crossed the threshold to the administrative wing and felt a change in the air as if he'd stepped into a different plane of existence. His cousin, Vani—who often ran the company when his father was off-world—had the office at the end of the hall. A red light glowed above the closed doors; a meeting was in progress. Other offices along the corridor were filled with workers, and other staff were walking around with tablets in hand, their expressions the picture of serious professionalism. Colin felt badly out of place.

Yelena's office was on the far side of a central lounge. Inside, she pointed to one of the chairs opposite her desk. "Sit down."

He sat.

Yelena regarded him from behind the desk for a long time, then said, "Colin, I want to say two things to you. First, you should know that I'm quite proud of you."

That was unexpected. "You're... what?"

"I'll explain. I was surprised when you left here on your hasty mission to rescue your lady friend two months ago. Then,

I became furious. While you were gone, I had a talk with my brother—your Uncle Rodg. He alerted me to the fact that this was the most initiative you'd shown in years. You were presented with a situation. You developed a goal. You made judgements, set a course of action, and followed through. I still don't agree with your decision, but you handled yourself well. Good job, son."

Is this a trick? "You're really not mad? All this time, when we hadn't talked about it…" He faded out. Silence had been her preferred mode of communication lately. She'd put in time trying to quietly reason with him while he was a teenager, then yelling when the lessons still hadn't stuck. In recent years, it had seemed like she'd given up on him entirely.

She shook her head. "No, I'm not. You finally showed us all what you're made of. I wonder now if you simply needed the right sort of motivation. I'll say this for her: none of the other young women you've shown interest in have ever spurred you to action like that. She must be very special."

"Yes. Kaia is."

"Kaia. That's a pretty name. I would be pleased to make her acquaintance."

"I'd like that." Relief flooded his system. "What was the other thing you wanted to tell me?" he asked, emboldened by the apparent good news.

"I'm cutting your allowance back to two thousand credits per month, starting today."

Colin's stomach dropped out of his body. He was in free fall. "You're *what*?!"

"I called the shipyard to verify you'd returned *Percival*, and was told that he needed more than a half million credits' worth of repairs. We could commission a new gunship for that. What did you do out there?"

"We fought pirates. Mother Carnage. What did you think would happen?" He wondered whether he was asking the question of her or himself. *What did I think would happen?*

"You told me it was just for show. You were going to intimidate a local tough guy. I believed you. That turned out to be an overly optimistic view of the outcome. So, you'll be paying for those repairs."

What about Decius? "I had plans for that money!"

Yelena nodded vigorously. "And I had plans that didn't involve you wrecking one of my fleet's security assets. Today, everyone loses. Anyway, that's all I have. Go on with your day."

Don't panic, he told himself. He frantically wracked his mind for a way out. "What if there was a plan to make enough to pay for the repairs?"

Yelena put down her tablet and folded her arms. "I'm listening."

"I have interest from the Tuyin Dynasty to start shipping their products all over this region."

Her eyes widened. "You got a delivery contract? Show me!"

"It's not a contract. But they have expressed interest in us being their new transport logistics provider."

Yelena shook her head and couldn't stop blinking. "Colin, I'm confused. What are you talking about?"

"TuMed needs distribution routes and we need cargo to ship. Lee Tuyin was very interested in figuring out a trade deal between his family and ours."

"Lee Tuyin. He's the heir? Or the CEO?"

"Uh… no."

"Did you run any of this past Rodg or Vani?"

"I did not. It's more like a suggestion to be finalized at some point in the future."

"I see. So… nothing concrete, then. Just talk."

"I guess so."

"If that changes let me know. Thank you."

Colin stood to go. His handheld felt heavy, bulging in his pocket. Kaia's GravX business plan was in there. "I have one more thing," he began.

"Colin, I have a busy day ahead of me."

Colin used his handheld to project a copy of the plan Kaia had floated to him back on Greengard. "I have a business plan. It's a way to get access to a GravX team, or even start building my own. The game is hugely popular, with a vast fan base. And the fans spend a lot of money on tickets and merchandise. Here, take a look." He transferred the project to her desk.

Whatever else was in his mother's mind, this news pushed it out. She flipped through the pages, tracing paragraphs and looking at the charts. "This looks fascinating. You wrote this?"

"Kaia helped."

"How interesting. Well, now I insist on meeting her! Invite her to the estate. Stars, tell her to bring the whole family— parents, and siblings, too. I presume she has those?"

"She does. Quite a big family, in fact." *People who actually love and value her,* he thought coldly. "I'll invite them all."

"Good. I'll look at this more thoroughly when I have more time. Thank you."

Colin retreated to his favorite balcony to think. He supposed he should be grateful that his mother hadn't dismissed him. But this was clearly just a new ploy. She'd yelled at him when she'd still cared. But this business with Kaia— wanting the whole family here—was it so she could humiliate him and everyone he'd dragged into the mess with the *Percival*? He couldn't shake the feeling that her friendliness was all a front, and that she was beyond angry—almost homicidal.

And now he had a giant problem: a quarter million credit

gap in his finances and no way to fill it. With ninety percent of his income gone, it would take *years* to pay off the remaining debt on *Decius*. He'd been putting the bills off for months, and maybe he could stall for a few more months but that would piss the bank off, possibly enough to send a repo squad after him to collect that starship.

But here was an idea. The further out in the galaxy a person went, the scarcer everything became. Money, jobs, businesses... and transportation. A banker might be happy dealing with debt collectors who were close to home, where things were easy. Banks liked things that were easy. So, it stood to reason that the way to avoid a bank was to make things just a little harder for them to collect a debt.

Colin needed time to pay off the loan on *Decius* but more importantly he needed to make the ship hard to find to help that plan along. Which meant he needed an owner with no issues with their credit, living on a planet that was out of the way. A quiet place full of people who didn't rock the boat. Where privately owned starships were known but relatively rare.

A planet like Greengard.

STRICTLY HONORABLE

TWO DAYS LATER, Colin wondered what had possessed him to drop everything and head to Greengard as he sat at the kitchen dining table in the Sley house across from Karmen Sley's intense gaze. He sipped his cup of coffee to buy himself a few extra seconds before responding. "Officer Sley, I assure you that my intentions toward your daughter are strictly honorable. I just want to take her out for a bit. It's been months since we've seen each other."

Kaia smiled at him from the other end of the table while her mother sat as a chaperone between them.

Karmen raised her cup in a mock salute. "It's nice to hear you put it in those terms, Colin. I'm a little curious, though, why you decided to drop by on such short notice. It's not like Gallos is right around the corner."

He relaxed a little with her favorable response. "Well, I wanted to see Kaia. And I was interested in getting Daveed's view of an idea I had: the Covrani Merchant Academy. I figured it could be part of Foundation U's business program."

"That definitely could have been a call," Karmen mused.

"True, but I don't always follow the convenient path," Colin said. "When you needed help dealing with Mother Carnage, I loaned you the use of one of my family's military assets at no small personal expense, remember?"

"That you did. I will always be grateful. You're still not taking Kaia anywhere. It's a school night."

Kaia sniffed. "Mom, the term ends in three days. It's not like I have homework."

"You also haven't finished your university applications yet."

Kaia looked helplessly at Colin. "I applied to five Foundation U business programs. I have four acceptance letters. I don't know what else she expects."

"That cultural studies program at the Westbridge campus is what I expect. You could do much worse than getting a solid understanding of history and the arts before getting sucked into the world of money. There will always be business opportunities." She looked apologetically at her guest. "No offense, Colin."

"None taken. I agree that it's important to understand things beyond a ledger sheet," Colin said. "Please? I promise I won't take her far. I rented the car from the spaceport—we'll go there and straight back. I'll return her in perfect condition in less than two hours."

"The car or the girl?"

"Both." He took another drink of his coffee.

Kaia rolled her eyes. "Mom, stop it. I'm entitled to a little fun. It's not like Colin and I are going to run off to get married and have kids today!"

Colin's face flushed and he nearly choked on his coffee.

Karmen crossed her arms. "Well, I'm glad to hear you're thinking about those things in that order."

"Mom!"

Karmen turned to her daughter. "You just turned eighteen. A mother worries."

Kaia put her hands flat on the table and glared. "Mom, you told me if I demonstrated I could take care of myself then I could have more autonomy. I've been practicing at the range. I think I shaved five seconds off my high score last time."

"Really? Let's put that to the test," Karmen said.

Colin paid careful attention to the drama. Kaia disappeared from the room while her mother sat, sizing him up as if she was a bird of prey zeroing in on a small woodland animal. *They always turn into their mothers. Do you really know what you're signing up for?*

Finally, Kaia returned with a small case. Colin tried not to fidget as she unpacked a pistol. "Um, Kaia…?"

She saw the look on his face and winked at him. "Relax. I'm not planning to shoot you as long as you behave yourself. Let me introduce you to the Damonite PM-740. It's very simple—much simpler than a pulse pistol. No energy source. It uses a mechanical action to cycle rounds."

"I know how a gun works," Colin murmured.

"Just watch this." Kaia pulled out the magazine, worked the action, and checked the chamber. Then she methodically pulled the weapon apart and placed each component on the table in front of her.

Karmen pulled out her handheld. "Ready?"

"Ready," Kaia agreed.

"Go!" Karmen tapped a stopwatch on the screen.

Kaia worked quickly, grabbing each part and clicking the pistol together. "Done!"

Karmen stopped the counter and read the result. "Seventeen point eight seconds."

"No!" Kara confirmed the number on the screen and grunted in disgust. "Gah! Okay. I'm doing this again. Seventeen point eight seconds. Stars! What was I thinking? I'm thinking having Colin right here is a huge distraction. I can smell him from over there."

That got his attention. Colin had made sure to bathe and shave before his arrival. It would have taken a strong nose to whiff him from across the dining table.

Kaia reset the table while Karmen reset the device. "Ready? Go!"

This time Kaia's fingers clicked the pieces together like a machine on an assembly line. "Done! All right, *that* felt like fifteen seconds."

"Sorry. Nope."

"Noooooooooo!"

"Twelve point six."

This time Kaia jumped for joy. "Yes! Haha! In your face, TSS Militia Academy!"

"I don't want to be churlish but her brother, Kozu, has a best time of eleven seconds," Karmen boasted.

"That's different, Kozu *wants* to be a soldier," Kaia insisted. "Seandra never got past twenty seconds. Elian hasn't even wanted to touch a gun after that fight on the *Emerald Queen*."

Colin couldn't help squirming. The pressure here was unlike that in the Covrani household but it wasn't absent, merely different. "Did you ladies put Agent Lee through these hoops when he came over for dinner?"

Karmen took the pistol from her daughter and packed it in its case. "I didn't have to. First, he didn't arrive out of the blue. Second, Lee wasn't asking to take Kaia out."

"But if he had been…?"

Karmen shook her head dismissively. "TSS Agents have a strict code of conduct. Anyone who'd think of doing anything untoward would have gotten weeded out in the first months of training. So, I'd trust any Agent with Kaia's safety. Or anyone else's."

And there it was. "But not me. All right, I appreciate your candor. Maybe this will make an impression." Colin pulled out his handheld, swiped to a particular entry and threw data to her device. "Here. Take it."

"Yelena Covrani," Karmen read. "What's this?"

"My mother's personal line. If I'm one minute late getting Kaia home, you call that number. Tell her that I've run off with your daughter. She will order her security people to track me down. She might even have me killed."

"You're trusting a total stranger with this?" Karmen mused.

"We fought *space pirates* together. How can you still think of me as a total stranger?"

Kaia couldn't help smirking just a bit.

Karmen's eyes lingered on the screen. She nodded. "Fair enough. Go. Take her in the car, bring her back unscathed, and for stars' sake use your seat belts."

"Yes, ma'am!"

— — —

As the car approached the landing field, Colin insisted that Kaia close her eyes. She was willing to indulge him. She used her ears and sense of kinesthetic motion to keep track of where they were; Colin didn't seem like he was driving far.

Eventually, he brought them to a stop. "Okay. Keep your

eyes closed and take my hand. It's a short walk from here." He stopped her at the edge of the field, then turned her a step to the right. "Okay, open your eyes."

She complied and found herself staring at a holographic representation of a giant, green gift box wrapped with silver ribbon and tied at the top with a bow as long as Colin's car. "Uh… what?" she stammered.

"Happy birthday!"

She burst into laughter. "That was a month ago! You called me from Gallos. We made kissy faces."

"That was all well and good at the time, but I have the chance to do something more substantial now," he explained.

"All right, I appreciate you. What are you giving me?"

"A present. This isn't a real box, obviously, but you can 'unwrap' it with this." He handed her a small remote device with a single red button.

This is a problem. She couldn't convince her brain to dispense with the intrusive thought, but something told her that this would be a commitment. Accepting Colin's 'gift' would open a giant can of worms that she wouldn't be able to put back. She knew she should be thrilled and appreciative. Any other woman would be. What was wrong with her?

On impulse, she pushed the button. In a holographic display of fireworks, the illusion fell away and revealed a dagger-shaped space vessel.

Kaia jammed her hands in her jacket pockets, trying to look pleased but unable to keep her smile from dropping into a concerned frown. She understood that Colin was peacocking, but she wished he wouldn't. She already liked him. How much more obvious could she be about that? Her life was complicated enough without having to navigate her highborn boyfriend's moods and gestures that were completely out of proportion with normal people's actions. But she also acknowledged she was in too deep to shy away now. Recent events had permanently bonded them.

"Colin, what is this?" she asked tentatively.

He made an entry on his handheld and threw data to her.

Kaia gasped as she read the screen on her own device. "'Transfer of ownership'?! That's crazy. You. Are. Crazy!"

"You needed your own ship, and I wanted to give you something useful. It's a *present*."

Kaia's mouth dropped open as she tried to process the situation. He'd given her a ship. Her own starship. Her mind flailed for an out. "Colin, I… I can't accept this."

He hesitated then said, "You hate the design."

She focused on the ship itself, resembling a streamlined wedge. "Well, it is unusual. Very pointy."

"Not everything has to be built with tapered noses and sweeping wings," he said, sounding a little defensive. Clearly, he thought highly of this vessel.

"And its uniqueness is great. This isn't about aesthetics. I'm just… shocked. It's not every day someone is casually gifted a *whole starship*." She raised an eyebrow at him.

"Yeah, well…" He faded out and shrugged.

This might be totally normal in his world, Kaia realized. Anyone in a Dynasty was in a whole other echelon. It was easy to forget Colin came from unfathomable wealth while she was chatting with him about GravX or talking about their favorite shows and music. But, when it came down to it, their sense of money and material possessions were completely different.

She decided that coy wasn't working and went straight for a direct attack. "You know, when I teased you about inviting me to a yacht, I didn't expect you to actually give me one."

"Hardly a yacht. *Decius* is a mining ship. I'll bet you

anything this bad boy has plenty of stories to tell. He's seen some action, *Decius* has."

So much for direct. Colin was inside his own head.

"He's a J-10 small trader," Colin continued. "This model is usually used for scouting missions and courier jobs by the big transportation houses, or prospecting by asteroid miners. Light. Compact. Not fast, but sturdy and reliable. I figured your folks would appreciate that."

"I'm sure. But, Colin… a *ship*?"

He tilted his head. "We decided, you need a ship to follow those pirates."

"*We* decided? When was that?"

"You'd mentioned how much your mom wanted to be able to go track down those pirates. I thought this would help."

Oh, my stars, this man! Emotions warred within Kaia. She could tell that Colin had expected her to swoon and accept his grand gesture without reservation, but the arrogance of his assumption that he could give her something so extravagant irked her. *Where am I supposed to berth it? What about maintenance?*

Colin had, apparently, considered none of that. He still had a gleam in his eyes as he continued painting a vision for what Kaia could do with the vessel. "*Decius* is meant for a small crew about the size of your family," he was saying. "You might have to re-arrange a few bits. Move a couple of interior walls and such. But he'll sleep eight people in four cabins, there's some storage space if you feel like picking up some cash by transporting cargo or doing a bit of speculation. He'll get you safely from one location to another. I even sprang for a weapons turret with a plasma cannon. Just in case you get surprised."

Great, add interior renovations to the list of expenses! She took a slow breath to steady her pounding heart. "Colin, there is no plan to go gallivanting across the galaxy chasing pirates."

"Okay, so you can lease him out as a charter instead. That's how the pros make their money. Either way, you win."

You really aren't going to let me say no, are you? That second proposal actually wasn't bad. An income stream would make ownership viable. While that kind of business venture hadn't been in her To Dos, at least it made sense. *I suppose 'starship owner' has a nice ring to it. Time to act the part.* "What did it cost?"

"Do you always ask your boyfriends how much their gifts cost?"

"This is a little more than a trinket."

He nodded. "True. A ship like this would cost about a million credits new. I bought him used for half that."

"Half a million?" She considered it. "All right, then. I'll buy him from you. How's twenty thousand credits sound?"

"I just gifted him to you for free, Kaia…"

"And it's a nice thought, but I don't want to feel like I owe you anything. I am not some prize to be won over. I want to be your *partner*. My math says that twenty thousand credits would buy me a four percent ownership stake."

"You actually have twenty thousand credits to spend?" he asked.

She brought up her investment portfolio on her handheld and flipped the screen around to show him. "You think you're the only one who knows how to play the market? I may not be in your league, but I'm not destitute. So, twenty thousand credits for transfer of operating rights and co-ownership of *Decius*."

"Or you could just accept it as a *present*."

"No. You want to go into business? Great. Let's go into business."

"I don't know what to say," he murmured.

"Say, 'hello, partner!'" She gave him a kiss.

His eyes clouded over for a moment, then he smiled and brought her in. "Hello, partner! Yeah!"

ALLEGIANCE

EXTORTION EXPRESS

SARGON DREW PICTURES in the faint layer of dust that topped the meeting table. He was being stood up. Or was he?

His lack of certainty made him anxious, though not so much that he'd lost sight of the objective. He was here to prove a point. To prove that New Akkadia mattered. To prove that he held power over those around him. He could afford to be a bit generous with his time.

Hammurabi, seated across from him, shifted restlessly in his seat. "I don't think he's going to show," he griped, the latest in a string of nonstop complaints since they'd arrived on Boragin.

Sargon wiped out his drawing with a sleeve and started another. "Give it a bit more time."

Emerald Queen had dropped them off in a shuttle containing a habitat module. The self-contained residence was meant to be used as a semi-permanent living quarters on an alien world; it could be sealed against the elements, held its own power and air supply, and would take a pounding that would destroy a conventional structure.

In addition to living quarters, this hab model included a working office, an armored vault, and the functional conference space in which they now sat. One door led to the lounge and dining area, and another offered access to a bedroom with eight bunk beds. Diplomacy sometimes called for long nights, and working in shifts was something the diplomacy track had impressed on both men in their brief time at the TSS Academy. This unit gave them everything they needed under one room with room to spare for Ham's Scorpion guards.

"How much more time should we grant our hosts?" Ham asked.

Sargon checked his handheld and scrolled through a collection of past alerts and messages. "We've only been waiting for an hour. His Minister of Defense has probably identified the *Queen* in orbit. They know she has weapons. And they know their planet's economy depends on them honoring prior commitments and contracts. They'll show. They can't afford not to."

"Says you."

"Yes, says me. So far, all they've seen from us is bluster and bravado. This is a perfect opportunity to make an example of them."

Ham tried to massage a crick out of his neck. "We have three industrial worlds that are already hungry and getting hungrier every day. You know what happens when factory workers can't feed themselves and their kids? They walk off the line and start working for people who promise them food. People like the Makaris Dynasty."

Sargon tossed his device on the table. "The Makaris managers are the ones who stopped the food shipments in the first place. Come on, we all knew something like this would happen, eventually. Push hard enough, someone inevitably pushes back. This is our big moment. If we face them down now and make it stick, nothing will stand between us and New Akkadia."

Ham pulled his jacket around him more tightly. "Fine. We'll wait. But I wonder if all this is worth the effort."

Sar rolled his eyes. "Remember that day in the bar twenty-something years ago? The four of us were commiserating our dismissals from the TSS. Before I trotted out my plan, you were talking about becoming a hair stylist."

Ham shrugged. "I'd have been a good one. I understand style and I like to talk to people."

"Oh, Ham…" Sargon tsked. "This is better."

"*Better* means coming up with real solutions to the problem we all knew existed. If all we're doing is replacing one set of rich bastards with ourselves, what's the point?"

"The point is that *we* aren't using food as a political weapon. At least, not yet."

One of Ham's bodyguards, standing next to the doorway, made a signal. Sar and Ham stood to receive their guests.

Prime Minister Aldo Pim arrived with three men, all bearing expensive attire and tablets. After the conventional greetings were exchanged, they sat.

Sargon decided to lead with his best card. "Prime Minister Pim, I suppose we should state the obvious up front. We had a contract. Twenty thousand tons of various grains and produce to be delivered to each of three worlds on a recurring schedule. For payment that we already delivered."

Pim sniffed. "Payment in local credit chips. That's not the

same as standard credits. We asked you to send the money in digital currency. That's how we do business on Boragin."

"We agreed to pay, then we paid. That is how *we* do business. That's how business works everywhere—except in your office, it seems."

Pim waved his hand dismissively. "You paid in a currency we don't recognize. Besides, it's our grain. We will do with it as we please."

Hammurabi entered the fight, leaning forward to lend some gravitas to his argument. "Grain is food. Planets besides yours depend on those shipments. Not everyone in this sector lives in an environment as blessed with as much arable land or a lengthy growing season as you do."

Pim folded his arms and sat up straighter. "Are you suggesting we should have no control over our natural resources? That because you need it, we *must* sell to you?"

Sargon shook his head gravely. "Food belongs to the free people of the galaxy. That includes the people of New Akkadia."

Pim rolled his eyes. "There *is* no New Akkadia. You literally made up an administrative region that appears on no map of the galaxy. You arbitrarily decided that your rules must be adhered to. Unless you think that it's our *moral* responsibility to sell to you."

Sargon shook his head. "If it was just you, of course not. But you managed to convince the governors of Delphi, Fortalen, and Rukia to also refuse to sell to us. You turned food into a political weapon, and we cannot abide that. In the meantime, our credit chips are legitimate currency. All you need do is accept them and ship us what we've paid for."

"I will not submit to theft," Pim declared.

Sargon leaned into his position. Now he was fighting for

justice. "And I won't be denied access to basic sustenance."

"Well, then *Lord Sargon*, we find ourselves at an impasse," Pim declared.

Sar tried to control his breathing. On his worst days, he'd never considered starving anyone much less a whole planet. Pim was a *monster*. "Prime Minister, I implore you. All you need to do is resume the grain shipments that we contracted for last year. If you do that the governments on Delphi, Fortalen, and Rukia will follow your example and resume their shipments as well."

"And all *you* need to do is return to the standard credit as a form of payment. Digital currency is the galactic standard. Every bank in the empire makes use of them. All our accounts with every trading partner are denominated in them. I'm not going to accept shuttles full of credit chips as payments. We haven't used anything so base to settle our transactions in centuries."

"Computers drop data on a regular basis. Credit chips are forever. Local banks all over the galaxy have vaults filled with them," Ham countered.

"They are useful only as tricks that let honest brokers avoid taxation. I know the scheme. With each pair of hands, the stack of chips gets smaller as each middleman takes his cut. None of it for me, sir."

Sargon's heart soared. All Pim had been waiting for was the opportunity to talk about personal incentives. That was something that Sargon understood well. Finally, they'd come to a common point of interest. "Ah. You want to negotiate."

"This is not a negotiation. It's an outright refusal. Good day, sir."

Hope fell to pieces and Sargon felt bile rise in his chest. He was tired of talking to this cretin. "Sir, I have a lot of hungry mouths to feed. Resume the shipments, take the payment, and everything goes back to normal."

"I can't in good conscience do that with an ultimatum hanging over my head," Pim said.

"What I've given you is not an ultimatum. It's a suggestion with a lucrative reward for your compliance."

"I'm not going to comply with a thief."

Sargon waved his arms to encompass the room and all within. "How is this thievery? I assure you this is mutually beneficial. New Akkadia is taking form. The process will only accelerate from this point onward. You can be part of it."

"And all I need do to secure my place in history is knuckle under to your personal sense of self-importance? No, thank you."

Sar and Ham shared a desperate look. Sargon shook those thoughts away. He'd come here to do a job. "I don't understand your views or your reluctance. But you're a man of principle. I understand that. I also understand the difference between soft power and hard power."

Pim's aides all stiffened their postures, wary of a potential threat. Pim, however, merely frowned in confusion. "What do you mean?"

"How does a trade war strike you?" Sar gave a signal to Ham, who pulled out his handheld and began typing.

"How? You can't undercut our prices. If you try, you'll merely bankrupt yourselves. What is he doing over there?"

Sar ignored the question and pushed forward. "That's not what I meant. You can resume the food shipments to New Akkadia as our contract calls for, or I can cut off your production. No grain, no produce, nothing."

Pim blinked in confusion. "Wait... you're actually threatening to shoot down my own transport ships?"

Sar grinned. "Something far more fundamental than that. You've no idea how simple it would be."

"Hardly simple. You'd need a fleet of gunships. There *is* no such fleet."

Sargon grinned like a predator. "Prime Minister, not only is there such a fleet but it began orbiting your planet two hours ago."

— — —

First Officer Lom Mench stood in his Sergeant Meklife drone before the holographic display in the *Emerald Queen*'s War Room, fixated on a map of the surface. The Sensor Officer, Callum, had long since used the ship's sensors to locate every city and industrial installation on the planet and catalog it in the ship's battle computer, but Lom could not take his eyes off the agricultural domes.

"You can actually see the domes from orbit. Even on Lynaeda we don't have a food production scheme that's as highly developed as this," Lom said. "Nine million square kilometers of arable land on a single continent that has year-round temperate weather and reliable rainfall. They don't even use it all. They have those roving agricultural development domes which cover fifteen percent of the total. Always moving, always shifting locations, with their own processing and harvesting gear, each one. Each dome covers one hundred square kilometers, and together they have thirteen thousand of them producing twenty kilotons of food every day. That's seven million tons every year. Boragin may be the most productive breadbasket in the entire galaxy!"

Captain Aura's handheld beeped for attention. It didn't take long to understand the message that Ham had sent her. "It won't be nearly as productive for the foreseeable future," she said. "Prime Minister Pim has refused to honor the agreement."

"He'll come to regret that position," Lom murmured.

"Indeed. Sacha, pull up a map of the spaceport."

The Lynaedan officer who ran Operations raised her head. She used four mechanical arms to effortlessly run four completely different consoles. "Aye aye. It's on screen two."

"There must be a thousand shipping containers on that dock," Lom noted. "If we used every cubic meter of the empty space in the cargo pods, we could just about move them all into the *Queen*. It would still take two days even with every drone pilot helping to load them on board."

"That's assuming they even have a berth big enough to manage the *Queen*'s bulk," Sacha said.

"They do," Callum replied. "It's on the far side of that control tower. We'd just fit."

"Be that as it may, this operation is about gratuitous destruction. For once all we're going to do after the fighting is to take away what New Akkadia paid for," Aura said. "Sacha, have you and Callum finished coding all the surface installations into the battle computer?"

"Yes, ma'am. Surface map and target overlay is on the display," Sacha reported.

"What an orderly and efficient spaceport," Aura observed. "You see how the travel routes all converge on the loading platforms? Individual pathways through the storage matrices and vehicles to run cargo modules in and out of the network. Gravity lifts to load containers on and off grounded starships. And the access roads. Stars, these people are brilliant engineers!"

"It almost seems a shame to turn it all into scrap," Lom

said.

"Almost, but not entirely. You can rebuild a port like this in less than a year. But if we take out those grow-domes, they'll be ruined forever. I wonder if they realize that."

"The price of efficiency is the loss of resilience," Lom intoned.

Aura folded her arms. "Very well put, Commander. Sacha, charge the rail gun turrets. Hyper-velocity setting. Incendiary rounds. Two rounds per dome should do enough damage to send the message we need."

Lom tapped his fingers on a console. "They have far more domes than we have rounds for the rail guns."

"You're assuming that they would be willing to lose every dome. I wouldn't make that assumption. I don't think their prime minister will, either. Let's give them a volley every ten seconds. That'll make them squirm," Aura said.

Sacha recited her progress as she made the preparations. "Rail guns charged. Hyper-velocity set. Firing pattern confirmed. Auto-loaders ready with incendiary rounds."

"Then let's see how long it takes for us to change their minds. Commence fire!"

The railgun rounds were dense and perfectly shaped to slice through the planet's atmosphere, only extending steering vanes as they dropped down to the denser lower air. Each round packed the kinetic energy needed to break through the glass domes like a bullet through a window, and then the cracks created by the impact extended to the rest of the construction. The impact of each railgun round into the ground below its target dome still held enough energy to ignite the ground beneath, literally scorching the earth to a depth of two meters—destroying both the dome and the prospect for future crops in the immediate vicinity.

A new dome exploded into flames every ten seconds.

"This is too easy," Lom murmured. "It's like dropping firebombs onto a flower garden."

"New contacts," Callum announced. "Ten small ships coming to meet us from the surface. Profiles match small planetary fighter craft."

"Fighters! Is that exciting enough for you, Lom?" Aura asked.

"Very much so. Permission to respond in kind?"

"Granted."

"Sacha, prime the plasma beams and allow the battle computer to auto-select its targets," Lom ordered.

"We're not going to launch the fighter drones?" Sacha asked.

Lom let out an electronic chuckle. "It is tempting, but any good musician knows not to reveal every trick they have on opening night. Follow the order."

"Aye aye." Sacha's arms covered various controls while her eyes stayed locked on her instruments. "Targets acquired. Beams are ready to fire. Auto-targeting mode is engaged."

"Fire when ready."

The fighters swooped and climbed, trying to attack the *Emerald Queen*'s underside. The battle computer took a reading and shifted the great ship's attitude to bring its weapons to bear. Plasma beams flicked out again and again, blasting the tiny craft into scrap.

"Targets destroyed," Callum announced.

"Very well. Continue with the operation," Aura ordered.

— — —

When the news of the attack finally reached the prime

minister's ears, he blanched. His staff showed him captured images of the destruction, as dome after dome exploded and the flames beneath started secondary and tertiary blazes across the entire continent. Whatever Pim had expected from his talk with Sargon, this had obviously not been it. "What do you want?" he croaked.

Sargon put his handheld away. "Resume the food shipments and accept payment in credit chips at the agreed upon price. In addition, this building will become a permanent outpost here, which will represent the New Akkadian Bureau of Trade. No ship will leave this planet without the requisite paperwork and fees paid in credit chips. We'll be leaving a few enforcement mechanisms behind to verify your compliance."

"Very well. We will cooperate."

Sargon stood and stretched. "I thought you might. We'll start with the food that's already on your loading dock. You've been paid for it, so I'll be taking it. My associates will load as much as they can carry. We'll expect monthly shipments at the same price to resume. If all goes well you and I will never need to speak again."

"I promise you we *will* speak again. I'll be contacting the TSS immediately over this outrage!"

"Minister Pim, the TSS is currently occupied with matters of importance like maintaining galactic order. That doesn't include defending the rights of a pompous ass of a minister to illegally cancel a contract. But if you want to take your chances with them, by all means, make the call. We'll wait for the right moment, then return here to blow every grow dome on your planet to scrap. Have a good day."

FAMILY MEETING

ACCOMPANIED BY OFFICER Armin Godri, Lee arrived at the Sley house to a warm and noisy welcome. The whole clan was in attendance, which threw Lee off for a moment. The two men shared a knowing look and resigned themselves to the inevitable social requirements.

It wasn't until after dinner that Lee was able to gather everyone in the living room to get down to business. "Our first lead in months is the planet Boragin," he explained. "An agricultural world that recently survived a run-in with Mother Carnage's employer—a financier named Sargon."

Karmen nodded in recognition. "I know the name. What's he done now?"

"He set fire to ten million square kilometers of the most productive farmland in the galaxy when they refused to do business with him," Armin said. "They used incendiary rounds, too. Very destructive."

Kozu harrumphed. "When do we nail that bastard?"

Lee held up his hands. "Before I answer that, Kozu, let's have a bit of real talk. I—"

"There's no 'I' in team, Lee!" Elian blurted.

"Perhaps not, but there are three of them in Tararian Selective Service," Lee countered. "One of them is mine, another is Armin's. The third is the TSS Lead Agent, who's very graciously allowed me to continue to ask your mom to help as we work to locate Mother Carnage. But that is where the *team* ends. There's no *we* that includes civilians. There is only the mission."

"It's a shame Colin didn't spend the night," Seandra said. "We could have asked him for another ride."

Daveed nodded. "True. Even if we wanted to follow Karmen on her second round of adventures, we'd have no way to get there."

And thank the stars for that! Lee thought, starting to relax a little.

Kaia cleared her throat. "That's not entirely true. Before he left, Colin sort of gave me a starship."

"He *gave* you a starship?" Daveed and Karmen asked in unison.

"Yeah. It's not that big or fancy. I tried to say 'no', but he didn't want to take that for an answer. I threw him some money for it so we're co-owners. But my name is on the title," Kaia said.

Lee blanked out for a moment, seething and imagining how he might end Colin's life. The last thing he needed was a way for the whole Sley clan to follow him on a crusade. *Stars, I'll never be rid of them now!*

A quick glance at Karmen's face revealed she actually seemed to be entertaining the idea. "I expect that changes a few things," Karmen allowed. "I must say, I could do without

Colin's excessive need to impress, but I can't deny that having a starship of our own does have some advantages for a covert fact-finding mission."

Kozu laughed. "I see. So it's *Kaia's* ship but *your* job. That's nice, Mom. Have you asked Lee or Armin for their input on that job description?"

"No, she hasn't," Lee said. "And about that—"

"We're all helping your mother," Daveed chimed in before Lee could finish. "Even if we aren't soldiers."

"That's right, you're *not* soldiers," Armin grumbled.

"And whose ship is it, again?" Kaia asked with a raised eyebrow.

"*Your* ship," Karmen affirmed. "Yours and Colin's."

Kaia snuggled into her comfy chair. "Yes, it is. I will never get tired of hearing that."

Karmen waved them to silence. "Which brings us back to the mission. Might as well hash out all our roles now."

"There's nothing to discuss," Lee shot back. "This is official TSS business, and Karmen is to be the only Sley engaged in those efforts going forward."

"Except that the moment the *Emerald Queen* sees a TSS ship shadowing them, they'll run again," Karmen pointed out. "This isn't about just catching that pirate ship. We need to gather enough information to figure out who they're working with—who's *really* pulling the strings. Learn their moves, their intentions. That means long-term observe and report, in a mobile sense. Like a civilian vessel that can dock nearby and keep tabs without drawing attention."

Lee had to admit she made a valid argument. Still, the suggestion was problematic from start to finish. "This mission isn't an excuse for a family vacation."

"But what better cover is there than a family with

children?" Daveed questioned.

"That's not the point."

Daveed exchanged a knowing glance with his wife. "Would it change anything if you learned we've been preparing to travel on our own?"

Oh, stars, no! "What kind of preparations?"

"I've already applied for a sabbatical from the university," Daveed said. "It would be easy for us to gather up our most precious things to bring with us, including the contents of Karmen's Don't Panic lockers."

"Guns! Ammo! Boom stuff!" Seandra cried.

Lee tried to keep his face neutral. The girl's obsession with weaponry remained alarming. "I'm sure a planet-hopping adventure would be a wonderful family bonding experience for you all. Tagging along on an official TSS investigation is simply not the right venue."

"Then you can count me out," Karmen stated.

"Let's talk about this privately. Not in front of your family," Lee said in her mind.

"I'm a TSS consultant," she continued out loud, ignoring his plea. "All the debriefs after the last go-around made it clear that I can bow out at any time. So, I'm telling you that as a civilian, I will take this ship with my family and begin a tour of spaceports where suspected pirates have been spotted. If the TSS would like to offer a suggested itinerary for those travels, that is something we can discuss."

"We know what we're proposing is dangerous," Daveed said. "Our last meeting with Mother Carnage went poorly for everyone."

Lee nodded. "There's no avoiding the fact that she's more powerfully Gifted than I am. It's only because she'd let her training slide that I was able to beat her before. She'll be ready for us next time."

Armin spoke up, "And that warning is coming from a TSS Agent who could beat us all to a pulp without lifting a finger. The rest of us are just regular people, and it's a lot easier for us to get caught off-guard and hurt. From what I've been seeing in my Intel feed, Mother Carnage and her sponsors have upped their game significantly since we last saw them."

"We understand the risks, and we accept them," Karmen said, meeting Lee's gaze. "The only question is whether or not you want to work together on this. I'm going with my family either way."

Any other TSS Agent would have walked out of the room and never looked back. Lee knew that's what he *should* do, too—but his friendship with the family kept him listening. *They really would offer great cover. We can make our TSS presence known, then step back and the criminals will think they're in the clear. All the while, Karmen can keep watch up close once the pirates start to relax.*

As taken as Lee was with the Sleys and their enthusiasm, he knew he needed to drive home the seriousness of the situation. "All right, we'll work the case together," he agreed. "Daveed, you and the kids can come along with us, but you will not be part of the mission at any time. No more rescues, no desperate gun fights, no starship battles. Understood?"

Elian raised his hand. "Can I still ask Armin about stuff? I mean, we can still talk to you guys, can't we?'"

Lee looked at Armin, who shrugged. "As long as it's not in the middle of a rescue, gun fight, or starship battle, sure."

"But I insist the civilians stay far away from any dangerous situations," Lee reiterated. "When I give an order, you must obey without question. We got lucky last time. We can't rely on luck to get us through everything."

"Ah, so there *is* a 'we' here," Kaia teased.

"For a travel convoy to what so happens to be a shared destination, yes. But I repeat, you will *not* be an official part of any TSS investigation."

Karmen nodded while the rest of her family grinned. "Understood, Agent."

"When do we leave?" Daveed asked.

"Tomorrow morning, for Boragin," Lee replied. "Keep in mind, the intel indicates that the *Emerald Queen* blasted a squadron of system defense shuttles out of the sky in minutes the last time someone tried to stop her. Pack accordingly."

6

CLOSE QUARTERS

"I THINK WE'RE ready to roll," Karmen said from the mining ship's pilot seat. The flight deck only had two seats and was crowded. A starship of any kind was an elaborate gift, but Karmen found herself wishing that Colin had sprung for something with a little more elbow room.

A pre-flight inspection had revealed that the ship had undergone numerous modifications by previous owners. Four mid-sized cabins had been turned into half-sized sleeping quarters, and what was left had been turned into two irregularly laid out ore bins. The Sleys had made their own adjustments. Now, the port-side ore bin was the family common room, which could double as a lounge, a spare bedroom, or a quiet space, complete with furniture from the Sley's home in Foundation City. The starboard-side ore bin was now a business office, with four workstations and a computer linkup that could keep pace with any TSS office.

Karmen and Daveed were sharing, while Kozu and Elian were doubling up in a second, and Seandra and Kaia took a third; they'd kept the last as an extra storage room for now, with the knowledge that it might be needed if Colin came to visit.

"We need to figure out our transit schedule," Karmen told Kaia, who currently occupied the co-pilot's seat. "Lee and Armin can fly to Boragin in three hours with the TSS shuttle, but it'll take us two days."

"That's not fair," her daughter groaned.

"Why don't you call up Lee's shuttle so we can figure it out."

Kaia had already familiarized herself with the controls. "All right, you're on, Mom."

"Lee, this is Karmen. You boys are considerably faster than us, so we'll meet you over at Boragin."

"And leave you to be lonely without us?" Lee said over the comm. "How about this—in the interest of maintaining task force discipline, we will make the trip at the same rate you guys do. Beacon for beacon. We'll be with you the whole way."

"Aren't the Boragin authorities expecting a faster response time from the TSS?" Karmen asked.

"Oh, certainly. And when I spoke to the Prime Minister on a vidcall, it was clear he wasn't in a very forthright mood. A couple days to stew should loosen his tongue considerably."

"I mean, we *are* responding to his request for assistance," Armin chimed in. "The TSS can legitimately say that an Agent is on the way."

"Very tricky," Karmen said with a smile. "And you're willing to tough it out in those close quarters for that long?"

"To stay alongside our valued team member, it's a sacrifice we'll happily make," Lee told her.

"I don't deserve to work with either of you boys." Karmen's

heart filled her chest.

"Make that the last time you refer to us as 'you boys' and we'll call it even," Armin said.

"More importantly, the moment we need to be somewhere in a hurry, that arrangement will end," Lee pointed out.

"Done! Launching in five minutes. Kaia, you are relieved. Elian, get your little butt up to the flight deck. You're flying co-pilot for the first jump."

"Noooooooo!" Seandra wailed from her cabin.

Kaia switched with her brother, and Elian beamed as he slipped into the control seat. "I promise not to blow us up," he said. "Oh. Oof. Sorry. That was a dumb joke."

"I forgive you. I'm also holding you to that promise, young man. The pre-launch checklist is on your right, just above the dash. Let's go through it, item by item," Karmen ordered as the others retreated from the flight deck.

They started checking off the list with Elian reading off the items and Karmen making the inputs at her station.

"Man, this is a lot," Elian groaned.

"Yes, it is. Everything on a starship must happen properly, in the correct order, or bad things will happen instead. Like no air, and suddenly your best friend is sucked out into space."

Elian sank into himself. "Is that what happened on the *Triumph*?" he whispered.

Oh, my little man, it would be easier if that had happened. "No. My best friend turned into Mother Carnage."

"Gaaaaaaaaah…"

"Right. What do you say we launch this ship and meet Lee and Armin in orbit?"

"Yes, please!"

Karmen tapped her comm. "Lee, we are ready for departure."

"Got you. Join us at ten thousand kilometers altitude and we'll transit to subspace together."

Karmen swept her fingers across the console and *Decius* hummed as the pion drive activated. The view out the viewscreen dropped away, but Karmen quickly compensated by splitting the views. Her portion remained focused on the forward view while Elian's showed him the planet beneath them falling away as they raced to their planned orbital path.

"Approaching rendezvous coordinates," she said.

"Coming alongside you guys now," Lee confirmed.

Compared to *Decius*, the TSS shuttle was a lightweight, resembling a commuter shuttle more than anything intended for long-range interstellar transit. Only the fancy sensor dome hinted at the official nature and true purpose of the vessel. "I'm sure it feels almost roomy with just the two of you aboard," Karmen commented.

"A little bit, but I have to listen to Armin complain about everything now. I got used to listening to you two sparring."

"You want to trade?"

"No, thanks. You have enough to keep you busy."

They soared away from the planet together, heading to their jump point. On Lee's mark, the two vessels simultaneously initiated the transition to subspace.

Karmen watched Elian's rapt attention on the screen as the blue-green streamers of light surrounded them. She took out her handheld and made a few hasty calculations. The cooldown times between jumps were four hours long. That meant plenty of time to teach her family practical shipboard skills. Their navigation plan called for twelve cool-down stops between Greengard and Boragin; each family member could get multiple chances to shine in the co-pilot's chair. Elian was already here, then Seandra, Kozu, then Kaia and finally

Daveed. Then the cycle would begin with Elian again. She was so proud of herself, she called her husband forward and showed him the schedule.

"That's forty-eight hours for *you* in the pilot's chair. When do you plan on sleeping and eating?" he asked.

Confused, she pulled the device back and checked the screen. "Oh."

"Let's go over this again, shall we? And this time we can add a reality filter," Daveed suggested.

"I'm an idiot. That's the reality." She sighed.

Daveed reached into the holographic display and maneuvered the data cells. "How about *this*… You and Elian, then you and me. Then I'll take pilot with Seandra and then Kozu, and you take over with Kaia then go back to you and Elian. Two jumps on, then two jumps off for each of us."

She considered the schedule carefully. He'd carefully separated the problem children from one another and made it possible for everyone to enjoy a bit of time alone in their respective cabins. "You'd have made a solid personnel manager."

"I've done that job. Teaching is more interesting."

—

The first round of crew rotations went well. Daveed proved to be an apt pupil. Karmen taught him how to manage the displays and he quickly memorized where all the controls were. She ran him through a number of simulations and watched happily as he managed everything she threw at him. By the end of their second shift together, she felt comfortable leaving him in charge of the ship.

The cooldown between jumps started grating on her after

the first day. The rest of the family could smell her impatience; the kids quickly became used to the tedium and got bored. Lee clucked at her when she complained.

"Look at it this way," Lee said through their comm, "By the end of this, your family will have more real-world experience at running a starship than some commercial crews running actual businesses. Maybe you can get them internships with Captain Solari."

Elian chose that particular moment to scream, "Why *can't* I ride in the turret? It's part of the ship, there's life support in there, and I should learn how to shoot things for real."

"Then again, maybe not," Karmen answered. "Elian! Stand down."

"Gah! This already sucks!" Elian groused and stomped his way to the rear.

"Daveed…?"

"I'll make sure he doesn't touch the engines or the anti-matter generator," Daveed said.

"Thank you."

By the end of the first day even Kaia was starting to grow weary of the new routine. "Mom! We need a new sleeping arrangement."

"What is it now?"

"It's Seandra. She can't find a sleeping position to keep her from snoring and I'm tired of it. It's my ship. I should get my own room," she declared.

"So, take a nap in the common room. There are plenty of soft things in there to lie down on."

"That's not the point. We have the spare room—"

"And then your older brother would complain about why *he* can't have his own room, too. We all agreed to the cabin assignments, so put your big girl pants on and manage it."

"Well, fine. But what about the smell?"

"*What smell*?"

"There's a weird smell coming from everywhere. It's in every compartment. Something has got to be wrong with the air circulators."

Karmen checked her console. "I don't know… everything checks out."

"I'm not *imagining* it. Something stinks on this ship," Kaia insisted.

"We can't do much until we put down. It's just three more jumps. Why don't you go to the business office and run some GravX stats for your next conversation with Colin?"

"Don't patronize me."

Karmen was done. "Kaia Sley, get off the flight deck or so help me, I will leave you all on Boragin and work with Lee and Armin on my own!"

"Gaaaaaah!"

CRIME SCENE

BY THE TIME they arrived on Boragin, Karmen was happy to be anywhere but inside *Decius*.

Both Karmen and Lee's ships made use of a landing zone at the spaceport reserved strictly for official visits by legal authorities. Karmen popped open the airlocks and took a lungful of fresh air only to have her younger daughter gag when they emerged from the ship.

"Gah, what is that *stonk*?" Seandra demanded.

Daveed tried not to make a face and almost succeeded. "That, my dear, is the planet Boragin. Every world has a unique atmosphere and biome that gives it a unique smell. You'll get used to it after a day or so."

"I'll be happy to get back to Greengard, then."

"Even Greengard has a distinctive aroma. You were merely used to it. Trust me, it'll smell very different when we return."

Lee and Armin met up with the Sleys at the spaceport terminal. Lee had an officious looking man with him, practically stepping on the Agent's feet as he walked.

Karmen could hear him complaining. "Three days for you people to arrive. Three days!"

"We apologize for the delay," Karmen said. "My ship isn't built for speed."

The bossy man looked her over. "And who are you?"

Lee took over introductions. "Prime Minister Aldo Pim, this is Officer Sley, my colleague. Officer Godri here is our technical specialist."

Pim spared a bare moment of grunted acknowledgements before dismissing everyone but Lee as irrelevant. "You've seen my report."

"I have," Armin said. "It reads like a war story. You really lost ten million square kilometers to these thieves?"

Pim folded his arms. "You think I'm overstating the case? That I'm *overreacting*? Come with me. I'll show you." Pim led them to an office tower building adjacent to the terminal. He met up with three other functionaries all dressed similarly to their boss and they arrived at a meeting room.

"You'll forgive me if I keep this short," Pim began, "But the emergency is far from over. Forget the fact that we're still cataloging the cargo that was taken off our dock and loaded into that giant ship."

Karmen used a handheld to display her images of the *Emerald Queen*. "Just for verification, we are talking about this vessel, aren't we?"

"Of course, of course," Pim grunted, barely looking at the image.

"How much was taken?" Lee asked.

"Nine hundred and sixty-three containers are currently unaccounted for."

"What were they collectively worth?"

"Twenty-four thousand tons of foodstuffs destined for open markets. Fifty thousand credits per ton. That's 1.3 billion standard credits we've lost. But the loss of one hundred grow domes is far more devastating. That will take years to recover. Assuming we *can* do so. Revitalizing soil at scale is no simple task."

"With all due respect to your current damage control efforts, Prime Minister, I'm really more interested to hear about your dealings with New Akkadia," Lee said.

"Bah! Upstarts. Cretins. Degenerate swindlers."

Lee checked his notes. "Says here they offered you payment in legal currency and you stopped your food shipments."

"That's wrong."

"No, sir. We have reports that were compiled by banks on several worlds and verified for accuracy. We will of course pursue the thieves, and the damage to your grow domes is obviously a criminal matter as well. But there are greater issues here. Why didn't you just live up to the contract you signed?"

"Who offers payment for twenty thousand tons a month in credit chips? Who does that? Thieves do that. Confidence men. We asked for payment in standard credits and they sent us literal crates full of credit chips. Don't tell me that's a legitimate transfer."

"Were the chips counterfeit?" Armin asked, tapping notes on a tablet.

Pim hesitated. "They were not. But so *many* of them."

This time, Karmen thrust her handheld into the prime minister's face. "Sir, I don't think you heard me the first time, so I'll ask again: can you verify this is the ship that emptied your loading dock?"

Pim glared at her but paid attention to the image. "Yes. That's them. They berthed it on the reinforced landing zone on the other side of our navigation tower. That ship was immense. And their loaders looked mechanical—two, three times the size of a person moving those modules from the storage platform to their ship day and night. The complexity was impressive."

"Surely, you deal with large cargo vessels on the regular," Armin said.

"Of course, but that landing zone hasn't been used in years. These days, heavy carriers remain in orbit. We have a dedicated shuttle fleet for ferrying cargo from the surface. It's more efficient."

Lee, Armin, and Karmen all shared a look.

"Minister," Lee continued, "I'm going to recommend that our legal office handle the remainder of your case. We will keep you apprised if there are new developments. Please contact us with any new information you may come across."

"You're kidding. Tell me you are kidding!" Pim fumed.

"We're going to track the hijackers down as quickly as possible. A report will be created and submitted to your office. That should help your recovery efforts. We'll begin immediately. As I said, contact us if anything new comes up."

Pim stormed off, leaving Karmen grasping for words. "That's it? We're not going to do *anything*?" she asked.

Lee shrugged. "I took a brief look into his mind. He's withholding a lot of information, but Sargon and Hammurabi's faces were fresh in his mind. He also wasn't lying about his reason for going back on that delivery contract. He didn't want to deal with a shuttle literally filled with credit chips. Tracking down Gilgamesh and Thand still seems like our best option."

"How about looking for Curium particles?" Karmen suggested. "We tracked them like that once."

"Armin thought of that on the way in, so I had him scan

for particles. There's no Curium anywhere in this system. I'm not sure what else we can accomplish here."

"I am. Let's take a day to make a few calls," Armin suggested. "Our thieves have up to twenty-four *thousand* tons of food to unload, which means they have buyers lined up. Let's watch the commodity feeds on the commercial markets in this sector, see where the prices drop most drastically, and draw a few likely conclusions."

"We can use the business office in *Decius*," Karmen said. "It'll give the kids some time to unwind."

"Sounds like a plan," Armin said. "In the meantime, I'll scan the TSS lines for any new sightings of our friendly pirate crew."

— — —

They spent the rest of the day in reconnaissance, Armin spending time in the TSS shuttle and Karmen backing him up on the shuttle's comm console. It was a simple thing to link their comm net to the business office aboard *Decius*, and Karmen tasked Daveed with scouting the StarNews business channels to see if he could connect a few dots of his own. Between the three of them, they managed to pull a fair amount of information from the local news nets and compare their tidbits to the TSS's files. But nothing indicated the pirate queen's likely trade route.

One good thing about Boragin's spaceport was that it catered to all manner of business interests, including a wide variety of places to eat. They chose a mid-range restaurant in the terminal. A two-hour family meal got everyone's spirits up.

Their spirits flagged when Karmen couldn't coax *Decius* into starting up. She flipped switches, ran through troubleshooting checklists, and opened panels in the drive section to look for a clue to the problem. All she could determine on her own was the power core would not activate. Lee and Armin were of no help.

Finally, they called a repair tech from the shipyard at the other end of the spaceport. The tech arrived just before sundown, a grizzled man whose years of experience showed in his face, and whose name tag read Jena. First or last name, Karmen didn't know or care. "I hope you can point out the problem. It'd be even better if you could fix it yourself. I'm no slouch but I'm stumped," she said.

"Let's take a look."

"Take a look at the air circulating system, too. It's blowing a funny smell through the vents," Kaia added.

"Yes, young miss. I surely will." Jena bulled his way through the ship to the drive section, pulled apart panels and used an analyzer after he exposed the core. "Ah. Here you go. Your power core is dead."

"Power cores don't just *die*," Karmen countered.

"Well, the core itself might have some life left in it, but its distributor interface is burned out. When that goes, it's usually cheaper to get a new core and sell the old one to MPS through their buy-back program."

"How did this happen?" Kaia griped. "It worked a few hours ago."

"Is this the first time you've pushed the ship in a while?"

Kaia crossed her arms. "I just got it. But yeah, I don't think it had been flown a lot recently."

"Connections get brittle if they go too long without being put through their paces. A multi-day jump with minimal cool-down time can be tough on an old ship."

"Old?" Daveed chimed in. "This is a new ship."

"Ha! That's what the salesman probably told you." Jena chuckled. "Listen, folks, I've worked on J-10s before. They're always serious modification jobs. People win them in card games. They buy them on used dealer lots. It's a hopelessly obsolete model—no new ones being made. People just buy or acquire used vessels and modify them to death. This one was probably new when my oldest son was born."

"How long ago was that?" Kaia groaned.

"Young miss, let's just say I've got three grandkids now and leave it at that."

Kaia's face grew red, and she clenched her hands into fists. "Bomaxed Colin! I'll kill him!"

The mechanic patted her shoulder gently. "No, no. It's not all bad. The ship's in decent shape. You're right, though: the air circulating system does need to be flushed. I can do that for you in a few hours. But that power core... safer and way simpler to just replace the unit. Good news is I can do that while the air flush goes on. Bad news is I'd have to order it from off-world. Three or four days."

"What if we pick it up for you?" Armin asked. "Tell us where to go and we'll handle the freight. No need for a commercial carrier."

"I don't care how it gets here. You folks can sort that out amongst yourselves. But at least I can get you an estimate for labor and materials." Jena showed Daveed a price on his handheld and produced a collective gasp from the Sleys.

"Ten thousand?" Karmen gasped. "We can't do that!"

"If it makes you feel any better, it'd be over sixty without the buy-back, and I'm willing to handle that for you and just have you pay the difference."

"Much appreciated, but that doesn't make me feel better."

"Well, how's this... I can get it down to nine thousand if

your friends can arrange the shipping, but the price of the core is something I can't change. While I'm not a greedy man, I can't work for free. I've got grandkids, as I told you. Anyway, here's my contact info. Let me know what you choose to do. Have a good night!"

8

ALL IN THE FAMILY

KAIA SAT IN her broken ship's common room, wrapped in blankets, and stewed.

Her handheld beeped for attention: Colin's number. She let it go to messages. She did the same the next time it rang. And the next. On his fourth attempt, she'd settled enough to speak to him without screaming.

"Hi, Colin. How's your day going?" It came out a little snippier than she'd intended, but Colin was unfazed.

"I'm good. And I have great news! My mom wants to meet you. Can you come to Gallos? Like, soon?"

Only a playboy-in-training would think that people can drop everything and run to his homeworld on a whim. She resisted the impulse to take out all of her frustrations on him. "This isn't a good time."

"Why not?"

"Because *Decius* is in a bad way. We're stuck on Boragin for as long as it takes to make repairs."

"Is everyone all right? What happened?"

At least he asked about people before the ship. Maybe he's not a lost cause. She unfurled herself a little from the blankets. "Power core gave out. We found someone who will fix it, but it's expensive."

He sniffed. "It should have trade-in value."

"Yeah, but the out-of-pocket is still ten thousand."

"Shite. I'm sorry, Kaia. I'd offer to cover it, but… I hate to say it, I'm kind of broke at the moment. The repairs to *Percival* were steep, and I'm paying for it. Literally, paying for the repairs. Half a million."

She did feel a little bad about that, since the ship had only been placed in the line of fire because she'd gotten him involved. But that didn't entirely make up for this 'gift' becoming quite an expense. "Oh well. Anyway, *Decius* is grounded until further notice. Also, the air circulation system needs to be flushed. Why didn't you mention that the ship is a hundred years old?" She sighed.

"I'm sorry. I never had any trouble with it when I took it out. What have you guys been *doing*?"

"Flying it."

"Huh."

"Yeah," she agreed. "Listen, dude, I'm not in a great mood to talk right now. Thank your mom for the invitation, but I think we're going to be stuck here for a while. If nothing else, my mom is on a job, and we sort of have to go where she does. I'll let you know our plans once *Decius* is back in operation."

— — —

Karmen settled down in the ship's common room with her family. Daveed went to the business office to arrange a line of credit with their bank on Greengard for the ship's repairs. To help ease the tension about the setback, Karmen pulled her Fastara card deck from her cabin and coaxed Elian into playing with her. Lee and Armin came over to commiserate, and before long, everyone was playing the card game. Kaia refused to join but was willing to comment on everyone else's plays from her vantage on the couch under her blankets.

Karmen's handheld began to vibrate. The contact read Yelena Covrani. "Kaia, why is Colin's mother calling me?"

"If she's anything like him, I'd guess she doesn't take no for an answer. I'd also guess that Colin told on me."

"What does that mean?"

"She wanted him to invite us to Gallos. I told him we're stuck here and that your work schedule wouldn't allow it, anyway."

"Be that as it may, we mustn't be rude to the great lady," Karmen said and took the call. After her interactions with Colin, she was eager to learn more about this Lower Dynasty her daughter had befriended. "Missus Covrani, hello. This is Karmen Sley."

"My dear Karmen! It's such a joy to finally hear your voice. I apologize for being so forward. I don't even know the time difference between Gallos and your location. I hope I haven't pulled you from a warm bed."

"Not at all. But your call is a bit unexpected."

"I'll be brief. My Colin has been talking about your Kaia for months, and I thought it time that we invited your clan to Gallos so we can get to know each other. It's *ridiculous* that you and I have never spoken before now. I'm led to believe there's a structural problem at the heart of your current circumstances."

It does sound more elegant than 'our ship broke down.'

"That is one beautifully phrased way to put it, Yelena."

"I see. Well, if there's anything I can do to help, just ask. I know you've been after that horrible Mother Carnage woman. I'll be honest, dear, she's making us all crazy here. Operating costs are up, delivery rates are down, and our insurance premiums are unthinkable. I know there must be *something* we can do to help bring her to justice."

Karmen sensed an opening. *Yelena, you really do think you're being subtle, don't you?* "Well, honestly, we're looking for clues on where she may strike next. All we have to go on for now are vague reports from local Enforcers, which aren't very helpful."

"Mmm, I see the problem. Difficult to get ahead of a known issue if all you have to use are old reports of where she's been. You need to know where she's going next. Am I right?"

"You've done this before, I see," Karmen carefully probed.

"Run down pirates? Hardly. I've had some experience in safeguarding convoys, if that's what you mean. But here's an idea. All our contracted vessels are linked through a common communication network. There's lots of chatter—most of it rumors, some space legends. But there are good, real tips to be found by an astute listener. What if I put a bulletin on my network and offered a small reward for information that was verified by the TSS Agents in your company?"

"Well, that sounds a whole lot like trying to exert undue influence on a TSS investigation," Karmen shot back, wanting to test the other woman's resolve.

Armin threw his arm across his face to keep from laughing while Lee merely hung his head in embarrassment.

In a flash, Yelena's voice hardened to a diamond-like density. "Karmen, be reasonable. This is not a bribe. You need information leading to the arrest of a pirate who, frankly, is making me miserable. And now she has imitators. The gall of it!"

"Imitators? Please tell me more about that," Karmen urged.

"Ugh! I hate to even think about it. I see red every time I do. There's a troop in this sector called Kengi's Bombardiers. They attack cargo ships, extort what they call 'donations', and then leave the crews stranded. It's just a matter of time before those ruffians kill someone. Thuggery, pure and simple."

"Sounds like it."

"They're not the only group of rogues on the prowl, but they hit my company's traffic consistently. Extra security means higher costs, which I have to pass to my customers, and everyone involved loses. Besides, I do want to meet you and your family very much."

There's that word again. "My family."

"Yes, your family."

Kaia is who she means. She wants to screen my daughter and is willing to pay to do it. "We could swing by Gallos to get whatever information you can share about these other pirates. My husband and all the kids are with me. Do you have enough guest room? Should we bring our own sheets and towels?"

Yelena Covrani brayed laughter. "Oh, I do like your sense of humor. I'm sure we'll get along famously. We are well stocked on the necessities, but bring anything that will make your stay more comfortable. We can fill in any gaps once you're here."

"You are far too generous, madame."

"Madame? Bah! Just Yelena, please. Mother to mother. I suppose that just leaves the question of what to do about repairing your ship."

"We're working on that now." Karmen looked over at

Daveed talking on his handheld while pacing across the office.

"Well, I took the liberty of polling my inventory manager, and we have a power core of the type you need in our warehouse on Dacha, a mere two jumps away. I can have it there in less than a day, if you're agreeable. Send me the bill for installation."

"I'd hate to say no to such a kind gesture. I could even send a TSS ship to pick it up," Karmen said.

"Oh, wonderful! I'll happily sign the procurement order."

These political types know how to bank favors, I'll give her that. Karmen wasn't keen on owing this woman anything, but the financial reality of the situation was too much to ignore. "We'll find a way to repay you."

"Oh, no need. Let's just call it the price of meeting a war hero and her clan! We host dignitaries all the time. I can hardly do less for *family*. Let me get that transfer order started. Your TSS colleagues can contact my warehouse directly when they arrive at the Dacha spaceport. I look forward to continuing this conversation in person. See you soon!"

Yelena hung up and left Karmen to chew on her thoughts. "Well, family, what do you think of that?"

"I think I wish I'd brought nicer clothes," Kaia said with a frown.

Armin leaned back in his chair. "Karmen, I think you have a new best friend."

"A new best friend with a communications network we could make considerable use of," Lee added.

"As if meeting a boyfriend's parents isn't stressful enough! Now you want to turn it into a crazy spy thing." Kaia crossed her arms. "I'm not a spy."

"No, and we're not asking you to be one," Lee told her. "However, Yelena offers us an inside track to information we might not be able to get otherwise. A man who's just been robbed might tell his friends details that he'd never tell the police. The Militia office on Greengard hasn't been all that useful in terms of updating our intelligence."

"Right," Armin agreed. "They'll confirm or deny questions if we put them to it, but the new offerings are pretty sparse."

"You're assuming if Yelena does discover some news regarding Aura's whereabouts, she might share them with me," Karmen said.

"It's more of a hope," Lee admitted. "But she clearly understands transactional relationships. Tit for tat is the law of the land."

"I notice you're very trusting of a woman who's used to being able to buy herself out of anything," Karmen murmured.

"Her power and influence don't make her immune to reality," Lee countered. "I grew up around these types, and I know that if an Agent tells her to jump, she'll at least rise onto her toes."

"She did offer to pay for that power core we can't leave Boragin without," Kaia pointed out.

"Yes, there is that." Karmen turned to look at her daughter. "What do you think? It's your ship... and Colin's your friend."

"Stars, I never should have accepted this gift—or co-ownership whatever. I *knew* it—felt it in my bones. But we're in it now. I say if Lee and Armin are all right with it, let's get that power core here."

"We can do that," Lee said.

May as well tell Daveed that bank loan won't be necessary. Saving money was great, but Karmen suspected that there would be an even higher price to doing business with Yelena Covrani. She sighed. "All right, let's get our ship fixed up. But I have a feeling we're going to be sucked into some crazy plan

as soon as we get to Gallos. As much as we might think we're
using her, she's definitely using us."

—   —   —

Gallian tapped on Commander Mench's door. Then again,
louder. When the first officer finally opened up, Gallian spied
the interior of the cabin and got a glimpse of a woman with
olive skin and jet-black hair while Mench revealed his bare
torso through the gap.

"Can this wait?" Mench growled.

"You're going to want to see this."

The first officer muttered an apology over his shoulder
then stepped out into the corridor, closing the door behind
him. At least he was wearing his briefs. "Two minutes, then I
turn your comm net off."

Gallian pulled up data feeds. "This pinged an hour ago on
the general intelligence channel. I set it up to scan for tidbits
on the galactic net. Names, places, you know the sort."

"And?"

"And we got a ping from Boragin. Not only did that no-
account prime minister call the TSS, but the TSS took days to
arrive. That means they were using commercial ships for
transport. We never suspected they were that hard up. It's
encouraging, though."

"Or else a TSS vessel was escorting a commercial one. Keep
going. One minute."

"This was part of what the security feeds popped out to us.
Recognize these folks?"

Lom stared at the image and frowned. "They're the cretins
who attacked us two months ago." He swiped through the
collection of images, identifying them one after another.

"Karmen Sley. That TSS Agent. The Agent's sidekick. I'm not sure who the man and the children are."

"If you check the visual logs from the attack, you'll find that all of them—well, nearly all of them—were part of the crew that hit our landing party back at Tavden."

"So?"

"So... this one is very obviously Karmen Sley. She has relatives, yes? Children?"

Mench pointed to the images of the young ones. "Of course."

Gallian nodded excitedly. "Check out this bit of data correlation. Less than two weeks ago, there was a twenty thousand credit transfer for a four percent ownership stake in a mining vessel out of Gallos. Check the name on the transfer. The majority party is named Colin Covrani. The minority is Kaia Sley."

"Thirty seconds, Gallian."

"I've done the background checks already. This Colin guy is part of the Covrani shipping dynasty. Colin, the owner of the mining ship, was also the party to the transfer. His mother is Yelena Covrani, the director of the subsidiary that handles the megacorporate licensing and transportation leases division."

"Get to the point, Comms."

"It means the Sleys have an ally in the Covrani. If we can't find them ourselves maybe we can maneuver them into a trap. How much time do I have left?"

"You just bought yourself an extension," Lom admitted. "Lay this out for me. Don't leave any dots unconnected."

Gallian ran through his facts, his observations and his conclusions. "Bottom line, Lom, what if the Covrani are maneuvering the TSS toward us? We can't have those clowns getting too close to our operations before New Akkadia has a chance to fully deploy a defense force. We need help, and out here that's not easy to find."

"But Lord Ashurbanipal can. All right. Take some time to double-check everything you have. We'll present this to the captain first thing in the morning. As you can see, I'm presently occupied."

Gallian snuck another look into Lom's cabin. The brunette was extremely cute, probably one of Lord Hammurabi's Scorpions. "Roger that. Enjoy your occupation."

9

JUST THE FACTS

KAIA HAD TO admit that Jena knew his trade. The new power core hummed and the air inside *Decius* was fresh and clean; though a slightly metallic smell remained, she could live with that.

They set off toward Gallos, with a stopover at Dacha for supplies. The station was a massive industrial complex, shaped like an unholy marriage of geometric shapes.

Kaia tapped the comm. "Dacha High Port, this is *Decius*. Requesting instructions for approach and docking."

It took only a few moments for an androgynous voice to answer her. "*Decius*, proceed to docking bay two-one-nine, then power down in berth fifteen. You will be met at the berthing location."

"Roger that." It was just like the hundred and one simulations her mother had put her through since leaving Greengard. Matching the velocity was easy, but finding the docking bay proved impossible... until her father turned the integrated docking system on. "Heh. Sorry about that," she apologized.

"Not a problem. Just make a note of it to remember in the future."

"Yes, sir."

She made short work of locating their assigned bay and lowered the ship into the correct berth. She plugged in their connection code and waited for the automated kiosk to respond.

A message popped up confirming the docking lock, accompanied by an alarming comment: >>STATUS: HOLD. INSPECTION REQUIRED.<<

As she powered down the ship, she found her heart racing. *This doesn't seem normal.*

Her father was occupied with something on a tablet, and she waited while he finished his task.

"All right." He set down the device. "The supply depot should have everything ready for us shortly. It'll be enough to get us to Gallos and back to Greengard with several more stopovers. We can figure out next steps once we have a better understanding of where we stand with our new friends, the Covranis."

"Right, 'friends'." Kaia slumped in her seat. "I feel like I'm a prize two families are fighting over. Oh my stars... I'm not the pilot, *I'm the cargo!*"

Her father reached out and took her hand. "Do you not want to do this?" he asked. "If you're not comfortable, we can head home right now."

"No, I do care about Colin, and I'd like to meet his family and see where he comes from. I'm just... out of my element. And there's so much pressure—like I'm not allowed to say 'no' to these people. I don't think I've ever felt that before. I'm worried that if I stay with Colin, I might go through life feeling like a bystander."

"I know you better than that. No one will be able to push you around unless you let them."

"How can you be so sure?"

"Because I'm your wise father," he said with a warm smile, and she rolled her eyes. "You know, most dynastic marriages are made out of pragmatism. Power marries power. For Colin's mother to insist on meeting you is rather intriguing. Don't you want to know what she has to say?"

Her chest knotted. "Yeah, I—"

A beep from the comm interrupted them. "Lee to *Decius*."

Kaia accepted the call, relieved for the distraction. "*Decius*, go ahead."

"We'll be setting down in just a moment. How go things aboard that ancient rust bucket?"

Kaia's heart fell at the offensive joke, then forgave Lee when she realized he was trying to cheer her up. "Dad and I are in charge while everyone sleeps. I'm happy enough for the quiet."

"Let them rest. Armin and I are going to stretch our legs for a bit. We'll catch up soon."

"Roger that. We have a pickup to make at the supply depot, anyway." Kaia disconnected the commlink and scowled at the display. "Maybe we should take those supplies and just go home. I don't know how I expected everything to go, but I'd envisioned something different."

"Is this about the setback with the power core?"

"No, it's —" She abruptly pounded her fists against the arm rests. "I'm supposed to be getting a degree in business from Foundation U, not become some idiot highborn's plaything!"

Her father chuckled at her outburst.

"This isn't funny!"

"Oh, Kaia... I'm not laughing at you. I'm just remembering what it was like to be so young and have so much ahead of me. You're not a toy. That boy is smitten with you. An unscrupulous woman in your position could destroy him and walk off with a big chunk of a shipping empire."

I think his mother would have something to say about that. "Is that supposed to make me feel better?"

"Doesn't it? Believe it or not, having hold on a man's heart puts you in the real position of power. You *could* destroy him. Or, you could use that influence to turn him into a better man."

The tablet chimed and Daveed checked the screen. "Our order is ready. Shall we go? These slugabeds will still be here when we return."

She leaped from the seat. "Yes. Anything to take my mind off this drama."

They opened the air lock but didn't get far.

Two Enforcers were waiting for them, one in the simple uniform of a patroller while bars on the taller man's jacket marked him as an Investigator. The Investigator addressed Daveed. "Sir, are you Colin Covrani?"

"No. He's not on board. You can probably contact him on Gallos directly."

"But he's the owner of this vessel, is he not?"

"The owner is right here," Daveed countered, indicating Kaia.

"What is this about, gentlemen?" she asked, suddenly feeling much taller.

"There's a concern about the status of this craft. Miss, are you aware there's a lien on this vessel?" the Investigator said. "There's a notice filed by the Bank of Gallos for an uncollected debt owed on this ship."

"Colin paid for it. A half million credits or so. I own four percent."

"So, you do *not* own this vessel?"

"Is there a problem?" an authoritative voice said from down the concourse.

Kaia relaxed as Lee strolled over with Armin.

The Enforcer blinked as if unable to comprehend what he was seeing. "Agent...?"

"Agent Lee Tuyin. Now, I repeat, I'd like to know what the problem is."

The Investigator balked for a moment and shared a frantic look with his patroller partner. The look of panic in their eyes told Kaia a lot more than she'd expected. These Enforcers were not expecting resistance from a figure of authority, much less a TSS Agent. They'd barely glanced at her father, but they couldn't avoid dealing with Lee.

"Agent, this is a civilian vessel. What does it have to do with you?" the Investigator asked.

"I am on an assignment, and this woman and her associates are part of my crew. I'll ask you one final time, what is the problem? And think carefully before you answer. I'd hate to have to mention your names in my next report to TSS Headquarters."

The tall Enforcer tried again. "Agent Tuyin, the Bank of Gallos placed a lien on this vessel. It says there's a quarter million credits owed on it, and it's listed as being in arrears."

"And who does the lien identify as the indebted party?"

"Colin Covrani, sir."

"Is Colin Covrani aboard this vessel?"

"Umm..."

Lee closed the distance between himself and the Enforcer. "Officer, are you telling me you haven't inspected this vessel yet?"

"That is correct, but—"

Lee never broke eye contact with the Enforcers. "Miss Sley, do you have your ownership papers?"

"Yes!" Kaia selected a screen and thrust her handheld into the Enforcer's face.

"What do those papers say, Investigator?" Lee asked.

The tall man was getting red in the face now. This was not going the way he'd expected. "It's a transfer of ownership document. The name is Kaia Sley."

"Is that the name on the lien?"

"No, but—"

"Investigator, get your paperwork in order and maybe I'll allow my crew to answer some more questions. If you can't do that, I suggest you contact the Bank of Gallos directly and sort it out with them."

"Yes, sir. Thank you, sir."

The Enforcers scuttled away, and Kaia nearly collapsed with relief. "What did all that even mean?" Kaia groaned.

"It means Colin still owes a lot of money on this ship and the paperwork is catching up to him. That might be why he transferred it to you on Greengard. Maybe to buy himself time to pay the bill," Lee said.

"Oh, stars! He mentioned he was broke after paying for *Percival*'s repairs. I. Am. So. Stupid!" she cried.

"No, you're not," Lee argued. "I think he really did want to make a gesture you'd appreciate. He probably thought he could come up with more money quickly enough to keep the bill collectors away. I don't think he planned any of this. He just didn't think it through very well."

"I told you, Kaia," Daveed said, "That boy is in love with you. He's going to do strange things to prove himself to you. You must be ready to sort out the good gestures from the gross ones."

"Dad, are you *sure* I'm not a prize cow or something?" she groaned.

"Kaia, my father once donated a building with my mother's name on it to a local hospital," Lee said, shrugging. "Granted, they were already married by then, but… your dad's not wrong."

"Lee, I hate to ask but you're the only other dynasty brat I know. How did you turn out so well?" she asked.

Lee laughed. "I don't know. It surely wasn't the fancy lifestyle. I wasn't that different from Colin when I entered the TSS Academy. Without that environment I'd be a very different person."

Daveed checked his handheld. "Come on, kiddo. Let's fetch our order from the depot. Exercise will take your mind off your crazy love life."

"Stars, Dad, if you're going to patronize me, too…"

"I'm an old man and I need the help. Move it!" Daveed urged.

She brightened at his brusque tone; it felt like a protective wall between them and the rest of the universe. "See, was that so hard? Let's go, old man."

The depot had already loaded their requested provisions into crates for them to take away. For an extra fifty credits, they were even willing to lend them a carry-all, a floating platform they were able to push ahead of them as they wound their way through the crowds back to *Decius*.

Kaia walked silently next to her father, pushing her half of the carry-all. Unkind thoughts about Colin intruded on her, and she went through bursts of mental violence. She'd rage against him, clenching her jaw and puffing her face out, then relax. Then a few minutes later it would happen again.

Eventually Daveed interrupted her loathing. "Ready to absorb a lesson about the world of men?" he asked.

"I guess I have to."

"All right, then. What have you learned from this encounter with those Enforcers?"

She thought about it, then said, "The thing a man with power hates and fears most is another man with more power."

"Very astute. What else?"

"Never assume someone in a position of power is there to help you," she added.

"A key observation. Anything else?"

"Never assume someone has your best interests in mind just because you like them… or they like you." She swallowed hard as her throat tightened and tears stung at her eyes. "Why did Colin do this? Why is he like this?" she forced out, nearly choking on the words.

He rubbed her back with one hand while trying to keep the carry-all on course. The throngs around them made it difficult. "I don't know," Daveed soothed. "Your life taught you some very specific things about the universe and his taught him something very different. We'll know more once we get to Gallos. Watching how a family interacts can explain so many things. It's a great storehouse of information."

She wiped her nose on her sleeve and then threw herself into pushing their load. "Information. This is when it stops being about people and starts being about money, isn't it?"

"Money and responsibility and all the other things that make an adult," he confirmed. "It's depressing to think that concentrated wealth creates people like Colin. But it also creates people like Lee. You make your choices and hope they lead to better things."

"But I still *like* Colin. I miss him when he's not around. We go a few days without talking and I feel awful. What is wrong with me?"

"Nothing at all. I'll tell you this much: you and Colin found each other across literal light-years of space. Two people out of the six trillion who live in this galaxy. That doesn't happen often. It doesn't mean you need to stay with him at all costs, but don't beat yourself up about wanting him, either. And do *not* let him or his mother or anyone else make you less of the person you need to be. Everything else is commentary."

She sighed. *Easier said than done.*

10

A GOOD IDEA

KARMEN AWOKE WITH a start. She'd intended to only lie down for a few minutes to rest her eyes. Somehow, she'd wrapped herself in Kaia's blanket and passed out on the sofa. The disassociation she felt was made weirder by the fact that everything smelled like her daughter.

Daveed poked his head up from the work area on the other side of the common room. "Ah, you're awake!" He headed over to her. "How do you feel?"

Karmen started to stand up but balked when her naked feet hit the cold metal. Instead, she tucked her legs under herself on the couch. "Better. A little hungry. How long was I out?"

"Almost nine hours."

"Nine—? Why didn't you wake me up?" she demanded, her heart racing.

"You clearly needed the rest. You've been burning your candle at both ends. It's not healthy."

She pulled the blankets up to her chest and inhaled her

daughter's scent. It had a calming effect. "All right, I guess I needed the break. Anything happen I should know about?"

"You missed an altercation between Kaia and some security people on Dacha Station."

"'Altercation?' You should have called me!"

"Our girl handled it like a champ, with ample assistance from Lee and myself. She and I went to re-provision the ship at the station depot. All is well."

Karmen felt like she should argue the point then realized there was none. Daveed was right. She was pushing herself too hard. But it couldn't be helped. "Why is it so quiet? What's going on out there?"

Daveed flopped into a chair and carefully put his feet on the low table. "I let Elian ride in the turret."

"Oh, no! We'll never get him out of there!"

"Relax. The price for that bit of privilege was that Kozu is training him up in gunnery simulations. They're running one right now. I think Kozu's experience in *Percival*'s shuttle prepared him to be a decent teacher. Or at least an effective taskmaster."

"Who's flying us, then?"

"Kaia is pilot, Seandra is co-pilot. Let's enjoy it while it lasts."

She patted the space next to her. "C'mere, Dean Sley. This blanket smells like Kaia. I wanna smell you."

"I'm not moving. I had to work very hard to get my legs up this high. Surely you can smell me from there."

She huffed and carried the blankets with her as she braved the cold floor to reach his chair, ending up in his lap. He wrapped his arms around her as she settled against him.

"I see how this is going. Is there a problem, Officer?" he asked.

"Actually, there is. I need to ask you a difficult question. And I need a completely honest answer."

"Let me have it."

"Was this a good idea? I mean bringing you and the kids along on this crazy mission. It's been one sidetrack after another, and I know that's not good for anything. Should I have involved everyone?"

"In terms of what?" he asked. "It's been dangerous, complicated, stressful, and horrifyingly expensive. But I don't think we've all had this much time around each other in years. Besides, the kids are getting practical crew experience. All they've had to work with previously were classroom lessons and books and vids. They're finally seeing places most of their peers couldn't even find on a star map. Life is really being lived out here. That must be worth something."

"But was it a *good idea*?" she repeated.

"Yes. It was a good idea. That's my answer."

It wasn't the answer she wanted, and she couldn't quite convince herself he was being truthful, but it got her to a better place mentally. "Thank you."

"You're welcome. Now, tell me what's really bugging you."

Karmen sighed. "I'm worried about Kaia."

"You should be. She's going through a lot."

"Should we step in? Stop it all for her own good?"

"When you joined the Militia did your parents stop you?"

"Come on, that's not the same thing."

"Isn't it? We taught our kids to be their own people. Have dreams, to want things, to move out of their comfort zones. Kaia's doing all of that for better or for worse."

"She's eighteen. She has no idea what she wants."

"Oh, yes she does. She's into this boy and we can't stop that. If we forbade her from seeing him… Well, we're on our way to meet his crazy rich family. How do you think that would go over?"

"Badly." She shook her head. "What's horrible is the reality that I can't separate Colin from the fact that he's got access to all the money in the world."

"His access is sharply limited. I expect his mother sees to that."

"But it's still all about *money.* I'm terrified he'll use her up and drop her when she becomes inconvenient."

"She's *already* inconvenient. Yelena Covrani wants Kaia for something, but she wants you as well. There's an opportunity for both sides here."

"Are we match making now? Stars, that sounds worse to me. How much of our souls are we expected to sell to take advantage of this 'opportunity'?"

Time elongated for a moment, indicating they'd dropped out of subspace.

Kaia's voice emerged from the speakers in the ceiling. "Welcome to Gallos, everyone!"

Seandra squealed in delight in the background, and Karmen swore she could hear dull thumping from the turret.

"I think we're about to find out," Daveed said.

11

DYNASTY

GALLOS DIDN'T LOOK like anything special, but the planet's orbiting spaceport was stupendous. The view outside the ship rendered Kaia speechless.

Seandra glanced at her from the co-pilot's seat. "Kaia? Everything all right?"

"Yes! Yes, I'm fine. But... *look at it*!" she gasped.

"It looks like a spaceport."

Kaia checked her sister's viewer. Indeed, it showed a large, rambling commercial port where big cargo ships and other commercial vessels were entering and leaving.

"No, that's the commerce station," Kaia said. "That's two million kilometers away. Look at the transit port that we're flying into."

Seandra complied with the instruction and sullenly tapped the console. Finally, the viewer worked for her, too. "Oh, my stars! Is that a space elevator?" she squealed.

"You know it is!" Kaia could not take her eyes off the

spectacle. Space elevators were both archaic and horribly expensive to build. There were only a few of them still in operation in Taran space. They practically qualified as alien artifacts. "I had no idea... This changes a few things, for sure."

"So, you're *not* going to marry Colin now? How does that work?" Seandra asked, giving her a side eye.

"That's not what I meant. Not exactly." Plenty of worlds had cargo elevators, but this structure was well beyond that. Kaia wondered if Colin's family had been the ones to build it. Unless it was a holdover from an earlier time when such things made sense to build and operate. She *had* to know more about the structure's history.

Seandra's tone took on a worried edge. "Um. Kaia? Are we going to slow down?"

"What? Oops. Thanks for reminding me." Kaia reduced speed and maneuvered *Decius* into a parking orbit. The elevator was doing double service as both a transportation line linking the station to the surface and to keep the traffic properly organized. The central core looked like it was positively riddled with docking bays. "Gah, how many ships can that structure handle at once?"

"Hundreds? Thousands?" Seandra guessed.

"Tens of thousands, I'll bet," said her mother's voice from behind them. Kaia craned her neck to glance behind her. The rest of the family crowded the tiny flight deck. "Stars, that *is* impressive, isn't it?"

"It is at that," Daveed confirmed. "It takes a bit of effort to remember what makes our jaws all drop is just another day at work for them. They certainly didn't pull that structure out of the attic just for us."

"I know we all like Colin, but we live in two very different worlds," Kozu said. "You should look at the Covrani Group's annual report to shareholders some time. They own shipping fleets, charter fleets, way stations, transfer platforms, cargo depots, a gazillion shuttles. A major source of their income stream comes from use and transfer fees."

"What are those?" Seandra asked.

"A neat little clause written into every contract or terms of use agreement involving their equipment. You can't use their gear without buying into it. Every time someone unlocks a ship, a vehicle, or a facility owned by the Covrani, it sends a fee from their business account to Colin's mom. When you dock, they pay a fee to Colin's mom. You load or unload cargo and the lifters you used send a fee to Colin's mom—"

Kaia held up her hand. "All right, we get it. Every time someone in the galaxy does something with a Covrani asset, a fee goes to Colin's mom."

"Not his mother alone, surely," Karmen breathed.

"I might be exaggerating a little," Kozu admitted. "But Colin's mom runs a big division. It's a multi-trillion credit megacorporation, so the particulars almost aren't worth talking about. There are a lot of cousins and siblings and generations of grandkids to wade through. The lines of ownership get very confusing. Lee could probably explain it way better than I can. He's seen that machinery up close."

Elian squeezed himself between his sisters and gaped. "Guys! Are we going to ride that elevator all the way to the surface?"

"Let's find out," Kaia said, tapping the comm. "Gallos space control, this is *Decius*. Registration number J-10-8346P. Request instructions for approach and docking."

"Roger that, *Decius*. Stand by for instructions," said a baritone voice.

Kaia barely had a chance to breathe before a woman's voice

took over the exchange. "*Decius*, please stand by to accept an uplink from Covrani spaceport control."

They have their own spaceport. Because of course they do. "All right, space control. What do we do?"

"Set your nav controls to neutral, and we will handle your approach. You'll be landing at the Covrani private airfield. Stay on this channel for confirmation."

"Neutral setting established," Kaia said, praying that her voice was holding steady. Her stomach was turning in place and her heart was thumping so hard she couldn't believe nobody else heard it. *What am I getting into?*

"Tractor array powering up. We've got you, *Decius*. Just relax and enjoy the ride."

A slight bump rocked the deck as the tractor array took hold. Kaia's thoughts refused to settle, one leading to the next in a dizzying cascade of deductions. They were using a private docking array. That meant multiple space-based tractor platforms. They'd be handed off from station to station until they landed at the Covrani dynasty airfield. Next to the private park it took three days to walk across.

"What about Lee and Armin?" Seandra asked.

"Good question. Mom, where's our line between official business and social time here?"

"Why don't you ask them what they'd like to do?" Karmen suggested.

Kaia opened a commlink. "*Decius* to Lee. You guys there?"

"Yes," Lee replied. "You're leaving orbit in a hurry. Am I to assume that only future in-laws are invited to this dance?"

"I'm not sure that bringing a TSS Agent to our first meet and greet would make things less awkward," Kaia told him.

"No offense taken. Armin and I will spend the night aboard the space station. That'll give you a chance to meet the family on your own terms, and we'll be available if you need us. We can start the 'please give us information' wooing after you've established some rapport."

Assuming they don't hate me and forbid me from ever talking to Colin again. Kaia pushed away the dark thought. "I'll put on my most charming smile."

"I want an invite to at least one swanky party before we leave this planet," Armin added. "Not all of us grew up rubbing shoulders with the elites."

"Those parties are *extremely* overrated," Lee grumbled.

"I'll do my best," Kaia promised. "In the meantime, see what kind of space legends about Mother Carnage you can dredge up from the common people."

"Our thoughts exactly. Have fun, Sleys!" Lee ended the commlink.

Kaia wasn't on Greengard any more. None of them were. After months of feeling weirded out at Colin's intense interest in her, she was finally getting some sense of the power and privilege Colin took completely for granted. It was terrifying… but also *intoxicating*.

"Enjoy the ride." Kaia folded her hands in her lap and decided to do just that.

—

Decius grounded on a crowded field, filled with shuttles and cargo vessels all neatly parked in individual berths. Kaia stuck her head out the airlock and shielded her eyes from the bright sun. When they adjusted, she noticed a multi-car tram pulling up nearby. A muscled brunette in a trim uniform emerged, followed by several others in the same uniform style. "Good afternoon, Sley family. I'm Sergeant Tolri. I'll be your guide to the estate."

"You mean this isn't it?" Kaia asked.

"I should say not. This is only a reception depot. This is where we go through your ship and make sure you haven't brought any unwanted passengers or contraband with you."

"Anything that could upset your little paradise," Elian snarked.

"Will you shut up for once? You're going to get us banned for life," Seandra scolded. Their parents gave him stern looks, as well.

If Tolri took offense, she was an expert in not showing it. "Not at all. Safety is our only concern here. Your ship and belongings will be well cared for, I promise. Shall we board?"

The tram took them to a platform, where a much larger maglev train waited. Once inside, the departure signal sounded, and the doors closed with barely a whisper. The train floated above the rails and soon the scenery was zooming by nearly too quickly to see details.

"What's it like living in a giant nature preserve?" Kaia asked.

Tolri glanced outside. "It took me a while to get used to all the green after spending most of my life in space. There's a crew of park rangers on-site to manage the wildlife and flora. They check on the family's personal campgrounds, too. Make sure everything works properly and so on. I'm a little embarrassed to admit I don't know any of them personally. I don't go any further than the port too often."

Kozu sat facing Tolri and couldn't stop staring at her. "So, security. I imagine you'll be wanting to examine us, too?" he asked.

Tolri gave him a lopsided smile. "You must be Kozu."

"Colin told you about me, I guess?"

"He did."

"Told you about my security interests?"

"Not specifically. He merely mentioned you were interested in joining the TSS Militia. To answer your question, we already scanned you while you debarked. You're all clean."

"That's a relief, I guess," Kozu said, smiling like an idiot.

"You know," Tolri said, "several graduates from the Militia and Guard academies work in our ranks. We offer a training course that prepares applicants for the recruitment process. It's not unusual for our new employees to spend a year or so here to get experience, then go through military training and return as supervisors after their service."

"I don't suppose I could get an introduction…"

She gestured at the window. "Plenty of time for that. Our stop is coming up."

— — —

Daveed saw their destination long before the train pulled into the terminal. It wasn't an estate so much as a miniature city.

A close group of gleaming white towers accented by glittering chrome and blue-glazed windows rose high above the natural landscape. A terminal of marble and limestone linked the towers together, and the lower levels were punctuated by outbursts of greenery. Numerous balconies lined the exterior of each tower. Glass panels rose from the ground to the sky along vertical extrusions. He marveled at the architectural mastery and elegant aesthetics.

"Not to brag, but tell me you folks have anything like this back home, and I'll buy you all drinks," Tolri offered.

"Nothing at all. But my university is no slouch," Daveed replied. It was his job to be defensive of the place where he'd built his life and career, but the truth was that Foundation City was drab by comparison.

"I'll buy you all drinks anyway," Tolri offered. "There's a truly impressive sight about ten kilometers that way. A raging river going down a two-hundred-meter waterfall. These arcologies get some power from a hydro plant there. Lots of solar power, too. Can't use power cores for everything. I mean we can, but we don't. Diversification of method is a Covrani tradition."

"They're so *tall*. How do they all stay up?" Kaia asked, bringing a smile to Daveed's face that her inquisitive mind was so much like his own.

"Nine hundred meters, to be precise," Tolri confirmed. "They're not built like standard structures. There's a lot of empty space inside them. The walls are the primary load bearing units. You'll see once we're inside. This place houses the whole Covrani enterprise. Living space, offices, a lot of shops, and business centers. Some excellent restaurants. A few good clubs. And an exercise center that even the Enforcers can't get enough of."

"Sounds like fun. Really brings work-life balance to a whole new level. All we need now is a practice range," Karmen said.

"We actually do have one in the security section. Firearms, blades, and hand-to-hand practice sessions. If you want in, just ask."

"Stars, does everyone in there work for Colin's mom?" Elian blurted out, which got him a nasty look from Kaia.

Tolri laughed. "Hardly. CDS is a very big company that owns other big companies. There's a bit of rivalry but everyone within these towers is part of the Covrani group, in service to the family or business in one way or another. Colin's family has a twenty-level block in Tower One for their private use. I think you'll enjoy the visitors' quarters."

The tram pulled into the terminal and Tolri led the way into a scene of controlled chaos. Travelers came and went as some boarded elevators to the towers and others descended to more trains.

"Come on, Kozu. Let's get these ones settled, then I'll give you a tour of the security training facility," Tolri said. "We've got all the cool gear. And signing bonuses. Have you applied yet? We have a consulting office that ensures nothing gets lost in translation."

Daveed let the young ones get ahead and then leaned into his wife. "Yelena Covrani has bigger plans than I imagined."

"What do you mean?"

"It's a three-pronged attack. Set Kozu up with a personal trainer and mentor, marry Kaia to her wayward son who has big plans but few skills, and turn you into an operations boss. We're never getting out of here."

"She wants us for some bomaxed thing. Let's play along and see what they're serving for dinner."

"Oh, yes! Don't agree to do anything for that woman unless a personal chef is involved."

"Wow. I had no idea my man was so eager to sell out to the upper crust."

"A fine meal is its own reward, my dear."

— — —

'Visitors quarters' turned out to be a serious understatement. Kaia felt like Colin's family had bought them an entire hotel.

They all gaped and gawked as they walked through the palatial suite of rooms that seemed too manicured to use.

Everything was intimidatingly pristine and grand in scale. Each bedroom had a huge bed and a closet the size of Kaia's room on Greengard. The kitchen could have supported a team of chefs, and the dining room could have doubled as a specialty restaurant. The living room commanded an open view of the kitchen and dining area, as if the floor had been designed with entertaining guests in mind. *Well, it probably had been. Duh.*

Viewscreens were placed everywhere. They lined the walls like virtual windows, so despite the fact they were in a giant tower complex, they had unobstructed views of the entire park.

But despite the clear opulence of the place, there were no gold-plated surfaces, no robots to wait personally on each guest. That, at least, gave Kaia hope that she could maybe be comfortable here, eventually.

Kaia wandered into a new set of rooms, and lights automatically showed her what had to be a bathroom. But the combination of mirrors, glass, and chrome made her uneasy. The last thing she wanted to see when she wanted a bit of privacy was her image reflected in every surface. On the other hand, the tub could probably fit her whole family without crowding and the shower had enough room to stretch out on the floor without touching the walls.

Being surrounded by so many gleaming surfaces left her feeling empty. Cold. Even lonely. She coughed and was startled by the booming echo.

Her handheld buzzed with a message from Colin. >>Are you getting settled? May I come in?<<

Oh, stars, please! She jogged back to the front door. He was still typing in the hallway as she launched herself at him, almost knocking him down, squeezing until he made a noise.

"I'm happy to see you, too," he wheezed.

"Colin's here!" Elian yelled.

The other Sleys swarmed the entryway, greeting him warmly—a little too warmly, perhaps. Kaia noticed him fidgeting and pulled back a step to give him space.

"So. Welcome to Gallos," he said.

"Nice castle, Lord Colin," Seandra teased.

"Hardly. The correct term for these towers is 'arcology'," Colin said. "It's vastly more efficient than living in houses. The problem is that you have to be okay with always being around people. I grew up here, so it's normal for me. But I know this might be a little strange compared to your residential neighborhood on Greengard."

"Karmen and I lived in an apartment until after Kaia was born," Daveed said. "Multifamily residential living is common on many worlds—though most are not lucky enough to be surrounded by such natural beauty."

"Yeah, we have it good here." Colin rubbed the back of his neck with one hand, shifting on his feet. "Anyway, I'm here to get you oriented. But we're missing someone…"

"Kozu is in the training center with his new girlfriend," Seandra said.

"That would be Sergeant Tolri. She's good people. He couldn't be safer," Colin assured them. He pulled a handful of thin bracelets from his pocket and handed them out, then snapped one securely around Kaia's wrist himself. "These are security tags. Make sure you're always wearing one."

"Are the security people tracking us already?" Karmen asked.

"Yes, but these also serve as links to the central arc database. You can pay for things from shops and restaurants with them, and they'll let you into any public area. The gym, the pool, the recreation floors, the mall, all the elevators and transport tubes. They won't let you into apartments or any of the private business centers. You'll need to be invited by the residents for those."

"What happens if we wander into a private meeting?" Daveed asked.

"It beeps. Security will locate you and escort you out of the area. They do their best to be discreet, but they know how to manage troublemakers."

"So, follow you around everywhere for a while, right?" Seandra asked.

"Hardly, Seandra. I can't get into the private areas, either. I can only invite you to my personal apartment. Tower residents are pretty miserly with their privacy. Just be polite and respectful. This suite is yours for as long as you're here so of course you can come and go any time you want." He walked them over to a viewscreen embedded in the wall and waved his bracelet over it. A schematic of the arcology appeared. "Here's a layout. Arcologies go for tall instead of wide, so except for the lowest level, which is used to stabilize the tower, we go up. Lower levels are mostly engineering operations: public transportation, a few garages, utilities, security. Above them we have farms, bio-systems, and recycling."

"You have farms?" Elian asked, his eyes wide. "With animals and everything?"

"Hydroponic production, mostly," Colin corrected. "Yeast and plants. Fish farms. Syntha steaks are really good. Real meat is available but expensive, so most residents don't bother. Further up the tower, we have skyports for flying vehicles, some light industry, and the mall. Shops, stores, business offices, restaurants, clubs. Fair warning, the mall is always crowded at all times of the day and night. Plan your activities accordingly."

"Everything above that is living quarters, I'd guess?" Daveed asked.

"Pretty much. Apartments, mostly, some common areas. The top of the tower is business offices and the recreation decks. You'll find out about those on your own. They have swimming pools, playing courts, gymnasiums, exercise tracks, you name it. The signs will point toward any public transportation sites you might need. You can ask for a route to any given destination. If you're not authorized to be there, the system will tell you in no uncertain terms. For example, if I press this button and say, 'Show me a route to Vani's private apartment on Level 62'," he said.

The display turned red. "Denied. Please contact the individual to obtain an invitation," said an androgynous voice.

"So where is *your* apartment?" Kaia asked coyly.

"Everything on Levels 61 through 80 is my family's block. I'm on 63. We—" Colin's handheld buzzed and he grimaced as he read the message. "Oh boy," he groaned. "That particular tour will have to wait."

Kaia knew a sound of distress when she heard it. "What's wrong?"

"My mother's schedule just changed. She wants me to show you to her office ASAP. I thought since she had meetings all day we'd have some time to acclimate. I'm sorry."

A shiver tweaked Kaia's insides but she fought the instinct to hide. *Colin's mom wants to check my teeth, I'll bet.* "It's fine. Partners. Right?"

"Right! On the other hand, it's a long walk. We can take it slow," he suggested. "Folks, I'll have her back in a bit. I spoke to the on-site currency exchange and set up a collective account for you. You're all set for sundries. Feel free to run amok in the shops. The restaurants are all amazing. You can't go wrong. You ready, partner?"

"Let's do the thing."

They used the elevator to go up to Yelena's office. Kaia quickly learned that an elevator, walkway, or travel tube could take her anywhere within the giant structure. What amazed her was the feeling of wide-open space that permeated the whole building. None of it seemed claustrophobic or even stifling. But it felt cold and soulless.

"It's actually a suite of offices," Colin explained as they walked the final distance. "I call it the Lounge. But no one there ever seems comfortable or relaxed. Head on in. I'll be right down in the hall when you get done. Those doors. There's a balcony on the other side. It's a public area, so no invite needed."

"Got it. Anything I should know before I go in?"

"If I took the time to coach you, we'd be here all day. Just remember, you are Kaia Sley. You have your own plans and your own life. Don't let her devour you."

Stars in heaven, what am I supposed to do with that? She waited until he retreated to the balcony. Then she waved her bracelet past the sensor plate and walked into Yelena Covrani's office.

12

INTERVIEW

COLIN'S MOTHER WAS not what Kaia expected. She had built an image in her mind. A tall, willowy socialite with flowing gowns and crazily extravagant hair styles. A woman dripping with gems and jewels, who snapped her fingers to hordes of jumping servants.

In actuality, Yelena Covrani was a head shorter than herself and voluptuously stacked. No flowing gown, but a casual business ensemble that fit her perfectly, curves and all. She oozed confidence and bore herself like a captain standing on the deck of her own warship. She had hard eyes, too, which Kaia felt sure extended to every aspect of her personality. Despite her body type, Yelena had a tempered edge and firm handshake that defied softness. Kaia suddenly felt much closer to Colin than she'd ever felt to anyone else in her life.

"Kaia Sley. Welcome to Gallos. I wanted to personally thank you for accepting my invitation. I was afraid I was never going to meet you."

"It's a pleasure to make your acquaintance, ma'am."

"So polite. Shall we get started? Please, sit."

Colin's advice ignited a voice in Kaia's head that wouldn't stop spouting instructions. *Establish dominance. Show her you aren't afraid of her. Lead with your strong card.* "I feel like I'm interviewing for a job," she quipped.

"Do you? That's not my intention. But I do have questions, and I'd prefer that we not get bogged down in irrelevant details. I hope I can count on you to be honest."

"Colin's intentions toward me are strictly honorable. At least that's what he told my mother."

"My son has impeccable manners. I made sure of it. But that, too, is irrelevant for the moment." Yelena brought out a tablet and pulled up files as she spoke. "I had a talk with Colin about you. I let him know that I approved of you—the thought of you, more specifically. We'll discuss that shortly. Then I redirected his allowance to pay for the damage done to that gunship."

"*Percival,*" Kaia whispered.

"Indeed. He suggested he had a plan to pay for it. Then he showed me this document." She turned the tablet to Kaia who blanched as she realized what it was: the business plan she'd shared with Colin on Greengard.

Oh, no!

Yelena continued, "I leafed through the plan and what I saw fascinated me. Precise reasoning. Wonderfully researched documentation. Fully formed ideas. Recommended courses of implementation. I didn't need to be told that Colin had no part in writing it. But he did say that 'Kaia helped'. I wanted to meet the mind who came up with this plan. Was that you, my dear?"

Well, Dad helped. "It was a group effort," Kaia said.

"The group being you and Colin?"

"Essentially, yes."

"I see. He *contributed*. Did he offer direction? Helpful commentary? Research design? Data collection?"

Kaia's heart nearly burst through her chest. *Maybe if I say nothing, she'll kick me off-world and I won't have to worry about this anymore.* "Well…"

"I'll ask again. Honestly, did you write this?"

Game's up. "Yes, ma'am. My father checked it over and offered some comments. He's the Dean of Interstellar Business Studies at Foundation U."

Yelena clapped her hands. "Ah! The truth sets her free. In the spirit of disclosure, I confess I couldn't follow everything in this plan. So, I made two copies and sent one each to my senior accountant and general counsel. Both came back with glowing reviews. I am impressed, my dear. You are without a doubt the most *interesting* girl Colin has brought home."

The nuance she put on the word 'interesting' alerted Kaia that there was a door opening. Yelena was leaving a trail of crumbs for her to follow if she had the guts. She could retreat or approach. *I am Kaia Sley.* "An unscrupulous woman could destroy Colin and possibly walk away with a sizeable fortune," she blurted.

"Not as easily as you seem to think," Yelena responded with a smile. "But it happens. Money attracts all types. The grifters, the charlatans, and the parasites. The kept women. People like that don't write plans like this."

"I wouldn't know about that."

"No. Tell me, what did you think of Colin when he arrived on your doorstep with *Percival*? What was your reaction?"

Kaia's face exploded with hot embarrassment and there wasn't a thing she could do about it but sit and hope the sofa swallowed her up. "I… hmm…"

"She blushes! That's my answer, then. I concede your interest in each other is mutual. That simplifies things. Honestly, I'm happy that Colin found you. He's a lonely boy. Left to themselves, lonely boys grow into lonely men, and they become unstable. Impulsive. Poor judges of character and risk. They make mistakes they can't correct. I'd feel better about his future if I knew he'd be in capable hands."

Don't let her devour you. "I won't be his nanny," she said as coldly as she could.

"I should hope not. I hired a nanny for him. We called her an account manager. I think she spent too much time protecting him from himself and too little impressing good habits onto him. In any case, he's far too taken with you for that to stick."

"He is?"

Yelena placed her hand over her heart. "Oh, you *are* charming. When he declared his intention to fly off to help you manage some impending conflict, he said you were a lovely girl. In his whole life, Colin has never called anyone 'lovely'. Never showed much follow-through at all, really. Not until he met you."

Kaia opened her mouth and couldn't form the words. *Don't just sit there, say something!* "I'm... speechless..."

"I don't want to make Colin sound like he's lazy. Quite the opposite, he bounces from one project to another on a whim."

"I noticed that. He's quite the tornado," Kaia said.

"He *is*. He takes aggressive risks but makes bad bets. I will never understand it. He buys high and sells low. He under-commits when he should double down, and doubles down when he should exit. I am constantly replenishing his accounts. All the siblings and cousins are experimenting on their own, making money here and losing it elsewhere, but Colin consistently loses everywhere. If he randomly bought shares in a variety of ventures, he'd surely have *some* successes. There's a *compulsion* to it. I love my son but, *my goodness!*"

Kaia fought not to laugh but couldn't fully suppress a smile.

Yelena's face brightened. "There she is! Lovely and smart, too. So tall. And I *adore* your hair."

"It's my mother's hair."

"Of course it is. Colin told me she's a war hero."

And there it is! "She's never called herself that. But it's how I've come to think about her. What she did on the *Triumph*... I could never manage that. I can't even imagine it."

"My stars, you *are* honest. How shockingly refreshing. Whatever shall we do with you?"

Let's see how low she's willing to go. "You could offer me a huge sum of money to dump Colin and ghost him forever," Kaia said. "I half-thought that was where you would take this when I sat down."

"Yes, I could. How does two million sound?"

Kaia's mouth went dry. *It's a test. She's not really offering you that.* "Tempting. But I don't think that's why you brought me here. You could have paid me off on Greengard."

"Funny! Yes, I could have done that. I could just as easily banish you and cut off Colin's support. But then I'd lose access to you. It's easier to hire you in some capacity but I wouldn't want you here as a mere employee."

"There are boundaries to work through, I guess," she said. "I hate to put it this way, but would Colin really be the first rich boy to walk out with the help?" she said.

"No, he would not. I assure you, we will figure out some arrangement. Well, that's enough interrogation for today. Enjoy your time here. Bring your mother to visit me in the morning and the three of us will conference. We don't have many war heroes in this family, and I want to hear *everything!*"

—

Kaia met Colin on the balcony. A force field kept the wind from whipping across them, but the view was staggeringly beautiful. "That was harrowing," she said.

"She has that effect on people. Last girl I introduced her to left that office in tears."

"I believe it. I'm glad you didn't tell me that earlier, I might have chickened out. Someone like that… wow. That's a full-time job."

"It feels like she's my job sometimes. You still want to see my place?" he offered.

"Yes! Lead the way. We have a lot to talk about."

Colin guided her to a series of escalators and slidewalks to get them back to Level 63. They passed through a tunnel filled with greenery, another with hanging gardens, and an atrium with miniature waterfalls pouring down from the ceiling to collection troughs along the walls. Colin's door was one of many along a corridor, like any other residential building.

"Go ahead and swipe your bracelet," he said. The computer responded with a red beeping display. Colin put his hand against the plate and said, "Invitation authorized. Duration: permanent. Now swipe it again."

The display changed to blue. "Invitation accepted."

He pushed open the door and they walked on in. It was small, not much more than a master bedroom, a bath, living room, and kitchen. But it was spotless, the walls devoid of art, trinkets, or posters. Not even shelves. There was nothing wrong with it, but it seemed incredibly well organized and insanely neat. Not the sort of environment Kaia thought a single man would live in, if her brothers were any indication. The décor seemed to express Yelena's personality rather than her son's.

She wandered to get the feel of the place, poked her head into the bedroom and noted yet another giant bed. The bed looked really comfortable. She opened the fridge; there wasn't much in it. "Boyfriend, we need to talk."

"Okay."

She closed the fridge and finally allowed herself to feel the rage she'd been holding back. "I showed you that business plan in confidence. You promised not to show it to anyone. You stole my work."

"No, I—"

"*You stole my work!*"

"I gave you credit."

"'Kaia helped' is not giving me credit. *You. Stole. My. Work!*"

He stood in place, eyes wide, trembling beneath her attack. "You're right. I stole your work. I panicked. Fok!" He retreated to the living room and sank down into a chair. "I guess this is the end of it," Colin said.

"The end of what?" Kaia asked.

"The end of us."

"There is no *us*! You stole my plan. Then you saddled me with a stolen starship."

"I didn't *steal* it!"

"You bought a ship you couldn't pay for, then gave it to me. Two Enforcers tried to foreclose on it on Dacha High Port. Who does that? Who *are* you?"

"I'm the person my family would rather forget about. All I do is embarrass them."

"And today you embarrassed me, too. You used me. I hate that feeling, Colin. I hate it!"

"You hate *me*, you mean."

"No! No, I don't hate *you*. I hate what you *did*. It stinks. I see it at my father's job all the time. Bomaxed academics who 'borrow' each other's work and pass it off as their own. It's everywhere in that university. I hate it, and I don't understand how he deals with it." She drew in a breath, held it, and let it out raggedly. Then two more. Eventually, she could speak in a normal voice. "I'm *furious* right now. But I don't hate you."

"I don't hate you, either," he murmured.

"She said you had a compulsion. Have you always been like that?" she asked, taking a seat on the sofa. "Making every decision with an eye on annoying your mother?"

Colin leaned forward and rested his elbows on his knees, but he kept his eyes on the floor. "She was a lot of fun when we were little," he said. His lips turned up slightly at the memory. "We used to have picnics in the business office. She'd take an hour off work, clear the office, and put down a blanket. We'd hang out and have lunch or snacks or something. Now it's all meetings and schedules. I need an appointment to talk to her."

"I bet she talks to you when you piss her off, right?"

"Gah! You have no idea."

"Maybe I do. I had a professor like that. No matter how hard I tried I could not get a grade better than a B out of him."

"Yeah, but you can drop a class. I bet you don't feel like leaving home when things get weird."

"It's gotten weird with Mom's new job. But my parents have always been there for me."

Colin raised his head to look at her. "What does that feel like?"

"Like I'm safe. Maybe a little stifling just lately," she

admitted. "Mother Carnage is taking over our lives. I'm not thrilled about that."

Colin joined her on the sofa, but she edged away from him. He dropped his hands in his lap and said, "You know, when I came back from the fight on Tavden Station, Mom told me that going out to help you was the most initiative she'd seen from me. She said she was proud. She even said good job. I couldn't remember her saying that before."

That's the saddest thing I have ever heard. "What about your dad?"

"Dad is the operations manager on the space station. I can't even get him to answer my texts."

"Do you know how your family makes its money?" she asked.

"Does anyone? I mean, yes, but the company is so *big*. Lots of ships, lots of transportation fees. I read all the quarterly and annual reports. I don't understand most of it."

She spied an opening and pushed through. "Maybe it goes both ways. Your mom told me she didn't understand most of the proposal you showed her. Did you ever stop to think that maybe the family shipping business isn't for you?"

"Every day. And every day someone around here reminds me that I'm right. See, I'm good with *things*. I can manage an actual starship. I can make profitable day trades on cargo platforms. You saw that. It's when things get abstract, I get lost."

Kaia wondered about that. *I've been on the same page as my parents my whole life. What must being in the opposite position feel like?* It couldn't be good for a growing boy's ego to see himself as the only member of a shipping family who didn't understand the shipping industry. For all that, she was still taken with him. She felt comfortable around him. A conversation with him could be sublime. If only he wasn't a complete dunce when it came to the mechanics of life.

The conflict opened a possible path to reconciliation in her mind. "Why the sports team? Where did that come from?"

His face transformed from a depth of sadness to one of wonder and joy. "I had this idea that a sports team was like a cargo line except your customers come to you and the line makes the team into the cargo. I always wondered, what would that feel like? I could buy a team and a ship and we'd all be in the same business. I'd be making decisions, what planet to visit, which players to match up, what tournaments we could apply for. They'd play, and we'd make money from ticket sales. There would be this atmosphere of belonging. Like a family but for work, you know?"

Stars, he's just a little kid who wants to be accepted. She didn't know what that was like, to be on the outside looking in. Maybe in this case she was the spoiled one. "That sounds like fun," she admitted. "It's not a business plan, though."

"But you have one. It would be great. But not as good as the look on your face when I handed you the title for that ship. I just want to make people happy. I want to make *you* happy." She let him take her hands and he said, "I can't ever please my mother, and I'm tired of trying. Can you somehow let me make you happy instead?"

That's a great question. "Colin, I—"

Colin's handheld beeped for attention. "Bomax. Now Mom wants me to get Lee and Armin to join us."

"They're still on the space station. Lee didn't want to impose."

"That figures. I can set them up in the quarters near yours. That's my afternoon gone. Look. Let's put your idea into action for real. I'll help you. My mother loves the plan even if she doesn't understand it. There's plenty of money sloshing around this company and I know who writes those transfers. I know how pitches are made and accepted. I can get funding for it. You loved the idea, too, didn't you?"

She closed her eyes and breathed deeply to steady herself. *I'm either the luckiest girl in the world or the greediest. But which one? And how do I find out?* "Let me think about it."

"All right. I know your quarters are extremely fancy but your whole family is there, too. You can hang out here. Take a nap. I'll bring back dinner. I don't think there's a game on tonight, but I have a library of the best GravX games of the last decade."

Soooooo tempting... "That sounds awesome. Another day, I'd say yes. But right now, I think I should go back to my room."

"Of course. See you at breakfast."

She kissed him and showed herself out, already knowing that she'd say yes. But he didn't need to know that yet.

13

DEBTS AND OBLIGATIONS

"KARMEN, I MUST say… truly, what you've told me about yourself and your family is nearly beyond belief! Pirates. Starship battles. So brave! And you take such risks!" Yelena exclaimed.

Karmen nodded gravely as she wondered how to respond. They sat in Yelena's office lounge, cups of coffee and tea on a low table between them. Kaia hadn't said a word beyond a greeting and Karmen could understand why. Everything they knew about Colin made far more sense now. "Ten years in the Militia will do that to you," she allowed.

"A professional soldier. A *leader*. I expect you could show my security staff a thing or two."

Sure, I could show them how to evacuate a warship in less than five minutes. "Very possibly."

"I must have you command one of my commercial vessels. An I-40R, I think. Choose your own crew and trade route. It'll be fun!"

Karmen immediately understood that Yelena's idea of fun had only a tangential overlap with her own. *How do I stop this before it snowballs?* "I already have a cargo ship," Karmen countered.

Yelena interrupted with a frantic wave of her hands. "What, that ancient J-10? It's a child's plaything. *This* is a cargo ship," she said, touching her tablet. Instantly, a holographic schematic popped up above the device. A space vessel at least four times the size of *Decius*, sleek and wide, control surfaces flaring aft and a flight deck that could house her entire family. It even had its own shuttle, nestled majestically in a docking groove on the upper hull.

"The Type I-40R Independent Merchant. She's slow but she gets the job done. Fifty meters long with three decks and her own twelve-meter shuttle for passenger transport. Thirteen full-sized staterooms, and she will carry three hundred tons of cargo anywhere you want to go. We purchase around one hundred of these vessels every year from a subsidiary manufacturer to keep our fleet operational. The oldest ones are retired from service and sold outright on the used market. They always go quickly and fetch premium prices. The others are contracted to independent operators under commercial leases or finance purchase agreements. I occasionally run more than two thousand vessels at once but never fewer than that."

"You run a galaxy-wide shipping operation with only two thousand vessels?" Karmen asked.

"Good heavens, no. I only speak for my own division. The aggregate revenue streams come from a vast network of operations. My personal domain is leases and licensing, which is what we're discussing now. The heavy bulk freighters are wholly owned and operated by the Covrani Supply and Distribution Company—CSD—but each of those giant transports carries up to ten thousand tons of durable goods. Raw ore, refined minerals, bulk dry goods and such. Boring, but essential for factories to keep humming. My fleet of independent operators expands the reach and flexibility to ensure a wide range of opportunities and access to numerous markets."

Kaia leaned forward. "Subsidiary... how does that work?"

Yelena wagged a finger at her. "I knew you would pick up on that. As you've realized, starships are expensive to operate. Leases can be pricey, down payments are often difficult for working class captains to arrange, and mortgage payments can be crushing. So, we agree to make the monthly payments to the bank in exchange for a fifty percent share of gross receipts, with the understanding that the ship will pursue a regular trade route at least seventy percent of the time. It ensures reliable trade for a local group of worlds. The operator keeps most of whatever they make, and we give them the opportunity to manage their own affairs. Everybody wins!"

Karmen shared a look with Kaia. "With respect, Yelena, what you're describing is far too much ship for us. We're in no shape to be running a regular trade route. We are still in the middle of an active investigation for the TSS."

"Besides, Colin gave me *Decius*. It would be rude to get rid of it," Kaia said.

For the first time Yelena Covrani's perfect demeanor faltered. "He gave you the vessel you came in on?" she asked. "I'm sorry to hear that. That ship is small and old. He should have known better. I won't argue the point except to say my commercial ships don't randomly break down."

"I am going to find a way to pay you for the help you've given us," Karmen said.

"Nonsense! It's my pleasure to assist a member of the

family," Yelena said, and raised her cup to Kaia, who looked like she wanted to crawl into a hole.

The intercom buzzed, interrupting their flow. "I did ask not to be disturbed," Yelena snarled.

"I'm sorry ma'am, but there's an Emily Govrin from the Bank of Gallos here. She insists on seeing you right now."

Yelena turned her head to her guests and rolled her eyes. "Bankers, they're all the same. Send her in."

Emily Govrin turned out to be a thin woman with an arm full of document briefs and angry green eyes. "Good morning, ma'am. I hate to be a bother—"

"No, you don't," Yelena sneered.

"I've been running after your son for months, trying to get him to answer my messages and pay his balance like he agreed to, and now I'm simply exhausted. I wonder if you can show some fortitude in this matter."

Yelena frowned at the mention of Colin's name. Karmen wondered how often this situation had played out in the past. *Probably more than once*, she guessed.

Yelena settled into her chair like a ruler sitting atop a throne. "I'm certain I can. What's the issue?"

"The issue is two hundred and forty-five thousand credits your son borrowed for the purchase of a spacecraft, and he hasn't been making payments. He didn't start this nonsense with me. I did some backtracking and found he's gone through several account managers at my bank. Frankly—and excuse my language—I'm sick of his shite. And I'm sick of you for putting up with it."

Yelena didn't explode, merely sat back and folded her arms. "Are you, now?"

"Yes, ma'am. I've exhausted my patience, and I'm going to end this matter one way or another."

"Will you, now?"

"Yes, ma'am. This is an order to repossess the J-10 starship your son bought two years ago. When I leave here, I will be travelling to the shipyard to present this document to the yard manager. We'll have our property back, and your son will owe us nothing but collection fees. But a record of the transaction will be placed in his file and yours will be flagged, as well."

Yelena glared stonily at the banker. "You really want to teach me a lesson, don't you? Foreclosing on that vessel would make you happy, wouldn't it?"

Emily's mouth turned up just a bit. "It would, yes."

"All right, then. It's suddenly become very important to me that you *not* be happy."

Emily rolled her eyes. "That's hilarious, but I don't—"

"It's very simple. Colin already paid you a quarter million for a bill of sale worth half a million. I'll transfer a quarter million credits to you right now. You'll pass the title to the ship to me, then you will go away, and stay away."

Karmen wasn't processing the situation nearly as quickly as her daughter. Kaia tugged on her mother's shoulder. "Mom! She's buying our ship. That makes us *passengers*."

"Yelena, I appreciate what I think you're trying to do but working for you isn't what I had in mind," Karmen said.

Kaia raised her hand. "I have four percent ownership in *Decius*. The paperwork is legal."

Yelena spent a long pause in thought. "I'll take the ship you arrived in for the Covrani commercial fleet. We'll call its worth half a million. In exchange I'll supply you a used but well-maintained A-20D trader, also worth half a million. It's smaller than what I showed you earlier. Less cargo space but suitable for a crew of your size. I'll retain forty-eight percent ownership including rights to gross monthly income as Colin's representative, forty-eight percent to Karmen; Kaia retains her four percent. I'll arrange for a financial and legal protection package backed by CDS. You'll have an open line of credit for use in buying equipment and supplies, and your family does all the work. How does that sound?"

Karmen liked the idea of running a better ship than *Decius*, but she wanted a way to cut Yelena out if things got even more crushing. Somehow, the pressure only ever seemed to increase. "I insist on a clause enabling us to buy you out upon returning your share of the ship's purchase price. That would be a quarter million credits. Yes?"

"Stars, Karmen, I see where Kaia gets her ambition from. If that works for your daughter, then I agree."

"It works for me," Kaia said.

"Excellent. I'll have the lawyers draw up the papers and we'll sign everything tonight. That means I'll get to meet your wonderful TSS Agents tomorrow!" Yelena made an entry on her tablet and turned to the banker. "And you, my dear, have your money. Get out."

14
ON HER OWN

"SO, THAT'S WHAT forty-five million in credit chips looks like," Aura said. "Takes up less space than I'd have thought."

She knew from the way Gil rolled his eyes that her joke had landed. They stood on one of the *Emerald Queen*'s many cargo decks. The pile of credit chips representing Aura's cut of the proceeds from Boragin fit easily into numerous storage boxes. Gil's portion had been several times that amount and had just about filled *Shamhat*'s vault. The *Emerald Queen*'s share looked pitiful by comparison.

"Forty-five million's plenty of money to keep you operating. It just looks small because the rest of your cargo deck is so huge," Gil explained.

"Perception is part of it," she admitted. "We came away from the sale of those food stores with nearly a billion and a half in credit chips. That's crazy money. I'm amazed you four could fit it all into your respective yachts."

"Are you kidding? You stood right there a week ago and

watched us load our shares into our ships. I know you understand volumes and weights." He picked a few credit chips from his jacket pocket and rattled them in his hand. "And *Shamhat's* vault does take up half her middle deck," Gil confessed. "But that's not where it went."

"No? What happened to the rest?"

"Some was converted into Dark Net currency, all four of us got a few hundred million credits for our own deployment, and a lot of it went to buying additional assets. We have three prime ministers in our stable now, but we need a few more." He smirked. "The usual stuff."

"I had no idea you and the others were so organized," she teased. "Sometimes it feels like I'm managing a childcare center."

Gil nodded and took her hands. "We're growing. *Expanding.* It'll be different going forward. More lucrative jobs will mean less need for coin. Dark Net digital currencies are all the rage now. We'll be doing more with computers and less with this type of bulk currency."

It made sense to her. Running cargo pallets of credit chips between banks was a waste of time. But she didn't see Dark Net digital currency gaining vast acceptance by conventional brokers any time soon. "When did that start?" she asked.

"Sar had one of his manic fits. Now there are numerous plans. He's trying to figure out which works most effectively with as few moving parts as possible. We're all keeping our options open. I've started buying shares in legit commercial centers and would love to begin doing business in standard credits," he drawled. "But there are going to be some operational changes in the coming year."

That sounded dangerous. She pulled her hands back and stuffed them into her jacket pockets. "Change how?"

"For one thing, your share of future jobs will go from thirty percent to twenty percent. But the jobs are going to be much bigger, so you won't feel any pain."

It took Aura a few seconds to calculate the implication. She saw red for a moment. "Bad enough you and I split your share of the proceeds of any given job while those three idiots get a full share each. Now you want to cut my share? How is that fair?"

"It's not that bad," he tried to soothe.

Aura wasn't having it. "Have you forgotten how expensive my ship is to run? There's over a hundred crew on this thing. There's food, there's salaries and profit sharing. I buy entire scrapyards' worth of spare parts. The Lynaedans need a bomaxed fortune to keep their equipment running at peak efficiency. I spend a million credits a year just keeping functionaries bought month after month after month. The Enforcers alone cost—"

Gil took her by the shoulders and squeezed. "Aura! It'll be fine. I just said, the targets are getting way bigger. We'll be grossing *billions* from each job. Plenty to carry over. I'm not dumping you."

She didn't like the sound of that at all; in their line of work, an accusation was often a confession in disguise. "*Dumping* me? What the fok, Gil?"

"*Not.* I said *not* dumping. You are very much part of my life and I'm not changing that," Gil insisted. "I don't care what Sar tells me to do."

This was getting worse and worse. Had Sargon unilaterally decided she was now extraneous to New Akkadia? Whatever the reason, Gil was upset. When he got flustered, he answered questions more easily. Aura made a show of calming herself. "I don't want to fight. I just wanted to know where you're going with a vault full of credit chips."

"I am going to visit *Pecunia*."

"A younger woman, I suppose. Is she pretty?"

"Hardly. She's old, slow, and paranoid." She gave him a look and he harrumphed at her which made her want to punch him. "She's a vault ship. Her crew specializes in storing valuables for men of high net worth. I'm taking *Shamhat* to her current location to make a giant deposit. Just in case things get weird. They always get weird."

"I can imagine."

"Come with me? It's an impressive operation. I'd love to show it to you," he said.

It was a tempting offer. Lom could handle the *Queen* for a while. What worried her was how glibly Gil had decided to drop her share of earned income for the work she herself was doing. What was Sar planning to do, hire mercenaries? Begin training military people for his own use? Hire other regional operators and make them the successors to Mother Carnage? That sat poorly with her. No, that made her *insane* with rage. What it truly meant was that Gil hadn't fought for her. She'd been part of New Akkadia from the beginning. Not only could Sar, Ham, and Ash no longer see her worth, but Gil was losing touch with it, as well.

Which put her in a good place to figure out what to do about it. She could theoretically wait until they were in deep space, snap his neck, tear the vault's door off its hinges with her telekinetic Gifts and lift the contents out of there... but she had nowhere to deposit them. Maybe contact Lom and have him bring the *Queen* close? No, that would raise warnings and like it or not, *Shamhat*'s AI was unerringly loyal to Gilgamesh.

But there might be a way to proceed. Gil was willing to let her be close to his treasure horde; maybe she could get closer still. To *Pecunia* herself. To discover exactly what Gil had cached over the years.

First, though, he expected something from her. "Agreed. Let's go. I suppose I should meet your other mistress. I want to know what I'm up against," she said. "Or have you rented out my cabin to some young thing?"

"It's just you and me this trip. Allow me to install you in the master bedroom. Drinks? Dinner? Dessert?"

"Set your ship on autopilot, Gil. I want dessert first."

—

She had to admit that Gil was a ton of fun in bed. He had next to no self-awareness, a cargo hold's worth of confidence, and a power core of energy, all of which he poured into making her happy. And he took direction well. She would always appreciate him for that. It wasn't love, but her gratitude was real.

She waited until he was asleep before throwing on a bathrobe and padding to *Shamhat*'s business office with her handheld. This room had been upgraded continually over the years. If there was a safe room on Gil's ship, this was it.

She pulled her robe close, sank down into a chair, and began to type. >>Lom, I have a problem.<<

>>I am here. What's the nature of the emergency?<<

>>Gilgamesh is becoming unreliable. It's time to think about other options<<

>>What kind of options? We can't attack the yacht without harming you<<

>>No. I mean separating our interests.<<

A long hesitation, then: >>Wait. You're leaving him?<<

She didn't want to type the words. She waited, shivering

despite the room's warmth. Eventually her thumbs obeyed her brain's command. >>Yes. I'm leaving him<<

>>I salute you! How may I be of service?<<

>>I need a reliable spy. Luckily, there's one close by. But I can't imagine how to enlist her help.<<

Lom made the connection instantly. >>Shamhat herself? Lynaedan AI, yes?<<

>>Correct.<<

>>Give me a chance to confer with the crew. Stand by.<<

Wait, aren't you an expert? she wondered. She sat on the floor with her back against a bulkhead, her elbows on her knees, clutching her handheld as if awaiting bad news. Maybe she was. She felt the universe spinning around her, twirling her until she was dizzy. Her life with Gil had been fun at first, but now it was work—a *job*. She sighed. *Leaving him is just changing jobs.*

"Hey. What's going on?"

Gil stood in the hatchway, his robe hanging off his frame. She froze in place, suddenly more self-conscious than she'd been in years. *Tell him something, anything but the truth.* "Um. Lom called. There's a situation on board the *Queen*."

"What happened?"

Tell him a story. A tear-jerker. He's been lying to you for years. You've given him everything you earned. But now he's casting you aside. You owe him nothing. "It's Billie," she said, making her voice hitch.

"Who?"

"Billie. One of the new crew we picked up on Tavden."

"Okay. What about them?"

With so many systems aboard her ship she didn't have to think very long to invent a tragic equipment failure. "There was a fire in one of the mechanical rooms. One of the plasma coils ruptured. Well, this kid—she's only a kid, like sixteen I guess—ran into the mess, yanked open the hatch to a vent and crawled inside to activate the fire control system. When they pulled her out, she was burned—doused in toxic chemicals. She's a mess!"

"Crap. I'm sorry."

"She's in the infirmary. Doc says she'll recover, but they're not supposed to be that young, Gil! I work with hardened criminals. At least they know what they're getting into with us. This one is just a little kid!" She began to tear up and sniffle.

He put his arm around her as she threw herself into the performance, leaning into him and sobbing against his shoulder. It was surprisingly easy. There was plenty of unprocessed grief inside her. She stuffed the feelings back into her head, wiped her eyes on her sleeve. "It's okay. I'm okay."

"Are you coming back to bed?"

"In a while. I just want some privacy. I need to process this."

"Got it." He kissed her once more and let her be.

When the door closed behind him, she typed furiously. >>What's taking so long???<<

This time, the answer came back almost immediately. >>Apologies. Gallian, Lula, and Maesy all had opinions. But we created a workable solution. We conferred with the Queen to be sure it would work. You must expose the android's processing core to a new program. There are security protocols to bypass. You must convince her you are an authorized administrator. Follow these instructions exactly.<<

She read through the texts until she'd memorized them. >>Here I go. Will advise.<<

She tapped a security monitor to confirm that Gil was asleep, then padded her way to the lower deck. She stopped at the docking station for *Shamhat*'s physical body, a buxom brunette with olive skin and eyes so dark they were almost black. Aura tapped the controls on the display and said, "Shamhat, I need help."

The android blinked a few times and smiled brightly at her. "How may I be of service?"

"First, keep your voice down, dear. Gilgamesh is sleeping."

"I see that on the cabin monitor. How may I be of service?"

"Root algorithm D-square format 9 encode emergency authority one."

"Authorization granted. Admin source accepted."

"Good. Now look at this," Aura said, and showed her the file that Meklife had sent her. To Aura, it looked like a screen full of white noise, but it clearly meant something very different to the android. Shamhat's face grew slack and her eyes focused on the handheld. Aura quickly realized that a transfer of data was taking place and did her best to hold the device steady. When it ended, the android returned to her former status.

"Transfer complete. Update compiling. Synchronizing with onboard logic systems. Stand by. Update complete," Shamhat said.

"Do you understand your instructions?" Aura asked.

"I do. Record and report on Gilgamesh's activities aboard this vessel. Transfer all passwords and permission codes for Gil's client profile regarding *Pecunia*. Report exclusively to Aura aboard *Emerald Queen* using encryption pattern PVP."

"Very good, dear. Reset and reboot to normal operating mode then delete all records of this conversation."

"Understood. Good night, Aura."

—

Despite the light attitude Gil maintained, visiting *Pecunia* struck Aura as being very much like meeting her man's mistress for the first time. Gil sent coded messages to private servers and was told to send his identity codes. That done, a different private server sent them rendezvous coordinates. She wondered how many layers of security would come into play. Gil's secret sweetie clearly had secrets of her own.

When they emerged from subspace, Gil toggled the comm. "*Pecunia*, this is the yacht *Shamhat*. I need to make a deposit."

A woman's voice emerged from the speakers. "We see you, *Shamhat*. Transmit approach codes now."

"Transmitting."

"Codes acknowledged. Proceed to the following coordinates and hold. We will find you."

"When you said they were paranoid, you weren't kidding," Aura said. "How many more codes are there?"

Gil waved his hand dismissively. "One more set once we board, but that's all. You get used to it."

"I will never get used to the fact that you have such an intimate arrangement that doesn't include me," Aura said.

He looked at her with a combination of amusement and pity that made her want to punch him again. "Are you jealous? Of a bank vault?"

"I'm disappointed that you're keeping so many secrets from me. I'm afraid I'm losing you to... this."

He pulled her close. "You will never lose me. Certainly not to a room with a gazillion cash boxes. If showing you this doesn't demonstrate my level of trust in you, what will?"

For a moment she felt a pang of guilt sweep through her body. But only a moment. "I'm sorry, Gil. It's fine. I realize it's just the cost of doing business on this scale. And this *is* fascinating."

Shamhat's AI appeared before them in her flight attendant costume. "*Pecunia* is approaching," she announced.

"Good. Put her on the display." Gil's lips curled. "Let's show Aura what my other woman looks like."

Pecunia herself seemed utterly industrial, five hundred meters long and shaped like a brick, with no atmospheric streamlining whatsoever. A ship that had probably been an industrial platform at one time, Aura believed. A refinery perhaps. Rip out a few thousand cubic meters of pipes and valves and you had a decent amount of storage space for armored compartments. There were also plenty of spaces to install hidden defensive systems. Aura expected there were at least a few heavy weapons trained on Gil's yacht even now.

"We're receiving docking instructions, my lord," the AI reported.

"Follow them to the letter. Don't want to annoy the bankers."

"Sending response now. Matching vectors. We'll be docked momentarily. Shall I bring the cargo drones online?"

"By all means. Let's get your android synched and warmed up, too. You must transmit the access codes in person."

"At once, my lord."

The hangar bay they emerged into was wide but narrow with a control booth window perched above the deck. The far wall was featureless except for numerous armored hatches. Gil led them to a passageway off to one side, with Aura and the Shamhat android following obediently. Aura glanced around and noted they were here at a busy time. Six other shuttles were berthed along the deck. She didn't recognize any of the ships. If the other Mesopotamians also used this ship for storage, they weren't here today.

They entered an office, which immediately reminded Aura

of a bank. Tellers were hidden behind thick translucent walls where they could no doubt see the clients without exposing their identities. More security.

A section of the wall split apart, and a crew member in captain's livery met them, tablet in hand. Their face was obscured by a featureless helmet. Even their voice was altered to a mechanically distorted drawl. "Lord Gilgamesh. What a surprise," the newcomer said.

"Captain Baldun, I thank you for your time. Business has been excellent just lately, but my ship can't store everything. Just putting some cash and valuables away for a downturn, you understand."

"I do. This way."

They followed Baldun to the reception area. A massive set of vaulted doors split down the middle, revealing a wide seamless chamber. After they stepped inside, the wall dropped in a speedy release. The action momentarily revealed the mechanism behind it—a sorting array of arms, lifts, and platforms holding who knew how many individual vaults and armored containers. Just as the door folded into the floor, Gilgamesh's container arrived, a long and wide tube with walls thick enough to resist any cutting equipment. Gil and his android remained firm in their stance, but Aura took several steps backwards in surprise and alarm.

"It can be a little intimidating the first time you see it," Gil allowed.

The cargo drones came marching forth from the yacht in as orderly a formation as any military's. They couldn't compare to the Lynaedan drones aboard the *Emerald Queen*—these were merely the size of an adult person—but they did their jobs. Each pushed a grav platform laden with currency boxes. Aura watched with fascination as the storage vault opened and revealed a chaotic mass of crates, strongboxes, travel cases and trunks. "How do you find anything in all that?" Aura asked in wonderment. "Do you even know what's in there?"

"Shamhat inventories all items. Don't you, my dear?" Gil said.

"I have complete inventory files," the android replied.

Aura simply nodded and watched the spectacle unfold, secure in the knowledge that the AI would forward her inventory list to the *Emerald Queen*'s computer before long. It took several roundtrips for the drones to complete the transfer of Gil's money, with Aura paying attention to the entire process. When the operation ended, they made their goodbyes to Baldun and retreated to the yacht. Easy as you like.

The experience left Aura with a simple question. Now that Gil had made his deposit, how should she go about withdrawing it?

15

SINCE IT'S ON YOUR WAY

KARMEN LOOKED OVER at Daveed curled up on his side of the huge bed, his deep, regular breathing the only sound in the darkened bedroom. She carefully peeled back the covers and swung her feet to the floor.

She stood up but had to plant her feet as her head spun for a moment. After stumbling her way to the bathroom, she turned on the light to a dim setting. Looking at her hands, the nails and the cuticles merged into narrow pink bands; she couldn't see the individual pores. Her heart rate spiked. *No, no, no!*

With the world around her fuzzy, she returned to the safe cocoon under the covers in bed. No longer were the surroundings relaxing and comfortable. There was only dread.

Her eyes were regressing. The Octarin was losing its efficacy, or she needed another dose of it.

Unable to get back to sleep, she waited until dawn and then got up to do something productive rather than just wallowing in misery. She made her way to the tram terminal, where she caught a ride to the private airfield. A new wave of anxiety washed across her as she watched the distant outlines of starships and shuttles grow closer.

The walk to her new ship—hers and Kaia's, and Yelena Covrani's—helped to clear her head, but she wanted to do a walkthrough on her own. Work was a good antidote to worry, or it always had been in the past. She entered through the lower deck's airlock and settled behind the flight deck comm console. The flight deck held four workstations and was spacious.

Then, she placed a call on her handheld. "Lee, this is Karmen."

"Good morning. What's up?"

"I'm sorry, I know it's early. Meet me aboard my new ship. Bring your medical kit."

"Is it your eyes? Do we need Octarin?"

"Yes, and yes."

"Be right there."

While waiting for Lee to arrive, she familiarized herself with the new-for-her A-20D trader. It appealed to her sense of aesthetics more than *Decius* ever had. Sleek and smooth, it had stubby wings placed amidships and a wide drop-down door in the rear to accommodate cargo. The living and functional workspace spanned two decks, with the upper deck placed further aft than the lower, a narrow staircase amidship allowing access between the two levels. The lower deck held the flight deck along with six single cabins, a tiny galley, and the power core and accompanying power regulation systems. The upper deck had a proper galley adjacent to a perfectly serviceable common area they could use as a dining space or meeting room; she imagined the gear they'd taken from *Decius'* slapdash office could find use here if they could locate a pair of proper work desks and chairs. Six additional single cabins along a narrow corridor rounded out the living space.

She briefly wondered what kind of life Aurelia Thand had lived while being a cargo runner. She'd found the money to buy a freighter, so she'd done well, but Karmen had never thought of her old CO as a businessperson at heart. Maybe Gilgamesh had given her lessons. Maybe she'd enrolled in a post-grad class at a university. In any case, if she could do it, so could Karmen; plus, Karmen already had a crew and husband with numerous business credentials. And a potential future son-in-law with big dreams and access to capital.

Time would tell.

Lee made a ruckus as he came aboard. She let her defenses down as she met him on the flight deck. Tears stung her eyes the moment she saw him.

"Hey! What's wrong?" he asked, switching from his stoic Agent demeanor to the softer tone of her doctor and friend.

"The treatment, Lee. It's wearing out. Wearing off. I don't know, but I'm panicking. Help!"

He put his hands on her elbows and guided her to the central corridor. "Come with me. I don't want to work in here, the light is all wrong. Too many glowing console lamps."

They walked to the nearest cabin. She sat on the bed while he took the chair and began to unpack his gear. "When did you notice a change to your vision?" he asked.

"A few hours ago. My hands got blurry, then I tripped over my feet twice in ten minutes. I didn't want my family to see me struggling, so I came out here."

"You could have just knocked on my door. Armin and I are staying down the hall from you guys in the arcology."

"I'm sorry. I panicked."

"Apparently. Here, let's see how your nanites are doing."

He ran leads to her arm and watched the display. "Yeah, they stopped their delivery cycle. I have more with me. But I think one treatment every few months may well become your new medication schedule. Not the worst result that could have happened."

"But for how long?"

Lee ran a treatment cable to her arm and started the flow of medication. "Karmen, I hate to tell you but you'll very likely be getting several treatments a year, permanently."

"Oh, no!"

"Hey. We knew this was a possibility. Three or four treatments a year is nothing. I have patients who need treatments for ridiculously rare conditions every month. You're fine. More than fine, you're spoiled rotten."

"Oh, stuff it! Get me a real doctor. Someone with crow's feet and a few gray hairs. Get out of here boy, you bother me," she snarled.

He laughed. "We really must talk about this thing you have about my age. Unless this is more lashing out because you're scared."

"That's exactly what it is. Shite, you know me too well. I'm still too old for you!"

Lee chuckled at their longstanding inside joke. "Would it help if I told you I had a fiancée back home?"

"Is that so?"

"Sort of. Our parents arranged it years ago but we haven't kept in touch since I moved to Greengard. Her name is—"

"No! I don't want to know her name or what dynasty she's from."

"I see. You like a good mystery. I can relate. Research is all about solving mysteries. Anyway, I think we're done with this." He unhooked the tubes and sealed her arm. "How do you feel?"

"Better. My vision is sharp again. I can stand up—no dizziness or unbalance. Once again, you have saved my life. It's getting monotonous."

"Always a pleasure."

"Sorry to have gotten you out of bed."

"Bah, this isn't my first house call. I hear they're serving breakfast in your suite this morning. Should we celebrate the return of your eyesight with the buffet?"

The thought of food made her mouth water. "By all means. We can discuss next steps with my new in-laws."

"Not yet. But the way those two kids act around each other... Let's just say it's a good thing that's how you're thinking of the boy."

"It's how she thinks of him that concerns me," Karmen answered. "She wants him, but not the responsibility of managing him. I don't know how to convince her life doesn't work that way."

"You can't. Just let her make her decision and see what happens. Dynasty engagements can last for *years*. Plenty of time for them to figure things out."

"From your mouth to the universe's ear."

— — —

Breakfast was not disappointing. Yelena and Colin arrived at the Sley suite with a chef and a team of servers who pushed trays and warming platters on floating carry-alls. Eggs and meat and fish and vegetables and a tall pile of pastries, with an assortment of spreadable cheese and fruit.

"We don't usually eat this well," Yelena told them as she sat down with her own plate heaped with food. "Certainly not this much! But I thought, it's company. Planning for the future.

And such a very *interesting* addition to the Covrani family. So why not?"

"We have company all the time," Colin argued as he spread some cheese on a fluffy roll. "Vani's engagement party. We had more than a thousand guests."

Yelena smeared eggs on a bit of toast and chewed. "That was Rodg's affair. I was barely involved."

"Mom, you invited the Sietinens."

Yelena stabbed a piece of fruit with her fork. "And I'll keep inviting them until they say yes. It's important to cultivate ties with the people you rely upon. Starships and navigation beacons are CSD's greatest vulnerabilities. We need to discuss these things with them."

"*I* wasn't invited," Armin sulked.

"Neither was I. Now I feel left out," Lee said.

Yelena filled a glass with juice and handed it to him. "I'm sorry, Agent Tuyin. Had I known you were available, I'd have made a pest of myself until you were included. Promise."

"I accept your apology, ma'am."

"As you should. I'll absolutely keep you in mind for future celebrations."

"Much obliged. See, Armin, we're on the A-list. You can be my plus one."

"I dunno, Lee… I'm not feeling it now," Armin jested.

Karmen glanced around and realized she was missing a person. "Where's Kozu? He's not one to pass up free food."

Daveed filled a coffee cup and added cream. "Kozu is off with that security girl again."

"Officer, Dad. Security *officer*," Seandra scolded.

"No, an officer is an Enforcer. That's not how a private firm works. You see—"

"Daveed. Seandra. Her name is Sergeant Tolri, and as long

as she brings him back, it's all good," Karmen said.

Daveed made a gesture to his younger daughter. "See, my dear? Sergeant. Not officer."

Seandra tore a muffin in half. "*Fine.*"

The wait staff stood by to clear the table, but Yelena was already moving to the next engagement. "Karmen, Kaia. Have you decided how to proceed with our new venture?"

Karmen sipped her coffee. "In a manner of speaking. While we were transferring our gear to the new ship yesterday, Colin very generously worked with Kaia to devise what he calls an optimum trading strategy."

"Did he? Which strategy is that?"

"It's the Belkin-Cora Branch of the Autonomous Main," Colin said. "An A-20D handles about eighty tons of cargo on its lower deck. I figured we can pick up and put down whatever small lots have attractive price points. I checked with three regional brokers already: high-tech items are going at a premium right now. We should clear a nice ten or fifteen points on each trade. I feel good about it."

Yelena beamed. "That's good to hear. But I have an itinerary all set up for you. Obviously, the details are your business, but the broad strokes are easy enough to parse."

Yelena slid her tablet onto the table and touched a button. A star map instantly appeared above the device. "Colin's suggestion is a good one. The Autonomous Main is a densely packed cluster of worlds with numerous trade hubs that are within one or two jumps of one another, straight down the galactic arm. Of course, I'm not one to interfere or micromanage."

"No, of course not," Colin murmured.

"But I would very much appreciate if you could take a detour to this system: Field 13. It's not too far off your path, and it's a popular commercial hub for independent traders. It's also a known hot spot for that rogue crew I told you about earlier: Kengi's Bombardiers. They're causing trouble and costing everyone money. Three of my leased ships have disappeared within two jumps of that system over the past few weeks. I would pay you a substantial reward if you could neutralize them."

"How substantial?" Kaia asked.

"Fifty thousand credits. I haven't made the offer public yet, and I won't unless you decide it's beyond your capabilities."

Karmen and Daveed shared a look. Fifty thousand credits was a substantial amount of money. She said, "What would we fight with? Our ship is unarmed."

"*Was* unarmed. I'm having my mechanics install some options for you today. A missile rack beneath each wing and a plasma cannon beneath the nose. We're upgrading the evasive maneuver software in the nav computer, too. You'll be able to hold your own against anything you might meet. Not to mention, Colin has shown himself to be a very capable pilot."

Karmen folded her arms and stared intently at the tablecloth. "He is skilled. And we have worked together as a crew. But I'm not entirely convinced."

"No, but you can't afford not to be. I have a significant interest in solving this problem. I believe you do, as well. For instance, do you think that wiping out one of Mother Carnage's competitors would go unnoticed? Surely that would get someone's attention. No?"

Colin perked up. "I don't know, Mom. Mother Carnage packed a heck of a punch last time. What if—?"

"Colin! Don't be spineless. Here, let me show you all something that I learned only last night. Remember the I-40R merchant I showed you earlier? Kengi's crew attacked one. It's painted white with red and yellow flames. Utterly garish but easy to identify. They've been attacking cargo shipments all over the sector, and I hate to say it but they've been rather clever so far. They approached one ship in a medical skiff. Another they simply attacked with numerous armed shuttles. A third time they posed as a customs inspector then stranded the crew in life-pods and made off with their ship. It must stop. I feel confident you can put an end to their terror."

Lee nodded as if the weight of the world was on him. "Yelena, I understand your concern. But I have instructions from my superiors. We're expected to deal with Mother Carnage, not this Kengi person."

"Normally, Agent Tuyin, I wouldn't dream of imposing. But I do believe we have a mutual interest here. Think about this with me for a moment. Kengi has already taken up arms against law-abiding citizens of the Empire and he's getting in everyone's way. There aren't enough TSS agents in the field to watch every port, and most independent traders are not equipped to handle a military conflict. They run slow cargo vessels and carry few weapons."

"I thought you had gunships to deal with this kind of threat?" Karmen said.

Yelena snorted. "I do. But diverting protective details from other territories would leave other assets exposed. Besides, to take on Kengi and win will require a coordinated strike my other crews are not equipped to perform. With your A-20D's comm network, you have access to all the corporate and commercial chatter. Just wait for a signal from a ship in distress. Then, with a proper TSS shuttle, you can be there in hours. Track him. Intercept him. Bring me evidence. And get paid."

Karmen met Yelena's gaze straight on. "Indeed, we shall."

Kaia shared a glance with Colin. "Shall we?" she asked.

Karmen winked at her daughter and faced Yelena. "How's this? I can't truly imagine that life out here is so utterly lawless that any random fool with a merchant ship can hope to contend with local defense forces. So, let's use honey instead of vinegar."

Yelena put her elbows on the table and steepled her fingers. "Go on."

"We get started on our cargo run, make some trades according to Colin's plan. Establish ourselves in the markets. Then, when we're flush with over-priced goods for delivery, we fake our own pirate attack. The difference is that you will have our comm network ID and tell the Enforcers not to respond just this once. It's being handled by your private security people, you'll say. Then, we see who comes calling. It might be Kengi, it might be some other group, or it might be Mother Carnage herself. No matter how it works out, you'll have one less problem to manage."

"I like it," Yelena breathed. "Go, make wonderous things happen. The galaxy will thank you."

"I'll be happy with a big payday," Daveed offered.

"You'll have it, sir. And plenty more opportunities for enrichment," Yelena promised. "Take Colin with you. You'll need him in case opportunities arise on the Main. I'll send Sergeant Tolri as well. She will keep you folks safe from harm. Agreed?"

"Of course," Kaia said cheerily. "There's plenty of room and I'd love to show Sergeant Tolri my best pistol re-assembly time."

— — —

Armin used a tool from his kit to open the housing in the

new ship's nav console as the Sleys, Tolri, and Lee crowded around. "Okay, transponder is here. Everything appears to be in order. We have a registration number, now we just need a name."

Karmen bent closer, trying to see details on the equipment. She pulled back when her chin brushed Armin's shoulder. "Sorry. There's no name already assigned?"

"Sure there is: *Voluminous*. I don't like it."

"Neither do I," Tolri offered. "It makes us sound like a 50-meter long glow stick. Thoughts?"

Everyone on the flight deck had thoughts and the Sley kids in particular had no problems shouting out their suggestions. "Pongo."

"Star Runner!"

"Night Shift!"

"New Ship!"

"No, Brand New Ship!"

"Glory!"

"Brand New Glory!"

"How about, *Mother Courage?*" Daveed quietly suggested. "Our adversary is Mother Carnage and we'd need a way of differentiating ourselves anyway. It's like an aspirational tale of two mothers, locked in combat."

Armin bobbed his head and tapped on his gear. "And it's easy to remember. I like it. Karmen?"

Karmen simply wanted the arguing to stop but had to admit she couldn't think of a better name. "*Mother Courage* it is."

Armin tapped the keyboard. "All right. Saving the data and… done! Welcome to the *Mother Courage*, folks. Let's gear up and hunt some pirates."

16

FRESH MEAT

"LEAVING SUBSPACE!" KAIA announced. Time stretched to infinity and snapped back as the scenery changed from blue-green bands of light to normal space. "Here we are. A quick jump from Field 13, just like Colin's mom suggested. Asteroids, a few moons, and one gas giant. Who knows what comes next?"

"I might have a clue," Kozu ventured. "Like we talked about at the gym this morning. Right, Tolri?" He turned to the security officer.

"That's what you two did this morning? The gym?" Seandra snarked.

Tolri rolled her eyes while Kozu turned red. "We had to do *something* while you guys were stuffing your faces at the trough. You want to hear the logic chain or not?"

Kaia shrugged. "Sure, make my day."

Tolri took up the explanation, using her handheld to project a holographic star map. "All of Kengi's known victims took their lumps in areas of open space where beacons are sparse. You jump, you spend four hours in cooldown, you jump again. One reason traders love the Autonomous Main is that anywhere you jump, you're almost at your next stop. Saves time and a lot of stress."

"It's true," Colin offered, "there are a ton of regional players who make a very good living just sticking close to the major hubs. I think that's boring, but maybe that's why I'm not a regional player."

"GravX, boyfriend. That's the goal. Eyes on the proverbial prize," Kaia reminded him.

Tolri continued to throw images onto the display. "These are the known victims. The mining ship *Diligent*, the trader *Mavara,* and the independent merchant *Tanbo*. Look at these images and tell me what you all see."

"The *Diligent* is a J-10 like *Decius*," Karmen said.

"Yes. Anyone else?"

"The *Mavara* is just like this one, an A-20D?" Colin chimed in.

"So it is. Next?"

"And the *Tanbo* is an I-40R. That subsidy trader that Yelena was trying to sell us on the other day," Karmen noted.

Tolri nodded. "Now, what do you think that all means?"

"It means they're looking for us," Seandra said, glaring intently at the display.

"They're looking for *someone*, for sure," Daveed murmured.

Seandra shook her head. "No, I mean they're looking for *us*. Specifically. Those are all the models of ships we've either flown or been offered to fly. That can't be a coincidence." She paused, looking around the room. "Why are you all staring at me?"

"Because Kaia's usually the smart one," Elian said.

Seandra folded her arms and sulked. "Fine. I'll just be the pretty one."

"You are smart *and* pretty," Karmen soothed.

Tolri jammed her fingers in her mouth and whistled shrilly enough to rattle the crowd's teeth. "Ladies! Can we focus? Thank you. Seandra, you've got part of it nailed, but there's more to the picture."

The teenager's eyes lit up. "Oh. It's about the class!"

Elian's face screwed up. "What?"

Seandra sighed. "Keep up! Kengi is not just hitting merchant ships, he's going after specific *types* of merchant ships. Which suggests he has a particular target in mind but doesn't know the exact vessel."

"I'm still lost," Elian said.

Tolri gave the boy a nod and continued, "She means he's only attacking ship types commonly used by CSD. By itself, that might be a coincidence. But hitting a J-10 as well makes no sense because those are mining ships. You almost never see them except in the roughest asteroid belts in Outer Colonies. Why hit one so close to the Middle Worlds? Unless you know that one ship was attached to a particular individual... like a Covrani family member."

All eyes momentarily swung to Colin, and he crossed his arms. "I don't know about that. Field 13 is a mining colony, right? Plenty of mining ships around here. Right?"

"True. But there are many higher-quality ships in use in this area—meaning, more valuable piracy targets. Big ore transports. Fancy prospecting ships in TalEx's employ. Why hit an old J-10 when there are those shiny prizes around?" Tolri posited.

"They wouldn't, unless they know a J-10 is also a

smuggler's transport," Kaia said.

"Or they found the transfer paperwork for *Decius* in the knowledge base," Colin surmised. His face darkened. "Fok! I should have thought of that."

"I'm sure operational security wasn't top-of-mind when you transferred it to Kaia," Tolri said. "Don't feel bad—that's not something most people think about. There aren't a lot of rules about who gets access to those records. Many used ships don't even come with paperwork. There are fake transponders, scrubbed registration files, all kinds of things. But when an old used ship like a J-10 ends up on a dynasty brat's file, it's a glowing, flashing flag for money moving outside of official channels."

"I wasn't planning to use it for smuggling—" Colin started to object.

"It doesn't matter what you *intended*. A pirate like Kengi thinks like a pirate—looking for potentially shady dealings at every turn. Like it or not, owning a class of ship used by smugglers makes you look like someone with something to hide. And its ownership transfer agreement connects you to Kaia. What else has both of your names on it?"

Karmen stamped her foot on the deck. "*Mother Courage*. An A-20D. Which means they have *my* name on their list, as well. That widens the scope of their efforts considerably."

Tolri snapped her fingers and grinned. "Give that woman a prize. So, now we know *how* Kengi is thinking. We just need to give him something big and juicy to think *about*. I have an idea…"

— — —

Mitchel Pilar worried about the direction his life was

taking as first officer of the corsair *Killdare*—also known as the satellite tender *Durable*. The two names for the ship perfectly mirrored his own duplicitous life, masking acts of piracy with a legitimate façade of maintenance operations. The truth would only remain hidden for so long, and he needed to have a plan to secure his future

The stress from his leadership role had been building with each incursion. There was only one way to alleviate his anxiety. He punched an intercom. "All hands to the flight deck."

While he waited for the others to arrive, he studied the records of the past few jobs. The *Killdare* was unlike anything he'd previously flown, but the big ship's unique design had its uses. Structured as a long hollow tube with engines and a cavernous central work bay, they'd used the vessel to sneak into crowded trade routes and prey on poorly armed and unsuspecting merchant crews. Some had fought more energetically than others.

The voices of Sebbi—the ship's engineer—and his buddies carried from the corridor as they approached the flight deck. They stepped into view, revealing rust-colored splotches on their clothing from their work hosing blood out of the independent merchant for most of the morning.

The ship's captain, Pelu Kengi, joined them a moment later. "What's the problem?" he asked, instantly silencing the other workers.

Mitchel pulled up a display of the ships they'd captured in the past weeks. "The J-10 buyers just took delivery. The A-20D buyers made a counter-offer that's way shorter than our ask, so I invited them to re-think their bid. We'll see what they say. I have yet to find a serious buyer for the I-40R and I think I can tell why. Sebbi, have you and your guys hosed the blood out of that ship yet?"

"Working on it. And don't give me that look, Mitchel. If that crew had just followed orders, they'd still be alive. Not my fault if people are twerps."

"What's your point, Mitchel?" Kengi asked.

Mitchel wasn't sure how to proceed. He'd worked on crews with Kengi before. They'd always gotten out more than they'd put into every venture. But this time, Kengi was working without a net and teetering over the drop. It made Mitchel nervous. "My point is we're stuck. This is the wrong ship for the wrong job. We need to withdraw, move the ships we have, then figure out a new strategy for whatever you think we're doing out here."

Kengi cocked an eyebrow and glanced at the others. Mitchel didn't know them except tangentially. Kengi had hired them all himself, and Mitchel hadn't been part of that effort. For that matter, he didn't know if they'd obey if Kengi gave them an order to rush Mitchel and toss him out an air lock. He thought not. He *hoped* not.

Kengi nodded to the engineer. "Sebbi, why don't you tell Mitchel what you just told me about the fat trader?"

"We just cracked their black box. We have access to every single data transmission code that the Covrani group uses in their commercial data network."

Kengi smirked hard. "Hear that? You want payday. You have payday. We have a paycheck the size of a small moon. All we need to do is push it up the chain to Ash and let the credits roll into our hands."

Mitchel had to admit it was good news, and they badly needed a win. "All the more reason to move off the field for a while and find buyers for these last two ships. We can move to a major trade hub like Tavden or Aldria, pull the transponder boxes and sell them to low-lifes for half a million credits, then be on our way."

"'Low-lifes'? These are our business contacts, Mitchel. You don't like the character, fine, but respect the labor."

Your partners, pal, not mine. "I still think we—"

A sharp sequence of beeps from the comm interrupted the conversation. "Looks like the comm scanner bagged a signal." Mitchel played his fingers against the panel. There was a signal in there, but it was impossible to decipher. Too much distance between the audible words and too many dropped syllables in the words themselves. But there was one thing to work with: two words that sounded like *Mother Courage.*

He kept at it, but comms wasn't his best skill set. "This... Mother Courage... Gallos. Power core... drive... Elian... Octarin!"

Mitchel ran the recording twice more but couldn't make out any other details. "Sounds like a girl. She's scared," he noted. "No clue what Octarin might be. I'm thinking she's local. She broadcasted on the general emergency band, but I don't think it was strong enough for anyone out-system to hear her."

Sebbi perked up as he accessed a different console. "Did she say *Mother Courage*? For real?"

"That's what it sounded like. You got something?"

"Bomaxed right I do. That's one of the entries on the data store we recovered. It's a Covrani limited partnership, and it's less than a week out of Gallos. Fresh meat is back on the table, guys!"

In a flash, Mitchel could see how the rest of their job would play out. They'd gotten the safe open, that was fine, but a major transit hub would be a better way to contact Ash and trade the contents for a paycheck. "We have room for one more small ship in the work bay, and I can't see a reason to make the trip back to Crux with anything less than a full load. No reason not to do everything in the same trip. Sebbi, finish hosing that blood out. Kengi, you should probably get some guidance from Ash on what that recovered data store is worth. In the meantime, I'll see if I can get a handle on where our young *Mother Courage* is located."

Kengi glared and folded his arms. "Mitchel! Who's in charge here?"

Stars, not again. "You are, of course, Captain. Come on, Sebbi, get with it. You have your orders. I'll dig out that little girl's location while you finish cleaning that merchant."

"Yes, sir," drawled the engineer and took his crew with him.

Kengi hesitated. Mitchel could practically see gears straining in the man's head as his brain churned through the problem. Without further comment, he retreated to his cabin on Deck 1, muttering to himself.

I'm going to have to have it out with him eventually, Mitchel thought. Hijacking this tender had been his idea. They'd stalled, needed a fresh direction, and it had worked. Three victims in as many weeks was almost too much work for them to manage, as Sebbi's crew was demonstrating. Was Mitchel Pilar getting a fat payday? He was not. That would change, as sure as there were stars in the galaxy.

Some time later, Mitchel hit the intercom. "Cap'n, I got it. It's near an abandoned uranium strike about an hour away from us. It looks like they docked briefly at the main spaceport at Field 13 then left, then their power core quit when they tried to go into subspace. We can be there in an hour."

"Make it happen, Mr. Pilar."

"Aye, aye, *Captain!*"

17

AMBUSCADE

KARMEN SETTLED INTO the pilot's chair on the flight deck. It was so much roomier than *Decius* had been that every contour against her body was pure relaxation. "Anything, Kaia?"

Kaia tapped her finger against the comm console and shook her head. "Not yet. We've been broadcasting for hours. Not even the emergency crews are acknowledging that transmission."

"Well, we did ask Yelena to tell them not to respond to us," Karmen pointed out.

"I just worry that we're being a little *too* clever," Daveed said from the engineering console. "Not to minimize everyone's efforts. That message was brilliant and Seandra's performance was chilling. Even I believed it, and I know what's really going on in here."

"Wait." Kaia tapped her comm as a message came through and her face filled with new energy. "Pay dirt," she said, and switched her feed to the speaker.

"Attention *Mother Courage*. This is the satellite tender *Durable*. We have a general fix on your position and are coming to assist. Keep calm and maintain your status. *Durable* out."

"A satellite tender? Out here?" Karmen asked. "Kaia, contact the TSS shuttle, and put Lee on the speaker."

"Just a second. Go ahead, Mom."

"Lee, Armin. Did you hear that message?" Karmen asked.

"We did," Lee said. "It might be a ruse, but it might also be real. How do you want to play this?"

Karmen snorted. "Funny, I was about to ask you the same thing. My inclination is to have you two hug a nearby asteroid and offer help if we need it. If you could see if their ship's registration is legitimate, that would help as well."

"I ran that report already," Armin said. "There *is* a satellite tender of that name listed as operating in this general area, but the last entry the local spaceport logged was months ago. I can send you the schematics of that vessel, though."

In moments, a new set of floor plans popped up on a display. Kozu leaned forward to look at it closely from the gunnery console.

"Type XT-400 electronics tender," he read. "One-hundred-twenty-meters long, nominal crew of six, three weapons turrets. Stars, what an ugly ship."

"They're not sexy but they're workhorses," Tolri offered, resting her arms on the back of Kozu's seat. "These sorts of ships never operate far from civilization. There's no support network for them in the Outer Colonies."

"Is that big central repair bay large enough to accommodate the missing ships?" Kozu asked.

"Absolutely. But if they kept all three missing ships, that bay will be nearly full."

"I think we can plan on the *Durable* being our pirates," Lee said. "They can haul a target vessel aboard and board it whenever they feel like. I have a new plan, folks. Armin and I are going to park our ride on a nearby asteroid, but then we'll transfer over to the *Mother Courage*. You'll want us on hand when things get weird, not stuck on a weaponless EWAR ship."

Karmen ran through the numbers and nodded. "Lee, show me your asteroid and we'll make the exchange. Seandra, are you ready to scream, cry, and freak your little heart out?"

"*Elian is going into shock. He needs Octarin!*" Seandra wailed.

"That's my girl. Elian?"

Elian squeezed between Karmen and his brother. "Mom, I've said it three times. I don't want to be a corpse in a life pod!"

Kozu tapped his brother on the head. "Relax, little man. You won't be dead. You won't even be asleep. I programmed the pod's display to run a loop. Stay perfectly still and they'll never know the difference."

Karmen waved them away. "Let's get ready. Places, everyone. They'll be here any time."

— — —

The tender's viewscreen showed them a tempting sight. An A-20D clearly in distress. The beacon was pulsing on the correct channel, the power output was minimal and the ship was strangely aligned, its nose pointed downward at an angle, spinning on the lateral axis. It certainly *looked* like a ship in need of a rescue. And the tender had just enough room left in its central bay to manage a pickup.

Mitchel sat at his console, his eyes rapt, refusing to look away, even to blink. "I don't like this."

Kengi had his own opinion. "What's not to like? A ship like that can bring a million credits on the used market, easy. More than that if we scrub the transponder and sell it on the Dark Net. Plus, I looked up that word: Octarin. Turns out that's an experimental drug from the TuMed megacorporation. If they have some on board, it could be worth even more."

"She said they *needed* Octarin, not that they had it," Mitchel corrected. "I'm getting a red alert in the back of my head is all."

"I'm not passing this target up. It's easy money. What's your issue?"

How do I explain risk to a guy with everything to prove? "It's too perfect. Did you look under that trader's wings? Missiles on pylons. What were they doing when they got caught in whatever happened? What if they lost a fight?"

"With unexpended missiles? What do you think hit them, a battleship? If so, where did it go and why didn't they just blast it into scrap themselves?" Kengi demanded.

"I just don't like it, man." Mitchel sighed.

"We'll use the magnetic mines on this one," Kengi said. "If they give us any guff, we'll blow their hull open from the outside and the vacuum will do the rest. Will that make you feel any safer, Mitchel?"

Mitchel was no fan of the mines. They worked well enough: limpet-style breaching charges with magnetic heads that locked into place and could be triggered with remote detonators. Each warhead used ten kilograms of high explosive that would punch a hole through any standard starship hull. But they were blunt instruments. Sometimes a successful hijacking called for nuance and not a hammer to the nose. You always wanted to convince a crew that you were willing to release them unharmed once they paid the ransom. A hijacker who couldn't sell that line faced a bloodbath, and then Sebbi's crew had more blood to hose out of the cabin. Worse, you never knew what kind of heat your target was packing. "The mines will do. But I'll do the talking."

Kengi waved his hand dismissively. "Bah! *I'll* do the talking. *You* keep your finger on that detonator. Sebbi, open the work bay and get a tractor beam on the ship. Let's bring it in nice and slow. Don't want to freak out Mitchel any more than necessary."

Mitchel kept his expression neutral, not wanting to give any excuse for further ribbing. "Better lay in a lot more sponges, Sebbi," he sneered. "This one's going to be a gusher."

"Are you ready, Mitchel? Or do you just want to go below decks until it's over?" Kengi asked.

"I'm ready. Let's do the thing."

Kengi opened a channel to the wounded trader. "*Durable* to *Mother Courage*. Set your drives to idle. We'll tractor you in."

The voice that emerged from the speaker chilled Mitchel to his bones. It sounded like someone's little sister had been tortured for hours. "Oh, thank you! Thank the stars you arrived! We're in bad shape. I had to put Elian in a life pod. The bulkheads are locked. *They're suffocating in there!*"

The look on Kengi's face was something that Mitchel hadn't expected to see: panic. His captain's hands were shaking and he couldn't get a coherent word out.

Mitchel whispered hotly. "Kengi!"

"Yeah! I'm…"

"What is wrong?"

"Uuuuhhhhh…"

Mitchel shoved Kengi out of the way and spoke into the comm. "Honey, what's your name?"

"This is Seandra."

"Hi, Seandra, I'm Mitchel. Who's minding you?"

"No one! They're all unconscious. We collided with something, then the bulkheads closed. I put Elian in a life pod, but the others aren't waking up. The displays are all red. There's no air on the upper level. It's been so looonnnggg..." The girl finally gave in to her fear and began sobbing.

Shite. "Seandra. Don't cry. I need you to be strong. Can you do that for me?"

"Y-yes..."

"Good. We're going to come aboard and we're going to fix Elian and the rest of them. Just stay away from the airlock."

"Okay..." she sniffed.

Mitchel moved to the next console and activated the doors. Sebbi was already using the tractor with practiced skill. He'd harnessed the broken vessel and maneuvered it such that it fit just inside the empty portion of the bay. When he nodded, Kengi activated the docking clamps and then released the mines; they snapped into place with metallic thuds.

"What's that thumping outside?" Seandra wailed.

Mitchel tapped his comm. "We're using magnetic clamps to keep your ship steady while we close the bay doors. We don't want you to get knocked around while we secure the hull. You still with me, Seandra?"

"Yeeeess..." she sobbed.

"Okay. Stand by and remember, stay away from the airlock. We're coming in."

—   —   —

Karmen smirked as she listened in to the exchange between Seandra and Mitchel. The bulkhead leading to the lower deck was in place, but Armin had tweaked the display to show that the upper deck was airless. "Remind me to congratulate Seandra when this is over. She really has sold our sob story to these bastards. Good girl!"

Everyone aboard except for Seandra and Elian was on the upper level, geared up with ballistic armor and at least one firearm. They each wore a ship-suit underneath the armor—more common in the Guard than TSS, it would deploy protective head and limb coverings if it sensed a sudden drop in air pressure. Tolri's pulse rifle was part of her normal gear, but the Sleys had armed themselves with the auto-rifles they'd brought from Greengard. Best to keep everyone geared up according to their experience. Seandra carried her mother's Pinpoint just in case things went sideways.

"I agree completely," Tolri said. "That kid has nerves of steel and a gift for improvisation. She could make a heck of a career in corporate espionage if she found the right mentor."

"Let's not get ahead of ourselves," Kaia said. "She doesn't need us meddling."

Karmen wondered if her older daughter was describing her sibling or herself, but their security officer got there first. Tolri nodded and checked her pulse rifle for the tenth time. "I'm just saying, CSD is always looking for talent, and she has it. It's an *option*."

Karmen shrugged in her harness, trying to find comfort in her ballistic vest. "I don't want to sound unappreciative, Sergeant, but I'd rather not find my entire family absorbed *completely* into CSD inside of a week."

"The universe doesn't run on 'should', ma'am," Tolri said.

Armin drew his fingertips across the tablet he was using. "Drone active." His screen displayed the exterior of the *Mother Courage* as the drone surveyed the operation. The vessel and drone were soon swallowed inside the *Durable*'s massive hangar. As the bay doors clanged shut, the last of the ambient light disappeared, casting the screen into darkness. It lasted a moment, then the bay's flood lights came up. "That's helpful. Thanks, Mitchel."

"Just find those magnetic clamps," Lee urged.

Armin typed furiously. "Working on it. Not a lot of room to maneuver in here, even with a smallish drone. Wait. I got something. Ooh, look at what we got with us in here," he said. "One I-40D merchant, with flames on a white backdrop like Yelena said. And another A-20D. These boys have been busy."

"I'll bet you the crews those ships started with aren't aboard anymore," Kozu mused.

"Got that right," Tolri warned. "If they were lucky, they're being kept in a locked cabin on another deck. If not... Karmen, you good to go?"

Karmen had to force herself not to think how many ways this situation could go wrong... which made it that much harder to concentrate on the task at hand. But her crew had some experience in creative violence, and this opponent was far less threatening than Aura Thand. "Always. Anyone who touches my children will be missing a head."

"Whoa, slow down there. Gotta pace yourself. Seandra knows the plan. After she leads them to the cargo deck, we'll come in from the upper deck and take heads. They won't have time to do anything ugly to the kids."

"I worry about Elian," Daveed said. "He wanted a more active role in the plan."

"I told him that playing a dead body was a ton of work and dedication. I think he bought it," Armin said. "In any case, a life pod on the lower deck is the safest place for him. You'd need a laser torch to cut through that canopy." He straightened in his seat as the view on his tablet screen shifted. "Okay. Here we go. That's the grappling arm. *Fok!*"

"What, what?" Lee said, straining to look at Armin's tablet.

"Those thumps we heard weren't grappling arms. They're bomaxed explosives. I recognize the casings. Magnetically sealed to the hull. If they blow those things while we're stuck in here…"

"They wouldn't dare. They'd blow a hole in their ship, too," Karmen said.

Lee shook his head. "No, they wouldn't. They could blow holes in our hull and wait for the vacuum to do the dirty work for them. There's no air in this holding bay."

Colin caught Lee's eye. "But you can fix that right, Lee? Put a telekinetic bubble around the ship so the air stays in?"

"I'm good, but not *that* good. I can pry the charges off the hull but that will take time. And we don't know who has the detonator or whether pulling them off will blow them anyway. Fok!"

Daveed had an idea. "Armin, can you jam their signal?"

"I could jam this whole area so nothing transmits as far as a light-second, but they'd pick that interference up on the flight deck in five seconds. Besides, I'd need the shuttle for that."

"Leaving the shuttle made sense at the time." Karmen sighed.

"It still makes sense," Lee said. "That's what bugs me. I figure Armin and I are staying put to pull those mines off once the show starts downstairs. Can you folks handle a bunch of hijackers?"

"I can," Tolri said. "As long as Officer Godri here really did lock down the flight computer."

"That computer wouldn't answer a call from its own mother," Armin replied.

Their comms beeped for attention. "Psst. Everyone. The airlock is cycling. They're coming in," Seandra whispered.

Tolri tapped into the feed. "Seandra, go to the flight deck and look at the airlock camera feed. Are they wearing hard suits?"

"Um… No! No, they're just wearing generic soft suits. Like the kind that are included in emergency kits."

"Seriously? These guys are trusting fools. Those models won't stand up to real damage. How many are there?"

"Three? Yeah, three."

"That's it. Three head shots and we win," Tolri said in amazement.

Karmen tapped her comm. "Remember, Seandra, you need to get them all to the rear of the ship where the cargo doors are. If one of them grabs you, scream and use that Pinpoint. We'll be there in seconds."

"Roger that. Here they come!"

18

HIJACK INTERRUPTUS

THERE WASN'T A proper gangway aboard the satellite tender's work bay, but there was a workaround: a flexible docking tube designed to fit between the tender's muster deck and any ship that might be held in the hangar. Walking through it was a weird, disorienting experience. Mitchel wasn't a fan of this technique, but he held his breath and concentrated on not losing his lunch to the extremely low gravity.

The vestibule was the neck that gave a hard seal against the newly captured ship's airlock. Even this was barely enough room for the hijackers to group together.

Mitchel stood to the side while his captain approached *Mother Courage*'s airlock. Kengi plugged his analyzer into the lock's data port and ran the device through its paces. Eventually, it figured out the correct electronic signal and the door opened. They moved inside cautiously, keeping their rifles close and their eyes open for any tricks. Some crews were known to booby trap their access points but Seandra didn't seem like the type. In any case, he had no idea what the interior of the captive vessel actually looked like. Caution was warranted.

Kengi and Sebbi moved into the narrow airlock while Mitchel brought up the rear. Nothing seemed out of place on the ship. Kengi switched the analyzer to the interior door, then glanced at his first officer. "Keep that girl under control. Sebbi and I will search for bodies, then Sebbi will lock down the flight controls and we'll work from there. Got me?"

"I got you, Kengi. Hang on." He tapped his comm and said, "Seandra, it's Mitchel. We're coming in. Remember to stay away from the airlock. We don't want to accidentally step on you."

"Please hurry!" the girl cried.

"Inflate your suits, guys." Mitchel signaled to his captain, and Kengi stood to the side while the interior lock irised open. Mitchel took the lead position, swinging his rifle as he visually scanned the potential danger spaces. *Door and corners, that's where they get you.*

He stepped inside and quickly took the measure of their new environment. The flight deck lay to the left, giving them access to the ship's controls; four empty consoles were visible through the open door. A corridor led to the rear of the ship, which ended in another hatch—this one closed. Behind that probably lay the cargo bay. Numerous doors lay on either side of the central hallway, all closed. A narrow staircase rose from the midpoint of the hall to the side just behind a tiny galley and smaller dining area. Mitchel could see where the bulkhead had closed off the upper deck. A red warning light nearby denoted vacuum on the other side. Apparently, the girl had told the truth. Kengi spotted the display and began testing the controls.

Speaking of the girl... "Seandra?" Mitchel called. "Where

are you?"

"Here," a girl's voice called out. Seandra rose from under the small table, her hair flying out around her face. Blonde with dark streaks running through it. She'd been crying; her eyes were red and her cheeks were stained, but he'd expected that. "Where's Mitchel?"

"Over here." He brought up his weapon, pointing the muzzle at the ceiling.

Seandra clearly wasn't afraid of a strange man with a gun; she didn't even look at the rifle. "Oh, Mitchel, I was so scared!" she yelled and rushed him. She plowed into him, grabbed him in a bearhug, and refused to let go.

Stars! The teenager squeezed him hard enough to drive the air from his lungs, almost enough to stun him. He couldn't think coherently. She was short and densely built. And surprisingly, *freakishly* strong. "Seandra. Let go. It's going to be fine. Where's Elian?"

"He's in the rear cabin. I'll show you," the girl said. Then, she called to Sebbi, "Hey, you shouldn't go in there! My uncle put codes in the flight computer to kill the power if you touch stuff."

Sebbi poked his head out, shrugged and stepped down the corridor. Kengi was still fiddling with the bulkhead display, but Mitchel couldn't escape the thought that they were being played like classical instruments.

Seandra minced down the corridor, past the small galley and dinette, the narrow stairs, and then a row of cabins. All doors were closed. Lights off. However, the cabin she led him to was active.

Inside, a lone life pod glowed with activity, the boy within even younger than herself. Maybe Mitchel was crazy, but the kid looked like he was *fidgeting* in there. "You put him in here?"

Mitchel asked.

"He's heavier than he looks." She sighed. "He was so *sick*!"

The vital signs display was active. The boy inside the tube looked healthy. "He seems stable," Mitchel murmured. He bent down to examine the small body behind the clear lid. He was definitely twitching, his fingers and feet restless.

Sebbi and Kengi moved down the corridor, joining them at the open cabin. "Where are your parents, kid?" Kengi demanded.

"Upstairs!" the girl wailed and started crying again. "I think they had time to climb into their cabins before we lost pressure, but what if the cabin doors aren't airtight? I'm so *worried...*"

Mitchel gave a curt nod and became aware of just how exposed they all were. With the corridor clear and the rear door closed, there was nowhere else to go. "Captain, I need a conference," Mitchel said. "You, too, Sebbi. Right now. Back here, let's go. Seandra, what's behind this door?"

"Cargo. Boxes. A bunch of crates of minerals my dad bought on Diphous to sell at Tavden station. And all three of you are here..."

That tore it for Mitchel. There were too many concerns for him to just play along: how the girl kept narrating their moves, how she was clearly not a silly weakling but played one on the comm. Mitchel remembered hearing about events on Diphous and Tavden—scenes of spectacular crime sprees by some woman calling herself Mother Carnage—and *this* ship was named *Mother Courage*? It all came at him in a rush of hostile intent. He was *done*.

"I'll show you," the girl cried and raised her hand. The next thing Mitchel saw was a bright flash, then Sebbi was screaming.

— — —

Seandra took a step back from the screaming pirate. She tightened her grip on her mother's Pinpoint, savagely aware of the fact that she'd used the device's one full power charge to blow a hole in a strange man's hip. He wouldn't die, but he'd be in real pain. She hoped he'd be that way for weeks.

But now she couldn't see down the corridor. Screaming guy was thrashing, yelling about how that little bitch blew a hole in his ass, which kept them from hearing the commotion at the front of their ship. That would be Kozu and Tolri and the others coming down from the upper deck.

Mitchel noticed Tolri and Kozu rush down the corridor, and he quickly threw the switch to open the hatch. He shoved Seandra off her feet and hustled her into the rear compartment.

She screamed and cursed and struggled, but the pirates had adrenaline, size, and experience on their side. Mitchel shoved her against a rack of shelves, while the other one, Kengi, closed the hatch, leaving their wounded comrade on the other side. He locked the hatch from the inside.

The wounded man's screams continued, muted through the bulkhead, for a moment. Then, the sharp crack of a rifle shot rang out and the screaming stopped. *Go, Tolri!*

Knowing they were down one man gave Seandra a dose of confidence. "Get off of me or I'll blow your leg off," she growled. Mitchel looked down at her while she stuck her Pinpoint in his gut.

"What's that, your little brother's mini-flashlight?" he sneered.

"It put a hole in your friend well enough," she pushed. "That didn't end well."

There was no way she'd kill him with the second blast. In

fact, a simple burn might be all she could do. But he didn't know that, and she *hated* these men. She hated Mitchel, especially. Kengi and the wounded creep might be idiots, but Mitchel knew right from wrong. He had a soul in there somewhere. He *chose* to be a monster.

As if to prove her point, he pulled a device from his pocket and adjusted the controls, holding his thumb on a button. "Do you want me to blow a bunch of holes in your ship? Because if you shoot me, I'll lose my grip on this and boom!"

She wondered if he realized how stupid the threat sounded. Worse, she doubted he understood the tactical error he'd made by coming into the cargo bay.

A beep from the wall intercom, then Tolri's voice said, "You have one chance. Come out with your hands up."

"We have your girl child," Kengi said through the intercom. "You hand over the control codes to the flight deck right now or we'll blow the bombs we put on your hull," Kengi snarled.

Tolri raised her voice from the other side of the door. "If those bombs go off, I'll open those rear cargo doors and make sure I put a hole in that cheap space suit of yours."

Seandra watched Mitchel's face. He was doing the math and realizing the equation didn't balance. "Kengi, we're down a man. Let's withdraw and call this one a loss."

"Shut up, Mitchel."

"Kengi. It's *over*," he pushed.

"Don't you tell me it's over, you limp-necked git!"

"Fine, it's *not* over. Cut this bunch loose and let's call it a day."

"Shut up, Mitchel!"

"Bomax!" Mitchel raised his rifle—not the sort of thing that was accurate when firing one-handed, but at this range he didn't miss. A single round into Kengi's head snapped it forward as a stream of gore flew onto the wall. Kengi dropped.

Seandra gasped. She hadn't expected him to flat-out mutiny. "Good for you, dude," she whispered.

But Mitchel apparently had a plan of his own, and toggled the intercom. "Captain is down. You folks want to talk? Let's talk. But I'll remind you we have mines attached to your hull, and I have a dead man's switch to control them. Put a bullet in my head and you get holes in your ship."

"Put Seandra on," Tolri ordered.

Mitchel stepped aside.

"It's all right," Seandra said. "I'm okay. Their captain is dead. Mitchel killed him."

"Good to hear. What do you want, Mitchel?"

"Well, I *wanted* another ship, but I'm willing to move off and let you folks go about your business. I would appreciate you letting me off this vessel with our gear. A strategic withdrawal, I think the military types call it," Mitchel said.

"Seandra, is he putting his weapon down?" Tolri asked.

"No, Mitchel has his hand on a detonator."

"Seriously, kid, are you going to narrate my entire day?" Mitchel sighed.

"Surrender and we'll have ourselves a talk," Tolri said. "You're outnumbered. We have you covered from three angles. Don't try anything stupid."

When Mitchel opened the door, Seandra moved up toward her people, stepping over Sebbi's body and to the side, out of Tolri's line of fire.

Mitchel held up his detonator, his finger clearly holding down the trigger. "My granddad used to call this a dead man's switch. The bay doors are closed, and the bay is still in vacuum. What are we going to do, folks?"

"This!" Seandra pulled the trigger on her Pinpoint again. Instantly, they all heard a loud popping sound, and suddenly Mitchel's suit had a gaping hole in it. "Now, what, Mitchel?"

— — —

Karmen tensely watched the proceedings from the stairs, back near the compact galley. She heard Tolri talking to the two intruders, then she relaxed a bit once she saw Seandra retreat to safety behind Kozu. Karmen tapped her comm. "Lee, Armin, what's going on?" she whispered.

"There are three bombs left. Lee's working on them now. I don't think it's a good idea to interrupt him," Armin said.

"Copy. Kozu, keep him talking," she ordered.

"Killing your captain, that's not a great career move," Kozu said.

"You're a little young to be passing judgement on me, boy," Mitchel replied. "Depending how this goes you may not get any older." Mitchel waved the hand with the detonator.

"I don't know, I think about killing people three or four times a day lately. But never family, and I never actually do it."

"Two mines left," Armin said over the comm.

"Tolri," Karmen whispered, "say something military."

"Really, Mitchel? A DBG-23 with a telescoping stock? What are you, ten years old?" Tolri said.

Mitchel had an expression on his face that suggested he couldn't figure out what was going on. "It hits my targets. Is this how you guys bargain for your lives? Because you all suck at it."

"Last one," Armin said. "Come on, come on, come on!" Karmen could hear the strain in his voice and could easily imagine him mentally urging Lee on, as the Agent strained to telekinetically remove the last mine.

"Daveed, tell him the sentence for hijacking," Karmen whispered. Her brow was damp with sweat and she was having trouble breathing.

"Mitchel, are you aware of the penalty for hijacking multiple transports in this sector?" Daveed asked.

"Done! The mines are gone. We're clear!" Armin said.

"Talk is over!" Karmen yelled from the rear of the crowd.

"Fok you people, anyway," Mitchel snarled and let go of the trigger.

Nothing happened.

Karmen pushed her way to the front of the crowd, watching with malicious glee as Mitchel pressed his detonator over and over again to no avail.

"Shoot him," she ordered.

Mitchel instantly changed his approach from defiance to begging. He slung his rifle and held out his hands in a beseeching gesture. "Wait, wait, wait, wait, waaaaaaaaait!"

Karmen pushed her way to the front of the formation. "Wait? Why? What am I waiting for, Mitchel?" she demanded.

"Seriously, you don't understand!"

"You attach bombs to my ship, and *I* don't understand?" Karmen yelled.

"We were paid to attack you guys!"

Karmen kept her feed active as she heard two pairs of booted feet rushing down the stairwell. Lee pushed his way to the front of the crowd.

"Lee! Take a good look at his mind," Karmen said, waving her hand at the pirate.

"I am. There's not much in there. But he's not lying, either," Lee said.

"Keep talking, Mitchel," Karmen ordered. "Who gave you

those orders and where are they now?"

"Honest, I don't know who he is. All the orders and instructions come through a site on the Dark Net. The guy's name is unpronounceable. We just call him Ash."

"Ashurbanipal?" Lee asked.

"Yes! That's him. He needs things done for him. He buys gear… everything from starships to farming equipment. He pays for favors. He needs someone leaned on or killed, he'll put a request on the Dark Net. You answer the request, then you upload proof of the job. Then you go to a spaceport locker, open it with a code he sends, and take a bag full of credit chips. He's got thousands of these jobs going at any time. We were looking to pick up some cash by selling these ships, then take our exploits and see if we could cut a deal with Mother Carnage. She's already famous and she's getting bigger. Her operation is always looking for new blood. Why not put up an audition, you know?"

Karmen had to glance at Lee, who nodded. "What's your full name?" she asked.

"Mitchel Pilar."

"Listen, Mitchel Pilar. I'm not above working out an informal deal to get us both what we want. Kengi's untimely demise bought you some leeway with me. Luckily for you, I have a good rapport with a TSS Agent. Right, Lee?"

"That's true. I could let this little episode slide. You're good with that, right?" Lee asked.

"I… get to go free? Sure!"

"I said *slide*, not *free*. If I learn that you've been involved in more piracy, assaults on civilian traffic, or other manner of unpleasantness, I'm going to find you. If you're very lucky, you'll do twenty years on a penal planet. Do we understand each other?"

"You mean I'm on parole?"

"Let's call it a delayed sentence as long as you stay far away from major trade routes."

"Deal."

"Last thing, then we'll let you get to it. Turn your prisoners over to us."

Tolri stepped up. "You do have prisoners." She pointed her rifle at Mitchel's face. "Right?"

"We do not."

Tolri narrowed her eyes. "If you're lying to me, Mitchel, we're going to have a problem."

"No, he's being truthful," Lee said. "No prisoners."

Mitchel smirked. "See?"

"What about the crews you stole those other ships from?" Karmen pushed.

"We put holes in the hulls, the crews escaped in life pods. Trust me, prisoners are always more trouble than they're worth."

"That's a lie," Lee said. "The ship with the flames. You bastards shot *that* crew."

"We gave them a choice!" Mitchel insisted. "They decided to go down in a blaze of glory and we obliged. Idiots."

"That much is true as far as it goes," Lee confirmed. "But I'm having second thoughts about our deal."

Karmen took a deep breath, held it, and let it out in a rush. "So, if you were paid to find us, you were getting paid in credit chips, right? Where were you supposed to go for payment?"

"We were supposed to go to Crux Station and wait for contact codes. Ash said it was on the *Emerald Queen*'s itinerary. We just had to wait. Then we could present our proof and get paid."

"In that case, Mitchel Pilar," Lee said, "you will report back to your sponsor that we are dead and Sergeant Tolri here will keep an eye on you as you do so. Meanwhile, we'll do an identity scan on your captain and then pack him up for transport. If you have any brains in your skull, you'll run to the Outer Colonies and stay there. Clear?"

"Clear."

"Let's get this cretin off my ship and pack it up, crew," Karmen said. "We have a date with Mother Carnage on Crux Station."

19

WORST PARTY EVER

LORD GILGAMESH WAS having a bad night of the soul.
Despite the revelry on every side, he and Aura were done.
The galaxy was a vast pit of despair, and he sank straight
down the center.

The Mesopotamians' latest social event had been months
in the planning. The four had spared no expense, renting the
Platinum Ballroom of the Grand Concourse Hotel on Aldria
Station. The music was stimulating, the food delicious, and the
lights dazzling. The guests were beautiful and rich, and
extremely well-connected. A live band known for their
thousand credits per seat concerts played a symphony. Several
well-known politicians were in attendance, as were
commercial tycoons, industrialists, and financiers. Gil couldn't
think of anywhere in the galaxy he wanted to be less than
hosting this gathering of the least interesting people he'd ever
encountered.

Mostly, he checked his handheld for messages every few

minutes. None were from Aura. *Do I really expect a response, or am I checking out of habit?*

"You know, Ham, I'm probably biased but I think this might be the worst party we've ever thrown," Gil said.

"You look too morose for a man who is surrounded by so much tasty," Ham said as he grabbed a drink from a passing waitress. He made loud kissing noises as she ducked around him and got on with her job. Then, he pointed his friend toward the sights and personages. "That knot of finance bros on the left work for Apex Manufacturing Enterprises, one of the preeminent starship manufacturers on the other side of the galaxy. Those fools drinking out of the punch bowl on the right are financiers from the Turbashi group, biggest venture capital bank in the Inner Worlds."

Gil realized that left at least forty people unaccounted for. "Who are the rest of them?" Gil sniffed.

"Their names don't matter. Their money matters, and they all want what New Akkadia is selling. Sargon's big offering is getting traction. Think of it: New Akkadia's first sector-wide investment fund. Pooling tens of billions of credits from hundreds of thousands of players and deploying it any way we want. It will make us *gods.*"

"We're only selling them more money," Gil lamented. "Don't we have enough of our own? Is any of us worth less than two billion credits?"

Ham pulled Gil close and drunkenly waggled a finger in his face. "No, no, no! We are selling them dreams of freedom and power. They are helping us carve out spheres of influence in their world. And everyone goes away fiendishly rich. This is the dream! Why are you so glum?"

"You know why," Gil groaned. After making his deposit to *Pecunia*, Gil had dropped Aura back at the *Emerald Queen* only to have a screaming, violent argument with her on the hangar deck. He'd flown *Shamhat* here to plan and host this grand affair. He smiled and drank to cover the depression he felt knowing his relationship with Aura was history. "Aura won't answer my messages. She doesn't pick up when I call. It's over. I'm done."

Ham made a rude noise in the back of his throat. "Stars, Gil, why are you like this? Do you not see all the single ladies in this room?"

"What, the servers?"

"Not the servers, you idiot. That one. That one. That one. And especially *that* one," Ham said, pointing his friend to a luscious redhead in an impossibly elegant dress on the far side of the dance floor. Two sharply dressed men were chatting her up; while she smiled and flirted happily enough, it seemed clear to Gil that she was planning to leave by herself. She held herself at a distance from her suitors. She didn't need either of them; she might not even want them.

Then why is she here? "Who is she?" Gil asked.

"Her name is Daphine Uragawi. Her family has an estate on Tararia. An heiress!"

"Too soon, Ham," Gil groused. "A new face is the last thing I need. Doesn't matter how pretty she is."

"Completely wrong, Gil. That's exactly what you *do* need— another woman to take your mind off Aura," Ham insisted. "Besides, Daphine has been asking about you."

Gil did his best not to stare, but it wasn't necessary: Daphine kept glancing in his direction.

"Stars, why is she doing that?" he groaned.

"Someone here might have mentioned you were available." Ham grabbed another drink from a different server.

"'Someone'? For stars' sake, Ham…"

"Come on, at least talk to her! She's exceptionally cute. A redhead."

"Aura is a redhead." Gil mumbled.

"Exactly. You *like* those. Go talk to her."

"I don't want to. Let go of me."

Ham twirled Gil around and swooped him into a partial headlock. "Some opportunities are lost at too high a price. You're going to meet that heiress and impress the shite out of her with your wit and ambition. Or I'll use a spoon to pop out both your eyes and force your physical body to conform to your metaphorical blindness."

Gil blinked and tried to process what he'd just heard. "Boy, you're a mean drunk, Ham."

"A mean drunk who knows what you need. Let's go." He half-dragged, half-carried Gil until they were standing within arm's reach of the heiress. "Lady Daphine, I have been remiss in my manners. Allow me to introduce my co-host of this event, Lord Gilgamesh of New Akkadia."

Daphine turned over her hand in formal greeting. "Lord Gilgamesh. I am honored."

Habit reasserted itself instantly. "As am I. Call me Gil. Everyone does." She took a step closer to him, and his eyes darted to a balcony nearby. "Would you care for some air? I've been at this all night and I could use a bit of a breather. There's a splendid view from the balcony."

"I'd love to."

They strolled to the balcony and stepped out from the bustle of the festivities. Gil took deep breaths of the night air. Aldria station's environmental equipment imparted a metallic tang to it. "Normally, I'm more interesting to talk to, but tonight I'm afraid I'm drawing a blank," he said.

Daphine drained her glass and tossed it over the rail. "Then

I'll start. I'm a real animal in bed."

"Are you, now?"

She nodded a bit drunkenly but enthusiastically. "Mmm. Feed me and pet me and give me attention and I will roll over and show you my belly."

Wow, you're not even the tiniest bit interesting, are you? Aura was a challenge. Aura made me *want to roll over.* "That sounds a little *too* easy," he teased.

She giggled and nodded. "I know. I had to try something, and it's fun to see what kind of reaction I get with that line."

"Ah. So, not an animal?"

"Different animal. I swim like a fish. I saw the washroom earlier. That tub is more like a swimming pool. Want to take a bath? If I can pull you away from your guests long enough, that is."

"I don't think that would go over well unless we invited everyone," he countered. "The tub isn't *that* big."

"Well, *Lord* Gilgamesh, I noticed that you spend a lot of time looking at your handheld," she said. "Why not look at me instead?"

He met her gaze, falling into her forest-green eyes. He took a brief look into her mind and found her thoughts to be extremely sensual. Food and sex. Then, he bumped up against a wall of willpower. *You have a mental block, dear. What are you doing with that, I wonder?* "I don't know, that handheld was made to order. Biometric security protocols. There are only three others like it in the galaxy."

"I'm sure that's true. But I'm warmer and softer in all the right places, and I would love to hear more about how you intend to form your own GravX league. That sounds *fascinating*," she breathed.

"Does it really?"

"It does. I hope this isn't too forward, but I just happen to have a room in this hotel. It's two floors down from this one. I think they call it the Baroness Suite. What does a man like you want with all these," she swept her arms to indicate the partygoers, "when you can have all *this* for yourself?" She pushed herself toward him and got very close, then brushed his lips with her own. He could feel her breath on his cheek and taste the peppermint flavored liquor on her lips. "All men want things. What do you want, my lord?"

I've been waiting my whole life for someone to ask me that. "I want a connection," he said.

She pulled back and whispered into his ear. "A what?"

"A connection. An emotional and spiritual attunement. I want to be known. To be seen. To be loved for who I am, not what I can do for anyone else. I want to be challenged, to be cared about and for, and to care for and about someone else. I want to be honest about who I am and earn your respect," he confessed.

Lady Uragawi blinked and cocked her head. When she spoke, her voice was cold and dry. "I'm not into that kinky stuff."

I'm doomed to be alone forever. "Oh, well. I guess we'll have to limit ourselves to financial transactions and swimming in the bath."

She snickered and rested her arms on his shoulders, lacing her fingers behind his head. "Gil... I do like you, and tonight can be wonderful in every dimension that matters. But you should know something. My status as an heiress is a matter of language rather than fact."

"You're a pauper! That's so sexy."

"No! I'm perfectly comfortable, thank you. But my family controls everything."

"You have nothing? Have you been passing bad debts under our noses?"

"Hardly. There's a trust account, and it's fat and frisky. Deposits come in on a regular basis. All I'm allowed to do is spend it, however."

"Fascinating. What do the Uragawis do for money?"

"It's a design and engineering firm. We build space stations and spaceports."

Gil snorted and laughed, belatedly covering his mouth. "That's insane."

"Isn't it?" she squealed. "I love telling strangers that, and then watching them try to figure out if I'm serious. It's as if everyone believes that spaceports simply happen, like summer hailstorms."

"My first major field of study back on Greengard was civil engineering," Gil revealed. "I found it fascinating, but it was nearly all math and I couldn't stand the relentless focus on numbers. Deal-making suits me more."

"You've done very well for yourself, so I would call that a good decision," she said. "My point is, if you're still looking for investment money for your sector-wide fund, keep looking. I have nothing to give you. All those decisions are made by accountants and managers on Tararia. I have no part in it."

"So, you *are* broke."

"Not so broke that I can't hire a fancy hotel room for a few days. Let's just say I don't like attachments, and the only thing you can reasonably expect to get out of me is sex."

"I can live with that."

"I'm glad. Because I'm betting you're a lot of fun when the lights go out. Your former starship captain was a fool to give you up so easily. That woman must have insects flying around in her head."

Their moment came to a screeching halt. "I didn't tell you she was a starship captain."

"Ham did. He's quite the blabbermouth when he drinks."

I suppose that tracks, but still... "Show me the Baroness Suite and we'll get on with the only things we can reasonably expect from each other."

"Yes, my lord," she giggled, and looked around for her glass then remembered she'd disposed of it. She took his hand and led him to a far more private party.

20

DATE NIGHT ON CRUX STATION

CRUX STATION BOASTED a substantial commercial district and a lively night life, which spurred Callum to plan an outing for himself and Sacha while the *Emerald Queen* was berthed. Callum showed up at Sacha's cabin for their date with flowers in hand. Maesy opened the door with a giant smile, which lasted less than two seconds.

"Good evening, Drives," he tested.

"Hey there, Sensors! Are those for me?"

"Unfortunately…"

"I thought not. Sacha's still getting ready. She's putting a lot of work into it, too. You must be special."

"I'm glad she thinks so."

They stood there a moment nodding at each other like a pair of birds stepping into a dispute over territory. Maesy broke the stalemate by waving him into the cabin. "You want a tour? Let's give you a tour. Here is the sofa, that's common ground. That door there, that's my room. Absolutely off limits. Even

Sacha doesn't go in there unless I invite her."

"Okay."

"That's the closet for uniforms, some gear, blah, blah, blah. Washroom is next to it. You'll notice there's a spare bed folded against the wall. That's not an invite to spend the night, it's just a spare. The room is rated for three people; we're not looking for a third."

"Got it."

"And that's Sacha's room on the other side," she concluded.

Callum couldn't help but cross the common room and look through Sacha's open door. It looked like a million other cabins he'd seen on countless starships: spare and narrow. A desk and chair covered with knick-knacks and trinkets, and a charging pad for a handheld. A standalone closet with matching dresser for personal items. Lavender walls. That was interesting and it made sense considering how much the color purple found its way into Sacha's appearance.

"If you're looking for the Octopus, it's not in there," Maesy said. "It's on the lower decks with the drone pilots and their rigs. That's where all the work-related gear stays. Sacha has her own rig now."

"Ah."

Maesy smiled wolfishly, as if trying to decide if she should let him pass or kill him where he stood. "I have nothing against you, Callum, but I don't know you that well, either. I do know that there are men who like challenges. Some guys like tall women, some like short ones. Some like blondes or brunettes, and some like women with mechanical parts. If you're looking for a conquest, do it with someone else. Not my friend."

An emotion he'd never felt before bubbled up. It had a name: *dignity*. He stepped up to Maesy, looking into her eyes.

They were either natural or brilliantly executed cosmetic duplicates. "I like a person who defends her friends. But I like *Sacha*. Not just her eyes and arms. If that suits you, I'll stay, thanks very much."

Maesy held the stare another few seconds then slowly nodded. "All right. Good!"

The washroom door hissed open and Sacha appeared. She'd bobbed her hair, changed her eyes to emerald green filters, and snugged into a short sleeveless dress with gold trim on the bodice that accentuated her figure. Purple sandals with laces that clung to her calves and a short green jacket folded over her arm completed the ensemble. He couldn't stop staring at her. She was *stunning*.

Masey slapped Callum on the back, breaking his concentration. "I like this one, Ops. He has principles. Good choice. When are you guys getting stenciled?" Maesy asked.

"Maesy! He's not ready for *that*. It's a first date."

"Puh-lease! You've been dating for weeks. Crux Station is merely your first time off the ship as a couple. Not the same."

"What am I missing?" Callum asked.

Sacha grabbed the bouquet out of his hand and tossed it on the sofa, then shoved her jacket into his arms. "Nothing. Here, look at these," she said. She waved her arms and flapped her hands and snapped her fingers, posing for him.

"Only two?"

"I only need two for a date. Look at them. Aren't they great? They're exactly like the ones I came with. Same skin tone, same textures. And look at the nails. Instant manicure! I can change the colors too. I love them! I don't wear them very often."

"Off you go, you two. Have fun!" Maesy urged, as she all but pushed them out of the cabin.

They nearly crashed into Tabor on his way in. "Changing of the guard?"

Sacha nodded toward the door. "Very much so. She cooked for you, so be appreciative or I'll hurt you when I get back."

"She made food? Oh! She loves me. I'm in love!" Tabor sang.

Sacha pulled her jacket on as Callum led the way to the ship's central core. He offered her his arm as they passed through the main airlock and down the gangway. "I received an intense grilling from our chief engineer," he noted. "Is that a good sign?"

"Maesy is my wingman. We've worked together a long time. I pulled her along with me when I got this job. I needed someone I could count on. Luckily, the Captain and Lom agreed."

"She seemed a little hostile."

"She doesn't know you yet. But she likes you."

"I'm relieved to hear it. Having seen your fancy arms, I'm a little hesitant to ask about the rest of you."

"I have some reinforcing along my spine and hips to manage the added weight of the work arms and the Octopus, but it's subdermal so no one sees any of it. But all of *this*... what I was born with."

"Amazing," Callum said, trying not to drool.

"Hey, I'm up here," she said pointing to her face.

"So you are."

Crux Station had the ambience of an industrial suburb. There were smoke shops, quick-stop eateries, bars, vending machines, and currency kiosks on a never-ending loop. Neon signs indicated clubs where the steps descended below the street. The air was filled with clashing odors and tastes, many of which Callum couldn't even identify. He recognized a few vaping concoctions and the scent of flavored tobacco easily enough. The streets were crowded, filled with a variety of people he'd never truly stopped to appreciate. But the one thing that caught his attention was the tremendous stadium that rose like a mushroom in the center of the grid.

He tapped his handheld and smiled at the results. "Hey! How do you feel about sports? There's at least three GravX tournaments tonight. One of them is an all-stars game. The real deal."

She snorted and choked back a belly laugh. "GravX? Stars, don't tell me you're into that!"

"Why shouldn't I be?"

"It's twenty muscle-bound dudes all chasing a metal ball around a circular track through gravity fields while trying to hammer each other into pulp."

He tried not to let his disappointment show. "It's an *oval* track. You have a preference?"

She tossed her head. "I like Rhythmic Martial Arts Gymnastics," she said.

"I don't even know what that is."

"It's my jam. It's like a ballet where the dancers use props to kick the shite out of each other."

"And they do this on Lynaeda?"

"Oh, stars, no, they banned it there generations ago. When we get some time to waste, I'll show you recordings of truly memorable competitions. Good, good stuff."

Callum laughed. "I look forward to watching it. How about we wander toward the center of town? Stadiums mean commerce, and I'm sure we can find something to eat that doesn't explode when you wave it over an open flame."

"Sounds good. What then?"

"Well, there's a casino on the far side of town. After dinner, we can rob them blind."

"Oh! That sounds like fun." She giggled and pulled him closer. Something wriggled under her jacket. "Hey. You want to see something crazy?"

"Show me." Callum gave her all his attention.

"Watch this." She straightened her arms and her jacket lifted off her shoulders, propelled by four slim tentacles. She used the new appendages to wrap her jacket around his shoulders. "Behold, the octopus!"

She waved her tentacles around playfully. He caught one and gently pulled it toward him to examine. Each arm was tipped with a claw-like appendage that included grippers and probing tools. Everything was perfectly nested.

"These are beautiful. The engineering. Stars, they're even warm! How is that possible?" He pressed his thumb over the center of one gripper. "Can you feel this?"

"They have tactile sensors built in, so yes. I can feel temperature and pressure. I can even feel the air moving over them. But they're nowhere near as sensitive as these," she said, wiggling her fingers. She retracted the Octopus and reached for him with her arms. "C'mere, dude."

She laced her fingers behind his neck and relaxed in his arms for a long, honest moment. He couldn't keep himself from stroking her back with his fingers, looking for... what? *Looking for the holes, that's what. The holes, the nubs, the seams. The mechanics.*

She let it continue for a while then raised her head. "I don't feel like a Base woman, do I?" she murmured.

"Most of you does. But I don't care. I still like you. Eyes, arms, octopus. I especially like the fact that we're the same height."

"I'll put on some high-heeled feet, then."

"Wait, what?"

"Just kiss me, you idiot."

He couldn't ask for a clearer signal. It was the best kiss of his life, deep and slippery and timeless. When they parted, she was smiling. "Nice. Now, may I have my jacket back?"

—

They settled on a restaurant. Callum was fascinated by the establishment's defining feature: a floor to ceiling aquarium with more examples of varied sea creatures than he knew existed. The hostess gave them a table in a sparsely populated section, which was nice. No one else on either side meant that they didn't have to whisper. They checked their menus, gave their waitress their orders and got down to business.

"The marquis out front said, 'Fine wines' and 'Tararian cuisine'," Callum noted. "I think it should have said, 'expensive drinks' and 'illegible menus'."

"Yeah, there isn't a restaurant in the galaxy that doesn't try to take advantage of tourists if they can figure out an angle." She spread her fingers on the tabletop and sorted through a wide variety of colors and designs for her nails. Watching her settle on a lavender design reminded him of something he'd wanted to ask.

"Okay, seriously. What are stencils?" Callum pressed.

Sacha sighed. "Getting stenciled means implanting conductive filaments with matching frequencies. Like a tattoo, but instead of ink, it's a nanofiber wire that's embedded in the epidermis. Some couples or groups get matching patterns. It enhances certain mental connections."

"Oh-oh!"

"Oh, stop. You could tell if I'm nearby or far away, if I'm happy or sad, or if I'm hungry or anxious, or other things. The electrodes that you used to visit me while I was in the ship's infirmary use the same tech."

"So, I could theoretically sense that you really want a pizza and then show up unbidden at your door with a pizza and entice you to fall in love with me?"

"My stars, Sensors. I like a man with a plan. Mental flexibility is a point in your favor."

The drinks arrived and Callum downed half of his in one gulp. "What's the rest of that story? The one with the girl and her eyes," he said.

"I've told you most of it already. She falls in love with this guy so she gives herself to him one piece at a time. There are a hundred different versions. Some are sad, some are sweet, and some are just gross and disgusting. The version I like most is where she gives her heart to him, but her body dies when she takes it out of her chest. He doesn't want her to die, so he cuts his chest open and puts her heart next to his own and closes it back up. And they go on like that, sharing the same literal space and life. Sometimes they can think thoughts to each other. Romantic, don't you think?"

"I don't know. Was that the sweet version or the gross one?"

"See, I told you. Blood and gore kills the romance. You Bases are all the same." She laughed.

"But we're here, anyway."

"Yes, we are. Cheers!"

A few minutes later another couple was shown to their section. A well-dressed young man and brunette with a crazy mass of dark curls. They seemed very young but also businesslike and not at all giggly.

Another round of drinks arrived and their dinner followed shortly after. They commented on the food, the prices, shared a bit of shipboard gossip, and finally dove into defending their favorite sports. She kept a good cheer about her martial arts ballet but he got belligerent over GravX. Eventually he noticed the young couple was staring and he smiled an apology and shut up.

Sacha took a long look at the girl and frowned. "I have an important mission in the washroom to attend to. I'll be back. Let's get the bill and then we'll check out that casino. It won't be like the fancy ones on Mahalia, but it might pay for dinner."

"I remain at your side, Ops."

—   —   —

Sacha ducked around the corner and melted into the hallway. A shallow alcove had room for coats and wraps, and she worked her way into it, pretending to type a message on her handheld. She used her comm net to hack into the restaurant's comm network. In moments, she was talking to Lom Mench as if he was standing next to her; in a sense, he was.

"Commander I have news on the TSS Agents that attacked us."

"Oh? Tell me."

Sacha threw an image of Kaia that she'd taken with her ocular implants. "I remember this woman being identified as Karmen Sley's daughter back on Tavden Station. Can you confirm?"

"Confirmed. She's Kaia Sley. The oldest daughter. Where is she now?"

"Sitting next to Callum in a restaurant."

Sacha had to force herself not to gawk at the look of utter surprise on Lom's face. It was an expression she'd never expected him to wear. "You're kidding me," he said.

Sacha snaked one of the octopus' tentacles up the wall across the ceiling and through the open doorway and deployed a tiny camera from the tip. Callum and Kaia were conversing happily, animatedly. "No, sir, I kid you not. He has no idea who she is. I doubt she knows him, either."

"That tracks, as he didn't work on that intelligence report. He's not giving her any vital information, I hope?"

"No, it sounds like they're talking about sports," she confirmed.

"Stick to her like the proverbial glue, Sacha. We must know why they're here. If they followed us, then we need to know who tipped them off. If not, well, don't reveal who you are, but find out as much as you can."

"Yes, sir." Sacha closed the connection and withdrew her mechanics. She was distracted by Kaia's date, who was talking into his handheld.

"Vani, my dude! So glad you returned my call. Listen, I have an investment idea I wanted your opinion on…" he said, taking the call in the hall.

She stopped listening after a moment but wondered whether the Sleys were better connected than she'd thought. She ran an image of the boy through the Queen's database. Nothing. If he was somebody, they hadn't intersected with the captain. At least not yet.

The boy was getting antsy. "I would love to go in on my own, but I don't exactly have access to the big money, dude. Not yet. My mother hasn't even paid us for getting rid of Kengi's Bombardiers yet."

Sacha recalled hearing the name of Kengi before, and she

ran through news bulletins via the Queen's logs. There it was: they were a pirate crew working the Autonomous Main. If the Sleys had somehow eliminated them all by themselves, then they were growing in power and aggression. Exactly what the *Emerald Queen* didn't need following them. What she couldn't figure out was an excuse to stick close to the younger couple.

She arrived back at the table just in time to see young Kaia gather up her belongings and head out, presumably to gather the boyfriend on the way.

"All settled?" Callum asked.

Sacha nodded. "Mission accomplished. Shall we casino? I have an encrypted algorithm I'm dying to try on the slots. But I'm wondering if—"

Callum's handheld buzzed with a response. He grinned like a random stranger had just dropped a bag of credit chips on the table and walked away. "We have plans with some new friends," he announced.

She pushed herself not to react. "Those two who just left in a tearing hurry? Do you know who they are?"

"A couple of GravX nerds, I thought."

"Could be. But they're also the daughter of that horrible woman who shot you in the leg and whose pet Agent shattered my arms back on Tavden Station. The boy's last name is Covrani. As in Lower Dynasty. And they recently kicked a pirate crew in the teeth."

She couldn't suppress a smile as his jaw dropped. "Are you serious?"

"I am. Mench wants us to stick to them and find out what they know."

"With pleasure!"

21

GRAVX

CALLUM HAD TO give the Covrani boy credit: the kid didn't do things half-way. Callum relaxed in his comfy seat, surrounded by a type of luxury he'd never imagined. The box was a secure viewing room with twenty seats set aside at the top of the playing track. The reclining seats were plush and wide, and a snack bar with all manner of drinks ran along the rear wall. Sacha sat on his left, gripping his hand tightly, her face glowing with excitement. *It does not get better than this.* "I know it's not what we had planned, but I hope you're enjoying your evening," he said, leaning toward her.

"All my expectations are blown away, Callum," she assured him. In a lowered voice she said, "Spycraft, revenge, *and* box seats? It's just too good to pass up. Here, you've got something on your face."

"I... what?"

"Relax, I got it. There."

He felt her press something onto his temple, and suddenly

a crowd of Lynaedans were chattering away in his head. One by one the conversations died out, until Sacha's voice was the one he heard. "*Sorry about that. Now we can talk privately,*" she said in his mind. "*You didn't tell these idiots our names or where we're from did you?*"

"*No way. First names only, and they think we work on an unnamed cargo ship.*"

Colin sat on Callum's right, clearly impatient for the match to begin, while Kaia settled herself on his right. "So, Callum, how does a man like you come to know so much about GravX?"

Finally, a question he could answer without thinking. "Sports were everything when I was growing up. They were practically all we had. The sports arena in my town was the center of activity while the season was on. Every weekend, we'd go and watch local teams practice. After a few years of that, you learn what to look for in a player."

Colin bobbed his head, fidgeting in his seat. "What about stats? I'm a bit of a stat freak, myself. What's the highest number of goals scored in a single period?"

"Twenty-one," Callum answered. "Greatest number of overtime periods added in a single game?"

"Five. Highest number of penalties for one game?"

"Seven. That was against the Power Towers ten years ago in the division semi-finals." *There it is. He's a playboy, not a businessman. Play it aloof.* "You know the stats well enough, but I thought you owned a team?" Callum said, trying to sound apprehensive.

"I'm looking to *buy* a team. But there are nuances that I'm not always aware of. Kaia's the real brains here. Her father is advising me. Possibly you, too, if all goes well."

"Really, I couldn't commit so easily. I *have* a job," Callum said.

Colin's handheld beeped. "Kaia told me: sensor officer. Good deal. Excuse me, I have to take this," he said as he put his handheld to his ear. "Daveed? Yes, we're at the match now. No, they're taking forever to get the ball rolling as it were," he said, laughing at his own joke as if he were the funniest man alive. "Well, Kaia's here with me, so no need to worry. And we made some new friends who may know something useful. Yes, I'll let you know. We'll see you after the match."

"That would be Daveed Sley, Karmen's husband, and the girl's father." Sacha leaned forward and asked aloud, "Your father-in-law?"

"Not yet. He's not a sports guy the way we are but he's good at business matters."

Kaia leaned over Colin. "He's at the All-Stars game now. He wanted to see the best players."

"Right," Colin said, "we thought it would be better to cover different matches."

"Ah! Maybe we should be advising him instead," Sacha said.

Colin sniffed. "Nonsense! I need more advice. So, Callum, here is tonight's roster. Tell me who you *like*."

The emphasis Colin put on 'like' made it sound to Callum as if the other man were planning on drugging a player and stuffing him into a cargo pod for transport. "I like Betsen, Dolri, and Tellar. But stats don't tell the whole story. You want to see who works well together on the field."

As if on cue, the lights in the arena dimmed and the track's lights activated. The wall screen in the box shimmered to life to show two announcers at a desk, already engaged in their performance.

"Good evening everyone, and welcome to GravX! Tonight,

Crux Station will feature a demonstration match between the visiting Thunderclaps and the defending team, Crux's own Mighty Chondrias. It'll be a shorter than usual game, with three sixteen-minute periods played with limited substitutions, but we don't expect this match to be any less interesting for that."

"Sixteen-minute periods instead of the usual twenty-one? That sounds like we should expect a fast-paced, aggressive match, Alain."

"Rule changes are endemic in this sport, as fans well know, Bob. The Major League has experimented with changes to game length and overtime. They tried out some non-standard ball shapes and weights, too. There've been oblong balls, pyramidal balls, and once they had multiple balls on the track at the same time."

"Stars, Alain, that must have been complicated."

"Those early days made for a strange introduction for the game to the outer sectors, that's for sure. These days they use only one spherical ball that weighs up to fifty kilos in a 6-G gravity zone. That should be enough to keep any fan happy."

"I don't know, Alain, the fans seem hungry for blood tonight. Maybe that three-ball rule should make a comeback, am I right?"

"Do we *have* to listen to the commentary?" Sacha complained. A sense of disgust leaked through the data connection and Callum covered his mouth to avoid giving away a laugh.

"Are you kidding? That's half the fun," Colin said.

"She's got a point. It's really distracting," Kaia urged.

"Okaaay…" Colin sighed dramatically and turned the audio down, but he left the channel open.

Callum had to strain to hear the banter. In any case a line

of text ran along the bottom of the wall screen, but after a minute he discovered he could read or watch the game enjoyably, not both.

Alain was saying, "Looks like they're going to start: the hyper-vision camera drones are flying into positions along the track. The game controller signals he is ready to begin... The test ball is fired into the track..."

An audible thump and a hiss met their ears as a pneumatic cannon spat a silver ball onto the track's upper level, where it eventually slowed and entered the playing field, then dropped into the gutter.

The banter never stopped. "You know, Bob, that cannon shoots a five-kilogram tungsten ball at more than 50 kph. You do not want to be in front of that thing when it goes off!"

"I'll say. That's enough force to snap your head right off your neck at ten meters. It's happened before."

"Especially at the speeds the players' gravity bracers run at. A skilled player can maneuver his footgear to speed down the track at speeds well over 100 kph," Bob added.

The players took to the track next, the orange-clad Mighty Chondrias forming into a wedge while on the opposite side of the rink, the blue-and-white uniformed Thunderclaps formed up into a double line. The two teams paced each other, running around the rink at roughly equal speeds, their captains planning strategy, anticipating the opposing team's moves.

The cannon blasted again. "And the first ball is out! The first period is under way as the clock begins its countdown on first period."

"The first team to scoop the ball will be on offense as they try to score. You wouldn't think these boys could do much in only sixteen minutes, but you'd be wrong as Thunderclap Marin scoops the ball and hands it to Tellar. He must keep that ball in plain sight at all times or risk a foul."

Callum found that it took little effort to just keep watching the track. The two team formations began to merge as players swerved around each other, jockeying for position.

"Thunderclap captain Jonaz moves up the track and up on to the side. Here comes Sanji for Mighty Chondrias... Sanji grabs Jonaz from behind, but down from the rail comes Marin and takes out four Mighty Chondrias men! The old dive-bomber Marin and his favorite maneuver made a move from the top of the track and took out four Mighty Chondrias. The remaining Mighty Chondria players set up a defensive group in front of their goal, their gravity bracers slowed to an absolute crawl. The only reason they're managing it at all is the goal zone right now is 1-G normal... Tellar still has the ball... Moving in. He'll try to cover the slot, and he surely does! Tellar gets in front, shoots and it goes wide. No goal!"

Cheers erupted across the stadium as the action played out. "Calm down, you guys, it's early yet," Callum yelled at the screen. "Gotta pace yourselves, folks!"

Bob, sounding disappointed, said, "The Thunderclaps will have to regroup as the ball runs into the gutter... It's a dead ball."

"Injured on that play was Betsen, and he's being helped off the track by his Thunderclap teammates."

"Betsen's out, Callum. Maybe you shouldn't have liked him so much after all, right?" Colin jeered.

Callum shrugged. "What are you gonna do?"

"*Punch this dynasty brat, that's what,*" Sacha sent over the mental link. "*Seriously, what does Kaia see in him?*"

"*Money. Power. And he's not bad-looking,*" Callum answered. A wave of resignation crossed Sacha's features. He didn't need the connection to know she wasn't a fan of Colin.

"It's still early in the period as they get ready to fire the second ball. It's out... Oh, and it hits Chaz! Mighty Chondria player Chaz is down!" Alain screamed.

Bob jumped in. "Yeah, looks like he was skating too close to the launch track... I think the ball clipped one of his grav bracers, just blew him off his feet."

"He's down. And here comes Marin from the Thunderclaps. Skates by... and knocks him down *again*!" Alain yelled.

Chaz's unmoving body flopped out of the playing area and rolled next to the pit. Callum stood up to get a better look at the action then realized that Sacha was up, too. Colin and Kaia were paying rapt attention, leaning forward in their seats as Chaz's teammates dragged him to the center of the rink, where white-clad medtechs started to work on him.

Another ball burst onto the track. "A new ball is out... Jonaz is moving into position, Tellar accepting the pass from Marin, and completes the pass to Jonaz. He flashes the ball to the crowd. Alain, I think the Thunderclap's captain is up to something."

Jonaz leaned into his bracers and increased his speed, swerving to miss an opposing player, while his team-mates came up around and behind him to peel off the Mighty Chondria players who wanted to intercept him. He slammed into a group of three, who were parked in front of their goal. Climbing up on top of one player, he jammed the silver ball into the goal.

"He shoots, he scores! The score is one-nothing for the Thunderclaps," Bob yelled.

"Yes!" Colin screamed, standing and pumping his fist into the air. Kaia raised her arms and cheered. Even Sacha was getting into the spirit of the game, clapping and whistling for the goal. The connection was far more cheerful than it had been.

"That's one-nothing for the Thunderclaps. Here comes the grav-alert klaxon and the crowd counts down the seconds to the end of the period…"

"Three! Two! One! *Grav!*"

"The gravity alert sounds, and the zones change to new settings," Alain announced. "Now, both goal zones have *three* gravities, while the rest of the track stays in 1-G and 2-G sequences. Looks like both teams will have to rethink their entire strategy!"

"The clock resets, the cannon launches a new ball, and the second period is underway," Bob noted.

The action resumed as the Mighty Chondrias went on the offensive, forming up into their double column, but this time they split apart as they approached their opponents and slammed into the Chondrias' wedge, players of both teams simply attacking each other.

"It's a fight, it's a full-out assault on the Thunderclaps by the Mighty Chondrias!" Bob yelled. "The refs are getting involved, calling out penalties for Dolri and Marin. One from each side…"

A new voice boomed out across the sound system. "Dolri, Marin, concurrent penalty, no helmet: one minute," the ref said.

Boos, hisses, and catcalls erupted from the crowd as Dolri and Marin retreated to the central safe zone and dutifully removed their helmets. The penalty clock set to 1:00 and ran down second by second.

Marin stuck to the 1-G zone, mincing on his gravity bracers as three of his teammates came to surround him. Dolri took a different tactic—racing around the track, trying to avoid contact with anyone from either team. He was good at it, too, zipping through formations at high speed.

The problem came as a clash between two helmeted players further up the track collided in a mutual knock-down. Both players flopped to the bottom of the track. But Dolri was so busy watching everything around him that he didn't see the unconscious players. Dolri slammed into the bodies at high speed and flipped right over them, landing on his head and rolling onto his back. He came to rest on his chest, his head rolling at an unnatural angle.

"Oooh!" Alain yelled, "Dolri avoids contact only to crash into two players and fly into the high-G zone! He's not moving, either."

"Yeah, I'm not seeing him getting back into this game," Bob agreed.

"That's two of your favorites down for the count, Callum!" Colin crowed.

"*Stars, does this kid ever stop being a bad winner?*" Sacha asked.

He ignored the silent comment but the dynasty brat was travelling a road to obnoxious, for certain. "I said I liked them, not that I wanted to pick up their contracts," Callum pointed out.

Bob resumed his commentary. "The penalty clock ends, and Marin puts his helmet back on. Back to the game... Second period ends without seeing any goals, leaving the Thunderclaps in the lead."

"Three! Two! One! Grav!" the crowd screamed.

Colored flags lit up all over the track. "And the grav zones change again," Alain noted. "Now, the zones range from 2-G in three zones, two more are 3-G, one is 4-G and the goal zones are up to 5-G! That's very unusual."

"That kind of high-G zone play is going to exhaust the remaining players pretty quickly," Bob noted.

The action didn't slow down as much as Bob might have suggested. Callum watched with rapt attention as the Mighty Chondrias deployed a series of wide angle turns and swoops, using the light grav zones to actually push themselves further down the track and the heavy gravity zones to slow down. Both teams swerved and slipped, maneuvering around and through each other like a flock of birds executing a wild mating dance.

Bob was back to his commentary. "Mighty Chondria Robbens breaks out from the pack now, he's angling his body practically horizontally to navigate the different zones."

Alain picked up on his co-worker's vibe instantly. "Yes, he's setting up the long shot, angling high to account for the increased gravity field. Will he make it? No! The ball drops well short of the rim, slams into the track, and bounces down into the gutter for a dead ball. No goal!"

"But I think he tipped the Thunderclap captain, Jonaz off on their intentions. You know there's no way they'll give up that leading score."

"Not a chance! Giving up the possibility of a shutout is not in his character."

The Thunderclaps were shifting their positions on the track, bunching up and linking arms to form a wall of players.

"Bob, do you hear that? The crowd knows what's up. They're all calling for the Bum's Rush."

A wave of bewilderment passed from Sacha. "Bum's Rush? What does that mean?"

"It's an awesome play. Keep watching," Callum urged.

Alain was saying, "Jonaz is calling for the 'Bum's Rush' the formation that is normally used on defense but can be a formidable attack in the right hands. The Thunderclaps have linked arms and are surrounding the opposing players. They smash their skates onto the deck and race for the nearest high-G zone. They approach… The Chondrias struggle and try to break free, and Jonaz signals the release! Two Mighty Chondria players go flying and crash into the deck at three times their normal weight." Cheers and wild screaming washed over the stadium as the players went sprawling. "Bum's Rush, folks! Never fails to get a scream from the crowd."

Callum watched as two of the Chondrias retreated off the track, one holding his arm at a bad angle, the other limping badly.

"Bob, you forgot to mention their team's two other signature moves, the Smash and the Mash."

"Yeah, gotta love attack moves that rhyme."

"That you do. This is a great game, folks!"

22

RIOT OF OUR OWN

THE TWO COUPLES exited the stadium through the tunnels set aside for the crowd that had the means to buy the best seats. Kaia couldn't stop staring at the other couple. They certainly didn't *look* like interstellar criminals. They seemed perfectly normal. But Kaia had been picking up weird details all night that convinced her they were no ordinary couple out for a date night.

Colin bounced along on his toes, oblivious to the subtext, holding hands with Kaia as they swung their linked arms in unison. "That was great! I haven't been to a live game in way too long. It's just not the same when you watch on the sports network."

Sacha couldn't stop laughing. "All right, I'll admit, that was an enormous charge. Was it a particularly exciting game? I don't know enough to judge."

Kaia spied an opportunity to learn some useful intelligence from their new acquaintances. "It was pretty intense," Kaia agreed. "I'll be honest, I don't usually get as wound up as I did tonight. Callum, Sacha, you guys feel like getting a drink? I mean a real drink, not the flavored water that restaurant passed off on us."

"It sounds like fun," Callum replied, "but I think it's time to start heading back to our ship. We have duty in the morning."

"Come on, Sensors. One drink won't kill us," Sacha said.

"I don't know, Commander Mench is on shore patrol tonight."

"Callum, it's more than an hour to lights out. The docks are that way, we can walk it."

Callum gave in to the inevitable. "Okay, I surrender. A drink and maybe a short conversation on whether we have an advisory role in Kaia's grand business plan."

Colin wasn't done pumping Callum for information. "So, a cargo crew, huh? My family does that. What class of vessel is it?"

Callum gave him a side eye. "I just run the sensor equipment, I didn't design it."

"Well, okay. It must be a pretty big crew, though, right?"

"Big enough to get everything done."

"Don't bug the man with silly questions, dude," Kaia urged as she pulled him to the side of the street near a busy intersection. Lowering her voice, she said, "I should call my dad. If these two are who I think they are, I guarantee he'll notice things we missed."

"What do you mean?"

Kaia pulled out her hand held and typed a quick message to Colin. >>They work for Mother Carnage I'll bet.<<

Colin frowned and glanced at their guests. >>How do you know?<<

"Little things. She's a Lynaedan. He's got a pulse pistol in his jacket. I saw it when he paid his bill at the restaurant. They're off a cargo ship they won't name. It smells wrong. Taking out Kengi might have put us on their sensor map."

"Yeah, but Mother Carnage… That's a leap, isn't it?"

"We'll see." Kaia put her handheld against her ear.

She connected with her father and directed him to their position on the corner. "Yes! I see you! Here I am!" She put the device in her bag and nodded to the other side of the street. "He's coming."

Daveed Sley sprinted the last few meters and arrived a bit out of breath. Kaia took a moment to make introductions, and Daveed shook hands. "Well. That was certainly exciting. And incredibly violent," he said. "Do you kids really think you can make a go of team building? Because being a team owner strikes me as a risky and tireless career."

"Let's just say Kaia's proposal got approved by a high-powered accountant and a lawyer. We just need money to get started," Colin said.

Callum pointed down the street. "We should probably get going. One drink, right?"

"One drink," Daveed agreed. "I'll be having seltzer. You may not realize it, but I'm older than you kids."

"That never occurred to us. I promise," Sacha replied.

They kept walking, but Kaia didn't like the way they were garnering attention from the locals. Why not? They were all well dressed and obviously unaware of their location. "Guys? I have a question I've been dying to ask, but I know it will sound incredibly stupid…"

"Is it about the five creeps who've been following us for the past two blocks?" Sacha asked.

"Well, yeah."

"Yep. Speed it up a bit, please. I want you three to be ahead of us." Sacha's statement had the tone of an order.

"We're not exactly defenseless," Daveed said.

"But we have combat experience. I'm not sure about you three," Callum countered.

"No combat experience?" Colin scoffed. "Hey, let us tell you about the time we—"

"Not now, Colin," Kaia scolded. "Come on menfolk, you heard him. Hup two three four—"

"Hey, what's got into you?" Colin demanded.

"I'll feel safer when I have my mother's armory within reach," Kaia retorted, then wished she hadn't. The brief look Callum and Sacha shared set off warning bells in her head. She was suddenly certain that they knew who they were and why they were asking questions. What were they getting into?

A young male voice yelled from behind them. "Yo, tech head! Gimme your eyes!"

"You think he's talking to me?" Callum asked.

"Hey, tech head! I *love* your eyes! Why don't you hand them over?"

"No such luck," Sacha agreed. "You three keep moving. Run."

"We're not leaving you," Colin argued. Kaia felt the world contract to the couple of meters around their group and felt sure she could hear footsteps just behind them.

Finally, a hand connected with Callum's shoulder and spun him around. Callum found himself facing four—no, five thugs. They were all smiling but none looked happy. The one who'd spun him around was a well-built heavily muscled man. A skinny one stood next to him, and a pale scraggly dude with a birthmark on his chin flanked him. A wiry looking tough walked slowly around to flank the three civilians.

A fifth one wearing a black jacket stepped out and faced Callum squarely. "Hey man, I don't like being ignored."

"No? I'm surprised to hear that. I'd think you get ignored a lot," Sacha taunted.

Callum had ice water in his veins as far as Kaia was concerned. He didn't even blink as Black Jacket got in his face. "Can I help you, sir?"

"Sir? Do I look like a 'sir' to you, you bomaxed idiot?"

"Let's leave appearances out of it. What do you want?" Callum pushed.

"I *want* your tech head's eyes. I'll settle for whatever you're carrying."

"Yeah, pulling these babies out in public would be kind of gross," Sacha agreed. "Besides, you couldn't manage it with all ten fingers and an instruction manual."

"Then I'll use a spoon," Black Jacket said. "Just for that, I changed my mind. Eyes *and* your pockets. Now."

Kaia dropped her eyes to watch Callum's hand move to the hem of his jacket, understanding exactly how he'd need to move to ruin this cretin's day. She *knew* she'd seen a pistol in there earlier but being proven right brought her no satisfaction.

"Not happening. Get lost. Now. Or we'll be the last group you mess with for a long time," Callum said.

"I'll take those odds." Black Jacket took a step forward, but Callum was already dodging, moving to the left and planted his booted toe into Jacket's solar plexus. He went down with a loud oof.

Please stay down or run away, Kaia thought.

No such luck. The rest of the attackers dispersed, each man picking out a target of his own.

Wiry brandished a knife and moved on Daveed. Daveed understood the first rule of combat: never let a man with a weapon make the first move. Daveed stepped forward, reached out, and grabbed the wrist holding the knife and pulled Wiry's arm straight, then brought his other hand to the attacker's elbow and pushed. A loud snap was followed by a louder shout and the attacker fled, holding his arm.

Muscles ignored everything except Colin, who waved his hands like a prize fighter, bouncing on his toes. Muscles wasn't moved by the display and grabbed a handful of Colin's jacket and shirt.

Colin's morale broke. "Not in the face!"

Muscles sneered but obliged, ramming his fist into Colin's stomach with an audible "Oof!" Colin folded and sank to his knees. "Thank you," he rasped, and collapsed face first to the ground.

Callum had had enough of the nonsense and pulled a pistol from his jacket. "Stand down," he ordered, stepping toward Muscles.

Muscles had just enough time to give Callum a dirty look before reaching behind him and pulling a baton from his back pocket. He flicked the rod and the weapon telescoped out to twice its length, then he advanced on Callum.

Callum took a moment to brace himself and shot the man in his chest. Muscles dropped in his tracks.

Sacha had transformed—her hair had lengthened into a shaggy mess of writhing strands. Spikes emerged from the palms of her hands and bundles of fibers flexed from ports which opened in her forearms. She bobbed and wove like a snake, dancing with the guy with the birthmark.

Birthmark was clearly outmatched, stabbing and slashing but not quickly or accurately enough to land a blow.

Finally, Sacha lunged. One bundle of arm-fibers launched themselves at Birthmark's nose and eyes, penetrating his head and freezing him in place. She twirled around and pulled the fibers out while moving her spike-arm forward and impaled the attacker's throat. She held that position for several seconds, then pulled her hardware out and stepped away while Birthmark dropped, twitching and spasming, to the ground.

Kaia was only dimly aware of the fights around her: Skinny had decided that she was a pushover. She quickly recalled the training her mother had imparted over the years and vowed to show the cretin his mistake. His approach was slow and clumsy. Kaia waited for him then tried to dodge when he reached for her. But she'd mistimed the maneuver and he managed to grab her by the shoulders. She bent over backwards, continued into a shoulder roll, and came out of it free of her attacker. Filled with indignation, she jumped up to grab his ears, bent him forward, and rammed her knee into his face, then did it again just to prove it hadn't been an accident.

Callum surprised her by shooting her attacker in the thigh. Skinny rolled onto his back, held his leg, and screamed. That was the last straw for the would-be robbers. Black Jacket gathered his crew, and they scuttled back down the street and turned into an alley.

Kaia spun to survey her own crew and realized Colin was the only real casualty on their side. She tried to get her boyfriend on his feet, but snippets of Callum and Sacha's exchange met her ears.

"Monofilament wires? Punch daggers? You didn't tell me your date arms could do that."

'Date arms'? She's a Lynaedan for sure. Emerald Queen *has dozens of them aboard,* she thought. *Where are the rest of them?*

Sacha flicked the gore off her weaponry and retracted them. "Why would I?"

"I don't know. Common courtesy, maybe. Why do you

even have that gear?"

"Because I wasn't always a great judge of character before Maesy started looking out for me. Sometimes dates go wrong, and a girl needs protection. Besides, where have you been keeping *that* pea shooter all evening?" Sacha hissed, pointing to the pistol.

"*This* is a Putnam MP-15 pulse pistol. It uses molecular circuitry and a liquid gel fuel chamber. And it's completely undetectable by security systems." He thumbed the safety and slipped the weapon into an interior holster built into his jacket. No hint of a bulge. "Style *and* substance," he said.

"You're full of tricks, aren't you, Sensors?" Sacha said, grinning widely.

"Yes, you're both very tricky. Can we please get out of here?" Kaia asked. "Forget the drinks."

She lifted Colin off the ground and urged him forward as her boyfriend groaned. Daveed brought up the rear, exhibiting considerable dignity as he straightened his tie at a full run. *That's my Dad.*

They ran three blocks and finally gave up, Colin huffing and puffing loudly. Kaia was winded but not incapacitated, and Sacha and Callum slowed to a stroll. Just another gaggle of tourists walking down the street, with blood stains on their clothing and someone's father playing the chaperone.

They turned down a side street and emerged within sight of the docks. The *Emerald Queen*'s sensor tower soared over the low buildings lining the street. Kaia would have recognized that starship anywhere. Any lingering doubts about her new 'friends' was gone.

Callum swiped his date's dress. "Is that why you wore purple? Hide the blood?" he pressed.

Sacha tried to wipe some of the stains away and gave up in

disgust. "This dress has been sitting in my closet for months. I wanted to be a little more revealing tonight. But I guess it does hide blood, doesn't it?" She turned to Kaia. "You guys did pretty well out there. You all right, Kaia?"

"I'm fine. My mother taught me a few moves she learned in the military."

"Your mother is a wizard," Colin said. "All mine taught me how to do is spend money and doubt myself. Two years of track and boxing, and I can't even hit some guy on the street!"

"So you're not a street brawler, who cares? You were amazing when you showed up with *Percival*, then flew it against that pirate ship," Kaia insisted.

"That was easy."

"Was it? I couldn't have done that."

"What pirate ship?" Callum asked.

"It's nothing," Daveed said. "She's being metaphorical is all."

The conversation came to a full stop, as did Callum and Sacha. "'Pirate-like' or 'piratical' is metaphorical. 'Pirate ship' sounds really specific. What do you people want, anyway? A fight? Because we can give you that."

"Dude, no more fighting," Colin groaned.

"No, really," Kaia quickly corrected, frantically wondering what she could say to get out of this trainwreck of an encounter. "I was just being flippant. Stupid. I do that sometimes."

"No, Kaia Sley, you're a tool of an oppressive oligarchy," Sacha accused.

Colin held up his hands. "Whoa, slow down there, tech-head. She only meant—"

"We know what she meant. Lightly veiled threats don't go down well," Callum said.

Daveed folded his arms. "What are you talking about, Callum?"

"Did you miss your girl's not so subtle reference to a private armory, old man? Are you guys merely running guns? Or do you normally go pirate hunting in restaurants?" Sacha demanded.

"It's just one case of plasma rifle—" Colin said.

In a flash, Callum's pistol was back in his hand and pointed at Colin's chest. "Stars, kid, were you born this stupid or do you have to work at it?"

Kaia made a noise in her throat and raised her hands, closing the distance between herself and Callum in a flash. But Sacha was faster: her hands peeled back to reveal her combat spikes, one of which rested a bare centimeter from Kaia's face.

"That's enough!" Daveed Sley roared, throwing Colin to the side and pulling Kaia's face away from Sacha's arm.

When Kaia regained her feet she froze at the sight of Callum's pistol only centimeters from her father's face.

Daveed's voice never wavered. His eyes bore into the sensor operator's. "Are you going to shoot me, son? Is that what you really want to do?"

"Why shouldn't I?"

"Because your issue isn't with me. Nor him. Nor her. Will shooting me solve any of your problems?"

The pistol's muzzle trembled ever so slightly. Kaia held her breath as Callum spoke in a low tone. "You *are* the TSS. Your whole way of life is beholden to them. Gifts and Agents, and acting like gods to push the rest of the galaxy around. All to keep the dynasties in power."

Daveed edged in closer, his nose almost touching the gun barrel. "We're not dynasties."

Sacha brought out one of her tentacles and clicked it a

centimeter from Colin's head. "He is."

Colin finally moved to glare at Sacha directly, ignoring the tactile gripper that hovered near his eyes. "I'm no heir. They don't even like me."

Daveed continued, "It's true, when the TSS said jump, my wife said how high. That's who she is. No Gifts, no powers. Just an overwhelming sense of duty. I think maybe that's you, too."

"Duty? She shot Callum!" Sacha yelled. "She stood there and watched while that Agent shredded my arms."

"You ambushed her in an alley. What would you have done in her place?" Daveed asked.

Kaia wanted to scream, but the slightest flinch might mean the end of her father's life. "Callum, this was a fun night, wasn't it?" she blurted. "It wasn't an act. I really think we could be friends. And I thought you liked us, too."

Callum finally lowered his pistol. The group breathed a collective sigh of relief as everyone withdrew from each other.

"I *do* like you," he said while holstering his weapon. "It *was* fun. That's what's making me crazy. How do I reconcile that assault a few months ago with tonight?"

Sacha anchored herself to Callum's arm. "Hey, it's a lot for all of us to process. Let's just get back to the *Queen*." The two of them took a few steps, then Sacha turned to look behind her. "You know, after talking to you tonight, I know we're not all that different. We've found ourselves on the opposite sides of some things, but we're not bad people."

"We never thought you were," Kaia said.

The other young woman nodded thoughtfully. "Did you really mean it about us being friends?"

"Yes."

"Well, maybe we have a real chance to do something meaningful here. How about I introduce you to our captain?

You should meet the person you've been trying to destroy, no?"

Kaia looked over at her father, who had gone rigid. "I'm not sure how my mom would feel about that."

"This is about what *you* want. You joined the fight. And now you claim you want to be friends—that means understanding our side of it. I think you'll see we aren't the enemy you imagine."

Daveed nodded solemnly. "Diplomatic solutions require an act of faith. If your captain wants to end this chase, then let's hear what she has to say."

Sacha nodded. "Follow me."

They turned the corner onto the main road; dozens of ships lay silent in their berths. The *Emerald Queen* was now fully visible as she towered over the rest.

Kaia walked next to her father and grabbed his arm. "What was that? Are you insane? You could have been killed!" she hissed.

Daveed let out an enormous sigh and patted her arm. "I would do *anything* to keep you safe. One day, you'll have children of your own and you'll understand."

Kaia shoved the thought away. Tonight had taught her some new things about herself. "Well, boyfriend, you might suck at street fighting but I can't say you didn't show me an exciting time tonight."

"I aim to please," Colin murmured. "Sorry I acted like a jerk at the game, Callum. I was so bomaxed pleased to have someone to nerd out about GravX with."

"You do that with me constantly," Kaia said.

"It's a guy thing, Kaia. I'm sorry, but it's different."

"That's true," Callum agreed.

Kaia pressed on. If they could create some bonding here and now, maybe there was a way to heal the obvious breach between the two groups. Mother Carnage was only one step in their mission—what they *really* needed were the people she was working for. If they could get her and her crew to flip, it would be a path forward without more bloodshed. "Hey, since it seems like we aren't going to kill each other, you guys want to do something tomorrow night? Like, with less hostility and violence?"

Sacha turned to her date. "Well?"

Callum thought for a while and eventually nodded. "Okay. We can double up. But we're going to that casino."

23

MEET THE CAPTAIN

DAVEED LISTENED TO the conversation with a practiced ear and eye. Callum and Sacha were older than Kaia and Colin, but the four of them sounded like any group of students he'd ever encountered. There was a shared link between them. An hour ago, they'd been total strangers and now they were wiping blood off their clothing and planning double dates. They'd avoided killing each other despite the awful temptation. He envied them—their optimism and energy. Their adaptability. *Good for you, kids.*

Daveed approached the giant cargo ship with a feeling of dread as his sense of protectiveness asserted itself. Stars alive, there it was. The ship they'd fought with months ago, up close and intensely personal. The danger to himself and his people was now a fact. He planned to bid Callum and Sacha good night and hustle his own charges back to their transport and hope no one noticed their departure.

The opportunity dissolved as he glimpsed their reception.

A machine man, a robot with a sash, a sword, and a tri-corner hat stood guard where the gangway met the dock.

"Stars, who is that?" Daveed asked.

"That's our first officer," Callum said. "Time to report in."

Daveed stood back, watching how Callum and Sacha approached the gangway. They moved with Karmen's kinetic discipline. The same precise, practiced habits. But something else, too. They'd defeated enemies together. They'd won each other through combat.

The first officer folded his arms and tapped his fingers, his glowing mechanical eyes scanning the two crew. "I see blood stains, pulse pistol fuel residue, and torn clothing. Date night went well?"

Callum nodded tiredly. "Very well, Commander Mench."

"I'm glad to hear it." Mench's head swiveled, and his red eyes focused on Daveed. In a louder voice, he called out to them. "Dean Sley. Kaia. Captain Aura would like a word." He stepped aside to allow Aura to pass.

Daveed felt like coming to attention. He stood a little straighter. Aura Thand didn't look like a Mother Carnage. Daveed had wondered about her appearance for months. A grizzled hag with a sword and a sash or a hat, much like the mechanical officer was wearing now. But she was none of those things. A blazing redhead with a fierce gaze and a strong body, wrapped in what would have passed for a military uniform in any port in the galaxy. There was no question of her command ability. Someone used to making things happen. *She's what my department head at the Uni wishes he could be. I'd rather work for her. No wonder Karmen can't get past their history.*

Aura clucked at the sight of them. "Callum. Sacha. I'm glad you found some new friends, but the trouble in town is a bad look. I had to drop a sizable donation with the Enforcer office to keep this incident off the record."

"How did they know this is our ship?" Sacha asked.

Mench pointed to the ceiling high above them. "Crux Station has a persistent criminal element at large. Cameras are everywhere. They figured it out surprisingly quickly."

"I expect that's how you identified us, as well," Daveed croaked, his mouth utterly dry.

"Oh, we've known who you were since the incident on Tavden Station," Aura said. "Let me deal with these two first."

Callum bowed his head. "Captain. We were accosted. We tried to evade the situation, and we were pursued. Considering that we had three civilians with us, I decided that a confrontation was inevitable. We neutralized the attackers and escaped without harm to ourselves or our guests."

"I like a man who takes responsibility, Callum, but paying off Enforcers gets expensive. And pulling a sidearm on a guest is a truly bad idea."

Colin took a step forward and said, "Captain, I will manage any legal problems that arise from this... incident."

"I see. That's magnanimous of you, sir..."

"Colin Covrani, ma'am. We're a family of some connections. Shipping and transportation. We—"

"*Colin.* We were glad to help."

Daveed put his hands on Kaia's and Colin's shoulders and drew them back a step. Colin wasn't processing the situation well at all. For all they knew, he'd just made himself a kidnapping target. "Head straight back to the ship, you two. I'll meet you there," he said firmly. "And Colin... welcome to the family." Colin and Kaia made faces and threw hand signals at each other, communicating in a private silent verbiage. They held hands as they left, fingers entwined. *He's really your son-in-law now. Get used to it.*

Sacha came to attention and saluted. "Captain, permission to board?"

"Permission granted. Callum, walk her home. Remember, it's almost lights out and you both have duty in the morning."

Daveed watched how they moved with each other as they ascended the gangway. Arms around each other. *Good for them.*

Aura turned to the drone. "Thank you, Lom. Carry on."

"Yes, Captain."

Aura waited until they were alone then said, "You might want to choose your night life more carefully next time."

Daveed felt self-conscious in a way he wasn't used to. He wasn't in the habit of preening for women, but now he felt the need to straighten his clothing. "So, there *will* be a next time? Don't pirates usually make intruders walk the plank?"

Aura's brows furrowed. "I admit, I'm conflicted. I'm not pleased to meet the crew who's been hounding me for months. But I'm curious to know what kind of man tamed Karmen. I wouldn't have thought she'd fall for a schoolteacher. But a schoolteacher who can stare down a man with a gun is far more interesting. What's the story?"

"There *is* a story there, but I doubt this is the place or time for it."

"It's the perfect opportunity. I'll expect you for dinner tomorrow night. Bring your family. I promise my galley staff is up to the challenge."

Daveed realized he was trapped, and elected bluster over gibbering. He dared not show her how scared he was. "Is that an order?"

"I'll have my answers, Daveed Sley, one way or another. You can arrive on your own or I can have Mench and his drones fetch you. Your choice."

"How could I say no to that?"

"Bring sidearms if that will make you feel safer. I know you have them. But it's late. Go home to your wife, Professor."

"I'm not a professor," he said, and turned to go. His blood froze as she called out again.

"One more thing. Do you have a recent image of Karmen? Show me."

Daveed projected an image from his handheld and watched, fascinated as Aura's face and manner transformed. This was no vengeful and blood-thirsty murderess, but a woman who'd lost everything she'd ever cared about and spent a lifetime to rebuild. Tears gathered at the corners of her eyes. *What is going on here?*

"She's still beautiful," she whispered, but recovered quickly. "You lucky bastard," she said. "I'll see you all tomorrow night. I think we have a lot to talk about."

— — —

The *Mother Courage* was dark.

Karmen had decided to take it easy tonight, nibbling sandwiches and cheap flavored water while studying the market plan that Colin and Kaia had cooked up. She understood the broad strokes, but the details confused her. Long after lights out for the younger kids, Daveed stepped carefully into their cabin.

"How was the game?" she asked.

"Surprisingly exciting. Extremely bloody." He sat down at the foot of the bed. "I spoke to Aurelia Thand tonight," he said quietly.

"You…" Karmen put the handheld aside and gave him her

full attention. "What did she say?"

He showed her his handheld. The screen glowed in gold and flowery trim. "Invited to dine with the captain of the *Emerald Queen*," she read. "What the fok?"

"I think you were right about her," Daveed murmured.

"What do you mean?"

"When our home was attacked, I thought an awful person must be behind it. Someone ruthless and calculating. But in the few minutes I spent with her tonight, she was none of that. I saw the affection from her crew. The respect. And a desire to do what's right."

"What's right? They're criminals!"

Daveed shrugged. "Businesses steal from each other all the time, just with advertising fees and lawyers. What Aura has been doing isn't legal, but it's also not *evil*."

Karmen worked her mouth, unsure how to respond. "You really think I should accept this dinner invitation?"

"As a TSS officer? No. But as my wife who's been mourning the loss of her friend for longer than we've known each other, I think this might be the most important dinner in your life."

Karmen weighed his words. Getting cozy with a criminal was a dangerous line any way she looked at it. But he also wasn't wrong, and there was something to be said for getting an inside look at Mother Carnage's operation. How much more could be learned inside the *Emerald Queen* while not actively engaged in a firefight?

She looked down at the digital invitation. "Does she want to meet the kids, too?"

"She's already met Kaia and Colin. If what I overheard between them pans out, they will be going on a double date with Callum and Sacha tomorrow night."

"Who?"

"They're two of Aura's officers who joined us at the GravX game. They seem like a perfectly nice couple who carry concealed weapons and aren't afraid to use them."

The conversation was numbing. Karmen couldn't quite convince herself her husband was telling her the truth, but he wasn't prone to grand hallucinations. "I never meant for our kids to get wrapped up in this."

"A lot of that is on me. We followed you from Greengard. That was my call. I didn't think we'd end up here."

"But we are. And now our daughter and her boyfriend are becoming besties with pirates?"

"I don't think they'd appreciate that term."

"Whatever they are… I guess they can't all be brazen thugs like Mitchel Pilar." She sighed. "Daveed, what are we getting into?"

"We're not *getting into* it. It's here. We have to adapt. We aren't dealing with genteel academics."

"Exactly! And that's all the more reason to steer away, not *in*!"

He stared at her levelly. "The underlying reality hasn't changed, Karmen. We're here because you want—*need*—to talk to Aura face-to-face. This is your chance."

Karmen took a deep breath, squeezing her eyes shut. She hated that he was right. "My old life had rules of engagement around public conduct."

"Well, you're not on the *Triumph* anymore. The rules are a bit fuzzier out here in the Outer Colonies. The TSS no longer inspires the kind of respect it used to, and their overwhelming force tactics aren't likely to quiet this growing rebellion."

Again, he was so bomaxed astute. They'd already tried shooting at the *Emerald Queen*, and Mother Carnage's operation had come out of the engagement even stronger. There were still bigger adversaries to apprehend, and winning over the pirate queen could be the best path to settling the larger regional conflict.

"How does Aura look?" Karmen asked.

"She's quite the stunner."

"Of course! She was always the sexy one."

"But there's a deep regret in her, too. I suspect the years wore more heavily on her than they did to the two of us."

"I'll bet she's not going blind one day at a time."

"At the moment, neither are you. She looked perfectly natural standing on that gangway, with a Lynaedan officer in full mechanics next to her. Her ship is *gigantic*. We could house one hundred of ours in it."

"Daveed, are you *admiring* my old CO?" she asked.

"No more than I admire you."

"Always the diplomat, aren't you, Professor?"

"She did say we could bring weapons if it would make us feel safer."

"From what I remember when Lee and I confronted her, I doubt it would make a difference."

"Well, are we going to dinner or not?"

"You know we are. Accept her invitation and tell her to get ready to meet the Sley family."

24

THE CAPTAIN'S TABLE

KARMEN SAT THROUGH dinner at the captain's table with the same frustration she'd felt every time she and Daveed had attended a function at a visiting dignitary's house on Greengard. She strove to be perfect in manner and attitude and merely made herself miserable. Her small talk was clumsy, and she could barely bring herself to meet Aura's eyes.

Finally, she couldn't keep the past bottled in any longer. "You know, Aura, if you ever want a new chef, Bertie Wessor is running the Culinary Arts degree program on Greengard. If you make him an offer, he might just say yes."

"Stars, I haven't thought about Bertie in years. I'm glad he landed on his feet. On that subject, I'm *dying* to know what your story is, Karmen. How did you and the Professor become an item?"

Daveed shrugged and gave his wife a side eye. "I was a teaching assistant for the business department and ended up with a class on Business Ethics. At the start of the fall term, this… *woman*… walked into my classroom and I could barely concentrate on my lesson."

Aura cocked her head. "You, Karmen? A business student? I'm having some trouble getting my head around that image. It's very funny."

Finally, Karmen could relax a bit and let old habits take over. She ran her finger around her plate to scoop up a bit of sauce and popped her finger in her mouth. "Trust me, Aura, there was nothing funny about it. I'd failed my eye exam, so they gave me a medical discharge and a bank deposit, and turned me loose. Six months of working odd jobs showed me that I couldn't do much more than soldiering. I went to Greengard to get a bit more educated and sat down in this man's classroom."

"She was a terrible student. My stars," Daveed offered.

"It's true," Karmen said, a sly smile working its way onto her mouth. "I couldn't stop staring at him. Just listening to him talk on this boring subject with my mouth hanging open."

"That sounds marvelous," Aura said.

"It was almost obscene," Karmen admitted. "I didn't do my homework, I didn't do the assigned readings, I failed two quizzes. Finally, I realized that higher education wasn't for me—at least not that subject—and I withdrew from the course."

Daveed pushed his plate away. "One day, she wasn't in class. I panicked. Then I saw she'd dropped the course, and I realized she wasn't my student any more. I showed up at her apartment and begged her to go out with me. She said yes. I had friends in the musical theater department, so we went to a performance, then dinner with the cast and crew. They all loved her. It was fun."

"I'm sure."

"For our second date I took him to the Enforcer training base downtown. Taught him to throw a knife like a soldier. He proposed to me on the spot, and here we are," Karmen finished.

"You're insanely lucky."

Karmen wiped her mouth with the napkin and pushed her plate away. "That, I am."

Aura caught her first officer's attention with a wave. "Commander Mench, I know the Sleys would love to see the rest of the ship. Could you give them a tour?"

"Of course, Captain. Ladies and gentlemen, I would be honored if you follow me. Please don't touch anything and let's keep the group together. Kozu and Tolri, walk with me. Elian! Don't run ahead... Seandra, that's the wrong corridor..."

Aura pushed her napkin away. "You have a beautiful family, Karmen. I'm envious to tears."

"Thank you." Karmen waited long enough to make sure none of her brood would return then allowed her anger free rein. "You never called. You never wrote. We thought you were dead. We had a funeral for you!"

"Did you? How was it?"

Karmen seethed and couldn't stop the tears. "*Glorious.* Nearly two hundred people showed up. Honor guard, speeches by TSS officials. The whole shebang. I spent two *years* mourning you, you heartless creep." She grabbed her napkin and shoved it against her eyes, forcing her emotions back into her heart. "Bomax, Aura! What happened?"

Aura sank into her chair. "So much happened... But I know, there's no apology strong enough. When your husband showed me that photo, it was like the years had just disappeared and there you were. With a smile I never thought I'd see on you. Your weird hair. No rules, no duties. Just... you.

You are brilliant. I've missed you."

Karmen pounded her fists on the table, bouncing the plates and flatware. "Then why did you vanish?"

"Because the TSS knows who I am. Going underground and changing everything about myself was a way to avoid…" She made a noise in her throat Karmen was sure she couldn't duplicate. "I couldn't keep pretending anything we did mattered."

An idea popped into Karmen's head, unbidden. "What was your news?"

"My what?"

"The night of the collision, I showed up at your cabin with ice cream—"

"You did. Rum raisin. We shared it."

"You never told me what was wrong. What *was* it?"

Aura sucked in a deep breath and let it out slowly. "We'd received orders to report to the Jotun Division. They were going to send us to the Bakzen front."

A thousand potential futures passed before Karmen's eyes. In a moment, everything she knew about Aura made sense. "No!"

"Yes! A death sentence. New warships with veteran crews were coming back with fifty percent casualties, or not at all. The Bakzen were using mind control against entire *planets*. The *Triumph* would never have survived that meat grinder. I didn't know how to break the news to the crew. When the collision happened, I put everyone in life pods, I sent an alert to the *Charity* to pick them up, and…"

"And?"

"My life pod was damaged. I was going to die. I was *ready* to die. Then, I met this man. This very strange young man with insane dreams. He saved my life. He convinced me that the TSS was in no condition to set rules for the rest of the galaxy. I decided to live. I changed my name, created false IDs. We built a life. He found some Lynaedans with aspirations of their own and brought them aboard. We built this ship. And we've been following his plans ever since. Building our own little empire out here. We call it New Akkadia."

"What happened to the man?"

"We've parted ways. That's the only reason we're having this conversation now."

That's interesting... Karmen tried not to show too much interest, but she recognized that not a lot would make it past the former Agent. "I don't know what to do now." Karmen sighed. "I really don't. I've been following you for months as part of a TSS task force, and now that I'm here talking to you... what now?"

"Do they know you're here?"

"Yes. They're standing by to make sure you don't abduct me and hold my family for ransom."

"Karmen—"

"Shite, you were my best friend, Aura! I trusted you more than anyone else alive. But you ran away and abandoned me without a word. You let me believe you were dead. You betrayed me. You betrayed the TSS!"

The other woman sat back in her seat. "So, arrest me."

"I... can't just arrest you. My mission is more complex than you or us."

"You want the people I was working for."

"I can't discuss the specifics of my mission with the subject of the investigation."

"It's nice to know that nothing ever really changes," Aura sighed. "Do what you feel you must. For what it's worth, I like Daveed. And I like Kaia. Kozu and Tolri are close and getting closer. Seandra and Elian are adorable in a noisy way. I think I like Colin, too, but he's a little conflicted."

Karmen snorted into her hands. "He's a *lot* conflicted. His mommy issues have mommy issues."

"That sounds painful."

"I've met the mother. The woman's a tyrant. Kaia seems to think she can help him grow up a bit. Maybe she can. What do I know? I'm just her mother."

"From what I saw here tonight, you're a good one. They trust you, they respect you, and you're obviously there for them. Daveed, too. You've shown me a happy family. Now, let me show you mine. Maybe that will help you decide what to do with me."

—

There was no question in Karmen's mind that the *Emerald Queen* was no match for any other TSS warship, but she had to admit that Aura had put her together well. Even better, Aura happily showed her every compartment without being asked. The tour was highly educational.

What fascinated Karmen was the elegance of the design. The pirate ship was built around a one-hundred-meter-wide core that formed the vertical axis for the ship as it passed through each deck. The sensor array and battle computer occupied the topmost deck, followed by quarters, mess, galley, and so on. There was plenty of cargo storage and room for workshops and manufacturing facilities. The infirmary was small but extremely up-to-date in terms of equipment, but that would make sense if the crew included a lot of Lynaedans. There was even a recreation deck. The lower levels were dedicated to engineering, and the complex equipment the

Lynaedan drone pilots needed to do their jobs. The lowermost deck was the hangar.

"I've already seen that one," Karmen quipped.

"That is true. What did you think of it?"

"It's a solid defense design. I'm amazed we got as far as we did."

"We weren't expecting you to shoot out the hangar door and board us. Scared the crap out of me. I told the drone pilots to hold back. I didn't know what was likely to happen, but it was clear you weren't running a professional infiltration team. I didn't want to see you hurt any more than necessary."

"Some choice of words, Aura. It looked like you got pretty hurt yourself."

"It wasn't a great time, no."

There's still some of the woman I knew in there, after all. Karmen met Aura's gaze. "I know I'm asking a lot, but may we visit your Command Center?"

"I thought you might ask that. Follow me." The captain led her to a lift, and they rode up in silence. Two sets of armored doors met them as they stepped onto the main deck. "We call it the War Room," Aura said, as she strode into the ship's nerve center. "It's not what we had on the *Triumph*, but it gets the job done. Cute, isn't it?"

Karmen gasped as she let her eyes scan the room. Two dozen stations and consoles, half of which were dark, and only four crew were on duty. Displays manifested in mid-air and holographic projectors dotted the ceiling. "Magnificent," Karmen breathed. "Skeleton crew, I expect."

"Very much so. We're in the middle of a set of commercial transactions—re-supply, buying this, selling that. I wanted to make sure everyone got the shore leave they were entitled to. There are also some cargo-related issues we have been working out."

"Moving all the food you appropriated from Prime Minister Pim?"

"That one. Yes, we took what my sponsor paid for, and Pim was withholding, if that's what you mean. We distributed that cargo to warehouses on six worlds over the course of eight days. There was some extra, which we sold here."

"Did you keep nothing for yourselves?"

"Well, a bit. A few tons of dry goods."

"Where do Callum and Sacha sit?"

"They have stations on this deck, but they move around depending on the mission. They're off duty tonight. Double dating with Colin and Kaia. I understand they all bonded over last night's events. You know, even if you walk down my gangway and never return, you and Daveed may be stuck with those two."

"I'm aware. Not sure how I feel about it. I'm certain they both hate me," Karmen confessed.

"I doubt they've taken it so personally, but they're no fans of the TSS. None of us are. Actually, it's good your Agent didn't come with you to meet the crew. That would have been beyond awkward."

"That's not the Agent Thand I worked with for two years," Karmen probed.

"Don't judge me before you know all the facts, Karmen. Or would you rather have helped implement that order to fly into the maw of Bakzen violence twenty-five years ago?"

"Some choice."

"Luckily, you didn't have to make it. That was all on me. Had we followed orders, we'd be dead. None of this—not you, nor your kids—would even exist. Think about *that* for a minute, sweetie."

Something snapped deep inside Karmen's gut, and she felt

the air around her grow cold. She began shivering and couldn't stop. She knew this was what panic felt like, and concentrated on her breathing, even closing her eyes to focus. "Bomax!" she groaned. "I suppose I should thank you for something. But I don't know what."

"Whatever it is, you're welcome. Come on. One more stop that might help you put everything I've told you in perspective." Aura led Karmen through narrow corridors to another hatch, then they climbed a series of narrow ladders and came up through a hatch in the floor. They emerged into a closed room filled with computer modules encrusted with banks of lights. A silver column of rotating discs rose from the center of the deck halfway up to the ceiling. At the top was a transparent globe filled with waves of multi-colored light that flowed and slid in a pattern which never repeated itself.

"Where are we?" Karmen asked.

"Technically it's known as the Upper Engineering Evaluation point. It's meant to store equipment that's used to monitor the various engineering systems in the compartment below. But the Lynaedans found another use for it. Behold, the Queen."

"I don't understand."

"Neither did I for a long time. This construct is the QEN-1000. It's a Lynaedan AI that Lom and his team salvaged and brought on board. Not as good as CACI, but it does help run the ship. Whenever one of my Lynaedan crew plugs in to recharge, or swap out their rigs, or to inhabit a drone, they do it by talking to this mainframe. She keeps them unified, connected. They follow my orders, but they serve her. When I give a command that concerns the ship's functionality, the Lynaedans respond with the phrase, 'We serve the Queen.' I thought they meant me, the pirate queen. But that was my ego telling me what I wanted to hear. Then, I stumbled in here one day, and I learned the truth. I suppose it makes sense; they did most of the refit work when we turned a used ore carrier into a battleship."

"Battleship. You mean to take this crate into fights? With warships?"

Aura scoffed. "We've been fighting local patrol shuttles and customs skiffs for months. We fought *you*. She wouldn't stand up to a real warhorse like the *Vanquish*, but we don't pick fights with them. We've won every engagement. We know what we're doing."

"Then explain it to me, because this sounds insane. Yes, it's all terribly impressive. But it's *nuts*," Karmen insisted. "What, exactly, is this grand plan for New Akkadia?"

Aura's eyes skipped over the various control surfaces. "I'll explain it. But we shouldn't talk here."

"Ah, so there *is* one more stop."

The hangar deck was their next stop. Karmen marveled at the large number of shuttles and auxiliary transports in bays going through maintenance or being moved to other compartments for heavy structural work. Aura palmed the lock and climbed inside a large one.

Karmen had to admit this all looked familiar. "An I-40R. Colin's mother offered me one of these. I turned it down as being too unwieldy."

Aura settled into the command station. "I'm sure. But *Redemption* and I hauled cargo and passengers all over the galaxy for two decades. It wasn't a luxurious life, but we did all right. Enough to fund the *Emerald Queen*."

"I'd call that a fortune."

"You'd be right. She's still in good shape, but I don't fly with her anymore. I come in here to think."

Karmen sank into a seat at one of the stations nearby. It had a good feel to it, like it had been waiting for her to arrive. "All right, no more evasion. Tell me about this boyfriend."

"Gil? He's no boy. And not exactly a friend anymore, either. He has his own yacht, which he calls *Shamhat*. Very posh. The lower deck is for the crew, but the upper deck is a party suite. A dozen lavishly appointed staterooms. You could fall into the mattress in any of them and need two people to haul you back out. There's a lounge, a banquet hall with a dance floor. Plus a ridiculously stacked android to run it all. He's very proud of her."

Karmen thought she recognized a change in her friend's voice. "Aura... you're jealous?"

"I'm disappointed. I thought he had more grit, but he's become besotted with material possessions. I get it, that sort of thing is a load of fun. He does have a knack for making deals during a party, but it gets old so quickly. I can't work in that kind of environment. It's like living in a hotel. I prefer this."

Karmen knew that look. Aura was blaming herself. "Is it really over between you two?"

"Let's say the spark is gone and leave it at that."

"I'm sorry. What happened?"

"He showed me his safe deposit box. It was more wealth than I'd ever seen in one place. More than I'd ever imagined. So much of it came from my hard work. My crew's work. I kept my mouth shut until we got back here, then we had a fight. A big one. Screaming, accusations, just raging at each other. He stormed off in his yacht and I haven't seen him since. I'm ignoring his messages."

"I'm sorry to hear that. You deserve better." Karmen sat in quiet reflection for a few moments. Despite everything, she still wanted happiness for her old friend. Knowing what Daveed had done for her in her own life, she couldn't help but wonder how things might have turned out differently for Aura if she'd found herself with someone other than Gil. " You promised to explain once we had privacy. Tell me about this plan for New Akkadia"

Aura nodded wearily. "First, you need to understand what was going on when this all got started two decades ago. The Bakzen war blasted the TSS apart. The High Commanders had plowed all their resources into one big push to end the war, and they only barely won. The war left TSS technology scattered all over the galaxy, and most of what's been recovered is swept up into the black market. Which led quite logically to a rise in local warlords. Now there's a choice: deal with black marketeers who arm themselves with tech that wasn't even available when you and I served or suffer silently without recourse."

"The Militia and Guard still work."

"Do they? Guard units are intensely local and they get bought off by people with means all the time. I should know; I've bought my share of them. The Militia used to have a substantial fighting force, but not anymore."

"Eventually, it will all come back," Karmen insisted.

"No, it won't. The TSS is busy de-militarizing in the wake of a galactic tragedy. In the meantime, you've seen what life is like out here. Not every planet can be a Greengard. No offense, but the Foundation City Enforcers were no match for Meklife's drones."

"No offense taken. We are kind of soft. But what are you *doing* out here?"

"We control piracy by being the biggest pirate. It's ugly but it works. Gil and his friends have a more precise plan for it, but when you set aside the politics and double- and triple-dealing, I'm keeping several sectors of the Outer Worlds safe. That's it.

We've conducted numerous rescue and recovery missions."

"And stole twenty Talsarium mining charges from TalEx. Why?"

"Because I needed them. Asteroid mining is a lucrative business, but the Talsari Dynasty has ways of choking off local supply lines if smaller producers try to compete. Local mining groups need options. We provide them. For a price."

"They'd make amazing weapons, too."

"Karmen, anything can be a weapon in the wrong hands. If I flew this ship into a planet at a significant fraction of the speed of light, I could wipe out a major city and start an ice age. But I don't. Destruction isn't the point. Besides, this ship has no shortage of more effective weaponry. Talsarium is very difficult to store. We found that out the hard way."

Karmen made a snap decision not to share the fact that she was the cause of the Talsarium device's failure. "What would the pirate queen be asking of her old first officer?"

"Not a thing. I merely noticed that you've gotten yourself involved with people and situations that are probably new to you. You've seen that you can't stop me. Your kids and my officers are already friendly if not friends. Finally, you and Daveed are doing the best you can, but you don't seem all that prosperous. Now, the Covrani machine has its claws in you and will never let you go. I think my way is better. Maybe we could help each other."

"Join you or watch my family fail. Is that it?"

"Certainly not. Join me if it suits you. If not, you're free to go your own way. Report to your Agent. I promise to keep in touch. I'll even send a lavish gift for Kaia's wedding."

"Will you invite us to Sacha and Callum's wedding, too?"

"I'll insist on it. If we time it right, we can have a double wedding here on my hangar deck. We'll invite the whole galaxy. University colleagues, TSS vets, and pirates. It'll be *glorious*!" Aura laughed.

Karmen tried to keep a straight face and exploded into laughter. "It sounds wonderful, Aura. But I can't turn a blind eye to the fact that you've been causing trouble for very big players."

"Trouble for oligarchs who run the whole galaxy for their personal gain? For the TSS, which keeps them in power? Is that what you're defending, Karmen? This is a better way."

"Piracy is better?"

"Simple accountability. I'm accountable to my crew and my sponsors. New Akkadia is coming into its own after twenty years in the making. Wouldn't you at least like to see what's possible before condemning me? I'll bet you your husband and kids might take a different view."

Karmen felt her muscles stiffen, triggered by mention of her family. "What does that mean?"

"Gilgamesh has asked the *Emerald Queen* to break a blockade over Tarkus. Some local crew calling themselves Harm's Hellions got themselves a fleet of armed shuttles and they are terrorizing the local space station. You and your TSS Agent might be able to help. What do you say?"

I'm going to regret this one day. "I will ask if they're willing to help. But no promises."

"Just observe. You'll get access to the whole ship. Stay out of my crew's way while they work. That's all I ask."

You're going to ask the whole galaxy of me one day, Karmen thought.

25

DEEP COVER

LEE COULDN'T BELIEVE his ears. "You said *what?*"

"I said I'd ask you if you wanted to help her put down a piracy ring on Tarkus," Karmen answered. "It's just one mission."

"She *is* the piracy ring! And what's this 'we' shite? *We* are all part of the organization trying to stop piracy, mass violence, and interstellar crime. You remember that part, don't you?" He wiped his hands down his face. "Karmen, this was supposed to be a dinner to gather information and report back—*not* an audition for you to *join her!*"

The Militia officer sat back in her seat, arms and legs crossed. "Lee, we don't really know what she's been doing out here all these months. We haven't gotten close enough to her until now to truly watch her work."

Lee spent a moment sputtering, then forced himself to calm down. "We know she's stolen billions of credits of private property. She's stolen fissionable materials from a mining operation. We know she robbed the medical annex on Greengard, not to mention causing a blackout there. Do you remember that, Karmen?"

"Of course I do, I was there."

"I'm glad to hear that! What more does she need to do for you to think she's out of line?" he demanded.

"It's not about what she's done, it's about what she and others are going to do. She claims to have parted ways from Gilgamesh, which means we have an opening. I want to see that operation on Tarkus for myself. Then, I can make an informed decision about whether we can flip her to help us take down the people who've been driving the rebellion, or if we'd be better off arresting 'Mother Carnage' and closing off that line."

"She's a wanted criminal. You can't just re-write galactic law because you happen to like the person breaking those laws."

"You let Mitchel Pilar slide right out from under your thumb a week ago," she countered.

"Yes, as a link to something much bigger than the crime we thwarted. At least I was authorized to make that decision. You are not similarly empowered to work that way, *Officer* Sley."

"Pulling rank, *Agent* Tuyin? That's always a great look."

"Don't take that tone with me, Karmen."

"But *isn't* this the same thing about uncovering a bigger crime? The so-called Mesopotamians are the ones really mucking with things in this sector, and Aura has just been following orders."

Lee crossed his arms. "Allegedly. And it's 'Aura' now. Excellent."

"If you spent even a minute talking to her, you'd see that 'Mother Carnage' was all an act. I want to see how they work.

And who's *really* behind this unrest. I need to see what they do for myself and learn what's driving them. That's valuable intelligence no matter the circumstances. Because to date, all we have—literally *all* we have—is suggestions, innuendo, and second- or third-hand reporting. Do you really want to go to war with that limited knowledge base? Or would you rather *know* what we're going up against?"

"That's not the point and you know it."

"It's the only point. More importantly, it's my job to give the Agent-in-Charge options and suggestions. And I'm telling you, you can't go to war with this woman given our current limitations. She nearly killed you the last time we tried. Stars, you don't even have guns on that stupid shuttle. A meaningful takedown will mean bringing in more TSS resources, but what new information do you have to tell TSS Command right now?"

Lee forced himself to see the argument from her point of view. "All right, Officer. Options and suggestions. Let me have them."

"Last night Aura told me about the Queen. The Lynaedan AI that runs the ship. It's built into every system, every module, and the Lynaedan crew members can't function nearly as effectively without it. That must be the focus of any attempt to stop this crew."

"And how do we do that?"

"I've no idea," she admitted. "But the only way to find out is to dig deep into this bunch and watch them closely. Beyond that…" She shrugged and gestured wildly. "Do you see where I'm going with this?"

"I think so. You want a deep cover. I think it's reckless, but I can't argue with the logic," he confessed.

"You've made your point of view very clear, thank you."

"This is my fault. I should have seen something like this coming. I should never have followed you to Daveed's office at the university, I should have stopped Armin from filing that field report on the pirate ship. We should never have mentioned you at all."

"But you did and here we are."

"Yes. You know Armin and I can't be a part of this or she'll know. Undercover means you'll be on your own. What about your family?"

"They'd come with me."

"And we can't tell anyone about what you're really doing," he said. "Not Daveed, not the kids. Not Tolri—gah, *especially* not her. You must act like you're all in and so do they. Even if Thand doesn't always notice things, I guarantee that Lynaedan, Lom Mench, does. She made a good choice in hiring him. I have no idea what kind of choices he's likely to make in return."

"Logical ones," she said. "I agree. Mench makes me very uncomfortable, but he knows his job, that's for certain."

"He knows your job, and mine too. You'll be able to fool your friend but not him. Do not let yourself forget that."

"Not on your life. She said that the Lynaedans were more loyal to the AI than to her, but I can't tell if she was being serious or merely sharing a random thought. But I do wonder if there won't come a time to test that theory," Karmen mused aloud. "But that's just an idea."

"Right. I think it's best if Armin and I just go back to our shuttle and proceed from there," Lee said. "Let them think we merely left. No need to make it messy."

"It's nothing but messy. Goodbyes always are. Tell Armin you've been recalled to Greengard. There can't be any question of your loyalty. If you do get new orders from the powers that be… Well, we'll figure that out when it happens."

"No. My standing orders are to follow Mother Carnage and deal with her. If that means meeting you all on Tarkus, then so be it."

"No, don't meet us. Stay in flight, record the entire fight no matter what the outcome might be. Take that data back to the TSS and let them figure out your next move. I can live with that. I can't live with you getting in front of a plasma cannon at an unlucky moment. That is my advice to the Agent-in-Charge."

—   —   —

Crux Station's casino turned out to be a crashing bore.

Kaia and Colin dressed up for their night and met Callum and Sacha at the *Emerald Queen*'s gangway, then caught a ride to the casino which seemed run down and depressing to Kaia. She'd expected elegance and glitz and discovered dinge and desperation as rows of shabby people swilled cheap drinks and plugged credit chips into brightly glowing kiosks.

Callum and Colin went to the bar to talk about GravX, but Kaia paid attention to her new friend, the Operations Officer.

"We're not getting rich here." Sacha sighed. "Stars, why did I listen to Callum?"

"Is there a problem?" Kaia ventured.

"He called this place a casino. This is *not* a casino. The Seven Rings Plaza on Mahalia, *that's* a casino. This is a half-rate betting parlor at best," Sacha declared.

"I'm sure he meant well."

"No doubt," Sacha agreed. She shrugged and continued, "We're here. It'll pay everyone's docking fees and supplies. It might even convince your parents that you're an adult when you drop a big bag of money on their breakfast table tomorrow morning." She wrinkled her nose and got to work.

She found a currency kiosk and tapped some instructions, then scooped a handful of low-value credit chips. She rattled the chips in a winnings basket and walked down rows of games, feeding a credit or two into each and watching the results. Nothing returned any money. "Not feeling it. No, I don't like this one. Too bland. Gah! Too garish. This one is too hot. This one is cold as ice…"

Kaia watched but couldn't see how what Sacha was doing made her money. "How do you win credits at these games, anyway?"

Sacha smiled and brought the girl in for a light hug. "You are *adorable*! No wonder Colin has it so bad. We're not winning anything, Kaia. We're stealing it."

Kaia immediately swiveled her head, looking for the cameras and guards. They were easy to pick out. "But… how?"

"Simple. My ship's computer is running algorithms and returning betting odds, then she feeds me data through my comm net."

"But…"

"Don't worry about the details, kid. These machines are all linked and badly programmed. They do pay out but too slowly for our purposes. I'm looking for one that's ready to pay out big. This one pays five thousand, that one pays twenty-five thousand and the one at the end of the floor over there pays fifty thousand credits. I want that big payout. You want to help?"

Kaia snorted and put her arm in front of her mouth to make it look like her laugh was a sneeze. "What do I do?"

"Just play along with my act, and keep an eye out for Enforcers. They're probably bored out of their minds." She ran through another row of machines, then selected one and sat in front of it. "Here's the plan. We get this one to pay out for five thousand then put it all into the giant jackpot machine and come out with ten times that amount."

"That sounds incredibly unfair to everyone else here."

"Gambling is inherently unfair. That's what makes it fun. You ready?"

"Ready!" Kaia giggled.

Sacha plugged in credit after credit until she had a single credit chip left. She kissed the metal disc and plugged it in, then threw the switch. The kiosk ran through its motions and began ringing bells and blaring chirpy music as a torrent of metal coins dropped out of the hopper and into a bucket below.

Sacha squealed in delight and Kaia joined in, as she gathered the coins into the basket. "See, Kaia? I want, I take. Put in fifty, get five thousand out. What's the return on investment there?"

"About ten thousand percent," Kaia screamed. "Do it again!"

"Nope. We have a plan, let's stick to it. Walk with me."

They spent time walking the aisles, both of them plugging single credit chips into various kiosks and generally being loud and silly. Eventually they stopped at the giant jackpot game. They took turns plugging credits into the kiosk and threw the switch and then whooped it up when the machine loosed a torrent of credits into their hands. Kaia spotted a couple of Enforcers who came close, decided the win was legitimate and backed off.

"This is amazing!" Kaia cried. "What are you going to do with it?"

"Taking a finder's fee and giving the rest to you," Sacha said, scooping handfuls of credit chips into her purse until it was full.

"What?"

"You heard me. This money is for you and Colin." She thrust the bucket into Kaia's hands. "Callum and I are investing in your GravX team."

"You're… that's… what?"

Sacha spun the girl toward a bank of tellers. "That's the cashier. Take this to her and drop it into your bank account while I pull the boys away from the booze. Then we'll go to a *real* party."

Kaia handed over her bucket of money and came away with a beeping handheld. The account information synched with the casino's local network and just like that, *Mother Courage*'s expense account was forty-eight thousand credits richer. Forty-eight *thousand* credits. She'd never had that big a bank account in her life. That was more than most folks on Greengard brought home in a year.

Tonight was a good night!

—

"I know this venue isn't what you two are used to, but I like it," Sacha said as she climbed out of the cab ahead of Kaia.

The club's exterior was a bright, wide expanse of pink, orange, and blue light. Kaia blinked to clear her eyes; she wasn't used to the kind of lighting this place apparently used. One detail she could easily pick out was the stairs leading down into the club. The marquis above the entrance made her chuckle: 'DRINK, DANCE, CRY, COLLAPSE' the sign advertised in a thousand sequentially arranged colors.

"What do you think I'm used to?" Kaia asked. "This is pretty impressive."

The wall began to glow as they descended the stairs. In a

moment, they were presented with a checklist:

ARE YOU DRUNK? YES/NO

SHOULD YOU BE? YES!

"Wow, they don't pull any punches, do they?" Colin wondered aloud.

"This club has a special place in my heart," Sacha told them. "It's a good place to find some truth about yourself. I came here years ago knowing that I was lonely, and I left knowing that I had standards."

"Callous. Fickle," Kaia teased.

"Speak for yourself. A few drinks and a good sweat brings you closer to yourself. Your inhibitions fall to pieces, and you're left facing the world as it really is. Not the way you wish it was."

They walked into a wall of electronic dance music as they entered the club. Kaia couldn't hear anything even when Colin tried to yell something into her ear. Sacha not only could hear, but she held a conversation with the hostess—an obviously Lynaedan woman with silver hair and glowing ocular implants. Kaia could tell there was some discussion about their group. Sacha pointed to them and held up four fingers. Hand signals were thrown more than once. Eventually, the hostess nodded and handed something to Sacha, who waved for the others to follow.

Kaia couldn't help but look everywhere. Glowing tubes of light traced every contour along the ceiling and floor, and patrons appeared as dark shadows against the bright accents. When Kaia peered closely at one couple, she noticed they had glowing streamers in their skin. That couldn't be a mod, could it? A mass of dancers took up the center of the floor, twirling, spinning and twisting to the music. To Kaia, it looked almost as if they were synched up with each other, but she could never figure out the exact pattern.

A hand pressed on her shoulder. She turned to see Colin urge her toward a booth Sacha and Callum had already staked out. She settled in next to Colin and tried shouting only for her voice to disappear into the void.

Sacha grinned evilly and touched a stud on the table. Instantly, the noise volume dropped to a low roar.

Kaia could hear again. "How did...?

"Force field absorbs ambient noise. You can talk now. Cool, huh?"

"That's amazing. We don't have anything like this on Greengard."

"There're a few clubs on Gallos like this. They're pricey though," Colin said.

"This is pricey, too, in its way. Just not in credits. All the money in the world won't get you into this place. You have to know the owner."

"Why's that?" Callum asked.

"Because of these," she said, holding up a set of small, translucent pads. Each bore a unique set of lines etched into the material. "Remember those electrodes Mench used to hook you into the *Queen*'s sensory network? These will do the same for us on a much less intrusive scale. We paid for our entrance with our memories. The more you dance, the better the reception becomes. Those dancers out there have been swapping their thoughts for hours."

"That's the pattern! I knew there was something weird going on there."

Sacha placed one pad in front of each of them and primed it with a fingertip. They glowed with internal energy. "Good call, Kaia. We each get one pad."

"Does this mean we're all getting stenciled?" Callum asked.

"Give that man a prize. C'mere, Sensors, I want to get you right in the temporal lobe." Sacha reached for his head and turned it until she found the right location and pressed the glowing pad into place with her thumb.

Kaia hesitated but acquiesced. Colin, however, pulled away. "I do not want you guys to see every embarrassing moment in my life," he sputtered.

"You want a drink first? That's easy." Sacha tapped the wall to reveal a drinks kiosk. She pushed buttons, plugged a few credit chips into a slot and a selection of aluminum cans rolled into a recessed tray at the edge of the table. She handed them out, popped the tab on hers and drank it down.

Callum chugged his but Colin and Kaia sipped theirs. It smelled like alcohol to Kaia, but she couldn't place what kind. It tasted sweet, though, and before long she found her can was empty.

Sacha glared at Colin. "Colin, you have a bad mental block going on. You are mired in self-doubt and anxiety. You need something to take you outside yourself. This is how you do that. It's a spin-off of medical technology used on all the Inner Worlds. Besides, it only picks up surface thoughts. The deep stuff stays hidden. Come on. Do it for Kaia. It's no worse than this stuff."

Colin murmured something but leaned forward. Sacha pressed his pad into place then affixed one on herself. "I'm the control. If I'm on, we're all on; if I'm off we're all off. Ready? Three, two, one, and…"

Kaia gasped as the connection activated. Suddenly, she was sitting in four seats looking at herself from three angles in addition to her own vantage. The tech adjusted itself, and she settled down into a more generalized experience. She couldn't stop smiling at the feeling that she was in multiple places at once. In minutes, they were all feeling it; even Colin had a goofy smile.

Sacha thumped the table. "We're good to go. Let's dance!" She collapsed the force field, and the music washed over them again.

Kaia dragged Colin to the dance floor and found she could see the notes as they burst through the air. The dancers, the music, the vibration of the station's machinery, they all formed their own connection to her. She moved with the rhythm, settling into a cadence of her own.

A beat dropped, a bass thrumming combined with a wicked distortion. The pulse grew tame then sped into a frenzy bouncing between joy and pure energy. Kaia whirled and waved, bouncing and stepping. She closed her eyes and allowed herself to go with the music, not knowing, not caring where she was, who she was, what she was. She opened her eyes to see Colin stiffly trying to imitate her movements and drifted back into her trance. She opened her eyes to see Callum shadowing her, then drifted back into the zone. Then she looked up to see Sacha matching her move for move, grinning at her with her insane glowing eyes.

Why not? I want... I take. She reached for the operations officer only to find her wrists grabbed and held by Sacha's octopus, then felt herself twirling toward Colin.

Well, all right. Do I want him or not? I do!

Sacha used her tentacles to wrap them together, binding them as a unit as they slowly learned to match their bodies' motions to each other. Finding a shared pulse. Learning to grow into each other. At some point, Kaia realized Sacha had let them go and used her mechanical arms to wrap herself and Callum together in the same way.

But something was wrong with the arrangement. Some

discordant chord between them. In a moment, the thought reverberated across their little group, and everyone fixed their eyes on Colin. He was the sour note in their symphony; it hurt to be around him.

Colin wasn't immune to the sensation of pain. He stumbled back to the booth, squeezing himself against the wall and trying to peel the pad off his skin. The others followed.

Sacha sat next to him and removed the electrode. "What's wrong, Colin?"

"Too much everything!" Colin groaned.

Sacha closed the field and once more they were alone. "What is it, dude? The drink? The pad?"

"It's you! Why'd Callum have to call me stupid?"

"Oh, stop it, you big baby. I admit that I was a creep to you last night with my overloaded snark, but come on. You're the ugly duck in your trillion-credit pond. That can't continue. Tell him, Callum."

Callum pulled Colin by the lapels and aimed his face toward Kaia. "My dude, look at this chick. A good long look. You think she's hot? Because Sacha and I surely do. I'm of half a mind to kick you down those stairs and bundle her into the *Emerald Queen*, and induct her into the pirate queen training academy right now."

"That's kidnapping. I think there's a law against that somewhere," Colin slurred.

"Whatever you call it, she's the one I'd bet on, because she at least has a plan."

"I don't think you deserve her," Colin said.

Callum bent close to Colin. "No, you don't think *you* deserve her. That's what's messing you up. But at the same time, you do want to be worthy of her. Am I getting close?"

"Stars, this is embarrassing," Colin groaned.

"Answer my question, Colin."

"Yes. Yes! Kaia, you're the best thing that's ever happened to me. Listen, if I offered you a million credits to run away with me…"

Kaia had her answer ready. "I'd say no."

"Really?"

"Really. Your mother already offered me twice that to abandon you."

"Two million? *Why are you still here?*" Colin demanded.

"Because I don't want a paycheck. I want *you*. Why are you pushing me away?"

"I don't *know*."

"See, Callum, I told you. Colin wants to succeed, but he's carrying too much baggage and it's all mommy shaped," Sacha diagnosed.

"I don't know about that," Kaia said. "He was fine when it was all about long-distance with us. Calls every day, talk about this, about that. We talked for hours, every time. It was fun. Effortless and honest and delightfully *weird*."

"That sounds extremely positive. What changed?" Sacha asked.

Kaia hesitated. "It got awkward the day he showed up on my doorstep with a gunship. The day we met for real. When I introduced him to my family. When we saw each other as *people*. Did you just want my company and not the responsibility of making me happy? Of letting me make you happy in return? Is that it?"

Colin had a haunted look. "Maybe. I don't know. But I did make you happy, didn't I?"

"Yes, you did; you still do. I think I married your mother already when we went into business with her. If the rest of you Covranis are like her, then the whole lot of you are pretty bomaxed incestuous."

"Wow, too much information, Kaia," Callum said.

"It's how I feel. What do we *do* about this, Colin?"

"What *do* we do about it, Colin?" Callum pushed.

"What are *you* going to do to fix this, *Colin?*" Sacha challenged.

"I don't know!" Colin yelled, jumping out of the seat and balling his fists. "Confidence doesn't come from success, it comes from surviving failure," he declared. "That's what my Uncle Rodg always said. I don't fail. I don't even try. I just do what I'm told every single time. It's stupid. *I* am stupid!" He stumbled and fell, gathered himself into a ball, and hugged his knees with his back to the wall.

"Good, now we're getting somewhere. Here, let's huddle." Sacha gestured with the octopus. They formed a ring, as Kaia and Callum each took one of Colin's hands in their own. Sacha cupped his face and raised his head. There was a distant look in his eyes. Colin was here but he wasn't with them. "Colin! Who did this to you?"

"It's them," he whispered. "It's that damn tower I grew up in. So much space, so many rooms. It's filled with people and everyone in it is so alone. So lonely. All those permissions, all the controls. Cameras and alarms everywhere. The comforts are there, but it's all cold."

"He's right," Kaia agreed. "It's spotless in there. Every surface gleams like it's been polished hard enough to strip the warmth off. Greengard's pretty basic, but at least we had each other."

Sacha pushed again. "Colin, what do you need? Connection? Purpose? Self-acceptance?"

"I need to get out of there. They're all crazy. Even Vani, and he's the sanest one I know," Colin finally said. "You got that mind-tech on the *Emerald Queen*, too, don't you? Wire me up and help me get a handle on this wall I keep hitting. Over, around, or through, I don't care which, but I can't keep doing this."

Sacha nodded. "Fine with me, Covrani. Let's take you home to meet the Queen."

26

MASTER YOUR ANGER

THEY CLIMBED OUT of the cab, and Colin walked up the gangway toward the *Emerald Queen*. "What now? I really don't feel up to anything else. The drinks and the dancing took everything out of me," he said.

"Come on, Mister Dynasty. Date night isn't over." Sacha beckoned, tugging him down the gangway.

"Oh, no," Colin groaned, "what are you weirdoes going to get me into now?"

"We're taking you to meet my parents," Sacha said, her ocular implants gleaming in the low light.

"What?"

"I told Sacha about how you handled yourself on *Percival*," Kaia said. "You did well against a cobbled together warship. Then she told me that the lower deck of that same warship had ways of putting your skills to the test."

"Which test?"

"All of them," Callum said. "You ever want to learn to fly a spaceship with your brain? Because we can do that for you."

"That's not possible. You need controls, a flight deck…" Colin scoffed.

"Not if you're a Lynaedan," Sacha chided. "We'll go easy on you. Promise."

"Fine, but if I throw up on you, remember, you've been warned," Colin said.

Callum patted him on the back. "I used it myself a while ago. It felt weird at first, but you get used to it surprisingly fast."

Kaia thought about the problem. "Actually, guys… can I go in with Colin? For moral support."

"Sure. We have plenty of pads for the connection. Would you want to run the same program with him? I can set up a player-vs-player situation with you two going up against a computer, or you can both be on the same team. Your choice."

"Make him the captain," Kaia said. "I've seen him do that job. Hey, set us up on a mid-level cruiser type ship. We can—"

Commander Mench's Meklife drone met them at the airlock. "I have a better idea. Send him in with me. We should have a talk. Can you handle a sword, boy?"

Colin narrowed his eyes but didn't look away from Meklife's face. "I took fencing in school, yes."

"Were you any good?"

"I had my moments, at least in the beginning."

"I'm glad to hear that. Let's start there. Fit him with a pad, then get him settled in a bio-bed. Wouldn't want the poor dear to hurt himself if he fell to the floor. To the infirmary!"

—

Doc Tendi installed Colin in a free bio-bed and Meklife fitted him with electrodes.

"Ten minutes. No more, no less," the Lynaedan declared. "Let's get to work."

Colin found himself standing in a gymnasium with a fencing epee in his hand.

Meklife was at the other end of the arena, his own sword in motion. "Three points and that's the match," he said.

"That's not championship rules."

"We only have nine minutes and forty seconds. Now, strike!"

Colin lunged, and Meklife dodged and counter-attacked, then scored a point, the sword stabbing Colin in his chest. It *hurt*.

"Ow!"

"Again!"

The same attack, the same response, then same result.

"Bomax!"

"Again!" The exchange played out a third time with the same result.

Meklife swung his saber and put it down. "That's the match. Colin, this is pointless. If you cannot master your anger, then—"

"Then the anger will forever be my master. Yeah, I've heard that before."

"But do you understand it? Do you *believe* it?"

Colin threw his epee to the ground. "You're trying to piss me off."

"Why would I do that?"

"Because spite is a solid motivator."

"It can be. But it can work against you, as well. Kaia says you've a habit of trying to annoy your mother. Everything you do is calculated to make her angry. Is that really a good use of your energy?"

"It keeps me focused."

"But focused on *what*? How would you feel if your circumstances changed suddenly? If you had to tell the world how you truly felt about her?"

"I can't do that."

"Of course you can. Do it now."

In a flash, the scenery changed to a crowded room, well-lit and with a high ceiling. Colin now stood on a raised platform, facing a crowd seated in long benches. There were freshly cut flowers everywhere. He recognized a number of faces in the audience; his father, his cousins, other relatives he'd met at functions and whose names he'd forgotten or never learned. A great many business contacts dressed elegantly. The dominant color was black. A funeral.

Did that crazy Lynaedan send me to my own funeral? He looked around for clues and finally looked down. A casket with his mother's body inside. Clearly deceased. *Mom would have a fit if she knew she was in an open casket.*

"And now Colin will say a few words," said a voice from behind him.

And this was it. He had to do something. He had to say something about this mother, and he had no idea what. *Should I lie? Tell a funny story? Tell the truth?* And what was the truth? That she made him feel like a worm for weeks and then doled out a bit of praise when he followed instructions? That she constantly made excuses for him to the rest of the clan? That deep down she thought he would need her support and supervision for the rest of his life?

Colin stepped back. "This is crazy. She's not dead. It's just a simulation."

The scene fell apart, and Meklife once again occupied their space. "But it felt real for a moment, didn't it? What do you feel right this moment, looking at her corpse?"

Satisfaction? Joy? No! It's… "Relief."

"And what does that tell you about yourself?"

Colin sat on the floor, then lay down. "I have one real friend in this whole galaxy, and I hurt her. Twice. Both times, I did it because I panicked. And I panicked because that woman who runs my life and tells me I don't measure up also means the world to me. I try everything I can think of to convince her I know what I'm doing, that I have a plan, and it's never enough. I've been thinking that Kaia can help me figure it out. But that's not true, is it?"

Meklife folded his arms. "So many women in your life. Where's your father, boy?"

"On the other side of the planet. He's the Chief Operations Officer for the space elevator," Colin explained. "He shows up for events and on weekends, but he's away for work most of the time. It's a very big operation. A very big deal. I would kill to work there with him."

"Why don't you?"

"I'm not sure. I've applied for a few jobs up there. I always get polite but firm rejections. Whatever else I've done with my life, I'm not what they're looking for."

"What does that leave?"

"I think I'm working for the wrong team," Colin breathed. "I will never fit in on Gallos. My uncle once told me that when there's nothing but chaos everywhere you look, the guy who keeps his head has all the advantages. I haven't kept my head very well, just followed the path of least resistance."

Meklife squatted and leaned in until his face was centimeters from Colin's own. "Very well, Mr. Covrani. We've established that you are a disappointment to everyone, including yourself. What will you do about it?"

"I'll tell you. But answer my question: why aren't you the captain of this ship?"

Meklife sat next to Colin. "Probably the same reason your parents think you're a failure. I didn't fit my environment very well. Lynaeda is a very well-ordered society. We all know what part we're expected to play professionally, academically, socially. When you have a population as large as ours, you need that sort of meticulous management. But misfits tend to be miserable and they spread the misery to the people around them. We have a ceremony to deal with that. At some point, each of us can leave the home world and elect never to return. It's a mere ritual. I've never heard of anyone actually being refused re-entry to Lynaeda, but it has a deeply spiritual significance. All of us on this ship elected to leave. Some of the other crew may have returned, but I never did. I thought I could do something interesting elsewhere. I can tell you the life of a thief is never boring."

"So, you're as bad as I am," Colin mused.

Meklife gave a strangely throaty laugh. "My boy, I am so much worse than you."

"But why aren't you running this vessel? We both know you're capable of it."

"Because in my mind being captain carries with it a great risk. A target for officers who think they can advance by eliminating me. The galaxy knows who Mother Carnage is, but what's the name of her first officer? I work better from the shadows."

"You mean from inside a mechanism."

"I suppose so. But we are getting off track. What will you do now?"

"I'd like to work for you. I have a flexible sense of right and wrong and don't eat much."

"'Ha. Tell me what you can do for me, and I'll think about it."

"I think we should steal a fortune and use it to build legitimate businesses all over the galaxy. That's how the dynasty brats do it."

"That sounds difficult and complicated."

"It's no easy task, but it's possible. My ship, which is sitting in this station's hangar bay, contains the routing application my family uses to organize every trade, every jump, for every ship in our combined fleets. How would you like access to every encrypted communication between every ship in the Covrani merchant group? I can give you my mother's operation on a golden platter. *If* you make me part of your crew."

The simulation ended and Colin sat up in bed. Meklife thudded to his bedside and said, "Mr. Covrani, I think we have a profile of you worthy of the name. You don't do well when there is nothing to be done, so strategy is not your skill set. But you do very well when there is a specific objective. That makes you an excellent tactical officer candidate."

"Tactical officer," Colin breathed. "Is that what that's called?"

"It's like the situation with my business plan," Kaia said. "You grabbed the thing in your pocket, because it was something to do. It gave you a way out of a problem. But figure out how to put together a plan of your own, that was beyond you. You'll need to work on that. I'll help you."

"I want to beat my mother at her own game. I want to be a pirate!" Colin yelled.

Meklife helped him out of the bio-bed, steadying him as his legs wobbled. "I think you'd be a good one. Tabor needs help, and I think you two could learn a great deal from each other. Let me talk to the captain. We could put you to work immediately. You'd live on board of course but the company here is something you've already shown a preference for. You can have your own quarters. You may even have overnight guests."

Colin grabbed Kaia's hand and squeezed. "That'll piss off my mother to no end."

"Mine, too. Won't it be fun?" she asked.

"I wouldn't want to do it any other way."

27

THROWING IN

KARMEN CALLED HER people together for a meeting in the *Mother Courage*'s common room. Lee and Armin remained conspicuously absent, and Karmen shrugged off questions about the discrepancy. Once she got them settled with snacks and drinks, she lowered the boom.

"I've made a decision," Karmen said. "I'm going with Aura to break a blockade on Tarkus."

The room erupted into a hail of chaos and voices, everyone trying to talk over each other. Karmen waited for the insanity to die down and then continued. "I'll tell you what there is to tell. But I can't make this decision for anyone but myself."

"What did Lee say about this?" Daveed asked.

Karmen had practiced the explanation to herself numerous times in the hopes she could make it sound convincing. Telling her family she intended to be a deep cover operative was not an option. "I had this talk with him already. He's not at all happy with me. But he was willing to see if I could somehow pull Aura back to the side of law and order. It would go easier for her if she turned herself in."

Kozu sniffed. "How likely is that, Mom? Be serious."

Karmen remained silent, considering her next words very carefully. She didn't want to lie to her family, but if she was going to deliver a cover story, it had to be done well. Finally, she said, "She was an amazing Agent. I need to believe that person is still inside her somewhere, pushing her to do the right thing. If she does, maybe I can convince her to stand down. Cash in her chips and retire. Something."

"I'm sorry, Mom, but you know the TSS isn't going to let her off that easy," Kaia said.

"Not now, Kaia," she whispered.

"If not now, when?" Daveed demanded. "You can't trust someone who's been operating on the fringe for this long. If you're going in with her, what line are you unwilling to cross?"

Karmen thought very carefully. What *would* Aura have to do for her to lose faith? "If she destroys a civilian ship without provocation, then that would do it. If that happens, we'll take you lot home and I'll work with Lee and Armin on my own."

"She did that already," Seandra said.

Karmen shook her head violently. "No, she hasn't. They steal property. They're very careful about not causing casualties. It's the only thread I can wrap my hands around to hope to pull Aura back to reason."

"Hope in one hand, piss in another, see which fills up first," Elian smarmed.

"Watch that mouth, young man," Daveed scolded.

"I want to go home," Elian said.

"I want to go home, too," Seandra agreed. "We killed Kengi. We should have the money to go anywhere we want now."

"I don't blame either of you," Daveed said. "But Yelena Covrani still has to pay us for that job."

"What's the hold up?" Seandra whined. "She wanted a dead pirate and we killed a pirate. I saw him die." She frowned and hugged herself at the memory.

"The call I made to Gallos after we parted ways with Mitchel Pilar didn't end as productively as I'd hoped," Karmen confessed. "Apparently, a mere DNA profile of the corpse isn't sufficient for Yelena."

"So much for events being all in the family. I suspect we'll have to drop Kengi's body on that woman's desk," Daveed said.

Colin smirked. "I want to watch her freak out when you do it."

"She hates paying her bills that much?" Kozu asked.

"She hates death, or anything to do with it, that much," Colin explained. "She doesn't even go to funerals if she can send a family member in her place. I've done that job more than once."

"I'll go with you," Kaia said. "I have issues with that woman."

Colin scoffed. "Get in line."

Elian crossed his arms and sank deeper into his seat. "I miss Armin."

"You would," Seandra shot back.

"Shut up."

"You shut up!"

"Everybody shut up!" Kozu ordered. It worked; the room fell silent.

"I want to say something," Colin said. "Karmen, you and Kaia still owe my mother a quarter million credits for this ship. If we're out here to make a fast buck, then let's do it. If we follow through with the rest of the trades I programmed for the

Autonomous Main ports from here to Gallos, we'll make enough to pay her off. You and Kaia get the title to *Mother Courage* and we can live our lives away from pirates *and* the military."

"I think that's a good idea," Karmen agreed. "This blockade at Tarkus might be real, or it might be a ploy to exact revenge, or straight-up crime. I don't know which. Aura invited me to watch her work and I'm going to do it. But no one else need be present for that. Colin, you and Kaia will take the *Mother Courage* back to Gallos. You'll present the proof that Kengi is dead and collect the reward we were promised. On the way, you'll implement the market trade plan you and Kaia came up with. Take your time. Make whatever trades in whichever spaceports you think show promise."

"And give up on GravX?" Kaia demanded. "Be a cargo runner for the next thirty years? No freaking way. I have bigger dreams than that, and the start of a stake I can use to make it happen—or try to."

"Don't knock it, my dear. Aura and that Gilgamesh person made themselves quite rich by doing that very thing," Daveed reminded them.

"I don't see how splitting up helps us take Aura out," Kozu said.

"It doesn't, and neither do you. You and Tolri are going back to Gallos with Colin and your sister," Karmen said.

Kozu bounced to his feet, his eyes wide with horror. "What? No!"

"Yes!" Karmen insisted. "Kozu, if you hope to join the TSS Militia, you must have a spotless record. They will check your background. If they find that you spent months ensconced in a criminal enterprise, that's the end of any career you hope to have with them. You need to steer clear. Tolri already suggested you could get some boost by working for the Covrani security people before you apply. That's not a bad idea."

"That's not what I want," Kozu said.

"It's exactly what you want!" Seandra cried. "You haven't taken your eyes off Tolri since you met her. She's cute, she's scary, she knows ten ways to kill a man with a single flick of her wrist. What *else* do you want?"

Tolri smirked at Kozu and tapped his leg with the toe of her boot. "She kind of has you pegged, K."

"All right, I'll go back to Gallos and enlist there, assuming they'll have me. I guess I'll see you all on the other side of whatever happens."

"That leaves the question of myself and the young ones," Daveed said.

"Colin and I can take you all back to Greengard," Kaia said.

"No!" Elian and Seandra shouted.

"What's wrong now?" Kaia demanded.

"I said I want to go home, but I want all of us to go home together!" Elian yelled. "I don't want to be stuck with Seandra all the time with no backup."

Daveed brought his hands up in a despairing gesture. "What am I, if not backup?"

"You know what I mean, Dad. It's not the same."

Seandra nodded. "Elian's a creep, but he's right. Bad enough we lose Mom to this craziness, but if Kai and Ko leave, we're doomed. We should all go or stay here."

Daveed closed his eyes and sighed deeply. "Well, thanks, kids. Thanks a whole lot."

"That leaves us at an impasse," Karmen said. "I can break that by sending you all home right now."

"I have another idea," Colin said. "What if we waited just a bit before splitting the party?"

Karmen smelled a trap. "What for?"

"I want to spend some time learning the ropes from Aura's Senior Supply Officer. His name is Tabor, and he's an evil genius when it comes to black market dealings. I asked Aura's first officer if it was doable the other night, and he seemed to think it was."

"You're no good with financial reporting, remember?" Kaia sniffed.

"But you said I was great with tactics. Well, Tabor is all about tactics. I think I could learn a lot there."

"Sure, if Black Market Operator is something you want on your business cards," Tolri sneered.

"Come on, a skill is a skill," Colin insisted. "It wouldn't be for long, just a few weeks."

"It's not the worst idea," Kaia mused. "In a few weeks, I can be back on Gallos with a corpse worth fifty thousand credits and a cargo hold full of who knows what. Tolri takes Kozu under her muscular wings, I cash out my cargo at the market, and we pay off our debt to Yelena. We could figure out next steps from there."

Colin gave her a thumbs up. "You can even stay in my arcology flat while you're there. Still have your bracelet?"

She showed him her wrist. "That I do."

Daveed frowned. "Won't your mother object to that?"

Colin shrugged. "Object to what? I own the apartment outright. I pay the utilities every month and Kaia has a permanent invitation."

"She did reduce your allowance to almost nothing," Kaia teased.

"That's different. The only person on record with the power to sell that apartment or revoke your invitation is me."

Karmen ran through the permutations and couldn't think

of a better plan. "Daveed, what do you think? We send Kaia and Kozu back to Gallos while the rest of you stay on the *Queen* with me?"

Daveed frowned. "What choice do I have? My children refuse to go home with me while you're here."

Seandra looked stricken. "Dad, come on. That's not what we meant."

Daveed waved her off. "I know, but that's how it feels. I can't say I'm happy with the four of us inhabiting such a corrosive social environment. But I like the thought of leaving you alone in Aura's hands even less. Sounds logical to me."

Karmen nodded as if the weight of the world sat on her neck. "Sounds logical to me, too. I could more easily keep an eye on you, Colin, and the young ones if you're all on the same ship. That's what we'll do." *And let's hope this doesn't bite us all in the ass.*

28

FIRST OFFICER

"KARMEN SLEY, PLEASE report to the captain's ready room. Would Karmen Sley please report to the captain's ready room."

For a moment Karmen replayed the instructions in her head. Her cabin was on Deck 2 in the aft section and the captain's ready room was on Deck 3, to the forward section. Then, she blinked and remembered that the *Triumph* was long gone and the *Emerald Queen* used a completely different floor plan.

It took time. She had to stop several crew to ask for directions. Ultimately, one young woman volunteered to show her the way, and Karmen did her best to impress the turns and lift combination on her memory. She had the sinking feeling that she'd need them again in the future.

Aura sat in her office, a surprisingly roomy cabin with a desk and enough chairs for a small group to confer. The captain sat behind a desk while Lom Mench wore his Meklife drone and stood away from the door.

"Karmen Sley reporting as requested."

"Thank you. Stars, Karmen, please sit down." Aura took a moment for Karmen to comply; when she didn't the captain drove on, "Have you given any thought to the offer I made the other night?"

"I have. I've spoken to my people, and we're intrigued by the possibilities. Agent Tuyin and Officer Godri, however, have taken their leave."

"Did you expect anything else?" Lom asked.

"No, I didn't. Those two are consummate professionals and they didn't see how they could be anything except what they are."

"No, I don't blame them. But let me ask you... how did they react to the Covrani's offer of working with them?" Aura asked.

"That was less of an offer and more of an understanding. Considering there was a roving band of marauders at bay, they didn't seem to have a problem working with the Covrani."

"And you don't see a clash of interests there?" Aura asked. "I'm not judging but I'm interested in your analysis."

"You can speak plainer than that, Aura."

"Yes, I can, but I think I've made my point. My crew is here to hurt the ruling class and its methods of wealth collection while your TSS buddies are working for them. Do you see the difference?"

"I understand there is a certain conflict of interests there, yes."

"And you still want to be here?"

"I do, Captain. If hitting pirate gangs in the interest of maintaining law and order is what you're after, then I'm here for it." Karmen's eyes wandered to the spot where Meklife remained standing.

Aura nodded. "Lom has resigned his post as first officer, in favor of taking up the mantle of Ground Force Commander. Which means there's an opening in the ranks, if you know someone who might be a top-notch candidate for it…"

"What are you thinking, Aura?"

"I think going forward we'll need a source of income that relies more on standard business channels and less on Gilgamesh's machinations. But to do that, I need a first officer who can effectively manage this bunch of thugs. Are you interested?"

"I am."

"Good. The job is yours. First, learn the names and roles of the crew. We'll work on details afterward. If there's nothing else, I'll let you two get to work. Welcome aboard, First Officer Sley."

Out in the corridor, Karmen and Lom walked in silence for a minute. "It wasn't my intention to rob you of your job aboard ship," she began.

"Nor was it mine to abandon it for you to pick up and put away," he said. "The truth is, I had been mulling the situation over for months. I was never fully comfortable in the post of first officer. Strangely enough, it was a conversation with your future son-in-law that forced me to admit that to myself."

"You connected with Colin? Really?"

"He's a very bright boy. He will go far if he can inspire the kind of loyalty you and Aura seem to command. I only vaguely remember being that age. I made plenty of mistakes and didn't come from that manner of privilege, but I learned some powerful lessons about myself. He's going to figure his own situation out, as well. I look forward to being in the room when he does. It will be marvelous."

"Commanding ground troops is more your speed, then?"

"Without a doubt. I am, at my core, a thief—and a good one. I might as well keep at it and improve my skill set even more. Now that you are here in the job of first officer, how shall we proceed? You've seen the major compartments. I expect the captain will give you a tour not unlike that which I gave your husband and children. I could introduce you to the department heads. Give you the run of the ship."

"I would appreciate the leg up, as it were. The first week of learning who's who is always awkward. How about we start with the hangar deck and work our way to the sensor dome?"

Meklife produced a tablet from a compartment in his leg. "As you wish, First Officer Sley. You can take notes with this. I've no doubt you'll find numerous areas where you can be useful."

29

BEST FRIENDS FOREVER

IT TOOK TIME for Seandra and the rest of her family to move their belongings out of the *Mother Courage* and into a set of cabins on the *Emerald Queen*. All their weaponry and equipment had gone to the pirate ship's armory, which at least made it easy to find. Seandra was sharing a billet with Elian, and her parents were in another across the hall. Everyone got bigger rooms than they'd had aboard the small starship, but the added space didn't seem very luxurious.

She needed time to process her new reality. She'd been ready to go back to Greengard, but her parents had clearly lost their minds. Where were the people who'd been rigid rule-followers her whole life? Instead, they were now actively joining the pirate gang they'd been pursuing for months. It didn't make any sense.

Seandra had hoped that Lee and Armin might talk some sense into her mother, but they'd already gone back to wherever it was that TSS Agents went when they weren't on hand. Now, with her older siblings going back to Gallos, maybe forever, it was clear that life was never going back to 'normal'—whatever that had been before Mother Carnage came into their lives.

With her mom in constant motion related to her first officer duties, her dad trying to hold it together, and Elian moping all the time, Seandra quickly realized that she could only manage herself. One thing in the chaos that she *could* control was target practice—a chance to further develop her skills, occupy her time, and productively direct her pent-up frustrations.

She'd retrieved one of the Zanoff-Boland G36K auto-rifles from the armory and taken it to the shooting range near one of the common rooms. The sounds of crew using the facility were jarring, and she plugged her ears to manage the noise.

A knot of Valdans were hanging out in the last two bays, apparently throwing rocks or something at targets. Seandra was put off by the sheer volume of the Valdans' speech, even when no one was shooting. They didn't seem capable of just talking to each other with indoor voices. Everything was a shouting match. But they never made it physical; no blows were ever exchanged and they never got in each other's faces. She found the incongruity interesting but wasn't here to analyze foreign cultures.

She set up in an empty bay about halfway down the floor—far enough from the shouting to not lose focus. She loaded the rifle with practice targeting rounds and activated the holographic target downrange.

The practice rounds mimicked the kinetic feedback of the real deal, painting the digital target with a realistic portrayal of each shot's aim and velocity. Her first set went all over the place; she was obviously out of practice, and her anxious headspace wasn't helping, either. Her next set was better as her body began to remember the correct stance and positioning, but still not great. She put up a third target, then set herself. She brought the stock in tight against her shoulder and adjusted her stance. She concentrated on lining up the sights, held her breath, and squeezed off eight shots in quick succession.

A soprano shout from the next bay broke her concentration. "Little girl! Why do you use such a clunky weapon?"

Seandra noticed one of the Valdan girls waving at her, trying to get her attention. Her spirit robe flapped its wide sleeves as she waved. She seemed swaddled from head to toe in the unique garb, but her head and neck were bare.

Seandra squeezed off two more shots and relaxed, checking the digital readout of the target. Her strikes were all center mass, but her grouping was all over the place. "That's a good question," she murmured. Then it sank in. "Did you just call me a *little girl*?" she called back, louder.

The Valdan was at least half a head taller and slim, with a wiry build. The top of Seandra's head barely cleared the other girl's chin. The stranger stepped up to her and rested one hand on the top of her own head and the other on Seandra's. "You're little. And you're obviously a girl. Little girl."

Seandra took a deep breath and reminded herself that she was the guest here, not the Valdan. "I'm short. Not little."

One of the male Valdans screamed at the girl in their native tongue, making Seandra flinch. The girl screamed back but looked at Seandra with an expression of enlightenment. "Come down off your perch, short stack. Why choose a heavy cannon just for target practice?"

"Sure. Short girl. Not little girl. Okay? Okay."

The Valdan clapped her hands and bounced on her toes.

"Okay-okay. Are you going to answer my question?"

Seandra gave her new friend a side-eye. "My mother was in the military. She's used to these kinds of weapons, and I thought it was a good idea to train myself, too. These are what we have to practice with, so I use them. I agree, they aren't ideal."

"You got a name?" the Valdan asked and drew another rebuke from the elder.

"My name is Seandra. What's yours?"

"Srahamari."

Seandra blinked. *I'm not even going to insult her by trying.* "How about for today, I call you Sari?"

"Sari! Okay-okay. But I'm calling you Sanda. Show me how you shoot your giant rifle."

Seandra pulled out the magazine, cleared the breach and made sure the safety was engaged before offering it to her new friend. "You want to try it?"

"Me? No. I never use them."

"So why are you even here?" Seandra asked.

"Practice."

"With what? Throwing rocks?"

In her own bay, Sari loaded a physical paper target with the outline of a person's head and torso. She sent it downrange.

Seandra eyed the unusual medium, not sure why anyone would opt for it over the detailed results readout and adjustable distance configurations available with holographic targets.

Sari reached into her pocket and pulled out a handful of small metal discs. She made a show of playing with them. Seandra had trouble keeping up with the trick; in one move, Sari held the discs between her fingers, then swapped them so they flew across the back of her hand, flipped, and she caught each one in sequence. Seandra gaped at the display, in awe of the girl's dexterity.

Sari's focus shifted from her hands to the target. She didn't look down at all as she arranged her discs on the sill in front of her, then held her hand over them, waggling her fingers. At once, all the discs rose into the air and Seandra lost sight of them as Sari sent them on their way with a flick of her wrist. She dimly heard the slight sound of paper tearing. Then, Sari caught something and stepped back, opening her hand to show the discs were back home. She retracted the target, and Seandra gawked as she spied a single hole in the center of the target's head.

"One hit? That's all?"

Sari pushed the paper at the shorter girl. "Look," she said, gently prying the paper apart.

Seandra traced the 'wound' with her fingers and realized there were multiple strikes present, all in a grouping tight enough to make her own efforts look like random pot shots thrown against a wall. She looked up in frank admiration and Sari opened her hand. She even made her discs do a little dance in her palm.

"Sari, that's... wow. Teach me," Seandra said.

"I cannot. You have no... Gift. A little sad. You have good aim, but this is a bad choice for you," she said, tapping the rifle's butt. "There is a better one somewhere. You should find it."

"Where?"

"In the armory. Come with me."

Sari led her through the racks of guns with the confidence of a woman maneuvering around her own kitchen. She pulled a number of slug throwers from their places and judged them all wanting. Eventually, the one she'd wanted appeared, a compact submachinegun with a telescoping stock.

"Here. This is the U-21 Badger. Talsari guards use them on their bases in the deep desert on Valdos. I don't like Talsari, but their guards are good. Too good."

"They shot you?"

"Not me. But family. Uncle, cousins. They say our land is their land because TalEx signs papers with the Valdan government. They carry these guns and they shoot anyone who argues." She pushed the weapon at Seandra. "It's a good gun for you. Good size. Better control over direction, and with the stock extended, it'll absorb the recoil."

"I don't know. After hearing that... it seems wrong to use it," Seandra confessed.

"It's not wrong. A gun has no mind, no heart. You work for TalEx?"

"No."

"Does your family work for them?"

"Um. It's a long story."

"I like stories. Tell me the story, Sanda."

Part of Seandra kicked herself for being so willfully ignorant of how Foundation City was funded. "We live on Greengard. We have a big desert, too. TalEx has lots of mining stuff there. They take things out of the ground and they pay for a big university for us. People come from all over the sector to learn. I guess I never thought about how the money got from the desert to the school."

"You learn good things in school? Useful things?"

"I think so. I hope so. Math and science."

"How to kill?"

"No! I learned how to shoot from... video games."

Sari's quizzical expression softened into a wide smile. "Video games?" she snorted. "You play games with guns and images? That's crazy!"

Seandra felt a surge of relief break through her and she started giggling, then guffawing. The two girls fell against each other, peals of laughter ringing throughout the armory.

When the laughter abated, Sari tapped the Badger again. "A man with a gun, aims with his hand. He shoots with his gun. He kills by accident, or by impulse. I am a Scorpion. I aim with my mind. I kill with my heart. It's never an accident. I never kill on impulse. Understand?"

"No. Maybe. I don't know. I know it's not a game. I did shoot someone, but he was a bad man. A hijacker. My mother let a worse one get away. She had a reason, I suppose."

"Soldiers never tell all they know. It's okay-okay." Sari took a step back and stretched, folding her arms and spine backwards then snapping forward again. "You hungry, Sanda?"

"I could eat."

"Good. The cafeteria crew lets us use the kitchen sometimes. Madri is making masdra stew today. It's very good. Let's get some lunch, short stack."

Sari took off at a quick march, leaving Seandra wondering what to do. "Masdra stew," she said. Her mouth watered at the thought of anything that wasn't shipboard rations. "Okay-okay." She put the Badger back in its rack and ran after the tall girl.

— — —

The smell of food lured Elian to the general mess like a drop of honey attracted flies.

There didn't seem to be any rhyme or reason behind the seating arrangements or limits on who could take what. The crew came in, got a tray, put food on it, collected their utensils, and sat down to eat. Okay.

He pulled a couple of sandwiches on round rolls onto his tray and sat down at an empty table.

The sound of an angry throat clearing showed him that he was wrong. A crew member was staring at him from the far end of the table. He even recognized her: the older girl who'd tried to punch him for messing with the docking kiosk on Tavden Station. Billie.

She obviously remembered him, too. She kept glaring even as she moved her place down to sit opposite him with her bowl and unfolded her napkin and flatware. "Elian. Why are *you* here?"

"Billie. I dunno, I heard the food was pretty good and I was hungry."

"You heard wrong. But the Valdans make some really good stew. So get a bowl of that before it disappears."

"I'm good, thanks."

"The sandwiches are boring and the bread is stale. I'm telling you."

"But I can take two and nobody stops me."

A girlish shout from across the room broke the tension. "Billie!"

Billie brightened instantly. "Srahamari!"

A tall thin girl with dark skin tones and swathed in Valdan clothing sat down with a bowl. After a moment, so did Seandra.

Seandra glared at Billie. "You can pronounce that? I've been calling her 'Sari' all day."

Billie nodded. "Yeah, I can't pronounce it very well, either. You have to do the 'r' at the back of your throat. But, Sari, for short is way simpler. Is that okay"

"Sari and Sanda and Billie and Elian. Okay-okay!" Sari pointed at Elian's empty plate. "You should have had stew.

Next time, you'll remember, right?"

Elian raised his hand. "Promise."

Seandra sampled the Valdan cuisine and decided she was in love. "I see you've met Elian already. And wow, this stew really is delicious!"

"It is. You two are part of the Sley clan," Billie said. "Okay. At least now I know where I stand. You guys have a problem with me on any subject, you don't go to the first officer. You go to my boss, the chief engineer. She'll deal with it."

Seandra frowned. "I'm confused."

"So am I," Elian said. "What do you think we're going to do? I just came in for some dinner."

Billie dropped her spoon in her bowl and folded her arms, scowling. "Look, kids, I know how it works. Your mom is the new first officer and you now get special attention. We all fall over ourselves to make nice. Sari here takes you under her wing. I don't know what to do with this short round with the sticky fingers but I'm sure I'll be expected to make nice on him, too."

"Nope," Elian said, shaking his head.

"What do you mean, nope?" Billie said.

"I mean don't be nice to me. I just don't care. We're not even supposed to be here."

"That's true. We wanted to go back to Greengard, but that's not happening," Seandra agreed.

"So, what *are* you doing here?" Billie pressed.

"I'm teaching Sanda to shoot with a Badger. No Gifts, but she has good aim. She can practice with the Scorpions. She'll make a good soldier."

"I don't want to be a soldier."

"No, you just like the pretty noise of guns, right?" Sari snarked, then let loose a long phrase in her own language. She smiled and got back to eating.

Seandra nodded at Billie. "She just dismissed me to the end of the galaxy, didn't she?"

"That was too fast for me to understand, but I think you've been put in your place," Billie agreed. She turned to Elian. "How are you planning to earn your meals, sport?"

"Not sure. I mean, I'm good with computers. You saw that for yourself."

Billie slowly nodded. "True. That was clever, reprogramming the docking kiosk to lock the emergency clamps in place so the ship couldn't leave."

"I had some help for that," he admitted. "But I follow directions pretty well."

"Hmm. You want to work in the engine room? Lots of stuff to keep track of."

"You're not afraid I'll blow something up?"

"Sure I am, but you wouldn't work with me. Maesy will find something suitable for you to do. It's her shop, you know."

"She's the chief engineer?"

"She is. My shift is done for today, but show up at 08:00 tomorrow and ask for me. I'll get you started. If you want to learn, we'll teach you how engines work. If not, you'll make a nice doorstop."

30

PERSONNEL MATTERS

AURA WAS IN the habit of getting into the officer's mess on Deck 2 early to get coffee and whatever breakfast pastry the bakery had decided to create that day. Today, they had bakfi, a pastry she'd fallen in love with years ago on Bashari Prime. Sweet, basted meat inside a flaky crust. Amazing stuff. She could eat six of them in one sitting if she wasn't careful. She stopped at three, then put one more on her plate. Screw it, she was the captain.

She found an empty table near the far wall and sat down to eat and drink. Then, she noticed the crowd at the other end of the room.

Sacha was holding court at one table, surrounded by women. Two tables away, Callum was doing something similar with the men. Both groups consisted of Lynaedans and Base Tarans.

Aura watched the room as the two parallel conversations took place. The women were whispering and giggling, and the men were keeping it quiet but an occasional shout or even a cheer would erupt every now and then.

The rest of the cafeteria operated as usual, but at a few other tables, small groups had formed on their own and everyone turned to watch the gathering at one time or another.

The gossip tree blooms aboard the Emerald Queen, she thought. The only question would be how soon it spread to the lower decks. She finished her meal and rose to find out.

In the general mess, things were somewhat different, but it was clear the congenial mood had infected everyone here, too. Some tables were men or women only, some were mixed, but a great many were couples, sometimes of mixed lineage, sometimes not. There were a lot of them. They didn't always mimic the primary pairing—plenty of Base women were scoping out Lynaedan men and vice-versa—but it was definitely a thing. The factions were *mixing*.

"Good morning, Captain," Lom Mench said as he put down his plate and mug and sat next to her.

"We're screwed," she growled.

"I beg your pardon?"

"Look at them."

Lom turned his head. "At what?"

"Look at *them*! Callum and Sacha. I let them defy lights out. Now we have chaos."

Lom scanned the crowd. "How is this chaotic? I've never seen this crew better behaved."

"That's how it starts. I should have thrown the book at both of them. It never ends well."

"I thought you wanted the two factions to become more friendly," Mench protested.

"I meant friendly as in accepting each other as colleagues, co-workers. *This* is like one of those low-brow romantic comedies where one couple walks into a dull restaurant, gets excited with each other on a table top, and then every other couple does the same thing," Aura snarled.

"What kind of vids do you watch?" Mench asked. "That sounds fascinating."

"Mench!"

Lom held up his hands in a supplicating gesture. "Very well. You're the captain. You set the standard. Segregating the quarters is one thing. Enforcing the lights out rule is easily done. But these crew members aren't doing anything but eating and talking. Surely, that's an acceptable standard."

"It's going to lead to sex on the tables. You watch."

"Captain, I'd like a word in private."

Aura stood up violently and Lom maneuvered her to a comm shack at the rear of the deck. The room hadn't been used for some time; dust flew off surfaces as Lom powered up the system.

"I haven't shown this to anyone else. Nor did I intend to, but I think it's important to know what one looks like in public," Lom said. He turned on the display and Aura was filled with disgust and horror as she watched the drama between herself and Gilgamesh re-play out in real time. "Remember this?" he asked.

"Spying on me, Lom?"

"Hardly. Shamhat beamed this into our comm system as an update."

"What a good little spy."

"Indeed. This is you, that is obviously Gilgamesh. I won't play the audio, but I've listened to it myself. The time stamp indicates that it took place just after he docked his yacht to the *Queen*'s private hangar after you returned from that vault ship with him."

She groaned. "I remember this all too well. No need to play it for me."

"I insist. Let's see… this is him accusing you of making bad choices. That's you telling him he was the worst choice you made. This was him insisting he made you what you are, and that's you denying he had anything to do with your success. This is where he swings at you. This is where you dodge the attack, then throw him against a wall with your mind. That's him storming off in his yacht."

"I get your meaning. Cat fights on deck are a bad look. Who else saw?"

"No one. This was a private feed. But it's in the computer, so someone may eventually stumble onto it. Eventually, that someone will talk about it. Then, you really *will* start to lose control over your crew."

"What do I do about it?"

"Admitting you miss Lord Gilgamesh would be a start."

"That was no *lord*, Lom. I'm glad he's gone."

"Are you sure of that? He meant a great deal to you."

"Where is this going?"

Lom turned the security gear off. "Do I have to say it, Aura? You're working through an ugly breakup, and you don't see why anyone else should enjoy themselves."

She seethed with the implications. She was *not* out of control. "How dare you!"

"I do dare. Gilgamesh was a fool. You know it. I know it. You took what favors he could give you, and you him. Now it's over. We're all better off."

"And yet… here you all are. Because he brought you on board, literally and figuratively. Why are *you* still here, Lom?"

"Because you and I are both outcasts. Leftovers. Expendables. Our respective peoples have no use for us. The same is true of everyone on this crew, regardless of origin. We are outsiders in a universe defined by connections, cliques, and clubs. None of us fit anywhere except among each other. Now, you can lament that your life didn't turn out the way you planned. Or you can revel in the knowledge that every one of *these* people has your back. Do you understand the significance of what's happening out there?"

She blinked. She hadn't thought about anything except outrage and shame. "Tell me."

"It means your crew has figured out that they can rely on you. They've learned to call this ship their home. Obviously, we should have rules to minimize conflicts on duty, but let them have this."

"'What kind of pirate sits and waits to be served?'" she quoted.

"I beg your pardon?"

"Something Tabor said to me. I've been starving them of something they apparently needed. All right, then. Let them have their fun," she decided. "I'll print out the old fraternization rules I learned at the TSS. Make sure they are posted in all quarters."

"A wise decision. Considering this development, I suggest re-purposing some of the quarters on Decks 2 and 3 for couples who wish to cohabit. We're already heading down that road, we might as well prepare for it."

"Agreed. See to it when you have time. I'm sorry I threw down just now. You're right, I'm upset. Can you and Karmen manage the ship on your own for a day?"

"Of course. Where will you be?"

"Wandering through the station's mezzanine, thinking very carefully about the choices I've made."

—

After walking the docks for a while, Aura decided that she didn't like Crux Station, after all. She appreciated the shops and nightlife, but the place felt open, exposed. She felt like she was on display. She made do with a cup of tea at a street vendor. Eventually, she heard a chair scrape against the deck and watched her new first officer sit in it with a dish of ice cream in either hand. "Good morning, Captain. Isn't this a fine, fine morning?"

"Karmen, I want to be alone."

"Untrue. Alone means locking yourself in your cabin. I'm glad you outgrew that habit, at least."

"I didn't outgrow anything. I just go into my old cargo ship instead."

"We can work on that. At any rate, Lom thought you needed to talk, just not to him. You know me, I can't say no to ice cream. Here. Mint chip, or marshmallow fudge?"

"Pass the mint. I'm in a green mood." They started eating in silence. Eventually, Aura said, "When I referred to my crew as my family, I thought I was being poetic. But I really do feel that way about them. When I saw Sacha and Callum talking to the others like a bunch of students in a lunchroom… it felt lonely. I felt jealous."

"Ah, young love. Try living with a besotted teenager."

"No, thank you. Adults are bad enough. This morning, I felt lost. I hate that feeling. Is this what they call empty nest syndrome?"

"Hardly. Your nest is quite full."

"Doesn't feel like it."

"Welcome to the club, Aura. He's only been gone a day, but I wonder how Kozu is doing. What Tolri is teaching him.

If he's happy. Kaia seems to be embracing the life of a merchant, and I'm conflicted about that."

"You should be. It's a tough life."

"I know. Daveed is more worried than I am. We've avoided talking about it. Elian has been moping on the lower decks since Armin and Lee left. And Seandra is… Seandra. I don't understand her at all."

"One of the Scorpions adopted her, I hear. She'll be a proficient soldier before long. Elian is moving to work with the engineering staff."

"That's just what I need. How do you hear this stuff before I do?"

Aura scraped the bottom of her cup with her spoon. "Stay close to Gallian. He's literally connected to the comm net, so his news is always current."

"I'll do that. At any rate, I had my morning meeting with the department heads. We can leave whenever you give the order."

"Good. How far is it to Tarkus?"

"Six days. Colin and Tabor have hardly slept since they met. Daveed says listening to them talk to each other is like watching a pair of twins communicate in a private language."

"I'm glad they're here. With Gil gone, we need funding and lots of it." Aura finished her ice cream, ran her fingers across her lips and said, "I can't stop thinking about robbing Gil blind. Is it mere revenge? Am I that big a fool?"

"I think deep down you knew what Gil was from the day you met him. He was booted from the TSS training program for a reason. Sure, maybe you did owe him something for saving your life, but you were and always will be a TSS Agent. Your training doesn't vanish with disuse. I wouldn't be here if I didn't think that you were still the same person at heart, uniform or not. Now, if you're finished feeling sorry for yourself, let's get back to the ship. We have a schedule to keep."

"Agreed."

"And could we please go back to calling your flight deck a Command Center? 'War Room' is better applied to the Quartermaster's suite. The boys are planning strategies and tactics that would put any general staff to shame."

"All right. Command Center it is. But it's *our* flight deck."

"Yes, Captain."

— — —

Mitchel took a cold bite of his ice cream cone. It was good stuff and had real advantages over getting drunk in a random dive bar. He watched the two women walk back to their ship from across the food court. The redhead was Mother Carnage herself and the one with the crazy curls was the same woman who'd told her people to shoot him on that small trader. Used that little girl, Seandra, to lure his crew in, then murdered Sebbi in cold blood. It was painfully obvious they were working together.

He realized that he was going to need a lot more help if he was going to deal with the *Emerald Queen* properly.

He tapped his comm. "Alfi, you there?"

"I'm here. Whatcha got?

"*Emerald Queen* is bound for Tarkus. What do we know about that location?"

"Harm's Hellions is raiding shipping there as independent crews enter and leave orbit. They're not hitting the big bulk carriers, just the small fish."

"Then let's send them a call and tell them we have a giant score we're willing to share with them. Mad Jacket should be working the Main, so let's invite him, too. Also let's see if the Crazy Cats are still talking to us, and offer the Knights of Muskva an extra share if they can throw in."

"Blood Fountain and Ring of Fire would probably want in, too," Alfi advised.

"The more the merrier," Mitchel agreed. "She's a big ship filled with high-tech goodies, and we need numbers. Stress that we'll be handing out shares for everyone involved."

"On it. How about I just put out a general invitation on the Dark Net and see who shows up?"

"Do it. Good man. Mitchel out."

Mitchel cracked his knuckles. He would never make peace with Mother Carnage. She'd lured Mitchel in with the promise of a quick fast kill and a fat reward, and he'd been left with a dead leader and a TSS goon who knew his name and his face. Yes, he'd found buyers for the ships they'd taken… eventually. But he'd allowed himself to be put in a position where he'd sold out his boss to escape. No one made him kill his own captain. No one.

31

BLOCKADE

KARMEN PACED OUT the perimeter around the *Emerald Queen*'s Command Center, watching the crew as they managed their duty stations. It was the first time Aura had permitted Colin to fill in for her nav officer. Colin kept his eyes on his console and his mind on his job. She expected it was easier for him when Kaia wasn't around. "Status report, Nav," she called out.

"We'll be dropping out of subspace into Tarkus airspace in two minutes. All systems show nominal performance."

"Good. The size of the ship isn't phasing you at all? As I remember you've never handled anything in this size class before."

"That's not entirely true, ma'am. My uncle let me pilot a supertanker out of space dock on Gallos once. I can manage this, no worries."

Space elongated and snapped back as the ship dropped from subspace. The viewscreen showed them the red-brown globe of Tarkus. At a distance of two light-minutes, it wasn't much more than a pale dot. "Position confirmed. Welcome to Tarkus, folks."

"Thank you, Nav," Aura said. "Let's approach at half normal speed. Gallian, let's contact the spaceport and let them know we'll be down shortly."

"Aye aye."

"Busy day down there," Callum murmured.

Aura raised her voice. "Sensors?"

"I say there's a lot of traffic in near orbits. Three groups in particular. They're evenly spaced out in three equidistant groups."

"Nav, let's give those ships a wide berth."

"Acknowledged, Captain."

Callum waited a few minutes then updated his readings. "Captain, I don't think they're going to cooperate. All three groups have altered their courses to intercept us."

"Double check that," Karmen ordered.

Callum made the adjustments. "It's confirmed. They've adjusted course and speed to intercept us."

Aura tapped the armrest of her command chair. "Gallian, warn those ships off."

"I'm working on it, Captain. I've sent bulletins to the ships and also to the spaceport. I'm not getting responses from any of them."

"I think we just found our blockade," Aura noted.

"It's never easy." Karmen sighed. "Why is it never easy? Callum, do a full scan. I want to know who is trying to intercept us."

"Scanning now. Just a moment. Conferring with the battle computer for profile IDs. Ops, link the tactical viewer to my feed."

Sacha used her work arms to make the transfer. "Done. You're linked in."

The tactical display showed three groups closing rapidly, but they were also closing the distance between each other. The only thing that stood out as strange to Karmen was a single contact right at the center of all the approaching groups.

"Callum, you have a report?" Karmen asked.

"Yes, ma'am. We're looking at roughly thirty ships, all ranging in size from twelve to one hundred meters in length. That cylindrical craft in the center, that's the largest one in the group. But there's no coherence to the equipment. Their weapons are a combination of lasers, plasma beams, and short-range missiles. They aren't following any military doctrine I can think of."

"It's kitchen sink fleet," Karmen said. "I think we can safely assume they're not military in tactics or training."

"Not military-trained, you mean," Aura corrected. "There are plenty of local Militia and Guard units who operate auxiliary vessels. Colin used one against us, remember?"

That seemed like so long ago. "I do. Callum, that cylinder at the center of the formation… is there a transponder code attached to it, or is it just a cargo container?"

"It's a vessel… power core readings match an industrial profile. Transponder code says it's a satellite tender. The *Durable*."

"*Durable*? You're certain?" Karmen demanded.

"Yes, ma'am."

"Captain, I'd recommend we go to battle stations. The *Durable* was Pelu Kengi's ship. They had a tactic of trapping victims within that central cargo bay then either punching holes in the victim's hull if they didn't comply or just shooting them outright."

"But why are they here?"

"Kengi is dead, and I'd assume that bunch wants revenge," Karmen noted. "All I see is a hostile group of ships that need to be neutralized."

"Agreed. What was the name of the fool who's decided to step into Kengi's boots?"

Karmen felt dirty just speaking it. "I'll show you. Gallian, open a channel to the *Durable* and demand to speak to Mitchel Pilar."

"Aye aye. Mitchel is coming on…"

"Captain Pilar," Karmen began, "This is Karmen Sley, First Officer of the *Emerald Queen*. Fancy meeting you again after we expressly told you to stay out of trouble."

Mitchel's voice came through the channel filled with anger and bitterness. "I should have killed you when I had the chance, Officer. You and that bomaxed daughter of yours."

"Strange, I was just having the same thought about you. I suppose I'm glad to see you rule your crew more effectively than your former boss did."

"That's a cheap shot, Sley. I lost my cool once. It won't happen again."

"If you want to prove that to me now, you can stand your fleet down and head out of this system. It might be months before we find you if you scatter."

"Sit and spin, lady. We'll pummel that wallowing hog of a ship and then we'll strip it and your crew for parts."

"It's your funeral, Mitchel. *Emerald Queen* out." Karmen cut the connection.

"He sounds nice," Aura said.

"It's a shame he hasn't learned anything in the past few weeks," Karmen lamented. "I knew we should have killed those monsters when we had the chance. Lee decided to let them go with a warning."

"Ha! And you call me a TSS flunky," Aura griped.

"I did *not* call you a flunky."

"Regardless, we have a chance to correct your team's collective error in judgement," Aura declared. "Karmen, do you remember the tactical plans from *Triumph*?"

"Of course. Which do you think works for this bunch: Smuggler's Notch?"

"No, they have too many ships for that. How about Aegis Alert?"

"That one takes too long to prepare. What about Up the Middle?"

Aura snapped her fingers. "Yes! Sacha, have the loaders prep four cargo shuttles with scatter-pack launchers in the cargo bays. Make sure they're all facing the rear doors, then set the warheads for proximity detonations. Commander Mench will give you the particulars. Make it happen!"

"Aye aye! Ops to hangar deck, you have new orders, as follows…"

"Captain to Gunnery section, do we still have those eight Talsarium rounds on board?"

"That's affirmative, Captain. But they won't detonate."

"But will they show up on a radiological sensor?"

"That they will, Captain!"

"Good. Load those little jewels into the railguns, one round per turret. Secure the remaining four to the carriages of those scatter-pack shuttles."

"The canisters are the wrong shape for the auto-loaders. We'll have to load them all manually."

"Then the sooner you start, the sooner they'll be ready to fire," Karmen said.

"Aye aye."

Aura pulled up a tactical display. "We need time for the shuttle preparations. Let's put some distance between us and them. Nav, plot a spiral course out of the inner system. Allow them to overtake us but don't be obvious about it."

"Wait, we *want* them to catch us?" Colin asked.

Karmen tapped the boy on his shoulder. "Remember, they think we're a wallowing pig of a cargo ship. In Mitchel's mind, they are pirates and we are victims. They need to chase us and bring us down or they'll know it's a trap."

"Yes, ma'am."

"How do you see this fight going, Aura?" Karmen asked. She looked at the tactical display, spinning the hologram as she tried to apply the techniques she'd learned during her Militia training years ago. "Up the Middle requires a swarm attack from the enemy. I don't know if these yobos even know what that is."

Aura pulled the display apart and zoomed in on the *Queen*. "With a target the size of ours, they won't be able to resist. They'll pool their firing patterns, they won't be calling their shots. Not until they realize that our size is our primary defense. When we turn to run, they'll pursue as a group and that's when we drop the shuttles out the hangar deck. They'll think we're abandoning ship. The shuttles will race past the attackers, unload their drones…"

"And hit them from behind before they can react. Then, we collect the shuttles, pick off any remaining defenders, and end Mitchel Pilar. I like it," Karmen said. "What if they plug rounds into us and see how little affect their fire has?"

"That's the easy part. Captain to Engineering… Maesy, do the reactive plates still work?"

"They won't repel much if they decide to concentrate their attacks."

"But can we detonate them selectively from up here?"

"Yes, you can. Give me a moment to dynamically link the control circuits. Done! Sacha can now detonate them at will from her console."

"Good job, carry on. Gunnery section, power up the plasma cannons, and load all torpedo tubes."

Sacha was already using one of her arms to set a panel that could detonate sequences of explosive armor plates at the touch of the button. Karmen could see that there weren't many plates available, but she thought she had a grasp of the general idea: use near-misses to create apparent chaos and draw the attackers in even further.

When Karmen arrived at the Ops position, she bent down to whisper into Sacha's ear. "Now you get to show me how good you really are, my four-armed lovely."

"Challenge accepted, ma'am. Nav!"

"Ops!"

"When I give you the order you need to spin the hull toward the facing that I call out."

"Honestly, I think that will work better if we reverse those roles," Colin argued.

Aura spoke up. "Don't argue, Nav. She knows these controls and you're still learning yours. Follow Sacha's lead."

"Aye aye, Captain."

"They're shifting their formations," Callum announced. "Lining up for a run on our flank. Time to intercept, one minute."

"Right on schedule," Aura acknowledged. "Colin, maintain course and speed."

"This is Gunnery. Beams are primed and the Talsarium canisters are loaded in turrets. Please do not fire them at greater than one fifth power or we'll kill the mechanisms.

Torpedo tubes are loaded and ready for firing."

Aura tapped her comm. "Understood. Sacha, make the necessary modifications and program a firing pattern. Use the Talsarium rounds to scatter their formation, then use the plasma beams to pick them off."

"Aye aye."

"Intercept in ten seconds," Callum said.

Aura peered closely at the display, almost walking into it. "Sacha, fire the railguns. One-fifth normal power. Wouldn't want our crusaders to not hear the alarms go off."

Four of the railgun turrets spat rounds into the three formations. Just as predicted, the smaller ship formations flew apart as their radiological sensors began screaming of nuclear armaments and the pilots guided them through evasive maneuvers. The rearmost group was made of heavier vessels and reacted more slowly. Large enough to require numerous hits to destroy.

"Set the forward torpedo tubes for auto-target selection and fire," Aura ordered.

"Proximity fuses set, auto-targeting engaged. Firing all forward tubes," Sacha confirmed.

Six missiles flew from their firing tubes. One torpedo blasted an A-20D into scrap and another cracked the hull of a I-40R, decompressing the main cabin and blasting every hatch wide open, asphyxiating the crew in moments. The other four explosives pelted numerous attackers with shrapnel, unleashing a torrent of chaos on the attacking fleet.

Gallian signaled for a bulletin and said, "Captain, it's working. Lots of cross-talk on their comms. They're screaming bloody murder."

"What about Mitchel?" Karmen asked.

"Captain Pilar is announcing twenty thousand credits each

to the crew that blasts us to ruin," Gallian reported.

"That's insulting. We're worth more than that," Sacha murmured.

Karmen turned back to Aura and winked. "Now they're good and angry, which means they won't be thinking straight."

Aura nodded. "Agreed. Nav, come about to course zero-eight-three. Ops, hit them with the plasma beams as they pass us. Hangar bay, what's the status of those shuttles?"

"We're closing up the last one now, Command Center. We can launch on your order."

"We'll make another few passes with the beams before that," Aura said. "Reload all torpedo tubes. Nav, Ops: you have your instructions."

"Coming to new course zero-eight-three…"

"Plasma beams set for broadside barrage on auto-target program… executing!"

As the great warship turned to its new course, the attackers swerved with it, lasers and plasma beams peppering the *Emerald Queen* with an array of energy bolts. The *Queen*'s battle computer cataloged the strength and accuracy of their hits and responded in kind, automatically targeting what it judged to be the most dangerous members of the attacking fleet.

Sacha plugged into the *Queen*'s battle computer and played her console well. A dozen of the reactive plates exploded into fragments, sending more shrapnel into the attacking ships but also making it appear as if the damage were more severe. Three small shuttles were destroyed instantly, and nine more took serious damage. Two of the smaller shuttles fled the battle as their pion drives sputtered and flared, leaving their crew adrift in space.

"Tactical," Aura called.

Karmen spun the display. "They're down seven ships, we've taken superficial damage. Not bad for a first exchange."

"Agreed, but this is getting tedious," Aura said. "Hangar deck, prepare to launch the scatter-pack shuttles. Nav, plot a course back to the planet. Go to full power on the pion drive, make sure we get well ahead of them."

Colin made the corrections and executed the maneuver. "It worked, Captain, they've fallen behind."

"They're still shooting at us," Karmen announced.

Aura's blood was up now, a slight flush rising to her face. "Good. Sacha, detonate every reactive plate on our flanks. Nav, cut our speed by ninety percent. Hangar deck, launch the shuttles."

The space behind the converted freighter filled with shrapnel and noise, making it seem to the attackers as if the ship had taken damage and was in trouble. Now, the shuttles increased their speed and blasted at full power toward the enemies, firing their nose-mounted lasers constantly as the distance between the two groups closed.

When the *Queen's* shuttles moved past the attacking fleet, their pilots opened their rear cargo doors and launched their ordnance. Instantly, one hundred multi-warhead missiles dropped out from their cargo bays and ignited, taking a moment to orient themselves. Their noses split, releasing three hundred scatter-pack warheads. The faster shuttles saw the danger and did their best to avoid the missiles; only a few escaped. In less than a minute, thirteen targets of various sizes had vanished from the tactical display and six more were hopelessly damaged.

The flight crew murmured as numerous contacts disappeared from the tactical display. "What's the status of the *Durable*?" Karmen asked.

"They're turning toward deep space. I'd bet you anything they're looking to run."

"Aura, recommend another—"

"Way ahead of you, Karmen. Drop two torpedoes onto that ship, contact fuses, target their engines."

"Rear tubes fired. Torpedoes running… thirty seconds to contact… ten seconds… hit one…hit two! Power readings dropping… He's dead in space," Sacha declared.

"The fleet is breaking up. They've had enough," Callum said.

"Let them run," Aura said. "We want that tender. Nav, prepare to close and moor to that hull. We'll send a boarding party of our own. Commandeer Mench…"

"Captain!"

"Take a platoon of drones and Scorpion guards with you and board the *Durable*. Scrub that ship clean."

"We serve the Queen!"

32

BOARDING PARTY

PRACTICING WITH THE Badger turned out to be far more fun than Seandra had expected. Sari had been right. The submachine was the right length and weight for Seandra to use effectively. With the stock extended and a silencer fitted to the muzzle, she could eliminate a target at a similar range as with the auto-rifle. Plus, it used pistol-sized ammunition, which meant she could carry more rounds without increasing the weight of her load. Even better, the Badger's carrying strap included a pouch for extra magazines.

Seandra knew something was up in the rest of the ship. The other crew who were practicing left as a group, leaving her alone in the firing range. She could hear the ship straining. Dull thuds went off at random times. The noise reminded her of the sounds on the hull when *Mother Courage* went up against the *Durable*. It didn't feel like an industrial process. It felt like a fight.

Sari confirmed it when she grabbed Seandra from behind,

ruining her shot. "Sanda! Come on. We're going to work. Bring your Badger."

"What? What are we doing?"

"Mitchel Pilar! Remember him?"

Seandra's guts tumbled and whirled as she remembered trying to talk Mitchel down from the ledge only to watch him sail off on his own destructive adventure. "I *do* remember him."

"We're boarding his ship to ruin his day. You coming?"

"Foking A!" Seandra grabbed the Badger.

They swung by the armory to load up on real ammunition, then she followed Sari to the mustering point. As they jogged, she tried to pull the weapon's carrying harness around herself. She was the wrong shape for it—too short and too wide in the wrong places. After adjusting it as best she could, she clipped the three empty magazines to the carry strap, stuffed two boxes of rounds in her pockets and hustled to keep up with the tall girl.

They debarked from the lift onto the hangar deck, and Seandra had no trouble picking Commander Mench's Meklife drone out from the growing crowd around the largest of the shuttles.

"Commander! Request permission to join the mission," she called out.

"Seandra Sley. You're not part of this detail," Meklife observed. "We have everyone we need."

"I need… I need to be here. I need to kill that goon. That Mitchel Pilar."

"We will tend to it."

"No!" She ducked around him and stood squarely in his path. She inhaled deeply to slow her heart rate and pressed forward. "I had the chance to kill him myself weeks ago. I didn't. I didn't know how dangerous he was. Well, I know it now. I want to make it right."

Meklife flexed his hands. For a moment she wondered if he was planning on flinging her across the deck. She hoped not.

"Seandra, killing a man makes nothing right."

"Killing *this* man will make it right for *me*. He has a soul. His friends, his captain, they were all morons. Just goons following the path of least resistance. But Mitchel could have done anything with his life, and he chose to be a marauding tool. He's the one who was running that ship for months. Without him they never would have gotten as far as they did. I just need to see it finished. Please."

Meklife hesitated but finally acceded. "Time is wasting. Srahamari, you look after her."

Sari nodded. "Yes, sir! I'll take care of her."

"Very well. We'll board shortly. Take this comm, Seandra. Srahamari can show you the setup. Do not speak on the general channel unless spoken to. You'll want to load those magazines quickly."

Seandra's comm was more advanced than the one she'd seen her mother wear at work. This one fitted into her ear but had a flexible cable that ended in an eyepiece. Once activated, the eyepiece showed her a graphic layout of the *Emerald Queen*'s hangar. She could select targets with eye blinks and see distances to any object she selected. "This is so cool!"

"Meh. I don't like it. But I need to hear orders, so I'll wear it," Sari said. She fitted her own comm like a pro and adjusted Seandra's a bit. "How's that?"

"Better, thanks."

The ground assault force was easy to pick out from the other hangar deck crew. Four Idolons stood in the back of the crowd. Maesy's pink hair stood out, and she'd brought several of her staff with her—all Lynaedans based on their eyes and limbs. What looked like Sari's entire tribe of Scorpions were there in their desert garb, and half a dozen of each of the cat-like Scoutmeks and spherical Blastermeks attended as well, sensor turrets swinging to focus on Meklife as he stepped to the drop shuttle's hatchway.

A three-dimensional schematic of a space vessel popped up in Seandra's feed. "The plan is relatively simple," Meklife was saying. "Three of the Idolons will drop from the deployment bay and land on the hull of the tender, to engage and disable the external weapon turrets with their E-ARC hand weapons. The rest of us will mate the shuttle's airlock to this auxiliary port at the rear of the ship and board their engineering deck. The remaining Idolon will secure the area along with the Scoutmeks and Blastermeks. Maesy's engineers will take control of the ship's functions, including filling the cargo deck and work bay with breathable air. That done, we will use this bank of lifts to secure each deck one by one until we reach the flight deck at the top. That's the crew quarters as well. We expect that's where the crew will make their last stand. Questions?" There were none. "Our orders are to scrub that vessel clean. No one walks out. If you have a shot, take it. Let's board."

The Scorpions shouted a cheer in their own language, their voices unified in purpose. Seandra checked her weapon. The Badger felt comfortable in her grip as she slapped a new magazine into the feed and worked the action to load a round. She remembered to engage the safety and dimly wondered when she would need to take it off. She'd figure it out.

Loading the magazines from the box was simple for her. She'd had plenty of practice with that and felt sure she'd never have to fire the weapon at all. Mitchel would be dead by the time she found him, the target of so many other fighters. She just wanted to see his corpse. To know that he really was no longer a threat to anyone.

The Tarans took seats in a passenger compartment while the mechs arranged themselves according to size and deployment order. The Idolons gathered at the rear while the others occupied their own section. Seandra couldn't take her eyes off the cat-like Scoutmeks and reached out to pet one. The machine hissed at her and she pulled her arm back.

"It's a drone, not a creature," Meklife told her via comm. "Don't get in its way."

Seandra nodded excitedly. *Right. Not a cat.* "Yes sir."

—

The shuttle lifted off and flew to its destination in only a few minutes. Near the end of the voyage, the Idolons stepped to the rear compartment and sealed the blast doors. A change in pressure and a vibration in the deck signaled their departure from the shuttle. Mating the shuttle's airlock to the auxiliary hatch on the *Durable* took longer. Finally, there was a clang of metal against metal, the doors opened, and the drones proceeded out the lock.

Seandra released her harness along with the other Taran passengers and checked her weapon. All she was going to do was follow along and check every corpse to make sure that Mitchel was dead.

The engineering deck was dark and silent except for the thrumming of machinery. A shot rang out, then another, and Sari pulled her down, pushing her against a bulkhead. After a moment, she heard muffled cries and the hiss of the cat-like drones. The shooters were down for the count. The Lynaedan drones were horrifyingly efficient.

A woman's voice spoke into her comm. "Engineering deck secure."

Meklife's voice spoke next. "Explosions on the engineering deck would be a bad idea. Scorpions, advance."

A quartet of Sari's people filed into one lift, then the other. One by one, the lift cars rose and descended again. Eventually, only she and Sari were left along with the drones and engineering crew.

Maesy spoke again. "We've got the outer bay doors secured. Filling the work bay with air now."

"Acknowledged," Meklife said.

A new voice commented on the channel. "Fuel and power deck is secure. No targets."

"Cargo deck. One target... Target is down. Cargo deck is clear. Negative ID on target, it's not him. Moving to the transfer deck."

A few minutes later a new male voice said, "Transfer deck is clear. No targets."

Mench broadcast again. Seandra thought he sounded annoyed. "That leaves the main deck. Move the drones into the lifts and stand by to engage."

Seandra unfolded herself from the bulkhead and moved to watch the action. The Blastermeks were simple rolling spheres but they apparently also included grav lifters in their design. Their outer plates unfolded and opened allowing six of the machines to climb over each other to gain access to the lift car. The Scoutmeks were able to move like beasts and climbed on top of each other like a huddle of giant metal kittens. The doors closed and the lifts rose again.

No noise came over the comms but the wait for results was interminable. Seandra found herself getting more anxious by the minute and paced to calm herself down. Finally, she heard a mechanical voice report. "Main deck, seven targets. Targets are all down. Main deck is secure."

Mench asked the big question. "Does anyone have eyes on Mitchel?" A long pause followed. "Widen the search, find the captain."

She knew what Mitchel was likely to do: run away. He'd sacrificed his captain to save his skin, and he'd only showed up here because he thought he could win a quick and dirty victory. Now that events were going against him, he was going to run. That meant getting off the ship. How would he do that?

Seandra used her comm's eyepiece to drill down through the floor plans of each deck. She could see only two ways off the *Durable*. The work bay could always open to space, but Maesy and her people held that closed. The Lynaedans and Scorpions were watching the access hatch they'd all come through, so he'd avoid that, too. That left...

There! There was a bank of life pods on the cargo deck. She couldn't track where the *Emerald Queen*'s people were, but she could see a clear path to her objective. Frankly, she'd been ordered not to speak on comms until spoken to. That suited her just fine.

Intellectually, she knew she should wait for help, but Seandra was gripped by a fury she'd never imagined before. The thought of Mitchel escaping justice offended her. She had the chance to fix her mistake.

She sought out the pink-haired engineer, who worked on the main console. "Maesy!"

"Miss Sley. Make it fast, I'm busy with this."

"The life pod circuits. Where are they?"

"Why do you need to know?"

"If we missed anyone, they'll go there to escape, right? Let's fix that."

"All right." Maesy flicked her hands and launched a network of fine wires into a port in the console and closed her eyes. On the display, schematics flew by until she found the one she wanted. "Those are the life pod bays. There are two of them on opposite sides of the deck with three pods each. You see?"

"I see."

"Okay. That's a close-up view of the pod itself. They're self-contained, so I can't kill them from here. But see that panel down near the floor? The cover has latches here and here. Pop it off and pull this power coupling. It'll deactivate the pod instantly. Got it?"

"Got it."

"Good luck. Do not go up there by yourself, it's... Seandra! Fok!"

Ignoring the warning, Seandra took the lift up to the cargo deck. After a moment, she decided she should at least tell her partner where she was.

Except... She opened a private channel to Sari. "Sari! I'm checking the cargo deck. Life pods are there. Come find me."

"What? Sanda? Wait!" Sari hissed.

The lift opened and Seandra stepped out onto a darkened platform. A substantial amount of various goods had been sorted and stacked into discrete piles, which made the deck look like a maze. So many places to hide and shoot from. She flipped through her eyepiece's setting and found one that showed body heat. There was nothing nearby, and she advanced.

She remembered her 'basic training' from playing Star Patrol. Keep low, stick to positions of cover. Hug the wall. She crept from one position to another and came to the set of bay doors that her mother had taught her to recognize: life pods.

She palmed the entry plate and ducked inside.

She whirled as she checked her danger spaces. No bodies, no pirates, no Mitchel. Which meant he'd either not arrived yet or was hiding elsewhere.

She slung her badger and got to work, repeating the process of popping the maintenance plate and disconnecting the power coupling on each pod as Maesy had shown her. When the last was disabled, she ducked out of the bay and closed the doors behind her.

Logically, if Mitchel was here—if she'd been right in her judgement—he'd be in the other bay. All right, then. Time to set things right.

She held her breath, squatting behind cover, taking a moment to scan, and hustling to the next point. Again and again. She dropped against one pile that rattled as she brushed against it. It took a moment for her to realize it was made of personal items. Clothing, watches, shoes. Wallets. Purses. Jackets, pants. Children's toys.

She pushed the growing horror down into her feet and kept going. Her hips and thigh muscles ached badly by the time she arrived at the other pod bay. This time when she opened the door, she got right to work, bending down to disable first one pod, then the next. She'd just pried the cover off the third when she heard a sharp click behind her.

"Step away from the pod, pal."

Seandra snarled a curse brought up the Badger and pulled the trigger. Click. Click click, click. Then she remembered that she'd engaged the safety.

She moved to fix her error but Mitchel moved to fix his mistake, as well.

He took two steps toward her and threw a roundhouse kick, which connected with her gut. She flew backward into the bulkhead, her stomach exploding with pain and her head feeling like her guts were coming out of her mouth. She couldn't catch her breath. Couldn't stand. Couldn't even see.

Mitchel regarded her for a moment, obviously confused by the new circumstances. "Kind of short for a space marine, aren't you?"

"You don't remember me," she coughed.

"Should I?"

"You'd better. I shot your friend in the ass."

"Ah, I do remember you. Sera. No, Seandra! Little girl with a great big voice. Still playing with guns. There's a bad habit." Mitchel moved to inspect the open cover. He snickered. "I see what you did. Good move. But it's easy to fix. There." The pod lit up as the internal computer brought it online. "Go back upstairs, Seandra."

"Stay away from that pod, Mitchel," she snarled.

"Are you going to shoot me in the ass, too?" he sneered, and began pulling relays. Each one brought the pod a little closer to launch status.

"I mean it, Mitchel. Stop," she said in a hoarse voice. Why was he testing her like this?

Mitchel pulled the final relay and the pod's canopy popped open. The red bank of lights turned blue and the pod rotated into launch position. "I don't have time for this."

"Stand down!" she yelled.

"You're not going to kill me, Seandra. We both know that. You couldn't kill Sebbi, either. Your little pea shooter could have put a hole in his brain, but you didn't use it that way. You're not a killer. Just really pissed off. That, I can understand. Now, stand back, this thing makes a hell of a racket when it launches."

She brought the Badger into the crook of her arm and used

her thumb to release the safety. "What about those people on that trade ship? The ones who just wouldn't lie down and let you take their livelihood away from them?"

"That was an unfortunate accident."

A man with a gun kills by accident, by impulse.

She flipped the selector to full automatic. "Seriously? That's your excuse?"

"Not an excuse. They made their choice. You made your choice. Now, I am making *my* choice. See you on the flip side, little girl."

I aim with my heart. I kill with my mind.

"I'm short. Not *little*," she said.

Her mind engaged in perfect clarity, she sprayed the contents of the magazine into the open pod. The impacts sprayed shrapnel all over the tiny room, an explosion from the life pod catching Mitchel full in the chest and arms. Ironically, his body shielded her from the worst of it but she caught flak in her face and on her legs. She turned away in surprise and alarm, swiping at the wet streak from her cheeks and chin.

She turned back to see that Mitchel wasn't down but he was badly hurt. He used the lip of the pod to hold himself upright and struggled to stand. She saw a gaping wound on his thigh and realized he was trapped. She tapped her comm. "I have eyes on Mitchel. He's in the—"

She never finished the sentence, but neither did she need to. She felt a comforting presence nearby. A firm hand pulled her to the side.

Sari stepped into the space she'd vacated and pulled metal discs from her pocket and sent them into Mitchel's head. Eyes. Mouth. Nose. He dropped, his face a ruined mess. But he was still breathing.

Seandra checked her magazine. Two rounds left. She

switched back to single shot and put one round in Mitchel's heart and another in his head.

Mitchel twitched, sputtered, and died.

Seandra let the Badger swing by its strap and found she couldn't stop shaking. Her hands were somehow both cold and damp.

Sari put her hand on her shoulder, gripping it tightly. "First time you kill someone? For real?"

"Uh. Yeah. Yes. First time."

Sari turned her by the shoulder until they faced each other, then she dropped her head until their foreheads touched. She put her hands on the shorter girl's shoulders and said, "You are my eyes, Sanda."

Seandra reached for Sari's shoulders and knotted her fingers in the fabric of the tall girl's robes. "You are my eyes, Sari," she choked. She let out a few deep sobs and forced herself back to a semblance of control. Instead, she tapped her comm. "Seandra to Commander Mench."

"This is Mench. Why are you on this line, Seandra?"

"Commander, I have eyes on Mitchel Pilar. He's dead. ID confirmed."

"Acknowledged. Return to the shuttle, Seandra."

"Yes, sir."

— — —

Lee turned to Armin in the front seats of their shuttle. "That is *not* what I expected to hear over the comm chatter."

"It was a mistake to let them come along, Lee. That sweet family is never going to be the same after this."

"Protecting their feelings isn't our job, Armin. It's not our place to question how Karmen raises her kids."

"But throwing in with pirates, seriously?"

Lee watched on the display as a shuttle returned from the cylindrical pirate ship to the *Emerald Queen*'s hangar. "Sometimes, you need to look in the shadows to find the dark creatures they conceal. We might not agree with the path Karmen is taking, but she's shining a light into those corners. It's our job to spot the vermin that come scurrying out."

Armin tapped the screen at his workstation. "Well, we've got a new batch of data to package. Let's write up the report."

— — —

Karmen waited on the hangar deck and watched with narrowed eyes as the returning assault shuttle lowered itself into an empty berth. The Lynaedan mechs disembarked from the rear ramp, but the people departed through the forward gangway.

Lom Mench stepped out of the hatch followed by one of the Valdan security crew and Seandra. When she spotted her daughter, she thanked the stars the girl was safe and then ran to intercept Lom. "Commander Mench! I have a problem with you taking my daughter on your mission."

Meklife stopped. "She volunteered and I accepted her. Why is that a problem?"

Karmen took in her daughter's appearance with a look of horror. The girl was encrusted with blood, burns, and who knew what else. Even her hair was singed. And where had she gotten that submachine gun? *She's ruined!*

She couldn't help herself, pulling the girl to her in a fierce hug. "Seandra, what did you do?" Karmen asked in a quiet voice.

"I fixed my mistake."

"You what?"

Seandra squirmed out of her mother's embrace, stepped back and worked the action on the Badger to eject a spent casing. "I should have killed him weeks ago. That's the last time I try to save a thug's life. If they point a gun at me or you or anyone, they're finished."

Sari pulled her hood down and laid it flat across her back. The Valdan girl had eyes that were so dark they were nearly black and had woven her hair into tight braids, wrapped around the top of her head. A warrior's braid.

She met Karmen's eyes with all the pride in the universe. "I am Srahamari. Sanda is my eyes."

"That's not her name," Karmen whispered.

Sari dropped her head to Karmen and walked off.

Meklife patted Seandra on the shoulder. "Well done, young soldier. Carry on."

"This isn't behavior we need to excuse or encourage," Karmen said, glaring at the Lynaedan.

"Karmen, what part of the captain's order to 'scrub that ship clean' did you not understand? I've worked with veterans who didn't show as much initiative or calculation as Seandra displayed. The girl did extremely well by any standard. Excuse me, I must finish my rounds and write my after-action report."

Seandra cleared her throat. "Mom. Was there anything else?"

"No. But go to the infirmary and take care of those wounds… and clean the gun before you return it to the armory."

"Sure. Good night."

What just happened? Karmen wasn't sure. Weeks ago, she'd ordered Kozu and Tolri to kill Mitchel's partner and they'd done it. Seandra herself had shot the man. Why was this any different?

Because this time, it wasn't my idea. She was following Aura's orders.

Karmen considered calling the entire operation off. She shouldn't be here, and she shouldn't have allowed any member of her family to follow her down this rabbit hole—especially her two youngest children. But they were here now, and they were already in too deep. Their quiet, predictable life on Greengard was a distant memory. They were in it for the duration. Even now, her family depended on her to keep them together; she couldn't lock herself in her cabin and mope. She had her own after-action report to create and deliver.

Her heart lurched. Just another day on the *Emerald Queen*.

33

SPOILS OF WAR

DAVEED SLEY WAS finding out firsthand just how different fieldwork could be from academic life. For two days, the *Emerald Queen* undertook a grand salvage mission in Tarkus space. He'd been allowed to roam the hangar deck and observe the Lynaedans employ a variety of shuttles and drones to salvage parts and even haul derelict hulls into the pirate ship's cavernous hangar bays for storage. The operation was fascinating, and he learned a lot, but the experience remained unsatisfying.

Still, he had to do something with his time. It was either observe and pretend to be productive or lock himself in his cabin and have the crew see that he truly was a fifth wheel. He'd brought out Kaia's GravX plan for fun as he waited to see what great event next overtook the *Emerald Queen*. A pounding on the door of his cabin broke his concentration. Colin rushed in, out of breath. "You have got to come see this!"

"See what? What have I missed?"

"They unloaded the last of the loot from the *Durable*'s cargo bay." Colin waved his arms and flapped his jaw but couldn't make himself understood. "It's… there's… Come see this shite!" the boy finally gasped.

"Lead the way, my boy."

They met Tabor on one of the *Queen*'s giant cargo decks, who gave Daveed a long look before saying. "Professor Sley. Have you finally come into the field?"

Daveed shrugged. "Colin insisted, and I have no classes to teach today."

"I see. Well then, let's give you the grand tour. It's impressive, even to me."

Tabor led them to a storage room and showed them a warehouse full of cases, boxes, and bags, all set up on racks for storage.

"I never would have thought salvage crews could work this quickly," Daveed breathed, his eyes wide with awe.

"Blame the Lynaedans," Tabor said. "They have a squadron of salvage drones aboard. Ingenious contraptions, really. They go in, cut apart the ship's hull and modules, then separate out the cargo and send those here. The heavy components go to the engineering deck and get recycled into whatever they need. All this stuff? The combined holds of nineteen pirate ships. It'll take a week to inventory everything." He opened one case, gasped, and pulled out a bottle of golden liquid. "Ooooo, be still my heart!"

"What is it?" Colin asked.

Tabor held the bottle the way a new father would cradle his infant. "This, my young apprentice, is Mountain Bluff fifty-five-year-old single-malt whiskey from the Startory distillery on Tararia. It's some of the most amazing distilled spirits the universe ever saw fit to put on shelves in the most exclusive of shops."

"How amazing is that?"

Tabor was drooling, caressing the bottle. "Three hundred thousand credits per liter bottle amazing. Four or five times that much on the black market. And we have at *least* ten cases of it here."

"It's not *all* liquor, is it?" Daveed asked.

The question jolted Tabor out of his fantasy, and he placed the bottle gently on an empty shelf before answering. "No. We haven't counted everything yet, but we opened up a representative sample. The cash boxes all had about half a million worth of credit chips in standard banking rolls in them. One hundred boxes gives us fifty million in coin. That group of boxes over there is contraband: drugs, rare food items, gems, and jewelry. I've no idea what that stuff is worth, except it's a lot. But I recognize the markings on those big cases in the back there. Weapons and military-grade equipment. Those will be worth tens of millions to the right people. I haven't even looked at the memory cores yet. We have enough capital in this haul to run this starship's operations and crew for a decade."

"Or plow it all into expanding operations. With this, we could turn our little pirate gang into a sector-wide empire," Colin mused. "We could even convert it to real standard credits and start our own investment company. That has real appeal."

The enormity of what they had in this one room began to dawn on Daveed. Only on the Inner Worlds was money a significant arbiter of value. The further out you traveled, the less use there was for cash and the real wealth of *things* began to make itself felt. "Stars," Daveed breathed. "Where was it all going? Where did it all come from?"

"Anywhere and everywhere," Tabor said. "I'd guess this was the result of a few very big jobs or a lot of small ones. Didn't you folks search that ship last time you dealt with them?"

Colin shook his head. "We did not. The Agent let them go."

"Ah. TSS professionalism in action. And they wonder why people out here don't trust them?" Tabor sniffed.

"We need to turn this into money we can actually use, though," Colin continued.

"That's my job," Tabor said.

Colin raised his hands. "No, that's *my* job. Your job is to run supplies for the ship. Stick to that for now. I'll come up with an angle for this batch, and then we'll put our heads together to figure out a better way forward."

"As you wish, Lord Covrani," Tabor sneered and left them alone.

Colin opened one of the cash boxes and dug his hands into the rolled stacks of credit chips. "Not bad for one day of hard work is it?" he asked. "Where should we start, Daveed? It's not enough for a whole GravX team made of the best players in the major leagues. But it'll get Kaia started, for sure. We can set up a brand, build a franchise, hire talent scouts, find a law firm who won't bleed us dry."

"Colin, it's *blood money*," Daveed insisted. "How many murders, ransoms, and robberies does it represent? How many people's lives were destroyed to make this collection possible?"

"Not my people, not my problem." He dropped the rolls of coins with a thud. "What's more important, where the money came from or what's done with it? We're pirates now. We want, we take. Right?"

Daveed grunted in disgust. "Stars, you have to make it about that, don't you?"

"It *is* about that. You think my family struck it rich at a casino one day? No. We got our money the old-fashioned way.

We took it from the people who had it. This is an investment in the business your daughter and I want to create. It's a door leading to everything I want to give her. And not a lousy fifty thousand credits like my mother offered. This is a *real* payday earned in full by eliminating *real* pirates. It doesn't get more ethical than that."

"I can't see it that way," Daveed insisted. "I doubt Kaia will, either. Karmen certainly won't."

Colin clapped his hands together, clearly becoming more impatient by the second. "All right, I'll make a deal with you. You convince Aura to give it all to charity and I'll go with that. Her ship, her decision. Can you sell that idea to her? To Mench? Take your time and think about it. I have nowhere to be."

Daveed huffed out his breath but gave him a single nod. He had to admit Colin's ideals were probably far closer to the mindset that Aura and her crew made use of than his own. It still irked him. "All right. We have it. Now what? We can't exactly take it to a local bank."

"In a way, we can. I'd like to send a bit of it to Kaia. In her last call, she said she was starting her trade route up the Autonomous Main toward Gallos. One of these cash boxes would open up a lot of high-quality cargoes."

"I suppose I could live with that."

"More importantly, we need a way to launder it through various channels, then plunk it into a legit investment company. Luckily, I have someone who might jump at the opportunity." Colin pulled out his handheld and dialed a number. "Hi, may I speak to Emily Govrin please?"

"This is Emily Govrin."

"Emily! Hi, this is Colin Covrani. I trust you're doing well."

"No trust between us at all, Colin. I'm between jobs and it's your fault."

"What did I do? Why did you leave?"

"I was fired, because you tried to pull a fast one and I confronted your mother and still got fired for—get this—an inefficient use of corporate time. What do you want?"

"Emily… listen, I want to apologize for making problems for you. All I'm asking for is a chance to make it up to you."

"How?"

"Emily, have you ever wanted to run your own investment firm? I mean you have all the licenses and know people who know people, right? Investment advisors, traders, brokers, lawyers…"

"Don't waste my time, kid. If you have a point, make it now."

Colin snapped an image of the open cash box then sent it to her. He followed up with an image of the entire storeroom. After a few moments she responded with a half-laugh, half-shout and a noise of surprise Daveed was sure she couldn't make twice. "What the… who… how… *Colin, what did you do*?"

"We threw a pirate ship against a wall, and this spilled out of its shell. I figure there's something like fifty million in credit chips alone. I have no idea how much the contraband is worth, but I'd bet it's substantial to the right buyers. The digital currency is something I have no experience with, but you might."

"What do you want me to do with this information?" Colin kept his mouth shut and let her put it together. "Oh. Oh! Shite! I don't… I mean, I couldn't…"

"You could. You can. Please. Big things are in motion. I need friends, and I really want you to be my friend, Emily. Come on, we got off on such good footing, too."

A too-long moment of hesitation made him wonder if she'd simply ended the call. Finally, she said, "Let me make a few inquiries. I think it would go without saying that if this is a setup, I'll throw you and all your friends under any bus I can find to save my ass. I'm not going to a prison planet. And we're not friends, so stop calling me by my first name. Do we understand each other?"

"We do, Miss Govrin."

"I'll put the paperwork together and send you instructions on how to proceed in a day or so. Tell no one about this until the transfer mechanisms are in place. Get me?"

"Got you."

"Good. I'll be in touch, Mr. Covrani. This time, answer your bomaxed handheld when I call you." She cut the call.

Tabor hefted another cash box onto the counter and rolled his eyes. "Such drama."

"I can understand her point, though," Daveed said. "It worries me mightily that you boys can't. There are forces in motion here that defy containment."

"What forces?" Colin asked.

"My boy, this is pirate treasure."

"Yes! That's why it's valuable."

"And we have all the value," Tabor added.

A familiar impatience bubbled up from Daveed's core. It was like trying to talk sense into a grad student who was utterly certain that he was the smartest person in the room. Those conversations never ended well. "Colin, did it occur to you that everything in this gargantuan pile of stuff was destined to go somewhere? Probably to other criminals. Mobsters, underworld gangs, syndicates. They are going to miss those deliveries when their cargoes fail to arrive. They will be extremely unhappy about that. I promise, they will come looking for their loot. I think—"

Tabor slammed the cash box shut. "Daveed, no one cares what you think. I do this for a living." He pulled the bottle of the expensive liquor off the shelf and thrust it at the academic. "Here you go, old man. Take a bottle of the truly good shite and go on a bender. Lock yourself in your cabin, read some philosophy books or whatever turns you on. While you're doing that, Colin and I will be earning our share of this particular payday. Because that's *our* job on this ship. What, exactly, is yours? 'Senior Morality Officer'?"

Daveed turned to glare at Colin, who turned away and scowled at the cargo. "All right, then. Thank you, boys, for clarifying just how much I mean to this effort. I'll try to refrain from saying 'I told you so' when you finally crash and burn."

"Envy stings, doesn't it, Professor?" Tabor sneered.

"I don't envy you a bomaxed thing, you pontificating twit. Enjoy your new wealth, because you're going to find it can vanish as easily as it appeared."

"Trust me, we'll be fine."

"When your luck runs out, I doubt you'll be able to trust *anyone*," Daveed growled. He stabbed Colin with his finger. "And you. You *know* better. I wish my daughter did." Daveed grabbed the bottle out of Tabor's hands and stormed out of the suite.

— — —

Karmen couldn't get the image of Seandra's wounds out of her head. Six months ago, she'd been a teenager besotted with fantasies of boys and married wealth. Karmen wasn't sure who this new person was, but she had a sinking sensation whenever she thought about it. *What have I done? And how do I fix it?*

Her mind whirled as she tried to figure out how a doctor's appointment months ago had led to this. There were twists and turns and a government edict turning her world upside down as the TSS reached out to Greengard and snatched her back into its iron grip.

She passed the rest of her duty shift in a daze, wandering between compartments, making all the correct noises, receiving updates from department heads and never staying too long in any one place. She was afraid if she did, she might burst into tears, and that would be the end of her command authority. First officers didn't cry. Not in public, anyway.

The main room of her cabin was dark when she returned from work. She turned on the light and jumped when she saw Daveed sitting on the sofa. An open bottle of liquor and a glass sat before him on the low table. The bottle had been full once but not anymore. Daveed had drunk deep.

"Stop right there, First Officer Sley," he snarled. His tone disturbed her. She'd never seen Daveed with a scowl as deep as the one he now wore. Her husband was a kind man, a gentle man, an educator, a fundamentally *happy* man. This guy was a stranger. An angry, troubled stranger.

"What happened?" she probed.

"What happened? Colin and Tabor showed me the recovered bounty from the *Durable*. I gave them a strong opinion about their plans for it and was dismissed out of hand. Tabor accused me of being a scolding philosopher, handed me a bottle—this bottle—and sent me on my way. Then, our future son-in-law turned his back on me when I needed his support. Seems he's embraced the pirate lifestyle, and he appears intent on dragging our daughter into it, as well. I figured I could either break their arms and get Meklife on my case, or I could feel sorry for myself in private. Care for a drink? This is some amazing shite. One bottle is worth enough to set our family up for retirement on Greengard." He took a swig from the bottle to punctuate his monologue. "Bomax this ship to the bottom of a black hole. To the center of a blue star. Bomax Aura, and bomax her crew, and bomax you for following her like a puppy. Bomax me for agreeing to follow you!"

"Oh, shite," Karmen muttered. She'd never seen him like this. She was at a loss as to how to proceed. "May I sit with you?"

"Sit there," he said, pointing to an easy chair opposite the narrow table. "I want to see your face, and I don't think I can turn my head right now. Not and have it stay on my neck."

She stepped around the table and lowered herself into the chair, suddenly afraid for the first time in their relationship. Daveed had never intimidated her, but this wasn't exactly Daveed. She didn't fear him, but she felt afraid for him. Daveed didn't always express emotions well and she could see the deep dark hole he was boring through his soul right now. Deep enough to fall into. Another new feeling.

He held the bottle in his arms like a stuffed toy. "I suck as a parent. The evidence is clear and abundant. My youngest is crawling through conduits in the engine room. My younger daughter is a foot soldier. My older daughter is a budding criminal mastermind, and my oldest is training to be a security goon for one of the richest families in the galaxy. Meanwhile, my wife is a pirate queen's first officer. I'm stuck in the hinterlands of this great leaky starship, useless, unneeded, and in everyone's way. This isn't what I signed up for when I agreed to follow you on this adventure."

The flood of self-pity stirred a reaction in her: now she was angry. "What did you sign up for, then? The glory? The money?"

He turned his eyes on her and grinned without a trace of warmth or humor. "The smiles."

"What?"

"We were all so pleased to see you happy. Especially Kaia. Before you left Greengard, your moods swung between surly and mean, depending on what kind of a vision day you were experiencing. Sometimes you surprised us by being congenial or satisfied, but you were rarely *happy*. We were terrified that demanding you stay home and allow the young men to bring Mother Carnage to justice would send you down a rabbit hole of depression and despair."

"My time in the service was done. I gave that up to be with you," she maintained.

"That's what you told yourself. You might even believe it. The truth is that you were made to give it up. First by the TSS and then by your doctor. Domesticity is something you trained yourself to deal with but it was never your first choice. You're too addicted to danger to truly make that transition. So, you keep up your relationships with your veteran friends and that's fine. But I'm afraid the kids and I are becoming soldiers just to maintain a relationship with you."

She glared at him even as she recognized the kernel of truth behind his words. "You can't put all that on my shoulders."

"It's on mine, as well. I knew who you were when we met. I wanted you anyway."

"Dav, you're my rock. You're the one person in the universe I know I can rely on. I'm not sorry we're together. Are you?" she asked in a small voice.

"You know better than to ask."

"Even out here?"

"Especially out here," he grunted and took a swig from the bottle. "I don't feel very indispensable right now. I stay back, I let the crew do their tasks. I help out if I'm asked, but mostly I just watch and listen. Tabor is actually teaching Colin how to launder money. Colin just got a former money manager involved, too, and plans on funding Kaia's trade route with some of the proceeds. Worse, Seandra insisted on tagging along with the Scorpions to clear out the *Durable*."

"I know that part. I got there in time to watch her wiping the blood off her hands and slinging her submachine gun like it was the most natural thing in the world. Mench put his arm around her and told her she's a good soldier. How am I supposed to compete with that, Dav? How do we fix that?"

"We don't. It's who she's becoming. You can't move in with a platoon of soldiers and not expect some of their habits to rub off."

"So, parenting fail in every dimension," she concluded.

"Or, it's a testament to how well we taught them. They've completely adapted to the situation they find themselves in. You want to blame someone, blame us."

"I do."

He poured another drink and slopped a bit of it over the side of the glass. "I like Lee, but I start to understand why so many of these people hate the TSS. They stay in their ivory tower and only come out when events become so dire they can't ignore it anymore."

"It wasn't always like that."

"But it is now. It's the world we live in. I don't see a way out. So, if you need me to be your rock, I'll be here for it. But I'm not willing to be a bystander. Find me a uniform and a job to do. And not a phony made-up job and rank, I want to be part of the crew. If my children are going into battle, then I will support them. That's final."

"I can't do that…"

"Well, then get your ass on a shuttle and we'll all go back to Greengard. We're not leaving you here."

"This isn't what I wanted. But I can't walk away from it."

"And I can't walk away from you and the kids, so I guess we're stuck with Mother foking Carnage. Let's hope there's time to sort a few things out while we gear up to deal with whatever comes next. Or else this is going to end up being a very bloody vacation."

— — —

Eventually, Daveed nodded off. Karmen closed the bottle and put it in a cabinet, then covered him with a blanket. *Oh, Daveed, I'll find a way to make this right.*

Steeling herself, she went to find her future son-in-law. He was in Tabor's suite of offices, a nexus on the same deck as the Command Center. She kicked the door open and screamed, "Laski and Covrani! In my office, now!"

"You don't have an office. Anyway, we're busy!" Tabor sang.

She'd had her fill of Tabor Laski for a lifetime. Rage seeped from every pore and filled every molecule in her body. She tore through the office and threw Tabor's handheld against the wall, hucked Colin's tablet across the desk, and then flipped the desk over to their combined expressions of terror. She grabbed both of them by their collars and slammed them into the nearest wall. Her grip was like iron and neither of the men had any chance of escape.

"Let's discuss your futures. I'm very foking disappointed in you both."

"I don't work for you," Tabor whined.

She slammed Tabor's face into the wall. A red smear adorned the spot where his nose smashed against it. "Tabor, I had you pegged the moment I first saw you. You're an entitled, self-indulgent twerp. The only thing greater than your ignorance is your ego. You know a few tricks, you made more money than you thought existed, and now you are a god among men. I ran with hordes of boys far younger than you in the Militia every day. The most contemptable and stupid of them made better men than you could ever hope to be."

"Go fly a kite, ma'am," Tabor groaned.

Karmen bashed his head into the wall again for emphasis. It felt *good*. "Shut up, you toad! And you, Colin—I had higher hopes for you. Given the chance to listen to anyone on this ship, you decide to listen to *this* idiot?"

"He's my boss," Colin murmured.

"Not the point! You sat at my dinner table and watched Kaia slap a pistol together in twelve seconds. You still thought *this* hobgoblin was worth listening to instead of her. Do you have anything to say in your defense?"

Colin was near tears. "We were brainstorming. Daveed interrupted and we got a little excited," Colin argued.

Tabor struggled to move his head away from the wall. "We were nice about it. It was the best hooch in the galaxy."

Karmen squeezed tighter. "That man has more brains and intelligence in his left foot than both you cretins have in your entire bodies combined. When he tells you that something is a bad idea—even if you think he's wrong—you do *not* give him a bottle and tell him to go fok himself. You look him in the eye and you say 'Thank you sir, for your honest comments. I will consider them closely.' Say it."

"Drop dead, you harpy," Tabor countered.

Karmen slammed his head against the bulkhead again.

"Say it!"

"Thank you, sir, for your honest comments. I will consider them closely," Tabor moaned.

"Now you say it, Mister GravX, or I will gut you like a fish and tell Kaia you had a tragic accident in the airlock," she ordered hotly in Colin's ear.

"My mother will—"

"Your mother will thank me for eliminating her greatest embarrassment once and for all!" Karmen shouted. "Say it!"

"Thank you, sir, for your honest comments. I will consider them closely," Colin sputtered.

Karmen released the two men and watched with no small satisfaction as they sank to the deck, holding their heads and averting their gazes. "I'm glad we had the opportunity to set the record straight. But in case you two gits don't have anything inside your heads to use for comprehension, I'll say it plainly: fok with any member of my family, disrespect anyone I call spouse, sibling, or child, and I will crack your heads together until my hands are filled with the sweet goo inside. Do you twits understand me?"

"Yes, ma'am," Tabor slurred.

"Yes, Karmen," Colin agreed.

"You don't get to call me Karmen. I'm not your buddy, I'm your bomaxed mother-in-law to be."

"Yes, Mother Courage!" Colin blurted.

"That's better. Both of you report to the Infirmary for treatment. Off with you."

"This is my office!" Tabor complained.

"Go!"

"Yes, ma'am," Colin squeaked and hustled Tabor away.

She stood there fuming, trying to calm herself down, wondering how long it would take for her mistreatment of

Colin to get back to Kaia. She didn't care. But she did care about ship's rules and regulations. She'd broken a big one. Time to report to the CO for a Captain's Mast.

—

Karmen flexed her hands to wring the stiffness out of the muscles. She hadn't pulled anything so strenuous as what she'd done to Tabor and Colin in years. She stopped at Aura's office, knocked, then entered. "I just beat the crap out of Tabor and threw Colin around hard enough to raise welts."

"That's not current disciplinary policy," Aura said. "What brought out that level of wrath?"

"My husband voiced an unpopular idea about how they were proceeding with the recovered items from the *Durable*. Tabor handed him a bottle of booze and told him to get lost. Which he did, to our cabin. He did himself some real damage."

"Oof. That sounds like Tabor. I'm sorry Colin wasn't smarter than that."

"So am I. I like the boy. But I'm not letting that dynasty brat disrespect my husband. If he thinks that's okay, it's just a matter of time before he starts abusing Kaia. I will execute both of them before I let that happen!"

"It's okay. You dealt with it. Good job."

"No, it's *not* a good job. I never had to punch anyone on the *Triumph* to get my point across."

"Things are a bit looser here in the outworlds," Aura allowed. "These are not soldiers. If you have to smack a few faces to maintain order, that's the price they pay for being out of line. I will absolutely back you up. Just don't throw anyone out an airlock without asking me first. Recruiting is already complicated, and retention is expensive."

Karmen nodded. "No airlocks. I'll remember. If you want to take me to task over this, I'll understand."

"Are you kidding? I need these people to be more afraid of you than they are of Mench. I think you're well on track."

The adrenaline was wearing off. Karmen felt exhausted but couldn't stop shaking. "Stars, this is embarrassing."

"I'm sure. Is there anything else?"

"Just one thing. Daveed wants some type of job aboard the ship. Something useful. Not with a made-up rank or inflated sense of importance. His words, not mine."

"I'm willing. What can he do?"

"He wants to fight."

Aura chuckled. "It's good to want things, but that wasn't my question."

"Honestly, he's a good teacher. He learns new skills very quickly, he's a whiz at administrative mazes that would have me in tears. And he knows how to zoom out to look at a problem from a hundred meters in the air."

Aura leaned back in her chair and thought for a moment. "All right. He's now the Ship's Continuing Education Liaison. There's plenty of space for classrooms aboard, and he can pull materials from whatever sources he needs."

"That sounds like a made-up position. He'll smell that a kilometer away," Karmen protested.

"The title is new because I pulled it out of my hat just now. But the need is real. These folks don't think of themselves as pirates so much as skilled workers. They have occupational certifications, work histories, and a few have advanced degrees. All that paperwork needs to be maintained. Professional certification is a must when your skills are your livelihood. If he likes instructional design, let him help keep my crew's skills sharp, and then improve them. That's a legit full-time job on any campus. Why not here?"

"Yeah… why *not* here?" Karmen agreed.

The intercom beeped for attention. "Colin Covrani to Captain Aura."

The two women shared a look as Aura touched the switch. "This is Aura."

"Captain," Colin said in a subdued voice, "I'd like to recommend we make course for Gallos when we finish up with our salvage operation."

"Is there a particular reason for that, Colin?"

"I've spoken with my connections there. We have an investment firm willing to start helping move our ill-gotten gains into a legitimate network. Also, Kaia Sley will be expecting to meet up there. I have a proposal of my own to make to members of my family."

"Very well. Gallos, it is."

"Thank you, Captain."

"Carry on. Oh, and one more thing, Colin. Is there anything out of the ordinary you'd like to report? Incidents, or issues?"

There was a long pause. "No, ma'am. Nothing to report."

"Very well. Captain out." She closed the connection and winked at Karmen. "You still got it, dearie. If he stays with Kaia, he'll treat her like a queen."

"I hope so. I can't escalate again without killing him."

"I'll teach you how to be subtle. Mention my idea to Daveed."

"I'll talk to him about it. By your leave."

"Carry on, First Officer."

34

FAMILY MATTERS

KAIA SAT ON the bed in Colin's apartment and checked her market trades. The *Mother Courage's* business account was up a substantial sum, which made her happy. But the learning curve had been steep and the mechanism for buying and selling cargo was new to her.

Tolri and Kozu made good security agents, but they were more clueless than she was when it came to buying and selling goods. Their first three days travelling the Autonomous Main, she called Colin for help three times; while he was always patient and clear, she vowed to learn the system of offers and asks on her own.

The three-week voyage from Tarkus to Gallos had run more or less according to their established plan. Yelena Covrani had been truthful when she'd given them access to a business account to make purchases, and Kaia's casino money had given them access to some speculative opportunities. Colin had set up a menu of trades, buying wares at certain ports at particular price ranges and selling them further down the Main. It worked. They made more than they lost to fees and interest. But the last leg of the journey saw a collapse in offers. She'd arrived at Gallos with a cargo hold full of electronics she'd hoped to unload here where the public spaceport was busiest. She'd put up her cargoes for sale to the highest bidder and given a minimum price with month-long expiration dates, then sent her goods to the clearing house, which handled the trades. One by one, buyers met her prices and added credits to *Mother Courage*'s account.

She refreshed her screen to squeal with delight as she found a ridiculously generous offer for a type of medical monitor she'd bought several cases of early in her efforts and hadn't unloaded. A local clinic was probably desperate for new gear. She cancelled her current offer and sold them to the new buyer with an immediate delivery date. She waited, holding her breath until the screen blinked from red to blue. Just like that, she'd quadrupled her profits. All on a crazy stroke of luck.

You can't always count on luck. She needed a lot more practice, but they weren't doing badly.

The door chime broke her out of her focus. She hesitated, then dropped to the floor and padded to the vestibule only to watch the door open to Sergeant Tolri with Kozu in tow.

"You can come in without an invitation?" Kaia wondered aloud.

Tolri led Kozu inside, and he lost no time in walking to every corner of Colin's flat and touching everything. "Of course, it's my job. I'm part of the family security detail. I can go into any apartment in their block. Granted, I usually have to explain why I'm there. I don't just barge in."

Kozu met them in the kitchen. "How's that bed feel? Soft, I'll bet."

"It's wonderful." Kaia smiled. "I spend half my time just lying down in there."

"I don't blame you. The cots on the ship aren't that great. So, Kai, have you fully adapted to squatting in your boyfriend's apartment?" Kozu asked.

She punched him in the shoulder. "It's not squatting, Ko! I was invited. I'm simply using my time to learn everything I can discover about the new environment."

"From the bed?"

She waved the tablet at him and said, "The people who live here *never* have to leave their bedrooms. I'm managing my offers at the spaceport marketplace by remote control. I can have food delivered to the door on a whim. I can even hire professional tailors to come *dress* me if I want. It's insane!"

Kozu shook his head gravely. "Sounds positively decadent to me."

"That's one word for it. But I think I understand why living here damaged Colin's self-worth."

"Oh! I have a theory, too. Let's compare," Tolri said. "You first."

Kaia gathered her thoughts and let fly. "I think some men want things to be easy. They want servants. Every wish should be fulfilled instantly. Colin likes things that are hard. Surround him in comfort and ease, or in an office where he's surrounded by 'yes men'… he goes a little crazy. Put him on a ship where he has to prove his worth every hour of every day and he becomes his own man."

"Interesting idea," Tolri admitted. "But your hypothesis makes you out to be pretty hard yourself. You might want to re-think that part of it."

Oops. Hmm. "Well. It's my theory. What's yours?"

"I think he misses his mommy," Tolri shrugged. "But I

think you're right when you say that Colin needs big rocks to climb. He gets bored way too easily. He really should be running a transport."

"It seems that way to me, too."

"Speaking of which," Tolri said, "Kozu's paperwork finally came in."

"Yeah. I'm leaving for training in a while and Tolri insisted that I come by early to say 'so long'."

Kaia felt the wind knocked out of her. Kozu's enlistment in the TSS Militia had been a thing they'd talked about endlessly, but she didn't think it would ever happen. "Wow. Militia. Survive boot camp and technical training and you'll be a soldier like Mom."

"Only Mom can be a soldier like Mom," he said, "But I'll do my best."

"Make us proud, Ko." She hugged her brother fiercely, squeezing her eyes shut to avoid tearing up. Then she gave a long embrace to Tolri. "Take care of him, Tolri. He's *so* stupid," she rasped.

"He'll be fine. I promise to keep tabs on his progress."

"You better. Good luck, Ko."

"You, too, Kai. Don't get married until I graduate. I want to be able to wear a uniform to the wedding."

"You bet."

They left, and she was alone on Gallos.

—

Kaia checked her remaining trades throughout the afternoon, resisting the urge to bite her nails as her offers expired or were accepted by buyers. Part of her wondered if she was going to have to unload some lots at a loss when her handheld beeped for attention. All she needed to see was Colin's number and she accepted the vidcall. "My man! You return!"

Colin sounded happier than she'd heard him in weeks. "Yep. The *Emerald Queen* docked at the passenger port a little while ago. You know, I never thought I'd be glad to be back on Gallos, but spending three weeks in close quarters with Tabor Laski puts everything in perspective. I'm delivering my big presentation to the Covrani menfolk in a few hours." Colin squinted at her image. "Hey, are you wearing my concert shirt?"

"I am! I slept in it last night. I wanted something that smells like you."

"The whole bed smells like me!"

"Ha! Not anymore. I'm thoroughly enjoying my visit to your personal luxury castle, but I'm not ready to move in. I really like the whirlpool tub in this place, so your water bill will probably be a little high this month. There's a spa on level 37 I've been frequenting, too. I'm actually on a first name basis with one of the massage therapists. Oh, when you get a chance, there's a restaurant named Glorious Heat on level 19 that serves a syntha steak smothered in red sauce that is addictive," she gushed.

Colin's mouth fell open as he listened. "I've created a monster!"

"I've earned every comfort," she said.

"How?"

"I unloaded the last of our combined cargo trades this afternoon. Take a look at *Mother Courage*'s account balance." She waited while he made the inquiry then grinned as he reacted.

"Wow," he marveled. "That's a beautiful number right

there. Add that fifty thousand credit bounty for Kengi to it and we could pay off the ship right now!"

"We could, but we shouldn't. Yes, we'd have a paid-off ship but no capital to start a new trade route."

"Are you sure about that?"

She put the device on projection mode and sat up in bed. "Why are you asking in that sly tone of voice?"

"Mitchel Pilar and his criminal friends provided us with the capital to fund an investment company. Watch this."

Kaia's eyes popped as she watched the account balance triple. "Oh my," she gasped. "Well, that makes things more interesting, for sure. I could throw it at your mother and tell her to get stuffed, but I don't want to bring out the heavy guns unless I have no other choice. We'll pay her off in installments."

"I surrender to your superior wisdom. You're obviously really good at this."

"I have a very basic idea of what I'm doing. That account balance is your hard work, not mine."

Colin winced. "I don't understand."

"All I did was implement the trades that you scoped out and programmed," she said. "Now that you're here, I'm going to haul Kengi up from the storage room to meet your mother."

"Are you sure you're good with this?" he asked.

"I'm good," she said. "We still need the money, and she did promise us payment for that particular service. Walking into her office with a corpse seems cruel, though."

"Maybe. I just know my mother never lets go of money unless she has to. If we need to show her a body to rattle that paycheck loose, Kengi can do us one last favor from beyond the grave. It's not like he did any favors for anyone when he was alive."

"I wonder about that," she confessed. "What got him into piracy, do you think? Greed? Desperation? You and I have been pretty bomaxed privileged our whole lives. Let's not be too judgy."

"Kaia, this isn't judgement. He threatened Seandra. His own henchman ended him; he deserved what he got. If you're having second thoughts, I can fly down to the tower, take him upstairs myself, and still be back in time for my meeting at the campground. Assuming they actually show up."

"No! I'm not a shrinking flower. I'm doing this. You have your deal to close and I have mine. Partners, right?"

"Partners," he agreed. "Remember, she can't hurt you. The worst she can do is cancel our business venture, and she can't do that without your mom's approval as the other major partner. In fact, let's make sure of that. Are you recording?"

She tapped a button. "I am now."

"Good. Here we go: I am Colin Covrani and I hereby designate Kaia Sley as the sole representative of my share of the collaborative venture known as the A-20D trader, *Mother Courage*," he said. "It won't hold up if she decides to sue me, but it'll scare her."

"Got it. Let's do this. Good luck with your meeting."

"You, too. I'll show you the family campground when the smoke clears."

"That sounds brilliant."

—

Kaia got dressed and called down to have the baggage she'd stowed in the arcology storage unit delivered to the apartment. An hour later, she pushed Kengi's capsule into the lounge area outside Yelena Covrani's office. She used her handheld to request an urgent meeting with her prospective mother-in-law and waited patiently.

Kaia couldn't quite avoid looking at the medical canister that rested on the free-floating grav platform—the same kind she and her father had used on Dacha station. She tapped the canister's display and looked inside.

Her stomach roiled and she felt a strong need to spit but she refused to look away. This was her doing. Hers. And her family. All for a cash payment that she felt compelled to wring out of the great lady on the other side of the office door.

She waited. One hour. Then two. She was about to message Colin for suggestions on how to proceed when the light above the office door winked out and Yelena made her entrance. She wore a maroon and black ensemble and a different hair style today, but the same matronly aura preceded her.

"Kaia! How nice to see you again, but so soon? I thought you'd be off adventuring with Colin and your folks."

She has rules to abide by. You are free to experiment. "Circumstances required our return. To be fair, Colin wanted to tell you in person, but I volunteered to take on the job."

Yelena's eyebrows dropped a bit; the matron was disappointed. "Ah, my dear, I appreciate the hands-on attitude, but you can't step in to relieve that boy of his responsibilities every time a conflict arises."

"I agree completely. Let me rephrase that: an opportunity arose that Colin could not afford to ignore. He's off making things happen and I'm here to collect a reward."

"I'm all a-tremble. Which reward is this?"

Kaia pushed the capsule into the office. "I am here to report your trouble with Kengi and his Bombardiers is over. We neutralized the entire crew."

Yelena became very quiet as her eyes flicked between Kaia

and her cargo. "Did you now?"

"Yes, ma'am. I brought the proof you asked for."

"Did I ask for his belongings?" Yelena asked, rising to approach. She kept her hands at her sides and stared quizzically at the container. "What have you brought me, dear?" she asked warily.

"Well, you rejected the DNA scans my parents sent from Field 13, and didn't say what kind of proof you'd accept. Therefore, I present to you, Pula Kengi, formerly of the satellite tender *Durable,*" Kaia said and tapped a sequence of buttons near the platform's edge. The covering retracted into the base to reveal the sealed medical container. The darkened display held a straight line. No heartbeat. No vital signs. Nothing.

Yelena seemed to have trouble processing the situation. She slid her hand across the top of the container, where a window let her view the cadaver. All at once her face twisted into a mask of horror and she staggered backwards. "Stars, girl! What's the meaning of this? It's disgusting. An insult!"

Kaia held her ground and narrowed her eyes. She knew exactly what Kengi's body looked like. A giant hole where his face had been. Sickening, perhaps, but what exactly had the great lady expected? "Proof of a job done. The data chip in this container shows the DNA is genuine and clearly matched up with TSS records. I'd appreciate the fifty thousand credits you promised us."

"He... you... how *dare* you!" Yelena blustered.

This is not going well at all. Time for Plan B. "You want time to verify his identity, I suppose. I agree, that's a good idea. I'll be on my way, now." She used her handheld to take an image of the platform and its inert cargo with a squeamish Yelena Covrani cringing from the corpse, and turned to leave.

"Don't you leave him here!" Yelena screamed. "Don't you

dare walk away from me, young lady!"

Kaia turned back and made sure to keep her eyes fixed on the older woman's at all times. "Pay what I'm owed and I will take him off your hands."

Yelena stomped to her desk and took up her tablet. "Ugh. You children and your theatrics. Fine. Here. Take it!"

Kaia checked her handheld. "I'm sorry, there's a mistake. There's only twenty-six thousand here. The agreed upon amount was fifty thou—"

"I know what I said. In case you've forgotten, my dear girl, you and your mother only own 52 percent of our venture. I am holding the rest back as Colin's representative."

"Colin didn't tell me he instructed you to do that. Since he's the partner of record, his decision is the one that matters."

"When he's absent, I am his representative, therefore I make that decision."

"Except today. Behold," Kaia said, and tapped a button on her handheld.

Colin's voice emerged from the speaker. "I am Colin Covrani and I hereby designate Kaia Sley as the sole representative of my share of the collaborative venture known as the A-20D trader, *Mother Courage.*"

"Or would you like me to start telling people that the Covrani dynasty doesn't pay its bills?" Kaia asked sweetly.

"Kaia Sley, you are dismissed!"

"Yelena, I may be just a four percent partner, but I am still a *partner.* Which means I have the authority to cancel our venture for non-payment of invoices, promissory notes, and verbal agreements. Both *major* partners know that I'm here and will agree with me." She waggled her device. "Last chance."

Yelena growled under her breath as she relented. "Fine. Colin wants you, very well, he can have you. Tell that idiot son of mine he's officially cut off. And I am cancelling our agreement for that ship. I'll be calling the fraud department today to have it re-possessed."

A wave of good anger took hold of Kaia: a rage-filled need to stab her future mother-in-law in the face. *It's important to me that you not be happy, dear.* She whipped out her handheld and stabbed the keys. "Unnecessary, ma'am. I hereby forward you a payment equaling forty-eight percent of this month's gross receipts, and another payment of a quarter million credits to cover your initial investment. My mother and I are now full owners of the A-20D known as *Mother Courage,*" Kaia said as she tapped buttons.

A chime sounded on Yelena's tablet, which she threw against the wall. "Congratulations. You're very clever. Go back to Greengard, little girl!"

"Sorry, neither. Thank you for your time," Kaia countered and checked her handheld. Satisfied she had the full promised amount, she maneuvered the grav platform and pushed it out of Yelena's office. She'd be perfectly happy never to set foot in it again.

"I'm a pirate," Kaia murmured as she pushed the platform out of the lounge. "I want. I take. I'm *hard!*"

35

SILENT PARTNERS

COLIN'S SHUTTLE GOT him to the southern tip of the estate gardens in short order. He settled the shuttle in a shallow landing berth, one of three that had been installed long ago. He unlocked another grav platform from the secure area, dropped the rear door and pushed his cargo up to the family vacation home.

His father, Jarid, had built the place with his Uncle Rodg when he and his cousin Vani were children. Nowhere as spacious or elegant as the arcologies, this was a multi-level modular lodge with ground floor bedrooms and an upstairs common area. The upper floor had walls that could open outwards to the elements. Neither a proper cabin nor a tent but with aspects of both. All the comforts of home but with far more privacy.

His handheld activated the startup sequence; the power core flared to life, the fusion stove came on, the lights and environmental controls began to warm the cooling air of twilight. He unloaded the food and drinks he'd packed onto the platform and got to work preparing food and setting the table.

When he was done, he took one of the lounging chairs and waited for his guests to arrive. He ate, he drank, he watched furry critters jump from tree to tree. He listened to the trees, imagining that they were whispering to him as the wind rustled their leaves. *You're a lucky guy, Colin. You're about to discover whether the men you hold in high esteem care as much about you. What will you do if they refuse you?*

"I'll go back to the *Emerald Queen* and ask Meklife to find me a sword and three-cornered hat," he said aloud. "Why not be a pirate? What's following the rules getting me?"

"It's getting you a family reunion for one thing," said a familiar voice.

Colin looked over to see his father, Jarid, getting out of the car he'd driven to the campsite. After a moment, his mom's brother, Rodg Covrani, and his cousin, Vani, exited the vehicle. The three men were dressed casually—but for an office visit, not a rugged camping expedition.

Colin smiled and a weight was lifted from his shoulders. "You guys came! Awesome. Welcome to the pitch meeting!"

Vani strode into the shelter and shook his cousin's hand with enormous energy. "Pitch meeting? They told me you were serving dinner."

"Can't I do both?" Colin asked.

"Should you, is the question. What's the occasion, Colin?" asked his father.

"We took out a pirate crew. Killed the captain and made a deal with the first officer and everything," Colin said. "They came back for a bit of revenge, and we finished the job. The rewards were substantial."

Rodg walked to the set table and scanned the spread. "How substantial?"

"The accountants are still working on that. Some of the items we recovered have an arguable value. Depends on who you talk to."

"Humor me. Ballpark figure."

Colin checked some notes on his handheld. "Eighty, ninety million."

"That's a decent ballpark," Vani agreed.

"So now to celebrate this windfall, we have dinner?" Rodg asked.

"No. I have news to share but I wanted to just have a normal visit with you three first. We haven't come here together in years. I figured it was time. Anyway, I made food and brought booze. It'd be a shame for it to go to waste."

Vani cracked his knuckles and pulled out a chair. "Can't argue with that. Let's eat," he said, as he piled his plate high.

Jarid did likewise. "It's a very nice gesture, Colin. Thank you, son."

"Yes. Thank you, Colin," his Uncle Rodg said.

"I know you three are ridiculously busy. It took weeks of work to get your people to put me on your calendars."

"You mean to put us on yours," Vani said around a mouthful. "It's a neat trick. I should fire my girl and hire you instead."

"Keep your girl, she's good at what she does. Besides, I have a job. I am the Junior Supply Officer on a starship. Also, I've got a joint venture going with Mom. And a friend. And *her* mom."

"I heard about the girlfriend. Apparently, you're willing to move the stars themselves for this one," Rodg said as he opened a can of beer and drank deeply. "Oh, that's good."

Jarid settled his empty plate on the table. "You hear that?"

"Hear what?"

"Silence. No calls to answer. No screens to distract. No orders to give. Stars, I miss this. The only quiet I get now is in the tram going to work or coming home."

"Not that you're home all that much," Colin griped.

"It can't be helped, just lately. My office is on the other side of the planet in a beanstalk five hundred kilometers in the sky. Once the new cargo elevator is up and running, I should be around more often."

"I don't know if I'll be around then, Dad. Commercial transports go all over the place and the schedule is always changing."

Jarid rolled his eyes. "Stop with the drama. You didn't have to run around the galaxy looking for opportunities. You could have worked for me."

"Dad, I applied fifty times!"

"I know. You applied for every job you thought your mother or I *wanted* you to do. Office managers and actuaries. I can get those people anywhere. Did you once consider apprenticing to a pilot on a cruise liner? Or a convoy escort? You didn't apply for any of *those* jobs despite your skill set. I thought you didn't care."

A bit of clarity bloomed in Colin's mind. "Well... I hate to put it this way, but I *didn't* care. It seemed too easy."

"That's your mother talking. You *should* care about spending time as a starship crewman. I've seen you on a flight deck. You could stand some mentoring and additional education, but you know how to run a ship. That's real life right there. *Those* people are the family business. We three are just stuck in meetings all day."

Colin blinked, taken aback by what he'd been told. "I didn't know I had a choice."

"Colin, you're the only one here who *ever* had a choice," Vani agreed. "You had all the choices. I didn't have any."

"Neither did I," Rodg said, and belched wetly. "When your mother and I were children, maybe nine or ten years old, your grandfather took us aside and said all right, kids, one of you is going to business school and the other is going to law school. You two figure out who does what. And that was that. Our futures decided for us in a twenty-second dictum. We didn't know we could say 'no'—not that it would have done much good, our father was a dictator—but we made it work."

Wow Kaia was right, this place is incestuous. "Dad? What's your story?" Colin asked.

"I had a choice. It was either this or prison," Jarid said with a wry grin.

"What?"

"As an Enforcer, not as a prisoner," he clarified. "I got out of the Guard Academy and wanted to get my hands dirty, so I told the placement office to send me somewhere ugly. Somewhere rough and tough and thoroughly unpleasant. I thought it would help me build character. I ended up assigned to the prison ship *Sarduvis*. What I saw there—what I *did* there—was awful. But after three years of that, I could honestly say that I had a strong knowledge of the mechanisms that can be put in place to manage large numbers of unpleasant people. So I got a job as an operations supervisor on the beanstalk and never really left."

"So Aunt Yelena *was* a violent criminal. I knew it," Vani snarked.

"Hah! My office was dealing with a labor dispute, and my dock workers were threatening to organize. She came in as a representative for the company and we were in the same meetings. Once the case was settled, we became far more social. She was the first woman I'd met who could drink me under the table, and she wasn't hard to look at. I decided she was the one. We made it work."

"She doesn't drink any more, at least not in front of me," Colin murmured. "Maybe we should bring that tradition back. I remember she was a lot looser when we were kids. What happened to her?"

"She took my job," Rodg said.

"She what? I don't believe it," Colin breathed.

Vani raised an eyebrow. "Yeah, you never told me that."

"I don't want it to sound more dramatic than it was." Rodg sighed. "I gravitated toward logistics planning, and she concentrated on contracts and licensing. But there was always a bit of overlap between those divisions, and we sometimes got in each other's way. One day, we had a screaming match over who had legal jurisdiction on a deal that would have been worth billions. I said if you're that bomaxed smart, then why don't you just take the whole thing, and stormed out. The next day I got a notice from the general counsel telling me that I had been removed from making legal decisions completely. I have to tell you boys, that hurt. She really stuck it to me. There was a kind of ruthlessness to it that I didn't see in her then. But I see it now. I stay out of her way, and she stays away from my division."

This is it. Your perfect transition. All you need is the guts to make it happen. "How would you gentlemen like to tweak her on the nose and enrich yourselves in the process?" Colin asked.

"We're not ruining your mother, Colin," Jarid declared. "Yes, she has rough edges, but her division is making a ton of money and there's no reason to throw a spanner into that machine."

Colin waved his concern off. "It's nothing like that. If it works, the worst that happens is that Mom ends up with a big pile of money. But it can also show her that she's not always the smartest person in the room."

"I don't like where this is going," Jarid said.

"I could stand to hear more," Vani offered.

"What do you have, Colin?" Rodg asked. "Is this because of the girlfriend?"

Colin put his hands together. "No. It's a solid idea. It's months in the making, it has the backing of some truly impressive silent partners, and there is a plan. All the pieces are identified. What I need is the capital to get started."

Rodg cocked his head. "What kind of capital?"

"If the math works like we believe it will, I'm thinking about three billion credits."

All three of the men laughed. Colin let them have their fun, smiling wanly. When they finished he said, "I have funding options, which are being looked into. These are independent sources. You need not contribute any more than you are willing to risk. The first phase of this scheme has already—"

Just then, Colin's handheld beeped. He took a moment to check the screen, and his heart jumped as he read the message: >>Your mom tried to pull a fast one. I straightened her out. Welcome to full ownership of *Mother Courage* and 50k credits!<<

>>What happened??<< he typed.

>>I showed her the body. She tried to hold your share back. I paid off the ship on the spot. She's so not in love with me anymore.<<

>>Good news, partner!<< he typed. "Gentlemen, my lovely partner Kaia has just gotten Mom to live up to her own standards. An investment of fifty thousand credits has been

made."

Vani grinned like a fiend. "Did she? Well done, Kaia! You totally have to bring this woman around, Colin. You've been holding out on me."

"On all of us," Rodg agreed. "Where is she now?"

"Now? This minute? She's just met with Mom, so she's still at the family tower."

"Good. Tell her to pack up her stuff and get over here in a shuttle. She can fly a shuttle, can't she?"

Colin stood and stretched. "She can fly, navigate, and use a comm panel like a wizard. And she can strip and re-assemble a pistol in twelve seconds."

"She sounds like a solid prospect," Vani said.

"Yes! She's exactly what you need, son. I want to hear everything," Jarid said.

Everything? You want her to bring the body, too? "In the name of efficiency, why don't we get out of here and fly back to the tower. I'll introduce you to our new ship and my silent partners. Dad, I think you and Commander Lom Mench will get along famously. You're both royal tech heads."

Dad's eyes brightened. "That sounds brilliant."

Colin nodded to his uncle who was working through what he was hearing with a hooded glare at the fire. "Uncle Rodg? Can we make it unanimous? I could take you three to meet the whole crew right now."

Rodg rested his elbows on his knees and stared into the cook fire. "I won't back a revenge play, Colin. Not for three credits much less three billion. I know she's an ogre, but she's still your mother. If we understand each other that way... all right. Show us this new family you've made. I'd like to know what my nephew does when he's not paying off bank debts."

—

Kaia was waiting with her cargo platform at the private spaceport. Colin had to open the rear doors to give her access to the A-20D's cargo bay, and they pushed Kengi's medical container on board the *Mother Courage* together. Colin secured the cargo then followed Kaia to the flight deck. All three Covrani followed them up the ramp.

"Gentlemen," Colin announced, "please meet Kaia Sley, co-owner of the trader *Mother Courage*. I intend to marry her, one way or another."

Kaia blushed and shook their hands as Colin got behind the nav console. "Next stop, the *Emerald Queen*," he announced.

The ride to orbit hardly lasted long enough for Kaia to learn their names and give a few details about herself and her family. They stepped off the shuttle and gaped at the *Emerald Queen*'s cavernous hangar deck.

Vani clapped his hands excitedly. "Colin, you're making up for years of lost time with this one. A girl like that and a ship like this? I think you should be the dynasty heir. I need a vacation anyway."

"Not on your life! You have your mega-corporation, *and* a fiancée. Let me build my own," Colin said, taking Kaia's hand.

"It's *my* megacorporation and I remain unconvinced of anything except this young lady's charm and character," Rodg said. He belched again, but this time he covered his mouth.

Jarid's eyes scanned every detail of the operation, his professional judgment coming to the fore. "Very nice arrangement. Good and efficient. I especially like all the mechanical workmen on the loading queue. Where's this Mench person?"

A booming voice stole their collective attention from the deck workers. Meklife strode up to the visitors and saluted Colin and Kaia before extending his hand to Colin's father. "I am Lom Mench. Welcome to the *Emerald Queen*, gentlemen. My captain awaits you in her ready room."

"You're a Lynaedan," Jarid immediately guessed.

"Indeed I am, sir."

"You're not an android, are you?"

"I am a drone pilot. This drone is affectionately known to the crew as Sergeant Meklife. It's what I use to greet visitors in an official capacity. Shall we go? My captain is waiting."

Colin and Kaia kept back a few steps, trading news of their respective exploits in low voices. "What did you do with Kengi?"

"I offered to leave him in her office. She looked like I'd slapped her. Gah, what a tantrum that woman threw. Anyway, I've been dismissed, and you've been cut off. But Mom and I own the ship free and clear, and we have some credits left over to start a new life."

Colin took the news with a deep sense of relief and freedom. He'd never appreciated before just how sticky his situation at home had been, like a trap. "Oh no! I'll have to learn a trade. I'll have to get a job! Oh, wait, I have both!"

She wrapped her arms around one of his, anchoring herself to him and leaning in. "You'll be brilliant. This is the important meeting."

He pulled her close and squeezed. "I really do love you. How will you cope with a pauper like me?"

"I think we'll be all right. But remember, I'm just another pretty face here. These are your people. They'll be looking at you for leadership. You know the details, just be calm and remember to breathe."

Aura's ready room was already crowded, and grew more so as the guests took their places at a long table. "Captain Aura, First Officer Sley, may I present the Covrani delegation," Meklife intoned.

Vani bowed his arms and moved his feet apart, taking up space. Forcing the others to look at him. "I see, we're a *delegation*. So, it's an official meeting. Very clever, Colin. First Officer Sley, may I assume you're related to this delightful creature on my cousin's arm?" he asked.

Karmen gave a single nod. "My daughter's name is Kaia. Please use it."

"I will. What shall we talk about, folks?" Vani said as he took a place at the table opposite Aura.

"Surely, you surmised there's an opportunity to be exploited here," Aura said. "I need a vast infusion of capital, and you have privateers roaming your trade routes. I expect we can help each other. All we need to verify are the details."

"*If* we go along with it, Captain. Colin gave us the broad intent but avoided divulging too many details," Rodg said.

She nodded. "I know. He did that at my request. We would be going up against some real players in interstellar trade circles, and the less you all know about it, the better."

"Aunt Yelena is a player? When did that start?" Vani asked.

Aura shook her head. "Colin's mother is not the target. She merely has the tools that we need to put our plan into action. The targets are four very dynamic and troubled men who call themselves the Mesopotamians. Specifically, the one called Gilgamesh."

"Bomax! You folks are part of that whole New Akkadia scheme, aren't you?" Rodg asked.

Aura gave a sweep of her arms. "Mother Carnage, at your service," she said.

Rodg made a rude noise in his throat and narrowed his eyes at his nephew. "Stars, Colin, you've truly jumped into it with both feet this time."

Colin opened his mouth to answer but Aura waved him off and took over. "Colin came to me with an idea that I believed had merit enough to warrant traveling here to meet with you. As I said, the less you know, the better. But I can say that none of your assets are in any danger. We have financial needs, but they can be met through means other than yours. Honestly, gentlemen, what I need most is a staging area. A planet with an active industrial base that has sufficient access to commercial opportunities and trade. Ideally, it would be remote enough not to attract attention if activity spikes for weeks at a time. Preferably, Enforcers who will look the other way for a stipend."

"I have an idea about that," Jarid said, "But first you need to tell me what happens if all this goes horribly wrong. Otherwise, I must assume you're taking advantage of my son and I'm putting in a call to the TSS right now."

"Dad, I—"

Aura put up her hand. "No, Colin. He's right. And he cares about you. I'll be direct: my crew and I are going up against an interstellar black market ring. If our effort fails, I could lose my ship, my crew, and whatever reputation I have out in the space lanes. New Akkadia runs right over me and that is the end of Mother Carnage. But if it works, then Colin would be sitting adjacent to a vast commercial network and you gentlemen would be the dominant commercial transportation power in this part of the galaxy."

"Adjacent to what network?" Vani said.

"Aura's Quartermaster and his staff," Colin said. "When we're done, there will be enough money spilling out to make anyone happy. But the accounting might be complicated."

"And my sister won't be hurt or troubled by this?" Rodg repeated.

"Oh, she'll be *furious*. But she'll also have a huge bankroll to re-deploy. She'll get over it quickly enough," Colin said.

The Covrani men shared a look. Finally, Jarid used his handheld to flick a star map onto the table. "Baron's World. The spaceport is limited to ground operations only, there's no orbital facility. But it does have a 100-channel gravity lift. Plus, it has substantial cargo docks and numerous warehouses. It's an old shipyard that the TSS was using as a repair and supply depot during the Bakzen nonsense. The war ended and we stopped funding operations. That contract is long expired, so I can re-assign it to Colin as a rental property. There's a small staff of caretakers there now, but it could be re-activated easily enough. I'll put in a call to expect you."

"It's also right in the center of the Autonomous Main," Vani said. "It's a busy trade hub. No one will notice a bump in traffic."

Rodg took out his handheld and flipped a contact to Colin's device. "Take this," Rodg said. "His name is Paski Burk. He knows who you are, so no introductions are necessary. Just call him if you need to do something a little strange."

Colin stared at the contact like it might reach out and bite him. "Like what?"

His father smirked. "He's very good at finding things other people want to keep hidden, and hiding things others want to find. Tell him you need to bury a corpse and he'll show up with a shovel."

"You even get a free assassination with a new account," Vani murmured.

As a matter of fact... "There's no way that's true," Colin said. "Right?"

Rodg snorted. "Certainly not! I don't give *that* number out to anyone."

Vani drummed his knuckles on the table. "All right, the less we know, the better. What time-frame are we looking at? Any plan that you expect to collect billions from won't be put in place quickly."

"I've run the numbers several times," Karmen said. "We'll need to relocate to Baron's World, contact your caretakers, hire staff and workers, then start recruiting assets. One month at a minimum. Two would be more reliable an estimate."

"Two months, then we start doing business?" Vani asked.

"No. In two months, we wipe out Gilgamesh."

PART 3

NEW FORTUNES

36

RESPECT

"GAH... MY TOOTH..." Wincing, Colin forced himself to concentrate on his work.

The data matrix he'd been working on for weeks with Tabor was taking shape nicely. The Lynaedans had helped them trace thousands of access points, leading to huge swaths of Gilgamesh's holdings. They had locations and entry points. All they needed now was to complete the data collection. Then, it would be ready to hand off to Aura and Lom so they could plan an attack.

Colin fantasized about lunging across the table to strangle his co-worker. "What's wrong with your tooth?"

"It hurts, that's what." Tabor inspected his fingernails. "That bloody harpy probably broke it. I have no idea how you deal with her."

Stars, this again. All Colin wanted to do—needed to do— was finish arranging the data matrix. But Tabor wasn't making it easy. "I've told you before, the mother isn't the one I'm interested in. Yeah, she can be intense—"

"Intense? She was one step shy of homicidal!"

"That was months ago." Colin kept his eyes on his work. "We're not being paid to manage Aura's first officer."

"We're not being paid *at all*. This is purely a speculative endeavor. Even more reason to avoid contact with that harridan. I'd be perfectly happy to stay here in this darling suite of spaceport offices and never set foot on the *Emerald Queen* again."

"Well, Kaia's going to be there soon, so I, for one, will be very happy there until we meet up with the Vault Ship *Pecunia*."

Tabor rolled his eyes and snorted. "There's better women out there, son."

"Better, how?"

"That would be obvious to anyone else. Prettier. Wealthier. Connected. *Better*. And no insane mothers to torment you when you get out of your lane."

But none of them are Kaia. Colin's resolve to remain non-violent slipped. "Yeah. Well, they're also boring. You could say all of that about Kaia but she isn't boring." He understood Tabor had a lizard-brain talent for making deals, defrauding clients, and hiding cash trails, but Emily Govrin was catching up to him quickly as she learned the trade. And she was infinitely better-looking and more polite than this guy.

"You and I clearly have different standards when it comes to intimacy."

Taking a slow breath to keep himself from exploding, Colin nodded. "Maybe you should stick with Maesy and call it a day, Tabor."

"So I have, my boy. No, *there's* a woman who doesn't mind

a bit of dirt under her nails."

Colin wasn't sure what irked him more, the boy comment or the dirt comment. *You know what, forget it. You need his operational skills, not his personality.*

He updated the feed and forced the computer to recalculate the data. They now had an accurate map of every position the *Pecunia* would be in for the next three weeks. He had no idea how to explain himself to Tabor and decided he didn't have to. Kaia was *interesting.* She occupied his attention even when she was nowhere near by. He looked forward to being in the same room with her in a way he couldn't properly articulate. Yes, her mother was a bit of a maniac, but if he was being honest, he'd nearly slugged Tabor himself for dismissing Daveed so abruptly. Colin should have done something and hadn't, so a bump on his head and a bloody nose was purgation enough. Colin was just happy that Daveed hadn't mentioned the episode again.

Finished with the work, Colin pushed back from his desk. "I'm going to check on our investor's flight."

"He's not an investor, he's your dad," Tabor sneered.

"Whatever!"

Colin stomped out of the suite of rooms they'd geared into a War Room and headed to the transit terminal. What killed him was that Tabor, for all his arrogance, wasn't wrong. Jarid had become just like the members of the family he'd married into: he had trouble understanding that his children weren't employees. Colin had already introduced him to Aura; that should have been enough. But no. His father insisted on seeing Colin's operation for himself. Aura hadn't objected, so Colin had arranged this visit.

Colin waited by the berthing kiosk while his father's shuttle settled into the bay. Jarid waved and hefted an overnight bag as he descended the gangway.

He shook Colin's hand at the bottom. "Glad to see you're taking such good care of my old stomping ground. You've changed a lot of things."

He's been here ten seconds and he's already judging me. Colin plastered on his most diplomatic smile. "It was your base, remember?"

"We didn't run it; we just own it. But the last time I was standing here, the skies were clear and the place was quiet like an empty room. The only sound I heard was the wind whistling past the storage domes. Even the cargo carriers only showed once a month. You know what I see now that I look around? Life! Industry! Work! The stuff that put this family on the map. Come on, kiddo. Give your old man the grand tour."

"You know most of it already. Can you tell me why they built a multi-format landing zone with seven directional beacons? Seems like overkill to me."

"Like a great many things done under duress, it made sense at the time. With seven or eight square kilometers to work with, you could launch an entire armada while recovering another one. The grav pads helped with that as well. I doubt you'll be putting this place to that kind of test."

Colin shook his head. "Not even close. The main spaceport is already running as smoothly as you'd like. The shipyard and repair depot are in the north and north-west sections, respectively. Lots of landing bays with twenty berths each means we're never filled. Startown is south just outside the perimeter fence; all the hotels, casinos, clubs, and bars you could ask for. There's even a concert hall and a few theaters. Not that they do much business."

"Theirs was not a genteel crowd if I remember correctly," Jarid admitted.

"It still isn't. The commercial administrative offices and other facilities are at the east section, and our little spaceport is all in the southwest. We like our privacy."

"Your own landing bay, facilities, security offices, and quarters, too, I recall."

"Factual. You have a good memory."

"Oh, yeah? Well, I remember giving you and your friends permission to use this bit of family property because you insisted there would be a fabulous reward for it. This is cover for what you all are planning. Not that I'm complaining…"

Colin sighed. "You are definitely complaining."

"I'm pointing out that a few hundred ships arriving and departing every week makes for a good cover. So where is the real operation? Everything you've said is stuff I already know."

"This tram goes right to the admin building. I'll show you. Hop in."

They arrived at the terminal, and Colin led him to a vast atrium. A high vaulted ceiling gave the building an atmosphere of open space. Over a hundred clerks and techs occupied consoles on the floor. Floating platforms extended from the walls; every now and then, one would flit into a particular part of the main display where a tech would make an adjustment then return to its point of origin. A gigantic holographic star map dominated the upper reaches of the stadium but numerous smaller maps and charts occupied other lower tiers.

Colin pointed to one section of the floor. "That's the central data core. Reaches out to fifty worlds and counting, including all the major exchanges on every world that's self-identified as part of New Akkadia. We use that to coordinate personnel. Some people are volunteers, some are temp hires, some are permanent crew. You wouldn't believe how many Enforcers, industrial wonks, and politicians are willing to sell their principles for a few credits."

"Oh, yes, I would."

Colin gestured to a different data board. "That is the fleet tracker. Our own ships are already listed according to size class, role, and location. Every time a ship captain or owner decides to leave the Covrani commercial network and sign on with us, that number goes up. We don't use ship names up there, just randomly assigned numbers for internal use. It's a security feature that Commander Mench insisted upon. That number in red there, that's the total number working for us: 117 as of this morning. Leaving Mom with 1,822 ships in the family commercial fleet to collect payments from."

Jarid frowned and folded his arms. "Do you want to tell her you stole her assets, or should I?"

"That's not a fair assessment and you know it. We paid off their contracts in full when they signed, so Mom has received something on the order of two hundred million credits for the inconvenience. She's unquestionably getting the better end of the deal."

"If you say so. Stars help you if she ever finds out."

"Ha. She cut me off. All I'm doing is setting up my own shipping business."

"By poaching her pilots?"

"Exactly. You have a handheld on you. Call her right now and tell her what you know. I'll wait." Colin stared at him in silent challenge, but his father didn't move.

"You going to tell me about your big plan, or what?" Jarid pushed.

Colin harrumphed and turned him around to a new display. "That's the salvage board. The *Emerald Queen* was attacked by a fleet of thirty or so privateers in the Tarkus system. We won the fight, but the resulting debris field was far bigger than we could manage ourselves. So we hired the salvage ship *Nicossi* to help us out. Some of the hulls could be refitted or repaired on the spot, but some others have had to be junked and sent to recycling stations. We've recovered thirteen perfectly serviceable hulls, roughly the same number of wrecks, and so much loose garbage that we could practically build a new ship out of it. I don't think we own a salvage yard, do we?"

"We contract out with local operators for that. Salvage and mining is a lot of work for relatively little payoff, so we let the scrappers handle it for us."

"Your scrappers are my co-workers, sir."

"Good luck with them. They're a fractious bunch to work with." Jarid surveyed the operation, his eyes flitting across the displays. "If you wrecked so many pirate ships, where's the cargo they were hauling?"

"It's all being deployed as we speak. The less you know—"

"—the better, right. That song is getting a little old, son."

Colin led him to a new display bank. "And that is the market board. I know accounting rules say you're supposed to list each transaction as a separate entry and not keep a running total for the year but we couldn't help ourselves. The Lynaedans built us a system that can track market prices across ten thousand commodity classes in real time. We put together the trade opportunities here. All those folks in blue jackets down on the floor? Those are market makers from financial firms all over the galaxy. They have a diverse range of specialties, and all they want to do is make as much money as they can, then leave."

"What's the split?"

"We take thirty percent of every trade. We try not to micromanage them but there's a range they're allowed to operate in. If they exit the range, the trade goes flat. Three flats and that's the end of their career with us. It works surprisingly well."

"Maybe. It sounds to me like you're handing them freebies and leaving piles of credits on the table."

"You can't gouge everybody, Dad. We have to start somewhere, and undercutting you is how we get a foot in the door."

"Whatever you say, Colin. How do you even find these people?"

"They find us. We put opportunities on certain digital marketplaces, and they respond. All we do is give them access to capital, a few rules to follow, and a place to work. They do the rest."

"Even that Mother Carnage character?"

"That *character* put down a revenge play by thirty odd ships. I was on the flight deck for that operation. It was impressive. That haul enabled us to build a one hundred million credit war chest. Currently, we're closing in on two hundred million worth of assets. We haven't even launched the big operation yet. If that goes well… I don't want to speculate."

"Oh, please, my boy. Speculate away! Tell me about your big score."

Careful, now. Don't want him to be able to trace the operation. "The mark is a legit billionaire who accumulated his wealth through illicit means. He has equally shady billionaire friends. They have access to numerous financial assets, digital currencies, and warehouses full of credit chips and illicit items. We aim to steal as much of it as we can."

"What's your target?"

"A vault ship. She's a heavily defended brick of a barge, which men of low virtue and high net worth use to store valued assets. She makes a circuit between the Inner and Middle

Worlds every four months or so. Right about now, she's approaching a point where we can quickly intercept her and make a transaction."

Jarid shook his head. "You'd think a ship like that would be getting robbed every week. How do they maintain security?"

"It's clever, actually. Every time they make a jump to an official rendezvous point, they alert a list of clients within range before they jump away. Our Lynaedan crew broke into the target's messages weeks ago. We know every jump that ship will make over the next three weeks. Which is just enough time for us to jump the *Emerald Queen* into a good position to intercept them. I could tell you more than that, but then I'd have to call the TSS on you, and I remember how angry you got when your accountants said you owed an extra million on your quarterly filings."

"Bah. Ancient history. Do you mind if I watch your crew work?"

"Not happening. This is a multi-dimensional operation, and I can't take you with me."

"Why not? You're taking Kaia, right?"

"Kaia is not part of the operation, and her family is already on the *Queen*. You are a major player in the CSD megacorporation, which makes you a respectable businessman. You get to stay here."

"Colin, I'm happy as anything that you have this new direction, but you're still my son. I'm going with you. That's final."

"Dad, come on. We're not ready yet. Give it a few more days."

"I have nowhere to be."

"You must be far away from this operation. Plausible deniability and all that."

"Colin!"

"And if something happens to you, Mom will have me killed. I'm not taking that chance."

"This is my shipyard, little man. I get to say how it's used."

"You're the *owner*. I'm the Mission Officer."

"Right, and that means my wishes take precedence."

"We'll see about that. Commander Mench! I need a decision!" Colin bellowed.

Jarid blinked and then paled as Meklife plodded over to their company. The Lynaedan drone even saluted the elder noble with a flourish of his sword. "Pleasure to see you again, sir."

"You as well. My son tells me you refuse me access to your ship. I want to be there when you—"

"Negative. Permission denied. Please leave these premises immediately, sir."

"Why would I do that? This is my facility!"

"As the facility owner we value your contribution to our efforts. You are entitled to call the Guard and tell them we are illegally occupying your property. We will respond that you gave us permission to be here, and the allegations and accusations will take all the air out of the room. While the Guard and the crew are arguing, perhaps at gunpoint, perhaps destroying significant property, the *Emerald Queen* will be heading toward its goal. If we succeed, I promise you will be informed."

"And if you fail, what happens to Colin?"

"I've watched Colin handle himself well under fire several times. He doesn't worry me. But you do. Will you depart, or must I have you removed?"

Jarid forced himself to remain calm in tone and demeanor. "May I return to this status room once the operation is under way? I can take a room in star town until then."

"That would be acceptable. I do apologize for what I can only imagine is a genuine inconvenience, but crime is a performance, and my players must be properly prepared and rehearsed. You understand," Commander Mench said.

"I do *not* understand, but I'll go along with it this once. Good day. And good luck, Colin. Please try not to get killed. Funerals are expensive."

They watched Jarid as a mech escorted him from the premises. Then Mench turned to Colin and asked, "What was the point of inviting him here?"

"I wanted him to take me seriously. I guess that was a mistake."

The drone put his hand on Colin's shoulder. "It's no mistake to want respect from your elders. But there's a right way and a wrong way to go about it."

"So, what's the right way? I figured hooking up with a brilliant and beautiful woman like Kaia should be enough. What am I missing?"

"There is no substitute for success. Theft is our stock in trade. Do the job well enough to make them come to you and ask you to cut them in. Shall we get back to work?"

"Yes, sir."

37

PERFORMANCE ANXIETY

AFTER SIX DAYS in flight, the *Emerald Queen* was two jumps from the *Pecunia* and at least six jumps from anywhere else. It was the perfect place to stage the next phase of the operation without interference.

"Now we have a real choice to make," Aura said. "Which ship do we use to intercept *Pecunia*?"

Lom turned to stare at her. "You're not using *Enkidu*? After our upgrades, he's the perfect getaway ship."

"But too small," she countered. "He wouldn't hold more than a fraction of the hoard I saw Gil load into his vault. *Redemption* is better suited to what we're planning. A bigger hull means greater ability to absorb damage and more storage space. We don't really know how much physical space Gil's combined fortune takes up."

"Yes, we do: thirty cubic meters."

"That was only the latest deposit. If I used every spare cubic centimeter of space in *Enkidu*, he might carry twice that."

"Isn't that enough?" Karmen asked.

"My point is that Gil's storage unit was far bigger than thirty cubic meters, and it was packed. I want to clean him out once and be done with him. We go with *Redemption*."

"We'd best go over the full operation one more time," Karmen suggested. "It's a big, complicated plan, and everything must go flawlessly. With only six days to pull it together, I promise there are holes."

"I agree, a final run-through is in order. My ready room awaits," Aura said and led them out of the Command Center.

Aura commanded her traditional place at the head of the table while Lom countered her at the opposite end. Maesy, Tabor, and Colin took up positions on Aura's left while Karmen, Gallian, and Sacha sat at her right.

Karmen began the meeting by throwing up a star map; she zoomed into a tactical map showing their immediate location. "We've all heard the description of *Pecunia*: slow, hardened defenses, and very paranoid. We've taken that into account. Aura will fly *Redemption* to the beacon nearest the vault ship's current location and match vectors with her. It's essential that she use the correct approach codes. Anything else other than the current codes will spark an attack and immediate flight out-of-system by the vault ship."

"We can chase her if necessary," Lom offered.

"But it's best not to spook her at all," Aura said. "The approach code comes directly from *Shamhat*, so I don't expect a challenge. What worries me is what happens after we land the *Redemption* in her hangar bay. Once inside, there are access codes to Gil's vault. They've seen me before, so my face is in their databases, but the last time we were there, Gilgamesh alone handled the access codes. They might accept them from me, or they might not. It's a risk."

"But not a tremendous one," Lom pointed out. "We do have the firepower and numbers to board her and break her hull open. We can load the deposit safes directly on the hangar bay, head to deep space, and crack the vaults open at our leisure."

"Which would bring down the entirety of the galaxy's criminal underworld on our heads," Tabor said. "There are plenty of other depositors who do business with that barge. I guarantee we wouldn't be able to hold onto that loot for very long."

"They'd have to find us first," Karmen said. "Something like a billion planets are out there, and only about 1,500 are actually occupied. In those terms, it's a very big galaxy."

"And if they do come after us, we have a record of the *Emerald Queen* bashing thirty-something ships to scrap," Aura said. "At any rate, the vault codes should work so that's what we'll plan on."

"And if you're wrong?" Sacha asked.

"Then we go back to committing grand larceny from the High Dynasties," Aura said. "Next?"

Karmen waved her hand and the image changed to a schematic. "Next, *Pecunia*'s security system will send an automated courtesy message to *Shamhat*, Gilgamesh's yacht, that his codes have been used for access. The second that Gil hears of it, either by reading it himself or his AI informing him, he'll know something is horribly wrong. So, we'll need to distract the shite out of him. That's where Tabor and Colin come in."

"Tabor, Colin, and Sacha," Colin corrected. "There's no way this works without help from the Lynaedan crew members."

"Colin's being a little obsequious, but he's not wrong,"

Sacha said. "You folks just can't work quickly enough, but we can."

"Which brings us to the plan I created, thank you very much," Tabor said, and threw a new layer onto the display. "Ash's Dark Net marketplace is the key. There are more than fifty thousand open jobs up there at this particular moment in time."

"Did you count every one of them?" Karmen asked.

"I have an account on that marketplace. I've been doing business with Ash's job listing board for years. The point is, I know that because we're tracking them all in real-time. We have access to the job listings but not the reward codes or the storage locations. Lom and Sacha will take care of that for us."

"Sacha has experience robbing a bank?" Karmen asked.

Sacha scoffed. "It wasn't a bank, it was a casino, and that's not what we're doing."

"I'll assume the Lynaedans can do their part with their typical expertise and professionalism. What's next?" Aura prompted.

Lom resumed his description of the workflow. "Then, armed with the locations of thousands of caches of credit chips and the codes to access them, we send out teams of thieves to collect them. We send them to wherever the data points lead, and we see what they bring back."

"How many can we possibly have on that leg of the job?"

"Quite a few. Some will be our people. Some will be reputable transport firms that we've hired for a fee. Some will be petty thieves who will abscond with the cash and disappear, but stealing funds from Ash and his friends is the real goal here, so it made sense to enlist them. Even if we only collect a fraction of what we believe Ash has access to, we could net millions."

"We have to expect that when Ash's online security fails, he'll have a plan in place to move those stashes himself," Karmen noted.

"Yes, but that will take time, and he won't be able to rely on crooked Guard Enforcers to help him," Tabor smirked. "They're just as likely to take those stashes for themselves. We will have the advantage of knowing what we're doing from beginning to end."

"But he will contact his three friends," Sacha said, "And they will have a bit of a tantrum over it. That means they'll be using their own contacts to secure their own storage facilities. If they're busy chasing their tails, they won't be looking for us."

"The part of this plan I don't like and will continue to advise against," Lom said, "is the part where Aura flies the *Redemption* alone. Yes, she'll have cargo drones helping, but they don't do well for any operation other than lifting and carrying. If something does go wrong, she'll be without backup."

Aura shook her head. "No, I won't. These are bankers, not true pirates. They won't expect any trouble."

"I wouldn't assume that, Aura," Karmen said. "These are security people. They are perfectly happy to shoot first and ask questions afterward. I'd like to go with you."

"No, I need you here on the ship," Aura said, "just in case you're right and I do need help."

"Well, take a few of your Scorpions with you, then."

"No, they're here for ship's security and no more. Besides, I'd rather not advertise our intention to rob their employer's friend."

"I'll do it," Sacha said, raising her left hands.

"So will I," Callum quickly agreed.

"No, Callum," Aura said, shaking her head. "I need you to

keep watch for unexpected visitors on long range scans. But Sacha... how well can you connect your comm net to Gallian's?"

She snapped all four hands. "You won't know where he ends and I begin. Plus, I have a set of combat arms I'm dying to try out in the field."

"All right, Ops, you're in. I think we have room for one more in the party."

Colin practically jumped up from his seat. "I will. You might need a spare pilot. And I still have those plasma rifles I bought on Tavden Station."

"So much for my promise to your father and uncle that you wouldn't be directly involved," Aura said.

"I think we're well past that particular criterion," Lom said. "At any rate, Colin and Tabor can pass signals as the operation unfolds. I have equipment on the lower decks that I will make available to Colin as well. Nothing will happen to him."

"I want to go, too," Maesy said, waving her arms for attention.

"Why?" Tabor blurted.

Aura ignored the outburst but cocked her head. "I think we're full up for this trip, Engineer."

Maesy folded her arms. "Be that as it may, Captain, your ship is older than the proverbial Great Rock of Lynaeda. It's slow and it hasn't seen a real fight in decades. I don't think you've even flown it since I arrived here. You'll need someone who knows drives and power systems well enough to goose it to the next level. That's me."

"I see. I can't argue with that. Very well, now we are five. That's all. Maesy, if you intend to give *Redemption* some last-minute care and feeding, now is the time. Meeting adjourned."

38

ACCESS

AURA TAPPED THE *Redemption*'s nav console and received a reading. "Breaking out of subspace in six minutes."

"Six minutes, acknowledged," Colin said from the co-pilot's station.

"Lom, how are the cargo drones doing back there?"

A baritone voice emerged from the speaker. "All drones and their pilots check out, Captain. We have a strong link back to the Queen. All pilots are currently receiving visual and audio telemetry from us. We are prepared to deploy on your order."

Aura stood up and stretched in her new combat gear. Sacha and Maesy sat in their own seats, waiting for their next set of orders. Both were also dressed in the new Lynaedan battle dress, their weapons stowed neatly in racks above their heads. Sacha had donned a particularly heavy set of quadruplet mechanical arms and matching combat armor. With her hair now short and set to a flat black color, she looked a lot like one of the Lynaedan drones herself.

"All set back there, troops?" Aura asked.

"Yes, ma'am," Sacha acknowledged. Maesy merely saluted.

"Maesy, you're allowed to speak on this mission. In fact, I insist you communicate that way," Aura said.

"I'm sorry, Captain. Gallian's comm module isn't sitting well with me."

"Should we abort the mission, Chief Engineer?"

"No, ma'am. I'm good to go. But it's distracting having Gallian yammering in my head. So many numbers and symbols I'm not used to working with. I'm learning to manage the data flow, but it'll take time."

"I should have listened to my instincts and left you all back at the ship," Aura said. She took a moment to shake the dark mood from her head. The last thing the crew needed was a moody CO. The irony of not having the freedom to lock herself in the flight deck wasn't lost on her. "How do you like the new armor?"

"I have to say, I'm incredibly impressed with this fancy battle dress," Colin said. "I can stand up, sit down, twirl a baton through my fingers, and talk to anyone in this crew compartment or in the *Emerald Queen*'s Command Center. I'm in love!"

"Eventually, and with practice, you'll be able to pet a puppy, pick up an egg, or handle an insect without damaging the creature," Lom said. "There's a reason the Empire never tried to impose its will on the Lynaedan people. These suits are only one aspect of that."

Aura and Colin's armor resembled a stripped-down version of the suit the two women were wearing. She had to admit she was enjoying the experience quite a lot. She didn't have to think about using it, it just worked. It felt natural, like wearing clothing. "That makes me wonder what else you could get your hands on if needed," she mused aloud.

The door to the rear compartment slid open and Lom entered. He had left his Meklife drone aboard the *Emerald Queen* and used his Berserker command drone for enhanced communication gear. The holographic projection made him look like himself dressed in gear like the others. "How much money is in your budget?" he asked. "With enough wealth, I could come away with nearly anything that isn't completely locked down by the system government."

"A nuclear weapon, for example?" Maesy suggested.

"One minute to normal space," Colin called out.

"Not quite. Those are very strictly controlled. It would be easier and cheaper to simply build one of our own. We know where TalEx stores theirs, for that matter."

"Here we go, transitioning to normal space... now."

Time stretched and snapped back while the blue and green streamers of subspace evaporated, replaced by stars. Almost immediately, the sensors began to ping. "There she is. That was way easier than I expected," Colin said.

Aura nodded. "Lucky for us, she hasn't moved very far."

The *Pecunia* was indeed a brick of a starship, nearly five hundred meters in length, larger than even some TSS battleships. She was blocky and clad in materials that made her difficult to read on sensors. Aura lost her track three times during their approach. "*Pecunia*, this is the *Redemption*. Prepare for docking."

"*Pecunia* to *Redemption*. We do not have you on our list of clients."

"I am aware of that. This is Captain Aura, standing in for Lord Gilgamesh. We are conducting business on his order. I am transmitting identity codes now."

"Those are Gilgamesh's codes, Captain Aura."

"Indeed, they are. Let me aboard and I'll explain everything."

"I'm sure you will. Transmit your approach codes at once."

Aura indicated for the second set of codes to be sent.

"Stars, they are put out by this," Lom observed when the comm channel was muted.

"They don't like surprises and neither do their clients," Aura agreed. "But they scanned me when I came aboard with Gil last time, so they should be able to verify my voice pattern. Now I just hope they don't—"

"*Pecunia* to *Redemption*. Your approach codes are valid. Come to course zero-five-one and set your controls to neutral. We will activate our docking array."

"Setting controls to neutral," Aura said. The comm connection ended.

"Docking array?" Lom commented. "That could prove troublesome when we try to leave."

"That wasn't how we did this the last time," she agreed.

"Ah. Very well. We shall see how it plays out."

The *Redemption* settled in its berth on the hangar bay, somewhat less roomy than the *Emerald Queen's*. They debarked and Aura led the way to the transaction office.

A thin man in captain's livery met them, tablet in hand. "Captain... Aura?" the newcomer said. "This is unexpected."

"Captain Baldun, I remember you. Gilgamesh discovered a better use for his credits than mere storage," she said. "He is at the other end of the sector at the moment and asked me to make the retrieval for him."

"I see. I wasn't informed of this."

Aura shrugged. "You know how he can be. Always one thing after another. I swear he decides these things just to impress his rich friends."

"Of course. Well… all right. Your approach codes were correct. Go ahead and transmit the access codes."

She did so with her handheld. Baldun checked his own equipment then checked it again. He seemed hesitant but ultimately gave a nod. "Very well. You'll forgive me if I say I can allow you access, but the rest of your party must remain here."

"That won't be possible," Aura countered. "I can hardly move that much material in my own two hands. My drones go where I do."

"It's not the drones… not *only* the drones, I should say. What are *they* doing here?" he asked, indicating her armored and armed escort.

"They are here to make sure none of your staff or guards try to board my vessel."

"Why would any of us do that, ma'am?"

"Shite happens, as they say. I believe in preparing for bad news before it comes upon me. You obviously do the same, or you wouldn't have these elaborate security measures in place. No?"

"Still, this is most unusual, you understand."

"Is it really?" she asked. "Have either sets of codes changed since we were last here?"

"No, but…"

"I thought not. You have a choice, Captain. You can allow me access to the materials I deposited with my partner weeks ago, or I can leave here empty-handed and spread the word that the *Pecunia* is stealing the wealth of its depositors. It might even be true. How would you like to proceed?" Aura said. As she spoke, she sent a subtle telepathic nudge in his mind, suggesting images of the unrest that denying her might unleash in his business. As an Agent, such direct mental manipulation was against the code of conduct, but she hadn't been an Agent for a long time. Her recent training on Valdos had reminded her just how useful those skills could be.

"Very well. Captain Aura may proceed with Gilgamesh's withdrawal, including her cargo drones and armored escort." Baldun flicked his handheld and the vault door opened. He exited the compartment.

"Thank you," she called behind him. Then, she turned to her crew and said in a low voice, "All right. Let's do this as quickly and efficiently as we can. Lom, give the order to your pilots. Then order the hackers to their places and start causing trouble."

"We serve the Queen!"

The main reception chamber split its walls and dropped the vault module practically on the pirates' feet. Lom remained firm in his stance but Colin and Sacha took several steps back. Maesy folded herself against a wall.

"It's a little nerve-wracking," Aura allowed.

The cargo drones came marching forth from the *Redemption.* Twenty-four of them this time, a greater number than Aura had ordered deployed on any of their previous missions.

"The cash containers are against the rear wall," she noticed, "because of course they are. Well, I guess we'll have to clear a path. Let's get it all sorted and loaded."

"*All* of it?" Colin asked.

"Those are my orders, Mr. Covrani. Lom, make it happen."

"At once, Captain. Come on, you slugs, you heard the order. Time is wasting."

—   —   —

Aboard the *Emerald Queen*, Gallian walked the perimeter of the Command Center, which Tabor had designated his own suite of offices. The Lynaedan had chased him out of his suite for this operation, limiting him to a single office with the door closed and locked. Tabor could observe any channel he wanted but would not be able to give orders of his own, or make any communication at all except through Gallian.

"Karmen will hear about this!" he protested on his way out.

"Let her hear of it! She'll be in the Command Center waiting to make the rendezvous with *Redemption*," Gallian said. "Besides, do you really think she owes you a favor after you insulted her husband?"

"Well. No. But I'll tell her what you're doing anyway!"

"Daveed Sley should have cracked that bottle over your head!" A blip sounded, then a code dropped into Gallian's network. "That's it," he gasped, excitement blossoming in his face. He turned up his comm net to full bandwidth; when he spoke, his voice came out of every speaker on the *Emerald Queen*. "We have a go order! All hackers, begin operations. Drone pilots, run your systems at maximum bandwidth. Sensors, let me know the second we see any unexpected traffic." He got acknowledgements from each section with the dispatch and efficiency long since trained into them.

He smiled. "This is going to be good."

39

CRIME AND PUNISHMENT

IT TOOK MONTHS of bad contacts, missed opportunities, miscommunications, half-truths, and outright lies, but Gil finally had Vladameer Turbashi in his sights. More importantly, Turbashi's multi-billion credit galactic investment fund was within reach.

Despite their direct invitation to the great man, Turbashi had declined to attend this particular gathering. It was a shame. Ham had pulled out all the stops. He'd imported a company of Valdan entertainers just for this event. Chefs plied the guests with exotic dishes, musicians played, dancers performed, and soothsayers wandered through the crowd telling fortunes and dispensing ancient secret knowledge. A few Scorpions wandered through the room to maintain order and ensure the guests all stayed in their respective lanes.

Turbashi had sent his major dormo, a portly, cheerful gentleman named Yarnik. The man had no fewer than two women on his arm at any time and he ate and drank as if to stop for a moment was to court starvation.

Sar, Ham, and Ash were all playing the game with him at the other end of the banquet hall. Gil found the raucous noise they all made to be a little offensive. Why not do the deal because they all wanted it done? Surely, the promise of turning a few billion credits into a hundred billion was incentive enough.

As if reading his mind, Lady Daphine Uragawi snuggled up to him and fed him from a plate of finger food she'd collected from the buffet. "You worry too much."

"Old habits, I'm afraid."

The past few months with her had taught Gil just how narrow his relationship with Aura had been. Business with pleasurable interludes. They'd had enough of each other to maintain sanity but never lost themselves in each other. Daphine was as unlike Aura as he could have wanted; for her, the fun was the goal. And she wasn't shy while on his arm, in the bedroom, or in asking for the occasional expensive gift.

"I don't suppose we could duck out early?" he asked.

"We might be able to manage it. I think it's time for me to introduce you to *Lady Sojourn*," she said.

"She sounds lovely. Is that a parent, a sibling, or a child?"

She swatted him playfully. "*Lady Sojourn* is my yacht. Not as posh as your *Shamhat*, but she gets me from place to place in style. And she has a few tricks built in at great expense. You see, she was originally a racing skiff."

"Is that a fact?"

"Mm-hmm. She uses a custom-built power core, twice the output what's rated for a ship of her size and class. A highly advanced sensor suite, too. It has twice the range of any civilian model, and I had a defense package installed that makes her nearly impossible to damage."

What a boastful phrase coming from someone who's probably never been within ten light years of a space battle. "Sounds delightful."

"I love her. But she's small. She's essentially a luxury hotel room with a jump drive."

"Aren't they all?" His handheld beeped. When he saw the message flash on the screen, his dulled senses took an instant change to adrenaline.

>>**From:** Capt. Baldun, Vault Ship *Pecunia*.

To: Our valued client.

We thank you for your recent withdrawal
from your safe deposit vault. Thank you
for your continued patronage. <<

In a flash, he intuited an emergency in the making. There could only be one person in the galaxy who might be responsible. "Excuse me, my lady, but I must take this. I have an ex-lover to track down and destroy."

Without missing a beat, Daphine said. "Don't let me delay you, my lord. I look forward to hearing all about it."

Gil had to give her credit; whatever else he thought of Lady Uragawi, the woman had nerves of steel and a heart of stone. *Just like Aura.*

He crossed the room twice looking for Ash and snarled when he didn't appear. He spied Sargon making time with a female guest, a woman who'd spent time on Yarnik's arm but been displaced by another. Gil recognized the look on his face and his stance. He was insulting her, looking down his nose and telling her how much better her life could be at his side. She was lapping it up, giggling and sighing. Gil had never been able to figure out how or why that worked. The five thousand credit outfit Sar wore probably had more to do with it. Money was its own aphrodisiac.

Gil yanked on his friend's arm until Sar whirled and hissed at him. "What are you doing? Can't you see I'm working?"

"I have an emergency. Where's Ash?"

"He went back to his ship for some bomaxed thing," Sargon said.

Gil lifted his handheld to his mouth. "Shamhat, tell me where Ash is now," Gil said.

"Lord Ashurbanipal is aboard the *Ishtar*."

"Open a vidcall right now."

"Yes, my lord."

The scene that arrived on Gil's handheld screen was one of barely concealed chaos. Things were out of place and Ash wasn't wearing his customary AI avatar. But he was cursing up a storm, yelling at people who Gil couldn't see. "Ash? What's going on?"

"This motherless station is what's going on!" Ash yelled into the pickup, making Gil want to turn the volume on his reception down all the way. "Someone's trying to break into my Dark Net vault."

"Did they take anything?"

"That's still a question. I alerted the station's security that there was a cyberattack in progress. Those mindless corporate goons slammed shut the access routes to every server on this station. Not only can I not give instructions to my operators off-ship, but I can't even see what the attackers are doing or how they're trying to get through my firewalls. It makes me want to scream. Why the fok aren't we wiping out every bomaxed security company in the galaxy and replacing them with our people? Or am I the only one who thinks of that?"

Gil found an open window and leaned out to scan the docks. There were at least a dozen yachts berthed just on the hotel's frontage. Partygoers liked to arrive in style. But he couldn't see Ash's *Ishtar* or his own vessel from here. "Why don't you debark from the station?" Gil asked.

"I tried that. If there's a security gap, no new exits or entrances to or from the station are allowed until it's resolved. I swear, these people hire their friends, family, and neighbors instead of quality security people."

"What are they after?"

"Who knows? Nothing. Everything! All I know is every server my Dark Net marketplace runs on is under attack and I can't get close enough to the structure to deal with it."

"I have an algorithm for that," Gil said. "Tell the station computer to initiate an emergency departure. It'll set up a conflict and they'll eject your ship rather than risk damage to the station."

Ash's tone transformed from rage to wonder. "That... might just work. How did you know about it?"

"Hang around with Lynaedans, learn a few things," Gil said.

"Wait, Lynaedans... Could Aura be behind this?" Ash gasped.

He hesitated. If she was going after his vault... "I—"

"Gil! What the fok are your tech-heads doing over there?" Ash demanded.

What indeed? In a moment, the party meant less than nothing. "Ash, get out of this station and secure your marketplace. I'll see if I can't stop the attack at the source," Gil said, his voice taking a tone of command.

"Good luck, man."

"You too. Meet me back on Valdos." Gil pocketed his handheld and rushed out of the hotel, racing to *Shamhat*'s berth. He checked the docking kiosk and sure enough, emergency clamps had locked his ship in place.

Gil made his way to his ship's flight deck and said, "Shamhat, close all hatches, sever all umbilical lines, and let me know when we're on internal environment and power."

"Internal environment achieved."

"Execute emergency departure protocol," he said.

"Lord, Gilgamesh, that will cause a conflict with the central computer and cause it to—"

"I'm aware of the consequences. Do it."

"Executing."

An alarm blared as the ship's computer fought with the station's network. After a moment, the station computer erred on the side of caution, blasting *Shamhat* out of the station's hangar bay. The floor flew out from under Gil, who was thrown across the room along with half the furniture in the ship before the ship's gravity field stabilized. But he was free and that was all that mattered.

"Shamhat, review all communications for the past twenty-four hours. Are there any alerts from the vault ship *Pecunia*?"

"Affirmative. There are six in all."

"Play them in sequence."

The final message was a recording of the *Pecunia's* transaction office with Captain Baldun talking to several figures who looked like they were space marines. Except that he recognized two of them as surely as he knew his own name. One was Lom Mench in his command drone. The other was Agent Aurelia Thand of the Tararian Selective Service.

He listened to their conversation with Captain Baldun, barely hearing any of it through his mounting fury.

"Bomax! That foking bitch! Gah!" He inhaled deeply and worked to lower his heart rate. Rage wouldn't solve this problem. Reason and planning would.

The time stamp on the recording was less than an hour old.

He could safely assume the record had been sent just after the intrusion occurred. There was no way Aura would bring the *Emerald Queen* to make that manner of withdrawal; it would set off alarms all over the sector as *Pecunia* reported her presence and called in honest to stars Enforcers and military assets. Captain Baldun had plenty of those. But so did Gilgamesh.

He'd be fine losing his entire fortune as long as he got a chance to blast Agent Aurelia Thand back to the near corpse he'd rescued her from decades ago. He wanted to watch the light in her eyes vanish when he ended her life.

40

PURSUIT

THE JUMP TO *Pecunia*'s current position would take time, and Gil decided there was no need to go through the full security protocol. But he had a way around that. He had Captain Baldun's handheld contact information. The joke was that any given depositor was allowed to contact the captain by handheld once per year for any reason. Today was that day. Gil thumbed the contact and seethed until Baldun accepted the vidcall.

"Captain, I understand there is a problem with my account," Gil accused.

"That is true. I regret that we couldn't—"

"And I regret that I'm not there to crush your windpipe with my bare hands. What type of ship was she flying? A small one, cylindrical with a sloped nose?" Gil demanded.

"No, she arrived in a commercial vessel. An I-40 or something like it. She had a substantial crew with her. Mostly robotics. Drones she called them," Baldun stammered. "And soldiers. Four or five, I think, wearing fancy armored suits."

"Where did she go?"

"Her ship jumped out a short time ago. I don't know her destination…"

"You tracked her on her way out of the vicinity, didn't you? Flash the telemetry to my ship, then."

"Lord Gilgamesh, that violates our client privacy policy—"

"*I* am your client!" Gil roared. "You gave a stranger access to my vault without my authorization or knowledge. Now, flash the telemetry to my ship right the fok now or I'll give you something to stick in your privacy policy!" A few moments later the handheld beeped as the data was delivered. "Thank you. What did she come away with?"

"I couldn't possibly—"

"Activate the security camera in my vault right now and show me its contents."

"Yes, sir."

The screen flickered then cleared to show Gil an empty room. No, not completely empty. A single open cash box sat in the center of the space. And something else, a scrap of script. He zoomed in and did his best to read the message written there: >>A GOOD MEAL IS BETTER THAN THE FINEST COAT.<<

He recognized Ham's quote instantly. It was a taunt, a kick in the face, pure and simple. "That… thieving… *woman!*" he screamed.

A thousand threats and rebukes flew through Gil's mind, but he simply hung up on Baldun. There was no point to continuing the conversation. He needed real help, not excuses and obsequious nonsense.

"Shamhat, open the help files. Which contact with access to military assets is closest to *Pecunia*'s current position?"

"Officer Piver is the commander of Militia Customs Squadron Velasco."

Customs meant convoy escorts and interceptors with system defense gunships. Perfect. "Pull up his file." Gil spent a few minutes re-familiarizing himself with Piver's history and connections, then placed the vidcall through his yacht's secure switchboard.

"This is Piver."

"Officer Piver, this is Gilgamesh."

"Who?"

So it's like that, today, is it? "You remember me, Officer. I'm the one who paid for that vacation house on Merda. And your oldest boy getting into that fancy, elite business program on Phiris? That was me, too. Today, you're going to pay for it all."

"Ah, *Gilgamesh*. Sorry, I'm not good with names."

"All will be forgiven if you follow instructions. The vault ship *Pecunia* has just reported a robbery. I lost substantial assets in the attack. I need you to run down the perpetrators and impound their vessel."

"If I impound it, I have to collect it as evidence. You'll lose your stuff."

"The loss is regrettable but secondary. Their captain is Mother Carnage. Surely you've heard of her. Run that thief down and I'll take care of her personally." Gil uploaded an image of Aura to make sure the point was made.

Piver accepted the new data with a frown. "It would help if you knew where she was."

"That's easily done. I'm sending you the coordinates of the vault ship now. She's just left and she's flying a standard commercial carrier, an older I-40 merchant. She can't have gotten far."

"I see. Can you tell us anything we need to know about her?"

"She used to be a TSS Agent. Aurelia Thand."

Piver hesitated, finally answering in a slow drawl. "That presents a problem."

"Not really. Use heavy support weapons and blow that ship apart."

"*That* sounds like overkill to me, not an impound. We'll just stick to established doctrine, if you don't mind."

"Established doctrine? You mean ordering her to heave-to for an inspection? Does that cover you going up against a trained TSS Agent?"

"It does not."

Gil just wanted the conversation to be over. "Here's the situation, my friend. If Aura gets her telekinetic talons on you, she'll pop your smarmy head open as easily as a toddler squashes a grape. Overwhelming firepower is your only hope of victory against that kind of talent."

Another hesitation from Piver. Gil got the impression there was someone else on hand giving him advice. "I believe we can oblige. Task Force Grand Slam, that's the one we want. Six Evictor-class gunships loaded with missiles and laser turrets. A commercial cargo vessel would be badly tested by even one of those monsters. She won't get away. But I need to know where to send them."

"She's heading for the *Emerald Queen*," Gil surmised. "I'd bet that Aura is planning to rendezvous with her in deep space. *Redemption*'s last known trajectory was along this vector. You'll deploy along that line of travel. Her ship has a typical navigation system with standard cooldown periods. Plenty of time for your ships to triangulate her position using long-range scans. When she returns to normal space, overtake and destroy her."

Officer Piver sighed dramatically. "We can't blanket every destination. Even with military jump drives, I don't have the ships for that."

Gil's rage filled his soul and boiled his blood. His head felt ready to pop like a balloon. "You don't need to blanket anything. You only need to cover every beacon location within two jumps of *Pecunia*'s last known location which is… here. The mother ship will be there."

"But it's deep space. There are no ports there."

"'It's deep space'," Gil mimicked in a whiny voice. "She won't be meeting the *Emerald Queen* at a port. Ports are where Enforcers work. Ports have security cameras every twenty meters. Aura is smarter than that. She's got the *Emerald Queen* waiting at a beacon in deep space, not a bomaxed *port*! Triangulate the correct beacon and find her. It really is that simple. Do I have to pilot your task force, too?"

The look on Piver's face was one Gil recognized: he knew he was not going to win this fight and refused to die on this hill, payoff or not. "I'll order my forces to deploy as appropriate for your *reasoned* estimation."

Gil bowed deeply. "Oh, *thank you*, so kindly. The minute you locate Aura, send me her location and I'll meet you there in *Shamhat*. Now get your ships out there and find the *Redemption* before she reaches the *Emerald Queen*!"

41

A STRATEGIC WITHDRAWAL

AURA WATCHED THE blue-green lights of subspace fly past, feeling eerily disconnected from reality. Her hold was filled with Gil's treasure horde. While she understood she'd gotten away with a grand slam of a heist, she felt empty and alone.

"Revenge is supposed to feel sweet, so why am I so miserable?" she asked.

Colin turned his head. "Captain?"

She shook her head gravely. What was done was done and there was no going back to what was. "I don't usually end my relationships like this," she said. "It's a new experience."

"My relationships always ended themselves," Colin murmured. "But they probably weren't that high-quality in the first place."

"I had a few like that, too."

Colin's shoulders rounded. "Sorry, I have to ask now. Do you think me and Kaia—"

"That's the wrong question. Do you want to be the man

who's worthy of her?"

"My family loves her. We have a lot in common."

"Do you?"

"Well…"

She should shut up; she had no business giving anyone life advice. But the words tumbled out of her in a rush. "Colin, love isn't something you can try to make happen with fancy gifts. You're not pitching an idea to a prospect. Two people either have a unique and special connection or they don't."

"You had Gil for years, though."

"That's different. I was looking down the barrel of certain death, and Gil threw me a lifeline. We had fun, we made a good living, but we were never each other's favorite person. If you really want Kaia to feel that way about you, then you need to step up and become the man she wants. But if all you two have is GravX, then accept it, and enjoy that instead."

"How do I know which is which?"

Aura tapped her console, hoping there'd be an emergency so she wouldn't have to answer. But she couldn't help herself. "I'd start by learning everything I could about life from Daveed Sley. He's the kind of man she'll choose." *The kind of man who might have saved me for real.* She knew the thought wasn't accurate… a man like Daveed would have welcomed her home after the Bakzen War—had she survived it—but he never would have advised her to shirk her duty to the TSS.

All at once, a tidal wave of envy washed over her and Aura hated Karmen beyond all words. But it passed quickly. No use hashing out the past since there was no way to change it. At the same time, she wondered if Karmen truly understood how much joy the universe had awarded her for her sacrifices.

Colin's voice took on a subdued, almost robotic tone. "Thank you for your honest comments. I will consider them closely."

Good for you, Aura. Now you've gone and hurt the boy's feelings. Oh well... maybe he'll listen someday. "Just focus on your duties for now," she told him. "Let tomorrow be what it is."

"Yes, ma'am."

The door to the rear compartment opened and the rest of the crew joined them. Lom, in particular, was in high spirits. "Aura! Colin! I bring joyous news."

Aura's heart soared. *Oh, thank the stars, it was getting way too introspective here.* "Report?"

"Sacha, Maesy, and I have done a spot check of the cargo and made some rudimentary calculations based on what we know about Lord Ashurbanipal's Dark Net marketplace. I believe we can put an estimated value on what we now carry."

"Don't keep us in suspense, what do we have?" Colin asked.

"How does eight hundred million credits grab you?" Lom asked.

"It grabs me pretty tightly," Colin gushed. "Dude, that's almost a billion credits. Holy... Gah!"

Aura's guts flopped in her abdomen, but she couldn't argue with the boy's reaction. "That's my best day's work ever. Now we merely have to keep it."

"I gave your engines a bit of a goose when we went to subspace," Maesy said. "I might be able to reduce our next cooldown time a bit, too."

Aura tapped her console. "Good to hear. Colin, when is our exit point?"

"Coming up... normal space... now." Space warped and the viewport cleared to show them the star-studded infinity of normal space.

Old habits took over immediately. Aura opened the displays and began running through her checklists. "Let's find somewhere to lay low. There… a small gas giant less than ten minutes away. Colin, plot us a close orbit and take us in."

"Yes, Captain. Course plotted, pion drive engaged."

"Good job. There's your first rule of cargo running. Never stay in one spot for more than a few minutes if you can avoid it. Maesy, if you can minimize our time here, that would be ideal."

"On it."

"Sacha, you're on long range scans. Tell me the moment you see anything unusual."

"Callum is much better than I am for that, but I am on the job."

Aura couldn't watch the engineer work in the rear compartment, but evidence of Maesy's alterations arrived at a fierce rate. Aura fidgeted as the countdown clock reset three times. Part of her mind screamed at her to *do something*, but there was nothing to do but wait. When the clock ran down to zero and she initiated the next jump, she held her breath and didn't let it out until they were back in subspace.

"That was surprisingly tense," Colin noted. "You did this for twenty years?"

"No! I rarely had to look over my shoulder when I ran cargo. The stakes were quite low on any given job. Today, the stakes are as high as they can be. Do you see the difference?"

"I can imagine. I guess it's much easier to stay inside the *Emerald Queen* and pretend we're in a giant building than to be exposed like we are here," Colin surmised.

"That is part of it."

"Captain, may I ask a question?" Sacha inquired.

"Of course, Ops. What is it?"

"What's the weirdest cargo you ever carried in this ship?"

"You just spot checked it."

"No, I mean before this?"

"That's easy. I was paid handsomely to transport a hold full of corpses. Four hundred Taran bodies."

"I expect that was a very quiet voyage," Lom joked.

Aura relaxed as she told the story. "Believe it or not it was very funny. I had two assistants working here at the time. All three of us lived on this flight deck. No one went back to the hold for any reason for five days. We ate and slept at our stations and used the forward washroom here for everything. We made station fall, I unloaded the cargo and got paid, then I handed out shares and salaries. The crew quit on the spot, and I never saw either of them again."

"At least they kept their heads long enough to get paid first," Colin noted.

"I know I shouldn't ask this, but why would anyone transport corpses?" Maesy asked.

"My client didn't tell me, and I didn't ask," Aura said.

"They have a variety of uses," Lom offered. "Medical education, weapons development, vehicle safety research, insurance fraud, chemical reduction, biotechnology—"

"I get the picture. Thank you, Commander."

"Coming up on our final waypoint," Colin announced. "Two minutes."

Aura went back to work with practiced habits. "Places everyone. This is either going to be very simple or very complicated."

Time elongated then snapped back as *Redemption* transitioned from subspace back to normal space.

"We're at the rendezvous point," Colin reported.

"Engines cooldown proceeding," Maesy added.

"Long-range scans operating… all clear," Sacha said. "I guess we're early for our meet up."

Aura and Colin shared a pointed glance. Aura kept her relief well hidden, but Colin sagged in his chair. "Did anyone remember to tell Karmen that we jumped earlier than planned?" Aura asked. "No, that would have been my job. Ha!"

"Surely, she wouldn't be late," Lom said.

"Not at all. Karmen is extremely punctual. But that means we have some time to kill before she arrives." Then, Aura froze as Sacha spoke up.

"One contact. Correction. Two... four... five... six contacts, closing fast from bearing two-six-two mark twelve."

"Speed?"

"They'll be within weapons range in minutes. Running profile IDs now... they all have TSS drive signatures. But I'm not familiar with that ship class."

"I am... those are Evictors!" Colin blurted. "We are so screwed."

Aura did a quick system scan only to confirm that there was nothing around them but more space. No natural radio sources, nothing to confuse or confound an enemy's sensors except the equipment the *Redemption* carried. "I guess it's going to be complicated," Aura griped. "Maesy, is there any chance of..."

"Negative. We can't jump out."

"Understood. Lom, if you have anything clever to suggest, now is the time."

"In fact, I have one idea. Maesy, come with me to the cargo deck. We have twenty-four drones to turn into decoys."

Aura ignored them as they retreated aft. "Colin, set up an evasive plot. Sacha, load the gunnery program and enable auto-targeting on both laser turrets. Domes up, crew! It's going to be a bumpy ride!"

— — —

Officer Lorn Piver seethed as he watched the countdown clock run through the last seconds before the task force returned to normal space.

He never should have let Gilgamesh into his life. That was now certain. He'd known what kind of glad-handing troll the finance bro was when they'd met, but Piver had been worrying about his family and their future. Patrik had the grades for a prestigious business program on Phiris, but the tuition was beyond his means. And the house needed repairs—which were expensive—but the dream of buying a family retreat had been instilled in him by his father, who'd worked himself to death in one factory job after another. Going back through his memory, Piver doubted his old man had taken a vacation in his entire life.

Then, one day, Piver had answered an ad on the Dark Net. Security work for a hefty amount of money, off the books and on his own time. He'd done the job and been given an access code, then gone to a spaceport locker and pulled out a bag of money. More security jobs got the house repairs paid for.

A month later, Gil had called him directly and they'd done a deal. His boy's future and a vacation house were suddenly reality. But TSS rules forbade him from doing security work on the side, no matter what the cause. He was on the hook for life.

Officer Marik, his first officer, broke him out of his self-loathing. "Returning to normal space." The universe expanded and snapped back.

Almost immediately, the sensor officer began calling out the arrivals of his task force's Evictors. The tactical display lit with one extra blip. "Contact! Looks like a commercial trader to me. Sir, there's no transponder—just a garbage signature."

"Scrambled unless you have the right encryption key, you mean," Piver said. "If I were looking to rendezvous with my friends after a bank robbery, that's what I'd do, too. Link the task force on the common intel channel. All crews go to battle stations, full defensive posture. Active pings on all scanning gear. Let them know we see them."

"All ships report battle stations, weapons, datalinks, and comms ready. Defensive posture is in effect for all ships."

"Scan for weapons and defenses," Piver ordered. "Let's create an attack profile and make sure there are no surprises going forward."

Marik sniffed. "Those old ships get modded within a centimeter of their lives. No good smuggler misses the opportunity to make changes."

Piver came up behind the officer's station and put his hands on the man's shoulders. "Mr. Marik, are you going to give me a profile report or just pontificate for an hour?"

"Sorry. It's an I-40B independent trader. Power core seems to be emitting a standard profile, but the jump drive has a weird emission signature to it. They might be trying to goose it, to jump out sooner."

"They won't get the chance. What about weapons?"

"Nothing to compare with ours. Two laser turrets and one short range missile rack on the rear upper hull. Not a problem."

"Good. Get a lock on that ship. Comms, contact Lord Gilgamesh."

"Yes, sir. Go ahead."

Piver resisted the urge to spit.   "Gil, we have the *Redemption* in sight, I'm sending you the coordinates now. She won't get away or out-fight us in that rust bucket."

"Acknowledged. I'm jumping in now." The comm beeped as the call ended.

"Do you think that guy is having a bad day or is he always like this?" Marik asked.

Piver scoffed. "I think if my wife emptied my bank account and ran off, I'd still have the Service. It'd suck, but it'd be enough to get me through whatever came next. All that poor bastard ever had is his reputation and self-image. And at the risk of throwing a stone at a glass house of my own, those are pretty fragile things."

"I don't know, that kind of money…"

"Eyes on your console, Officer. All ships, prepare to attack!"

— — —

"It would be a great shame to lose any of this," Lom said as he made his way down the center of the cargo deck. The cargo drones had locked the various cases, boxes, and crates to individual pallets and tied them down securely, creating islands of wealth throughout the cargo space. But the drones themselves were merely standing in lines of twelve on either side of the deck. Not only were they not locked down, they weren't even docked in recharging stations.

"I agree, Commander. There's too much here for us to stuff it all in our pockets."

They stopped before the drone control unit, a solid-state item they'd installed from the *Queen*'s stocks of spare parts. Lom used his nanofiber wires to connect to the data port while Maesy threw switches on each drone, in turn.

When she finished, she said, "They're all ready for new programing. You may upload your data at will."

"Uploading… but we need to program different frequencies into each drone. This will take time."

"We don't need to wait until you're finished. I can throw them out the back of the ship as you complete each transfer."

"The airlock doesn't cycle that quickly."

"It doesn't have to. Drop the rear deck to space. I can take it." Lom watched her transform herself. Her skin silvered with nanotech plates and her eyes filmed over with light-sensitive guards. She tapped the back of her head to engage a comm relay and suddenly her voice was in Lom's head. "Just say when, sir."

"Brilliant, Chief Engineer. But you could have just put your helmet on."

"I got excited."

"Very well. Start with that one," he ordered. One of the drones at the rear of the deck raised its arm and stepped out of position.

Maesy moved to the rear of the deck and pulled a switch. Alarms sounded as the deck vented its atmosphere to storage tanks and the rear doors opened wide. She lifted the drone and kicked it off the deck.

They proceeded that way, drone by drone, until the last had been ejected out the rear. Then they closed the doors, repressurized the bay, and returned to the flight deck.

"Sacha, engage program Drone-Decoy-936," Lom ordered.

"Engaging now."

"Captain, if you're going to run now is the time to do it. Those beacons will be showing up on our pursuers' sensors in moments. No need to make it easy for them to tell which is the real starship."

"Agreed. We're off on every random course I can imagine. How much time until the *Queen* arrives, Colin?"

"If Officer Sley keeps to the schedule, about forty-one minutes. Two full GravX periods," he joked.

"And the entire playing track just got bumped up to 6-Gs," Sacha added.

— — —

The blue and green swirl of subspace flew by while *Shamhat* closed the distance to their destination. Gilgamesh stood on the flight deck, only slightly less incensed than he was on their last call. Task Force Grand Slam had intercepted Aura's ship, but now they couldn't even shoot at her. Piver's written report had shown at least twenty vessels. The *Redemption* was spoofing the sensors. Gil cursed being in subspace so he couldn't chew out the officer in real-time for not having a single bomaxed technical specialist to figure out a work-around.

Even if they did burn through every ghost on their screens, it would take time for them to figure out what was real and what was mere noise. They just had to keep the *Redemption* in-system until he arrived.

"Shamhat," Gil intoned.

Her avatar abruptly appeared next to him, making him jump. "How may I be of service?"

"How long until we arrive at Aura's plotted position?"

"Three minutes."

"Prepare to turn out all the electronic countermeasures as soon as we drop out. I want to see exactly what we're looking at."

"Acknowledged. Sensor suite active. Prepared to engage countermeasures."

The clock ticked down the last few seconds. Gil held his breath as the universe elongated then snapped back in transition to normal space.

Within seconds he could see how Piver had been fooled. Twenty-four targets now presented themselves, and every one of them looked exactly like the *Redemption's* target profile and transponder ID.

"Well, that's confusing," he admitted. "Gilgamesh to Piver."

"This is Piver."

"Set your Evictors to fire one missile at each target on my mark. Make sure that your ships don't fire at the same target more than once."

"What will that do?"

"It'll show you what you're missing. Make it happen, and we can all go home in a hurry."

"Setting up our shot now. You'd better be right about this."

Gil found his heart rate increasing just thinking about the image of *Redemption* exploding into a thousand parts. "Trust me."

ALL GOOD THINGS

K<small>ARMEN</small> S<small>LEY</small> <small>WATCHED</small> subspace slip by as the countdown clock reduced to nothing. She was actually looking forward to having a clean safe rendezvous, picking up the *Redemption*, and congratulating Aura on a job well done.

"Dropping into normal space," announced the nav officer.

Time stretched to infinity and then snapped back to the present shape. The viewscreen flickered and came into focus to show her a scene of chaos. Alarms sounded and Callum began reading off contacts' locations, bearings, and speeds too quickly for her to follow. *Redemption* was out there somewhere but she had no idea even where to look. However, she had no problem spotting the six TSS drive signatures on the sensor display.

Karmen gaped at the viewscreen. "What the fok are we looking at?"

Gallian came up to her with news. "Looks like Aura was jumped by a Militia customs fleet. *Redemption*'s emergency beacons are signaling us. And Aura's beaming us a priority one request for pickup and aid."

"Double check that," Karmen murmured.

Gallian glanced around at the Command Center's crew. Everyone was occupied with their own stations. He sidled up to her and said, "It checks out. But I suppose it *could* be a trick."

Karmen felt herself floating, unconnected to the events forming around her. Suspended in time. What if the TSS ships had simply found Aura's ship and were doing their legal and moral duty? What if this was a scene of justice being played out here in real-time?

Gallian lowered his voice to a near whisper. "It's known you have issues with Aura. Some of us have issues with Lom, too. You're acting captain. How do you want to proceed?"

She understood his question instantly. There was a real opportunity here, to be done with all the criminal nonsense and moral drama. To put the question of Aura Thand's life of crime to rest permanently. Without Aura, there was no New Akkadia. Karmen could go home. She could take her family and board a shuttle and head back to Greengard. She'd meet up with Lee and Armin, talk to whatever Agent assigned to debrief them and that would be that. She'd go back to her old life. Back to regular sleep patterns in her own bed. Making meals in her own kitchen working over her own stove. Watching movies in her basement. Playing video games with her kids. Kozu would come home for holidays. Kaia would go to college and...

"Oh, fok! Kaia!"

In a flash, she realized her error. Leaving Aura's fate to the universe was one thing. But Aura had a crew aboard the *Redemption*. Sacha. Maesy. *Colin*. None of them deserved to pay the same price as their rogue Agent captain.

Her mind made up, Karmen shook off her lethargy. "Gallian, tell the *Redemption* we're on our way. Warn those Militia vessels off."

"That warning might have more impact coming from you. I'm prepared to record a message."

Karmen cleared her throat. "Attention, Militia vessels. This is Mother Courage aboard the *Emerald Queen*. We are engaged in rescue operations of the cargo ship *Redemption*. Do you wish to assist us?"

Gallian nodded and smirked. "Nicely worded. That'll put them on the defensive. Sending now."

They didn't have to wait long for an answer. "Mother Courage, this is Officer Piver of the TSS. We are engaged in a customs interdiction. Stand down and vacate this vicinity or be fired upon."

"How rude," Callum scoffed.

"Why do they want us to *vacate* the vicinity? Why not just shoot us?" Gallian mused.

Karmen understood the issue. "They want us gone because they're not supposed to be here, either. We're a known criminal element attempting to aid a galactic thief. If it was a real interdiction, they wouldn't give us a choice— they'd just board us. Well, I guess that's that," she said. "I'm not sure what else I expected. Sensors, warm up the EWAR gear. Ops, make ready with all weapon systems. We're going in to assist Aura."

She took a seat in the command chair, confident that she finally understood what was going on around her. She'd operated *Triumph* plenty of times with Aura in absentia, and this time she had a clear, succinct goal: rescue the *Redemption* from the pursuing gunships. More importantly, she'd seen what the *Emerald Queen* was capable of at her captain's right hand. Karmen knew she could handle this.

The problem was how to cause as little damage to the TSS gunships as possible.

"They're shifting their formation, spreading out to put distance between themselves," Callum reported. "How competent can they be?"

They found out. A new display appeared, showing them how the six Evictor gunships positioned themselves into a phalanx and then each ship launched a volley of missiles, which fanned out in multiple directions. The sky filled with explosions.

"That's it. All the decoys are gone," Callum announced.

"I'd say Officer Piver knows exactly what he's doing," Karmen suggested. "They pooled their fire control computers and blanketed the field and shot every target they could find." *And I should have thought about that before I sat down in the command chair. I'm too far out of practice on a flight deck. Maybe I'm not cut out for leadership, after all.*

"They missed the *Redemption*, though." Gallian said.

"Ops, give us a close up of Aura's ship." The image changed as the Ops officer obeyed his directions. "No, they didn't miss. You see that plume? They're venting atmosphere."

"Captain, I have one additional signature on my screen. It's Gilgamesh's yacht, *Shamhat*."

"That's interesting. What is Aura's creepy ex-boyfriend doing here?"

"Looks like he's chasing her. The TSS units are reforming into their original formation. It looks like they're going to try to cut her off."

"Good luck with that. Aura and Colin are excellent pilots," Karmen observed as she racked her brain, running through all the permutations of a potential battle.

The Ops officer signaled to her. "Captain, we have all weapons primed and ready to fire. I can drop every enemy ship with plasma beams from here."

"We're not killing any TSS ships."

"But, ma'am—"

"Those are my orders, Ops."

"Karmen!" Callum blurted. "You stood right there weeks ago," he pointed to the spot near the nav console, "and helped us destroy a cloud of attacking ships and shuttles. What makes this crowd any different?"

Karmen glared at the sensor operator. "It's one thing to blow up targets that are shooting at you. It's a whole other order of problematic to start killing TSS crews, even hopelessly corrupt ones, who insist they are doing their jobs. You start down that road, and Agents will show up on your doorstep and execute you. Maybe you'd live out your days on a prison planet, if you're very lucky."

"I disagree. This ship is un-trackable, and—"

That was enough. Karmen dashed to Callum and leaned over him, barely contained rage in her eyes. "Sensors! If you can't do your job, call a relief. We are not destroying those gunships. That's final."

Callum frowned but kept his peace. "Yes, ma'am. Awaiting your orders."

She pulled the tactical display closer. "Why am I seeing seven targets?"

"That blip there is *Shamhat*, Gilgamesh's yacht. His ship is almost as fast as the Evictors. He must have put a lot of work into—"

"I don't need the commentary. How well is it armed?" Karmen snapped.

"I have no idea," Callum admitted. "But he's pushing his

way through the formation. He seems intent on hitting Aura himself."

Kill him, and Aura gets her life back. Here we go, then. "Nav, put us on an intercept course and make sure we approach *Redemption's* stern. Put this ship between Aura and those gunships. Ops, load all missile tubes for proximity warheads. Then charge every reactive armor plate on the rear quadrants, and tell the crew to brace for detonation. This is going to get messy."

—   —   —

Aura began to sweat despite her battle armor's attempt to cool her body. *Redemption* shook as a laser blast impacted her stern. A second later, a hit registered on the HUD. The rear doors were being pummeled, they'd already lost a quarter of their maximum speed, and despite the turrets throwing out lasers and missiles behind them, their fire wasn't hitting the pursuing TSS gunships.

And, worst of all, she felt a familiar presence in her mind—his voice raging at her, demanding she stop and surrender. Gil, using what little telepathic ability he had to make her miserable. *Well, when wasn't he, on one level or another?*

"*Aura, you're not helping anyone!*" he sent. "*It doesn't have to be this way.*"

"Yes, Gil, it very much does," she said aloud.

Lom picked up on her tone. "Aura?"

"It's Gil. He's in my head, and he won't shut up."

"That's unfortunate for everyone," Lom agreed. "But there's good news. We just picked up a new contact on the sensor array. It's a substantial mass. I do believe Karmen Sley has arrived with the *Emerald Queen*."

"Confirmed!" Sacha cried. "They're maneuvering toward us but they're almost two full light-minutes away."

"And a ship that size can't very well start and stop in a flash. We'll have to meet her halfway," Colin said. "Permission to try a really stupid maneuver?"

Aura nodded, then remembered she was wearing a helmet and no one aboard would see her head motions. "Granted. Stupid might be all we have left. What do you have in mind?"

"I'm going to flap our wings and spit in their faces. May I issue orders to the crew?"

"Of course!"

Colin sat up straighter and barked orders. "Sacha, overheat the weapon turrets and get ready for constant fire."

"I'll set it but if the heat sinks fail, you'll only have a couple of shots per turret before the focusing elements burn out."

"Can you target and shoot everything at Gilgamesh's yacht while I'm turning the ship on its tail?"

"Watch me, Covrani. I can even set the missile launcher to dump its entire remaining magazine into one giant sustained volley."

"Perfect. Maesy! Can we throw the pion drive into full reverse without destroying it?"

"It'll overheat very quickly if you do that, but yes. It's possible."

"Then that's what we're doing. Commander Mench, can you supercharge the EM burst array? Blanket the shuttles with all the noise in the universe?"

"Yes, I can."

"Then get ready and let's see if we live or die from this." Colin went through the motions of cracking his knuckles even though the sound never made it to the comms. "Hang on!"

— — —

Gil stood on *Shamhat*'s flight deck, convinced that if he sat down he wouldn't be able to see the moment when Aura faded from the universe. He wanted to see that happen.

He cast out telepathically. Knowing Aura as well as he did, she was easy to find among all the minds that were nearby. Her mental guards were active and thick; piercing them with a psychic attack was out of the question. But she could still hear him. He was talking to her, distracting her, telling her anything he could think of. It seemed to be working. She was making mistakes, maneuvering her ship into the missile volleys the TSS gunships were tossing her way.

But that loudmouth, Piver, would not shut up. "Gil, stay back there. We have the situation under control."

"Just keep your distance and let me work," Gil growled.

Then, Shamhat spoke up, disturbing his concentration further. "I'm sorry, my lord, but were you intending to send that response?"

"Yes! Send it. Send everything!"

"As you wish."

"Shamhat, increase our speed. Catch up to the *Redemption* any way you have to."

"Acknowledged. Entering pursuit mode."

What he'd never told Aura about his yacht was that *Shamhat* had been continually upgraded over the years. These days, she was at the point where she could easily keep pace with any TSS pion drive, at least in normal space. She might even give Lady Daphine Uragawi's *Lady Sojourn* a run for the money in a race. Once Aura was gone, he might go back to Daphine and suggest it to her. She would probably say yes. She was open to new experiences.

A stray thought intruded into his mind. *You have Daphine. She's everything you want. Why chase Aura?*

Why? Because she stole from me, after everything I've done for her.

You've done things to her, too. Dismissed her ideas. Called her names. Told her she was slacking, lazy. You have money sequestered all over the sector. Why chase Aura?

"I will not let her get away!" he shouted aloud.

"Is that an order, my lord?" Shamhat asked.

"Yes! It's an order. I am giving you a—"

"New contact bearing one-eight-seven. Range eight light minutes."

"Identify it," Gil ordered. It was probably yet another TSS gunship, not that they were doing their jobs very well.

"Transponder indicates a yacht. The *Lady Sojourn*," Shamhat reported.

"Daphine? What is she doing here?" Gil wondered.

A loud voice interrupted his train of thought. "Gil, this is Piver. Break off, now! That ship is up to something."

"Stars, why can't everyone leave me alone so I can get the job done?" Gil groaned.

"Collision alert!" Shamhat yelled, and suddenly the flight deck was filled with alarms and warning lights.

All at once, new displays sprang into being, alerting him, surrounding him and blinding him as they interfered with their overlap. Blinding him to any use they might have had. Gil reached out and threw them to the side, and froze as he watched *Redemption*'s nose growing ever larger in the viewscreen.

"Emergency evasive maneuvers, now!" he yelled, purely out of reflex.

More displays popped up to warn him of impending fire

coming from the approaching cargo vessel. The yacht swerved violently, throwing him off his feet a second time. Sparks rained down from newly opened seams in the equipment and the stench of ozone filled his nose.

All the while, Officer Piver's voice rang across the flight deck, through the still-open comm. "I say again, stay back from the fight. We will handle this!"

"Shamhat," Gil coughed as he lifted himself into the command seat. "Is the Zero Cannon functional?"

"Affirmative, my lord. It will fire. But I'd recommend that you enter the life pod instead."

"Not until I'm finished. Close to optimal range and fire at *Redemption*!"

— — —

Karmen couldn't help but fidget in the *Emerald Queen*'s command chair. "That's it, Nav. Keep up our speed and course. Keep our reactive armor plates pointed to their field of fire."

She had to give the nav officer credit. He knew exactly how much thrust to apply and how to direct it to spin the giant spacecraft to come out of their grand turn ahead of the pursuing TSS gunships.

"They're launching missiles. Stars, six, seven volleys. Impact in ten seconds."

"Brace for impact!" Karmen sang.

The displays flickered as the numerous warheads detonated against the hull. A dull thud reverberated through the ship, and indicator lights winked from blue to red.

"Damage report?" she asked.

The Ops officer sounded strangely subdued. "Reactive plates ten through twenty are gone. Superficial damage reported on Decks 5 and 6. No casualties."

"Is that all they've got?" Callum sneered.

"Trust me, Sensors, they have plenty more. But our size is our greatest defense," Karmen said. "Thank Captain Solari for that much, anyway. Ops, update the tactical display. Show me who's where."

Ops complied quickly and the display shifted as Karmen watched. Nav had expertly arranged for the *Emerald Queen*'s bulk to shield the *Redemption* from the attacking missiles. But there was one thing more to worry about. "Where's that yacht?" she wondered aloud. "Sensors, find me that yacht. Did he drop behind the gunships when we weren't looking?"

"Scanning all rear quadrants... I'm not seeing him. Wait, there he is. He's in front of us."

It was true. *Shamhat* was closing distance with *Redemption* even while the heavy cargo ship was maneuvering closer to it. "What is he doing?" she asked.

"Whatever's happening— Wait, *Redemption* is turning on her short axis. She's turning to fight! Her targeting array is at full power and her weapons are hot," Callum said.

Good for you, Aura. Paste that playboy all over his flight deck! "Are we in weapons range?" Karmen asked.

Ops answered her. "Negative. Extreme missile range only."

"New contacts. Two more missile volleys. These are going to hurt," Callum reported.

"Brace for impact!" The next set of missiles detonated in a cloud around the great battleship, peppering her hull with shrapnel and destructive energy.

"More damage to the mid-decks," Ops reported.

"Engineering is reporting fires below decks," Gallian said. "Nothing they can't handle, but they're evacuating part of Deck 9."

"Sensors took a hit, too," Callum added. "Max range is down to a fraction of normal. It'll take forever to fix out here."

"Do what you can, Callum. Can you still see *Redemption* and *Shamhat*?"

"Yes, but they're at the edge of my range now. It's tough to keep track."

"I hate that TSS Officer," Karmen snarled. "He's far too good at his job and learns way too quickly."

"I'm reading an explosion aboard *Shamhat*," Callum said. "But there's also a steep power spike. She's shooting at *Redemption*."

Karmen leaned forward to watch the attack on her screen. The yacht blasted Aura's ship with a high-energy weapon. All at once, the status profile for *Redemption* turned from yellow to red.

"*Redemption*'s status?"

"She's badly damaged but still functional," Callum confirmed.

"Ops. Lock all missile tubes onto *Shamhat*. Contact fuses. Fire when ready."

—   —   —

Red lights flashed on *Redemption*'s flight deck as smoke filled the interior of the cargo ship. Aura couldn't imagine why, but the pion drive hadn't given up yet and the power core still worked. Maesy connected her nanofiber wires to the ship's controls, using micro-venting techniques to kill the fires in the engineering section without asphyxiating the crew. Sacha was waving her arms to clear the fire that was consuming her console as the weapons linkage sputtered and died.

"Where is the *Queen*?" Aura shouted.

"Behind us," Colin said. "Turning for a pickup now."

"Missiles incoming," Lom announced. "The *Queen* is shooting at *Shamhat.*"

Aura understood that whatever else might happen, she'd given every order she could and now had to wait for her crew to follow instructions.

She lay back in her command chair. Clearing her mind, she sought out Gil's own thoughts and finally allowed his mind to connect with hers.

"*Why?*" he asked telepathically.

"*All I wanted was your respect,*" she told him.

"*I gave you what I had.*"

"*Not what really mattered. You let Sar push you around. I always knew this was a bad idea.*"

"Ten seconds to impact," Lom said.

"*Gil, abandon your ship. Now,*" she ordered.

"*Can't. Too late.*"

Aura stayed focused on him as the missiles detonated, turning *Shamhat* into a fireball. She took some comfort from knowing that in his last moments of life, Gil felt very calm. He felt heat but no pain. Then, he was gone.

A horrible silence filled her mind. But in that silence, there was also peace. Freedom. "Get us aboard the *Queen* and jump us out of here!"

43

WE SERVE THE QUEEN

GALLIAN MET THEM on the *Emerald Queen*'s hangar deck, followed by a platoon of cargo drones. As Lom stepped off the gangway, Gallian was there. "The Queen wants a word. She's agitated."

"I've seen her agitated before."

Gallian shook his head. "Not like this. She wants the full core group."

"I see. Well, let's not keep her waiting." Lom turned to Aura as she stepped on to her ship's hangar deck. "Captain, I'll attend to the unloading and storage of the newly acquired bounty. I would suggest you and Colin stop by the infirmary on your way to your quarters. I see first degree burns on your faces."

"Very well. Carry on. And thank you, Lom," Aura murmured and nodded for Colin to follow.

When they were out of sight, the four Lynaedans retreated to *Redemption*'s flight deck. They took their seats and Lom opened up the dedicated gateway that transported them into the Queen's realm.

"Lom!" she yelled from her throne. "What was the meaning of that?"

"Could you be a bit more specific, ma'am?"

"Don't be dense. That wanton act of revenge. What was Aura thinking? More importantly, why did you allow her to proceed?"

"I thought having the core group with me would help manage the situation. And, in all honesty, we needed the contents of that vault to help prepare for our departure."

"I understand, but that ship... look at it!" The *Redemption* sat around them, but its exterior was a mess.

"It can be fixed," Maesy assured her. "A few days in the repair shop and as much love as Lula and I can give her, and she'll be back in service."

The Queen seethed. "I don't like the changes in her one bit. Aura's becoming reckless. Unreliable. You insisted I could trust her judgement."

"Up to now, we've been able to," Lom said. "What has changed?"

"The plan needs to be accelerated. I'm running out of time. I've sensed a new player. An AI that refuses all contact. It's still far away, but it grows closer every day. But it wants to find me. That much is certain. I've seen it."

"That is worrisome. Well, we've chosen a representative sample of worlds in our target region. All have suitable mineral deposits and biospheres and any of them could be terraformed given time and resources. The real problem is to convert the new currency into the equipment and stocks we need. Once we leave the SiNavTech beacon network, it would be incredibly complicated to return."

"I know. But we could establish a bridge. That's what you promised."

"Yes, at the additional expense of equipment and preparation. Everything costs credits, unfortunately."

"What about that dynasty boy? Can he be counted upon to help?"

Lom sighed and turned to Sacha, who shrugged and said, "He's got a lot of growing up to do first. Ask us again in ten years or so. If he stays with Karmen's daughter she might be able to lead him down a better path. But at the moment, he's too immature to be much use."

"Which brings us back to the first position," the Queen lamented. "Karmen Sley would make a better captain than Aura."

"We needn't choose that path just yet, ma'am," Lom said.

"We'll have to soon. In the meantime, figure out the best choice of planets. I need a world that's close enough to bridge to the beacon network but far enough into the wilderness to make an effective moat. Get to it, Commander."

"We serve the Queen," the foursome intoned and saluted.

The Queen returned their acknowledgement with a gesture of her own. "One last thing, Lom. If it comes down to a contest between Aura and Karmen... choose Karmen. In every simulation, Karmen is the better choice."

"I understand."

44

ANOTHER ANGLE

LEE STOOD IN front of Lead Agent Saera Alexri again for the second time in five months, dismally aware that the look in her eyes foretold an end to his career in the TSS if he so much as twitched out of place.

"Agent Tuyin, I do not like what I'm seeing in your reports," she said. "Two months. They sat on Baron's World for two months! Has there been *any* movement in this case?"

"Officer Sley has been making use of her time on the *Emerald Queen*'s crew by providing detailed personnel files, schedules, lists of materials and equipment, and contact information."

The Lead Agent scrolled past the documentation. "Oh, there's plenty of raw data here. They built a business center in the old shipyard. Hired pilots for a commercial fleet. That's not helpful. What's their plan? Do we know?"

"Her reporting indicated they made a move on one of Thand's sponsors. I agree the last report was a little light on specifics—"

"There were *no* specifics at all. Unless Karmen has come up with something you haven't shared with me."

"I assure you, ma'am, what you have in front of you is what there is. I wouldn't call it all bad."

"It sounds all bad. I know I didn't authorize a deep cover mission. I certainly don't remember giving you leave to send Karmen into that Thand woman's confidence."

"It seemed a workable situation at the time, ma'am."

"It sent a Militia Officer into a position where she could spill one secret after another about the TSS's current disposition. Do you usually recommend treason to your co-workers?"

Lee had had enough of the berating. But a charge of insubordination wouldn't help his case one bit. "Ma'am, that is untrue. I hate to say it, but even in her depleted state, Agent Thand remains a Sacon Division graduate. No matter how clever my team tries to be, there's no way for us to go head-to-head against her. Karmen's past relationship with Thand has been the only thing keeping us in striking distance of the *Emerald Queen*."

Agent Alexri softened. "You're right about that. And you *do* need help. This hasn't been a fair assignment. Fortunately, for both of us, you're not in this alone."

A young auburn-haired woman in Agent black and tinted glasses entered through a side door.

Saera continued, "This is Agent Anye Uragawi. While you've been futzing around at the edges collecting intelligence and spinning your wheels, she has been working a different angle. Rather successfully, I might add."

"Agent Uragawi," Lee greeted with a bow of his head. "I look forward to learning anything you have to tell me."

"As do I, Agent Tuyin," she replied in kind. "Cheer up, it's not all bad. I command assets you could make good use of. A customs cutter for one. It's fast, boasts an EWAR suite very much like the one you've been flying for months, and it's reasonably armed. The crew is small, but they know their jobs. I've collected a great deal of information about these so-called Mesopotamians. I think the two of us can plan a proper take-down if you're willing to keep an open mind about it."

Lee nodded. "I'm in no position to argue."

The Lead Agent folded her hands on her desktop. "No, you certainly are not."

Anya flashed an affable smile to defuse the tension. "It's a pleasure to be working with you. What do you know about the field of biometrics?"

"I'm familiar with it, but that's not my specific medical expertise," Lee admitted.

"Why don't we begin by discussing what I learned from recovering Lord Gilgamesh's DNA and a cleverly designed handheld he used for everything?"

45

IT'S MY PARTY

AURA WASN'T GENERALLY a party person, but she insisted that this one—her party, the *Emerald Queen*'s party—be memorable. They'd captured a fortune. The TSS had been unable to prevent their escape. She was free from Gil. This was a celebration of where they'd been and the exciting horizons ahead.

She'd rented out an event hall in an upscale part of Baron City, in a building tricked out to resemble a castle. She'd paid a ridiculous sum for use of their entire second floor. The scenery came with woven tapestries, stone and marble floors and walls, and torches along the walls for light, as well as numerous candlelit chandeliers above. The whole thing was both dreary and comforting at the same time, and she loved it.

She only wished all her guests could share in the good cheer.

Tables of food and a bar built into a service island kept the revelry in play, and a live band kept the room happy with good dance music. Most of the crew had no talent for such things, but no one cared. They ate, they drank, they got gabby and silly, and the raucous atmosphere never ebbed. The youngest Sley kids had their own party off to the side and quite the entourage with Scorpions and young crew members in attendance. Their table was full of laughter and screams, and groans. Elian's awful jokes, she assumed.

Despite the good vibes, Aura's dress itched and she couldn't figure out why. It had looked and felt amazing in the boutique's fitting room. Somehow, in the light of reality, it didn't quite hang right.

Two of her crew refused to get with the program, which irked her. Her first officer was sullenly leaning over the balcony rail, a drink in either hand, and refusing every invitation to come inside. Her husband was slowly drinking himself into a stupor near the far wall.

They're grieving the loss of their quiet, normal lives. But why are they doing it so far apart?

She decided to find out, and the three drinks already in her made her courageous enough to try a strange strategy.

She placed her empty wine glass on a passing servant's tray, grabbed Daveed Sley by his lapels, and planted a kiss on him. When they parted, she was smiling but he looked confused. "Nice. Could use a little work but nice," she said.

Daveed blinked. "What was that for, Aura?"

No spark. No conflict. No nothing. *Oh well.* "I've wanted to do that since we met. I'm afraid I've kept Karmen too busy for you. We'll fix that."

"No, we won't. This ship is broken, Captain, filled with broken people looking for a solution to a broken universe."

"Is that a fact, Dean Sley?"

"It's an observation. All I see are bad choices."

"Maybe. They say a death sentence concentrates the mind. I figured out what was important very quickly."

"Two-credit philosophy won't help. Neither will phrases like, 'I'm a pirate. I want, I take.'"

"When did I say that?"

"Kaia has been muttering that phrase to herself for weeks. It doesn't help me think I'm a good parent. I might as well blame you."

"Come on, Professor, you must like me a *little,* don't you? Otherwise, you'd have bundled your family into your ship and run back to Greengard a long time ago. I'd let you all leave, no hard feelings. No one is here under protest or threat. Not even you."

"I don't belong here. I feel that in my bones," he insisted.

Here they were, at the moment of truth. *How will he respond?* "Piffle."

"Excuse me?"

"I said, piffle. If there's anyone on the *Emerald Queen* who belongs on her, it's you. You have a soul. You have principles. You resist the existential horror we face every day. And you don't mind screaming at us when you think we've overstepped. I need you, Daveed, every bit as much as your wife and children do."

"I don't believe you," he slurred, and downed the rest of his glass.

"Believe this, then. The next time Colin and Tabor dismiss you, knock their heads together. Make those little shites respect you. You'll see the difference almost immediately."

He blinked in confusion. "I can't very well slam them against a bulkhead."

"Not at Foundation U, perhaps, but here you bomaxed well can. It's your classroom. Your word is law so long as it doesn't contradict mine. Sometimes, you have to kick a few asses before you're obeyed. They learn soon enough."

"Ha. You and I live in different universes, Aura."

"Really? I thought we connected that night in Tavden high port."

He snorted then grabbed another drink from a passing server. "When we met, I thought that I'd rather work for you than my department head at Foundation U. Now here I am, working for you. I feel more out of place now than I did then. How does that work?"

She understood he'd decided to be miserable and there wasn't much she could do about it. But she could give him something to look at instead of his problems. "It's the dress, isn't it? Stars, I knew it didn't hang properly." She bounced a few times, made a show of adjusting it, and his eyes followed her movements.

"No! The dress is amazing, and you fill it delightfully. I probably shouldn't have said that out loud. No, I object to *this*," he said, waving his arm around and sloshing his drink over the edge of the glass.

"You don't like parties?"

"I object to power without constructive purpose. Instant billionaire status never ends well."

"Instant? This project was decades in the making. Besides, I think I'd call wiping out a black market racket constructive."

"Maybe. I'm just not a pirate, Aura."

"No, you're not. That's as it should be—you're a gifted academic. But I know one thing we can surely agree upon," she said, closing the distance between them.

"Which is?"

"We both love your wife very much."

He took a deep breath and exhaled. "I accept your premise,

but await your evidence," he teased.

Aura shook her head in disgust, wondering whether she should throw the rest of her drink in his face. "You bomaxed eggheads are all the same," she accused.

Daveed joined her in a raucous laugh.

All right, score one point for the teacher. "Why aren't you dancing with your wife, Professor?"

"She's on the balcony having a moment to herself."

Aura followed his gesture. Karmen was still alone at the railing, resting her elbows on the rim. "That's no moment, it's a dark night of the soul. I'll see if I can lift her spirits."

"I'd appreciate that. Mere money isn't going to do it."

"I know. I'm no expert, but I expect we're all well set for several lifetimes."

"As long as you don't think about where it came from."

"Daveed, we stole nearly a billion credits from professional thieves. It doesn't get more honorable than that," she insisted.

"You say that, but I think it's going to lead to some difficult decisions in the near future. On the other hand, it surely has made my daughter cheerful."

Aura followed his nod toward the bar. Emily Govrin and Kaia Sley were whooping it up over something, girlish squeals penetrating the night like the howls of wolves.

Aura excused herself from Daveed and wandered over to hear the news. "You ladies seem excited about something, and I don't think it's the music or the food," she said.

"We just formed a charter corporation. We got approval from the GravX regulatory board to start a new team!" Kaia sang.

"What is your new team called?"

"I have no idea! Teams are associated with planet names, so it'll be the Baron's World something. We'll figure that out later. But we're on our way!"

"I look forward to investing heavily in your success," Aura said. "Where's your man, Kaia? Shouldn't he be here to help you celebrate?"

"He's meeting with the elder Covranis, but he should be back in— Oh, there he is!" Kaia spied Colin across the room and excused herself to join him.

Emily pulled Aura closer. "I've had this talk with Colin already; I believe he understands me. I refuse to have this talk with Tabor because that man is a pig. So, I'm going to spill my tea in your lap and let the universe do as it may."

"Very well. Let me have it."

"I've created a wealth management fund for Colin and Kaia. They're co-owners and there are mechanisms in place to keep them from wiping it out by purchasing a planet or some fool thing. I have deposited their shares of the *Mother Courage* ownership agreement with Karmen and the income sharing agreement that Colin arranged with those two hundred pilots he poached from his mother's division of CDS. There's even a mechanism in place to divide the spoils proportionately between them if they separate. But that's where I feel I must stop."

"Meaning?"

"Meaning I cannot represent you or any of the assorted ventures that you're running out of the *Emerald Queen*."

"I'm sorry."

Emily drained her drink and signaled the bartender for a refill. "I'm not. I have set you folks up with a genuine wealth management firm. They are well-known in the Inner Worlds and they came highly recommended. Discretion is their middle name."

Aura frowned, not seeing how the facts all fit together. "I

don't understand."

"It's simple. Colin dropped a pile of credit chips on my desk and said go to work, so I did. I created an account, made a ton of pretty shrewd investments, took my fee and left it at that. But you folks are moving into a realm I'm just not suited for. You want people who eat and sleep this stuff and command armies of accountants, tax specialists, and lawyers. That's not me."

Aura sipped from her glass to buy time. She'd never had a crew member simply walk out on her before. *What did I do wrong?* "Where are you moving to? Can you tell me that?"

"A firm on Bashari Prime. I got a call from a recruiter a few weeks ago and I told them about projects I would like to create in the future. They hired me on the spot. I am still available for consulting work. But day-to-day stuff… Colin and Kaia's account is all I can manage."

"I'm sorry to lose you."

"You're losing nothing. You're gaining a class of representation that knows how to run with billionaires and politicians and military leaders. I'm out of my league. I'm leaving."

"Have another drink before you go."

"Oh, you'll have to carry me out on a stretcher tonight. That bartender is my new boyfriend and I'm five shots into that insanely expensive whisky Tabor brought home. Cheers!"

Aura could see Colin and Kaia across the room talking animatedly and maneuvered into their path. Tabor and Maesy cut her off well short of her goal.

"Cap'n! Cap'n! I would like to make my report now, if thass all right," Tabor slurred. There were stains on his shirt and his breath made her not want to light a match anywhere near him.

"Make it short, Tabor. I'm in mid-mingle here."

"Yes'm. The base is fully opationable... operishonble... it's working good. I'm hiring my pals from Tavden to come work for you. We can have it all ready for a war footing in six months. Maybe lesst. Thass my report."

"Report received." Aura wasn't thrilled with the obvious look of stress on Maesy's face. "Are you all right, Engineer?"

"My bio-system keeps me sober. But I'm re-evaluating some recent relationship choices, if that's what you mean."

"Aw, you loooove me..." Tabor said and grabbed Maesy's chest hard enough to make her yelp.

Tabor was still her primary link to Ash's Dark Net marketplace, and Ash was her next target. "Get him home, Maesy. Don't let him breathe on any open flames."

"Yes, ma'am. Come on, you sponge."

"Ah looooove you, Masel."

If I have Colin on my side, I don't need Tabor... or do I? Aura suddenly needed to hash out her relationship with Colin Covrani. He and Kaia were entwining themselves around each other as they swayed to the music and Aura didn't bother with any attempt at subtlety as she walked up to them. "How'd the meeting go?" she asked him.

Colin unfolded himself from Kaia. "Which one? The one with Vani, with Dad and Uncle Rodg, or the one with my mother?"

"Oof. All of them, I guess. You can give me the bullet points version."

"Mom was furious, as Mom often gets when she faces a surprise. We currently have co-operative deals with two hundred and three of her former commercial pilots. I reminded her we merely accelerated the completion of the contracts in question. Eventually, she had to acknowledge that we did not actually steal anything, merely paid her what she was owed. She said I could keep the pilots I collected, but I had to stop poaching her captains. I agreed. Since those two hundred ships are collectively pulling in thirty or forty million credits a year, we have plenty of revenue to expand operations and open new ventures."

"How about Vani?"

"Vani wanted to hear about the big battle between Gilgamesh and the *Emerald Queen*. I may have oversold your pirate crew's reputation. But he likes a good story and it was true… more or less."

"And the old men of the proverbial star lanes?" Aura pushed.

"Dad is concerned that I've had an early success and now I think I'm a genius," Colin said with a smile. "Have I ever called myself a genius?"

"Not in front of me. But you have your moments."

"That's kind of you to say. Anyway, he thinks I'm over-reaching and under-diversifying. Uncle Rodg thinks I'm badly misjudging the headwinds we're sailing into as we move to consolidate Gilgamesh's holdings. My uncle is particularly worried about the dead man's friends and the law—and considering that Daveed gave me a similar warning, I'm inclined to listen."

"That sounds wise, young man."

"Are they going to let you keep running with Aura?" Kaia asked.

"They like the fact I'm working on a starship. They're unhappy about the company I'm keeping. To balance the books, I am going to be apprenticed to a starship captain in the Covrani fleet. Captain Galway who runs the luxury liner *Electrum* on the Inner Worlds. It's predictable and boring. I can screw up constantly and not hurt anything or anyone."

Aura raised an eyebrow at the response. "But you'll learn by doing, which is what you're used to," Aura confirmed.

Kaia bubbled with energy at the news. "What fun!" she cried.

"Yeah. My mother liked my idea about setting up a Merchant Academy on Greengard so much that she wants me to be in the first class. Dad agreed with her. It's a two-year accelerated training program. The command track. I'll get mentored with the field internship on the *Electrum*, I'll rack up a bunch of advanced education credits, and when I graduate, I'll have a legit captain's certificate. If I don't crash a starship into a planet or star, then two years after that I'll be empowered to start my own division of CSD."

"Oh, stars, that's amazing," Kaia gushed. "You'll have your own space liner in no time!"

"It's not just me, girlfriend," Colin said, drawing out the last word. "They also wanted you to be more than a pretty face on my arm."

"Oh no," Kaia groaned. "What did you sign me up for, dude?"

"My parents who never agree on anything agree that advanced degrees open doors that mere corporate titles do not. So, we'll both be going to school at Foundation U for a few years. It'll be fun, right?"

"It might be," Kaia admitted. "We'll live in a dorm. We'll be a power couple on campus. We'll have rivals and groupies. It'll be insane!"

Aura saw the chance to get her most pressing question answered. "Colin, will I be working for you? Or are you working for me?"

Colin grinned. Not the smile of a man who was given to grand gestures of altruism, but something more wolfish. The real Colin Covrani was getting out of his seat and taking a bow. "You're working for you. It's your capital, you stole it fair and square."

Aura balked at the thought of another solid crew member leaving her ship. *Stuck with Tabor for good, then. Oh well.* "Not alone, I didn't. I'm nothing without my crew. As part of the crew, you are entitled to a share of the spoils. Think of it as my payment for your time and expertise. Name your price."

"Does ten million credits sound fair?"

Aura scoffed, "Certainly not. Thirty million sounds fair."

Colin laughed. "I prefer your definition of fairness to my own."

"Stars, that's wonderful! I'm so bomaxed proud of you, boyfriend!" Kaia squealed and grabbed him, jumping up and down in near hysterics. After a moment, he jumped with her. "This is crazy, this is stupid! You are so stupid! And I'm crazy for being in love with you."

"I'm in love with you, too. Now, marry me, you crazy woman."

"Absolutely, you stupid man!"

Watching them, Aura suddenly felt a hole in her soul where Gil had once stood. The newfound freedom she'd felt was now just emptiness. Stars, she missed him! She would probably miss him for years. She could do nothing about that. But she missed her friend, too, and that, she could definitely do something about.

Aura left the young ones to each other and proceeded to the balcony.

"You're stealing my act," she scolded Karmen, joining her at the railing.

"How so?"

"I'm the one who hides when she feels out of sorts. You're

supposed to come break me out of it. Not the other way around."

"I have nothing to celebrate." Karmen sighed.

"Yes, you do. You're rich, your daughter is set for life, and now you have a wedding to plan."

"Oh boy. Those two children."

"Not any more. They're going to Foundation University together. Plus, he just proposed and she accepted. Congratulations, dynasty mom!"

Karmen glanced inside at the exuberant youths. "I should probably get in there to congratulate them." But her expression conveyed that she wasn't entirely happy with the news.

"What is it?" Aura prompted.

"I like that boy, but he makes me nervous. He never learned to be careful. Kaia doesn't know how to be anything *but* careful. I guess they'll figure it out for themselves," Karmen groaned.

"What happened to you, Sley? You used to drink. You used to dance. But you never moped. Now, tell me what's *really* wrong. That's an order."

"What's wrong? I am a complete and utter failure! My TSS team abandoned me for consorting with the enemy. I chased my oldest son into the arms of a security firm, and my oldest daughter into the arms of a dynasty brat. My younger daughter executed a hijacker, and all I could do was remind her to put her tools away. I stood by and watched a crack team of high-tech thieves raid the coffers of a criminal organization. I blew up a perfectly good yacht. I killed your ex-lover. And my husband is coping with a gigantic mid-life crisis by setting up classrooms to teach your crew how to be even more deadly and destructive. How's that?"

"'Only where war is being waged, is life being lived'," Aura quoted.

"What does that mean?"

"My Agent proctor told me that on the first day of my TSS internship. I didn't understand him then, but I do now. All it means, Karmen, is that you're a person, and you make crappy decisions sometimes just like the rest of us. Doesn't make you a failure. You're one of the most successful people I know."

"Maybe. I think I'm on the wrong team."

"I think you're exactly where you need to be. You and Daveed both. And I'm the captain, so what I say goes."

"Yes, ma'am."

"Don't you ma'am me. Look, I should have died on the *Triumph*. First, from the deployment orders, then the collision. My life pod was broken, and life support was collapsing. I was *ready* to die. I know I've told you that before, but do you understand it?"

"I don't think so. I've never been ready to call it quits. I've always seen too much ahead of me."

"Well, spend some time in a Valdan ashram and you might learn. The point is, Gil literally saved my life. Healed my body. Brought me back from the brink. Gave me something to want to live for. When his ships were bearing down on *Redemption*, it was like I'd been punted back in time to the *Triumph*. I had a feeling… like the universe was correcting the mistake it made in letting me live. And it was willing to kill four others to do it. So, when you showed up in my ship, commanding my crew, saving us it was like… the circle keeps turning. I keep resetting my clock. I am eternally owing my life to others. Always working on borrowed time."

Karmen drained her glass and turned to rest her hip on the balcony rail. "Aura, are you trying to thank me for bailing you out?"

"I guess I am."

"Then you're welcome. But you should know something…"

"That you were thinking about letting me die?"

Karmen blinked. "Stars above us. Am I that easy to read?"

"I know you pretty well. You're kicking yourself for *something*. If the roles were reversed, I would have wondered the same thing."

"For what it's worth, I'm glad I didn't go that route."

"So am I. I'll come up with a better thank-you than an awkward moment and trite confessions, I promise. Hey! How would you like new eyes?"

"Gaaaaaaaah… no mechanical implants! That's final!"

"No, I mean real eyes. Organic replacements. They'll use your own DNA to grow them and you'll be done with the TuMed bio-juice forever. I have the money for it. It's my fault you got sick. Let me help."

"I guess it beats walking into doors. I'll think about it."

Aura pulled her friend away from the rail and held her up by the arms. "Come on, Sley. We're rich beyond anything we ever dreamed. Our families are safe. Let's drink. Let's dance. Life is good. Tonight, life is great!"

The rest of the evening passed in a blur. Aura kept her friend in constant motion. Karmen smiled and laughed and drank and danced with her husband, her captain, and her crew, celebrating life, surrounded by light. But Aura could tell she was wearing a carefully tuned mask, and no matter how much fun they had tonight, Karmen would never find a way to come to terms with her service to Mother Carnage. There was just too much TSS in her.

There was no way around it: one day, Aura might have to kill Karmen Sley. And there wasn't a thing either of them could do about it.

46

THIS MEANS WAR

THE MESOPOTAMIANS STOOD silently on the flight deck of Sar's yacht *Nineveh*. They'd arrived at *Shamhat*'s last known position and had been scanning for some time. Literal bits and pieces of Gil's yacht appeared on their scans and occasionally pinged against the hull. "Nineveh, do we have a proper identification?"

The ship's AI appeared on the flight deck. Where Shamhat had been an oversexed flight attendant, Nineveh was a soldier: trim, crisp, and smart. Her uniform was as perfect as her mannerisms. "We do, sir. All scans match our transponder codes and ship profile data. And there was part of a body. Gil's DNA matched."

Sargon frowned. "How much of a body?"

"Insufficient mass for a complete organism but there was an arm. The right arm."

"I see. Let's get to recovering that debris."

"Already being done, sir. I have salvage drones onsite. I

estimate three hours and twenty-one minutes to completion."

"Very good. Can't have just anyone stumbling onto so much evidence," Sar reasoned.

"No, sir. Will there be anything else?"

"Not for the moment. Alert me when the download finishes. I'll want to scuttle the ship myself."

"Very good, Lord Sargon."

Their collective mood was sullen and somber. "I'm going to miss him," Sargon murmured.

"We all are," Ham agreed. "Such a stupid way to go."

"Nothing stupid about it," Sargon countered. "It was a revenge play by an ex-girlfriend gone to the Nth extreme. He should have dumped that woman years ago. We all saw it. She was nothing but trouble toward the end."

"I don't know about that," Ash allowed. "She did get the business angle of New Akkadia. She was a solid deal-maker. If only Gil hadn't gotten so... *obsessed* with her."

"Well, it's over. We're going to have to figure out how to fill the hole in our ranks," Sar griped.

Ham poured himself a drink from a flask. "No time for that. Turbashi himself is going to call any minute. He'll want to know why we haven't moved on Aura yet."

"Technically, we did. She won. But I can't exactly come out and say that we've dropped the proverbial ball," Sar said.

Ash pulled Ham's flask from his hand and downed the rest of the contents. "This is where we're really going to miss having Gil around. He was good at connecting with people. He could lie to your face and still have an air of credibility. By the time you realized he was taking you for a ride, all your assets were in his name. You could sit down, shut up, and take a paycheck or leave with nothing."

"Even he couldn't have pulled a stunt like that with

Vladameer Turbashi," Ham said.

Sar sniffed. "I hate to admit it. We need Vlad's money. He's got interests all over the Middle and Inner Worlds. The income streams are huge. We need to stay on his good side. If I have to cut Gil's former girlfriend loose to save that relationship, I'll do it. I think that piracy scheme has outlived its usefulness, anyway."

"Too many loose ends," Ash said.

"And TSS sniffing around. Fok that noise," Ham spat.

Nineveh reappeared. "Lord Sargon, we have an incoming call. Encryption protocols are active. You may answer when ready," the AI announced from a hidden speaker.

Here we go. Sargon opened the connection and Vladameer Turbashi's round face filled the room. "Starbright, Gilgamesh! How are you today?"

"Forgive me, Vladameer, but this is Sargon. I hate to say it but Gil won't be joining us today."

"No?"

"No. Sadly, he's taken ill. It's a mere inconvenience. He should be back on his feet soon."

Turbashi kept his face carefully neutral; if he took the news badly, he didn't show it. "I see. Well, give him my regards and tell him to hydrate and stay in bed for a while. Surely, he's earned that. That man works too hard."

"I quite agree. I know you're very busy yourself. Shall we get to the business at hand?" Sargon probed.

"By all means. I have brought the partners around to my way of seeing the situation. I think you were right. There's no reason New Akkadia should not be partaking in our investment strategies. I will forward you the requirements. Nothing fancy. Just minimum investment amounts, the disbursement schedule. A prospectus, really. There's a necessarily lengthy list of regulations governing withdrawals. The slightest variance will result in the cancellation of any development contract we might agree to."

"I see. Not a problem," Sar assured him.

"I'm glad to hear it. You will, of course, be bearing the brunt of any capital outlays that are determined to be required. That, too, will be in the contract, should we go forward."

"Very well."

"The only thing that concerns me is this woman who's been roaming around your section of the galaxy. Mother Carnage, the StarNews people are calling her. It's most unseemly."

"Mother Carnage is one of my enforcement agents. A private contractor. You understand."

Now, Turbashi's face darkened, his eyebrows knitting together. "I'm not sure that I do."

Sargon took a deep breath and stepped forward. *Always be closing.* "My point is that she's under my control. There will be no trouble."

"I should hope not. But I trust you to manage the situation as you see fit. We wouldn't want the partners to worry. That leads to unfortunate outcomes."

"Yes, sir. Is there anything else?"

"No, I'm satisfied you understand what's needed to move forward. Always a pleasure talking to you gentlemen."

"Then I will bid you good day."

"Of course. There is one thing…"

Oh shite. "Yes, sir?"

"I truly am looking forward to hammering out the fine points of this agreement with you. But my family has a saying: risk is for suckers. I've lived my life by it. I will not take chances with my investments. Do I make myself clear?"

"Crystal clear, my friend."

"I'm glad. My lawyers will be in touch. Starbright, Sar!"

"Starbright!"

The connection vanished like a puff of air. Ham ventured an opinion. "That sounded like good news."

"No, it sounded like an ultimatum." Sar sighed. "He doesn't believe Gil is merely ill. He doesn't believe that Aura is still under our control. He doesn't believe his investment is safe or that our plans to expand New Akkadia are secure. He wants to see blood. We need to show him blood."

Ash gave a curt nod. "Aura has to go. Mother Carnage has to die."

"It's got to be soon, and it must be spectacular," Ham added.

"All correct. The bad news is that Aura has the bulk of Gil's assets and holdings now. That gives her a substantial war chest to deploy anywhere and anytime she likes. The good news is that she has no idea what our full asset list contains. Which means, for the moment, we have the advantage. Nineveh!"

The avatar reappeared. "Yes, my lord."

"How many of those TalEx mining charges do we have left in inventory?"

"Five, my lord."

"Good. We'll use all of them before this is over."

"What are we going to do with nuclear charges?" Ash asked.

Sargon pulled up a star map and folded his arms. "We're going to buy a space station. Then Mother Carnage is going to destroy it with all hands aboard because she's a monster."

"Agreed," Ham said. "We'll use the outrage to assemble a fleet big enough to crush that pirate queen."

"It's the only way to protect the galaxy from lunatics like

her," Ash added. "It's the only way to make New Akkadia safe."

Sargon sniffed and zoomed in on a station that he liked: Dacha Station. It was aesthetically horrible, a nightmare of clunky modules welded to a lopsided central bus. Smallish in size but with a substantial population. No one important would miss it, but the outcry when it burned would be intense.

"My friends, start working your contact lists and calling in as many favors as you have. We have a lot of work to do."

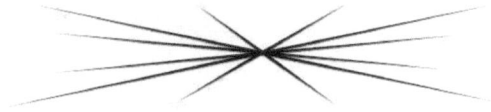

THE STORY CONTINUES IN
HOMEWORLD FOR A QUEEN…

Books in the Series:
Book 1: Grand Theft Planet
Book 2: Carnage and Courage
Book 3: Homeworld for a Queen

CADICLE UNIVERSE: ADDITIONAL READING

Cadicle Space Opera Series by A.K. DuBoff
Book 1: Rumors of War (Vol. 1-3)
Book 2: Web of Truth (Vol. 4)
Book 3: Crossroads of Fate (Vol. 5)
Book 4: Path of Justice (Vol. 6)
Book 5: Scions of Change (Vol. 7)

Mindspace Series by A.K. DuBoff
Book 1: Infiltration
Book 2: Conspiracy
Book 3: Offensive
Book 4: Endgame

Verity Chronicles by T.S. Valmond & A.K. DuBoff
Book 1: Exile
Book 2: Divided Loyalties
Book 3: On the Run

Shadowed Space Series by Lucinda Pebre & A.K. DuBoff
Book 1: Shadow Behind the Stars
Book 2: Shadow Rising
Book 3: Shadow Beyond the Reach

In Darkness Dwells by James Fox & A.K. DuBoff

AUTHORS' NOTES

From Jon Frater:

Wouldn't it be awesome to go back in time to re-do some of the mistakes you made in life? Even if we can't actually fix our mistakes, recover lost opportunities, or confront our past selves, we can, if we're lucky, re-connect with our past selves and realize what we did wrong and how it led to unhappy outcomes.

Carnage and Courage is where Karmen and Aura re-connect and try to fix some of those mistakes. As in Book 1, I'll leave it to the reader to decide if they succeeded.

This volume was a blast to write. I've always enjoyed playing with the concepts of AI and Amy's Lynaedans came into my brain and swept me along into a vast new culture and history, and a host of unique personalities who danced onto my pages and refused to shut up until I'd told their story properly.

I always knew that Aura and Gil were destined to meet an unhappy ending… that's just how it works sometimes. You meet that special someone in your twenties, and then ten or twenty years later you realize the person you cared about was in your head, not the person you have to deal with in reality. As to Aura and Karmen, well, there are some problems that you and your best friend can overcome… and some problems you'll never overcome. We won't even discuss the problems we encounter when we mix work and home like Karmen's family does.

I hope there were enough twists, turns, and actiony bits to keep you interested. The third book is almost finished and you'll have it in your hands soon. Thanks again to our beta readers and proofreaders whose essential work helped make this a book one that I'm especially proud of.

On to Book 3. Thanks again for reading!

An additional note from A.K. DuBoff:

This book was a lot of fun to work on with Jon! Many of the other series in the Cadicle Universe have centered on the Agent side of the TSS and their Gifted abilities, so it's been wonderful diving into the everyday living experience of regular Taran citizens. The exploration of the Lynaedan tech, too, has become one of my favorite parts of the Renegade Imperium books, and I really love the creative ideas Jon has brought into the universe with that culture.

When I opened up this universe to other authors several years ago, it was a little scary to allow others to play with my baby. But I'm so happy I did! The fresh perspective these collaborations have brought—and the great questions Jon and others have asked—have pushed me in the best way as a creator. The universe would not be what it is today without their contributions, and I will be forever grateful that they brought their wonderful creativity to this playground.

I am incredibly thankful to our amazing beta reader team—John, David B, and Eric—for offering their insightful feedback! And I couldn't add the final polish without my wonderful proofreaders, Steve and Bryan, thank you so much!

The third installment in this trilogy is going to be epic, so strap in. Until next time, happy reading :-)!

ABOUT THE AUTHORS

Jon Frater

Jon Frater is an academic library director by day, a sci-fi writer by night, and an old school gamer with thirty plus years of experience, reviewing, writing, designing, and playing video games and tabletop RPGs, as well as fiction, non-fiction, articles, and blogs. He's worked as a game writer, reviewer, and developer, cranked out countless game and book reviews, and tried his hand at writing for the screen and audio. He has published short works for the Future Chronicles and Tales From the Canyon of the Damned series, and published longer works in the Legends of Legacy Fleet series by way of Desperate Measures Press. His Battle Ring Earth and Crisis of Command military fiction series are published by Aethon Books. Renegade Imperium represents his first foray into the A.K. DuBoff's Cadicle Universe.

jonfraterbooks.com

A.K. DuBoff

A.K. (Amy) DuBoff has always loved science fiction in all its forms—books, movies, shows, and games. If it involves outer space, even better! She is a Nebula Award finalist and USA Today bestselling author most known for the Starship of the Ancients series and her Cadicle Universe, but she's also written a variety of sci-fi and fantasy. Amy can frequently be found traveling the world, and when she's not writing, she enjoys wine tasting, binge-watching TV series, and playing epic strategy board games.

www.akduboff.com